SPACES

(Properly, our children grow up in the spaces adults cannot occupy.)

C.S. GRAVES

Copyright © 2017 C.S. Graves.

All rights reserved. No part of this book may be reproduced, stored, or transmitted by any means—whether auditory, graphic, mechanical, or electronic—without written permission of both publisher and author, except in the case of brief excerpts used in critical articles and reviews. Unauthorized reproduction of any part of this work is illegal and is punishable by law.

ISBN: 978-1-4834-5064-3 (sc)
ISBN: 978-1-4834-5065-0 (e)

Because of the dynamic nature of the Internet, any web addresses or links contained in this book may have changed since publication and may no longer be valid. The views expressed in this work are solely those of the author and do not necessarily reflect the views of the publisher, and the publisher hereby disclaims any responsibility for them.

Any people depicted in stock imagery provided by Thinkstock are models, and such images are being used for illustrative purposes only.
Certain stock imagery © Thinkstock.

Lulu Publishing Services rev. date: 05/08/2018

Acknowledgements

To Mum, Lorraine, and Jim Kimmis

Spring,
As it eases into us, it softens almost everything.
Almost.

PART ONE

1

Saturday, 13 February 1982

...in rushed the rich, oily smell of crayons and paints. With little effort he was able to recall how rough and fat the wooden handle of the paintbrush felt enclosed in his small fingers. And now he was painting a butterfly with blue wings and yellow dots. And then he was scribbling down his first alphabet in a big, red jotter; and then it was milk at breaktime, cartons of milk all in a row row row, the pink straws sticking out of the tops so that, seen from a distance, the cartons resembled a bed of nails.

Once again he was listening to 'The Hobbit' being read out in class by Mr Powell. Then he was ordering his first book from the Book Worm Club, recalling how the pages had smelt that first time he had fanned them under his nose; woody, sweet, and kind of spicy, all at the same time.

Scenes, images, and noises played out on his senses, only to be hurried along by the next wave of scenes, images, and noises: he was running around a playing field, lap after lap, and his PE teacher was monitoring his progress, stopwatch in hand, nodding and smiling to another teacher standing next to him. Then he was at church with his nan and grandad, and as the fitful cadence of the vicar's voice moved through the ribs of the church, his grandad's head toppled forward and his false teeth poked out from beneath his top lip.

Scenes, images, noises...and then there was him, Jason, Mickey, and Ben. They were sitting around a table talking big things, making battle plans, discussing an enemy that required their full and immediate attention.

And there they were again, but now he was holding a big, yellow flower. He snapped the stem and a milky fluid trickled from the break. Jason, Mickey, and Ben all saw what he had done and laughed, and Ben shouted, 'Hey, look, the flower's spunked!' When he threw it away in disgust, his friends rolled around laughing until the teacher came along and threatened to split them up.

Scenes, images, noises…he was on the pier playing war games with his brothers, which involved a lot of laughing and hiding and running over the wooden decking, which popped hilariously under their feet as they ran and hid from one another whilst his mum and dad watched on, eating ice cream, knowing where each one of them had hidden, but saying nothing—even to one another.

Scenes, images, noises…he was on the pier once more, only it was a Thursday night, and he and his brothers were being treated to fish and chips by their nan and grandad after their swimming lesson. Feet dangling over the end of the pier, Michael was the captain of an oceangoing liner trying to avoid icebergs, David was in a spaceship with his crew hurtling through the solar system in search of new worlds, new civilisations, and him…he was a lone explorer at the helm of his small craft, Lookfar, *silently staring out across the horizon.*

Scenes, images, and noises, and then…

And then he was at a new school, Big School; new rooms, new teachers, huge buildings, impossibly massive playing fields. Wide-eyed, he was turning and turning, dead centre of a playground full of children, searching for a single face he recognised; Jason, Mickey, or Ben?

But no…no, they had gone to a different school.

Scenes, images, noises…and then his mum and dad were fighting, again. Only this time they were in the hallway and the front door, like their mouths, kept opening and closing in anger, and loudly. Until his mum suddenly reversed the order of things and his dad found himself staring at a door he had not opened…staring, until finally, but quietly, he went through it, not looking back.

And then his grandparents got poorly…and died; his nan first and then his grandad shortly after.

And now…now…

'Is anything the matter?'

Eliot shook his head, but sat a little more upright. It was the first thing his teacher had said on the way back. It was early evening; Saturday's lesson was over.

SPACES

The black Capri pulled up outside the school gates and he got out of the car. Mr Wilson said something about 'next week' and the boy leant forward and nodded. Straightening up, he watched the car pull away from the kerb. Absently, he wiped his hands on his jeans, adjusted his duffle coat, and without giving the school a backward glance, he started walking.

After ten minutes, he found himself up on the esplanade.

Somewhere down to his left, he heard waves breaking on the beach in the darkness; to his right, traffic noise broke against the esplanade: caught between these two sounds, he felt like the needle in an old radio set, searching for a station, a clear signal amongst the static.

Across the road, the occasional figure could be seen against the backdrop of the rising buildings, tilted and wrapped in layers against the cold, the gusting breeze and the sparkling air around them, into which the steam of their breathing evaporated.

A sea mist, formed out at sea, eased inland, dissolving edges and angles to a soft, grey-white as it advanced, so that buildings and other structures appeared partially formed, ghostly; or worse, not even real, only imagined.

He turned his gaze on the pier—the pier they were going to blow up in just under eight weeks' time.

It looked particularly old and helpless tonight.

'Press the Button!' the newspaper had promised the winner. The national competition had run for several months late last year, though the decision to forego further investment in the public building had been reached by the council two years earlier.

'Too expensive to maintain,' explained his dad, presiding over tea one night, his mouth stuffed with spaghetti bolognaise.

Eliot and David exchanged a sneer when their older brother, Michael, said, 'It's seen better days, that's for sure, Dad.'

Their dad grunted and chewed his food some more.

'Everyone goes tenpin bowling now,' Michael continued, 'or the cinema.'

'Exactly,' their dad declared, jabbing his fork in the general direction of those sitting around the table. 'They're forever repairing the damn thing…waste of bloody

money, plain and simple.' Again, he used his fork on his family. 'Who uses it now? Tell me that. Who?'

'Families do.' His mum said it so quietly that Eliot looked around the table to see if anyone else had heard her comment. But it seemed that no one had, which was odd because it was the only thing she had said all evening.

There was a moment's silence before their dad shook his head and pronounced judgement; 'No, it's had its time.'

Appearing pleased with this verdict (which annoyed Eliot), Michael then turned his attention on David, who was happily dangling a long line of pasta above his open mouth, and in a tired voice, snapped, 'David, stop playing with your food!'

Shocked, Eliot and David looked across at each other and then at their dad, but the sharp rebuke never came; their dad just pushed out his bottom lip and nodded approvingly.

The two brothers shared another look; Michael had gone too far this time.

Eliot looked at his mum, to see what she thought about Michael's superior, fake behaviour. But she had her head down, not eating, just rubbing her thumb over a chip on the edge of her plate.

Stopping at the lights opposite the Tourist Information Centre, he waited for them to change. A car horn blared, and hearing music and laughter, and someone shouting, he slowly turned his head. The dark-blue Allegro slowed as it approached his position. Pale, disembodied faces inside bobbed on cigarette smoke and the heavy bass of the music, which seemed to swell the car, making it fat, like a spider.

Predictably, the front passenger window had been rolled down.

'Spazza!' shouted the long-haired front passenger as the car drew alongside. 'What you lookin' at?'

Eliot opened his mouth, then shut it again.

'What was that, you little twat?' The big lad's words seemed influenced by the heavy beat of the stereo music, Pink Floyd's 'Another Brick In The Wall.'

A female face appeared at the rear passenger-side window. She pressed her tongue against the window; it resembled a leaf pressing. He stared at it, knowing that if Michael were there, his comeback would have been smart and deadly. But he was not Michael, and Michael was not there.

Grinning, the driver, who had a wispy moustache, leant across the lap of the front passenger. Capturing Eliot's gaze, he held it for a moment. And then, with a vicious snap of his wrist, he punched the furry dice hung over the rearview mirror and growled at Eliot, who flinched.

The front passenger laughed. And then the driver laughed. And then all three occupants were laughing.

Eliot shoved his hands deep inside his pockets and remained silent, as he knew he must; just as he knew his act of silence could make things worse, could be mistaken for an act of hostility.

After what seemed an age, the female stuck up two fingers, said something to the driver, and pulled her face away from the window. With a raucous sputter from the exhaust, the car slowly picked up speed.

Eliot waited until the red taillights of the Allegro had been swallowed up by other town traffic, then he crossed the road and disappeared down the next street.

And then the next.

Arriving home and slipping down the side alley, Eliot now stood just outside the skirt of grainy porchlight, watching his mum through the back door window as she scrubbed the kitchen floor. As always, she was wearing her dark-blue dressing gown and slippers. There was something about her efforts that reminded him of the old coin-fed rides on the pier; her slow, deliberate movements, her lunges and heaves.

It was a narrow kitchen, used. The ceiling seemed to sag, gathering along the uncovered fluorescent tube light hanging above his mother's head, and the walls appeared to lean in, giving Eliot the impression that they, too, were watching his mum work the floor. Along the joins, small ears of wallpaper curled away from the damp plaster walls. The clock above the hallway entrance was stuck at ten to nine, but the second hand twitched intermittently, like the tired efforts of a daddy longlegs caught in a web.

On the floor beside the washing machine there was a green plastic bowl, socks in soak. There was a heap of clean dishes on the draining board, but there were still more in the sink waiting to be washed. His mum had wanted a dishwasher for ages, but then she had wanted a lot of things; kettle, toaster, washing machine, new fridge. At one time or another, all these things had occupied the number one spot on her *'Gawd, the chance would be a fine thing'* list. Sometimes he wondered whether his mum was at all serious about her list because there was a brand-new mop down the side of the fridge, which she never used. He knew this because he had bought it for her with his pocket money, back when he used to get pocket money.

He watched as she sat back on her heels, dipped the brush into the bucket of soapy water, then rocked forward, slowly extending her arm as she applied the brush to the chequered vinyl. Water seethed through the bristles and spread out over the floor in widening, foamy spools as she worked the brush in tight little circles, really scouring the vinyl.

Eliot clasped his hands together and observed this communion of mother and kitchen floor in silence. As always, some instinct deep inside told him that this—whatever *this* really was—was something necessary, and should not be interrupted.

Every time she drew back, the ridge of her spine was revealed, like a range of hills beneath her dressing gown, and every time she thrust forward her long, dark hair fell across her face, causing him a moment of panic.

Occasionally she would sit back on her heels, raise the back of her hand to her forehead, like she was in pain, and his hand would start to reach for the door handle. But after a moment she would swap the brush over to her other hand, resume her work, and the moment would pass.

Wrestling with these difficult swells of emotions, which curled and contorted in his stomach like shapes in a lava lamp, he stepped forward and placed a foot on the back step.

The stains were not coming out.

The thought turned in his head as much as his stomach, one hard rotation after another.

He placed his other foot on the step.

The stains were never going to come out.

Why could she not see it?

Feet jostling for position on the narrow step, when his mum next thrust the brush forward, he raised his hands and gently placed them on the window.

Lips touching the glass, he whispered, 'Fuck him, Mum.'

He ran. He was a good runner. The best. The corridor of parked cars served to centre his thoughts and feelings. He found his second breath, and his legs worked the easy rhythm that so often promised his small body that he could run all night should he desire it.

The quiet streets accepted his passing, softening the sound of his trainers hitting the tarmac to a dull *pat, pat, pat*. An occasional face would appear at the front window of a house as he passed, hands reaching upwards, then coming together in silent supplication and collapsing the square of yellow in a rush of curtains—leaving him with one less person to worry about, one less witness who might say, '*Strange, where's that boy going? It's a bit late, wherever it is.*'

Ten minutes later, he entered a street that ended in a tall hedgerow. Like sentinels, two birch trees rose up the other side.

There was a rough gap in the hedge, made by the passing of a thousand children all desiring the same thing; a short cut into the park. It was a squeeze, and the depth of the hedge always took him by surprise. He held his hands out in front of him and pressed forward. Wet leaves brushed against his ears, his cheeks, his mouth. Holding his breath and closing his eyes protectively against the odd branch that slipped from his grasp and whipped backward, he felt the gravelled ground give way to soft earth beneath the soles of his trainers. A moment later he was out the other side, and he opened his eyes.

Bordered on all sides by trees and hedges, the park lay in shadows.

Just up in front of him stood a lamppost, bathing the brick path beneath it (which cut diagonally across the park) in soft yellow. Off to his left there was a playground. The swings and the see-saw lay still and the climbing frame was a bleak little construction, whose purpose the winter had nulled to a thing of structure, not play.

March was fast approaching.

To most people, the end of March meant the clocks going forward and the slow lengthening of daylight hours. To Eliot, the end of March meant the return of children to the park, and the end of his visits there.

Putting such thoughts out of his head, and detecting no other presence, he wandered over to the centre of the half-sized football pitch.

The miniature goalposts had long since lost their nets. The uprights were skewed, and the crossbars on both sets of goalposts were slightly bowed. He took his place in the centre spot, no more than a deep depression, muddy after the rain earlier that day...

He threw the ball back and wiped his face with the sleeve of his jumper. Who was next?

'Hey, sir! Sir?' Jason shouted. 'You should see Eliot in goal, he's dead good!' Knowing that Mr Sampson was watching, Eliot doubled his efforts to keep the ball out of the net. Ben stepped up and took a shot. Then Jason. Then Mickey tried his luck. He saved every shot. He felt a glow in his stomach, sensing that his PE teacher was clearly impressed. Other children had stopped practising and had come over to admire his goalkeeping skills.

Finally, Mr Sampson decided to take a shot himself.

This was it. If he saved the teacher's kick, he would be famous.

Tensing, he prepared himself for the shot.

The teacher swung his foot through the ball without mercy.

Eliot launched himself to his right...blocked the shot and rolled dramatically. All the kids cheered. Mr Sampson shook his head, astonished. Eliot held back his stupid grin when he stood, remained calm and serious. Who was next?

The sports teacher raised his hand. 'I think we've found our new goalkeeper.' He was suddenly surrounded, and everyone was clapping and cheering, and Jason was thumping him on the back.

He opened his eyes and looked up. A tall line of swaying poplar trees lay beyond the football pitch, forming a high, green boundary between the park and the busy main road beyond it. At times like these, he would play a game with the unseen cars the other side, imagining himself to be the driver—but not just any driver. He would be a hero on some emergency mission, or a secret agent fleeing from imagined enemies—usually Russian.

He heard a car approach from the right. He was a doctor, he decided, carrying a heart to a dying child. He had a hundred miles to go, but only an hour to get there before the organ spoilt and failed. He would make it just in time, but not before the surgeons had to stick wires into the heart so they could jump-start it.

Laughter.

Startled, he looked around, seeking the source of the noise.

There it was again, laughter.

It was coming from the direction of the bushes to his right.

Curious, he scooted along the touchline, reaching the bushes just as the sound of the intruders drew level with the other side. Two of them, he guessed, a man and a woman, by the sound of it. The two strangers continued talking, but he sensed that they had stopped moving.

He disliked the sound of the man immediately, but there was something about the woman's voice…it was unusually deep, and did odd things to his stomach.

The woman laughed some more and he worked his way through the bushes as quietly as he could. When there were no more than a few branches between him and the other side, he carefully pried apart the wet leaves to make a peephole. He found himself staring into the U-shaped courtyard at the rear of the library building. Until recently, it was a place he would visit on a Saturday if it rained. The old women were always friendly, and there were millions of brilliant books for him to get lost in. But of course, now he had his computer lessons.

Viewing the library from this position was quite a different experience, and the courtyard took on a new and mysterious quality. The lozenge-shaped security light above the fire exit established a weak perimeter of dull light that barely carried to the steps. Partially in shadow, the two figures stood to the right of the exit, the woman with her back to the corner.

As he stared at her, he could have been forgiven for thinking that she had just stepped out of one of his comic books. There was something exotic about the way her long, dark hair framed her raw-boned face. She wore red high-heeled shoes and black stockings. Her legs seemed to travel up for an age before they disappeared beneath a short, black skirt. He especially liked the way the thin blades of her suspender straps ever so slightly nipped into the white flesh of her angular thighs.

The woman shrugged off her small handbag and discarded it in the corner. Next she removed her black fur coat and tossed it behind her. Eliot grabbed the branches either side of him as his eyes traced the massively swollen contours of her red blouse. She wore no bra, and the hard nubs of her nipples budded stiffly against the stretched fabric.

The courtyard was suddenly filled with the little man's laughter. Shorter than her, the man wore an anorak over a dark sweater. His jeans were too long and puddled around his black loafers. He had blond hair, cropped short, and his head seemed too big for his body. Like a goblin's head, Eliot decided. The goblin was doing most of the talking, despite the woman's attempts to shush him.

There was something familiar about the man's swaying, awkward movements.

Get away from him! Eliot's mind yelled. *Don't trust him!*

The goblin reached for the woman but she pushed him away. 'Easy there, lover. You know the drill.'

'Aww, come on, sweetheart, you know me,' the man drawled.

'Aye, I do,' she replied.

The man made another grab at her but she pushed him away as easily as before.

'Twenty or nothin'. What's it to be, sunshine? I haven't got all night.'

The creature rushed at her again but she batted him away once more.

Eliot pulled a face. Was he stupid or something?

Grumbling something unintelligible, the little man relented and produced several crumpled bank notes, which the woman took and stuffed into her handbag before nodding. His hands went after her, and this time she let him through.

Eliot swallowed whatever protest was forming in his mouth when he saw the breast! It was more than he could have ever imagined; pale and huge, the nipple, dark and taut...better than anything he had ever seen in a nudey mag.

Wank material, Michael would have said, if he had been there. Or something like that. And Eliot would have laughed, ignoring the discomfort his older brother's comment would have brought him.

After a moment, the woman pushed the goblin away, carefully dropped to her knees, then slowly unzipped the man's trousers.

It was an awful size. Eliot tightened his grip on the branches, but he did not look away.

Then the woman took the man in the mouth.

No! Eliot wanted to shout. *God, what are you doing?*

The man groaned. Her mouth action was fluid, easy. The creature groaned again, only louder this time, and thrust his hips against the woman's mouth, crushing her lips. 'Fuck, yeah! That's it!' the man growled, grabbing a mass of the woman's hair. He lifted up onto his toes as though his soles were burning. 'Oh fuck…God…yeah, do it…come on!'

Eliot mouthed each word, each syllable, silently, and wondered at their potency. But he was cut short when the thin branch he was holding in his left hand suddenly sprang loose and whipped across his lips. He clamped his teeth together as the pain brought tears to his eyes.

'Bitch!' the man shouted.

Through watery eyes, Eliot felt a confusing surge of disgust and excitement as the goblin's anorak started to shake noisily. Reaching for the spot on his lips where the branch had hit, Eliot began prodding the precise impact area—prod, prod, prod, as though he were trying to keep the pain alive.

The shaking became more violent and then a tremor stiffened the creature's body. He started gibbering things in a strangled, unintelligible language.

Moments later, silence filled the courtyard.

Hawking up a gob of phlegm, the goblin spat to one side. The woman kept a careful eye on the little man as she stood and gathered her things from the corner, so Eliot decided that he would, too. But the man seemed somehow smaller now, and when he patted down his thighs, Eliot sensed a measure of awkwardness about him. 'Well then,' the creature said, nodding, but left it at that.

Ignoring the creature as he disappeared around the side of the building, the woman coughed into the tissue she had taken from her handbag, then tossed it. Next, she pulled out a compact and a tube of lipstick, and spent a moment powdering her nose and cheeks, applying the lipstick last.

Finished, the woman gave herself a once-over in the mirror of the compact, snapped it shut, dropped it into her handbag, and followed in the direction of the creature.

As he listened to the receding sound of her heels rasping on the gravel, Eliot stepped out of the bushes and went and positioned himself where only moments earlier the woman had stood. Turning around so he faced outwards, he summoned the image of her breast and masturbated quickly. He gagged as the dry, stabbing orgasm cramped up his stomach.

Seconds later he straightened up and slowly opened his hand, expecting for the miracle to have happened.

Nothing! Bringing his hand up to his face, he examined it thoroughly.

No, nothing.

It was getting late, time to be heading back. Reaching down, he picked up the crumpled tissue the woman had discarded and put it in his pocket.

Deciding he would return to the park tomorrow night, some guarded instinct warned him that he should keep this a secret, mostly from his brothers—especially his younger brother, David, who was devious enough to go sneaking up to the park behind Eliot's back, inevitably spoiling things for him with his...his childishness.

This was serious stuff.

Not for *divs*.

Michael was just about to get into the Mini when Eliot reached home. He was holding a large, blue sports bag in his hand.

'Mike!' he called out.

Michael hesitated, then bent down and communicated something to the driver and waited until his brother reached him.

'Mike,' he repeated out of breath, not quite sure what he wanted to say now that he had stopped his older brother from getting into the car.

Michael said, 'You're out late!'

Eliot looked down at the bag in his brother's hand and shrugged. 'Dad's been round.'

'Yes,' Eliot answered. 'I know.'

'Okay then. Your tea's in the oven.'

'Not hungry,' he replied, giving the sports bag another look. 'I thought you might be back at home tonight.'

'We've been through this,' Michael sighed, tossing his bag into the back of the car.

To Eliot, this action felt deliberate. 'What about Mum?'

Michael glanced towards the house. As always, the living room curtains were pulled across. 'She'll be okay,' he murmured. 'She's just a bit run-down.' Eliot could tell that his brother did not believe this.

They stood without speaking until the car engine started up.

'So?' Michael prompted.

Eliot knew what was coming. '*So*, what?'

'How was your lesson, Computer Boy?'

His reply was another shrug of the shoulders.

Michael took a deep breath and shook his head.

'What?' Eliot protested, shoving his hands into his pockets. 'What did you want me to say? It's Saturday. I don't want to do school on Saturdays.'

'So you've said a hundred times,' Michael sighed. 'You should think yourself lucky your teacher has taken an interest in you. Computers are the future.'

'You sound like Dad,' he snapped. 'Stop sounding like Dad.'

'Give it a rest, will you?' Michael said, sounding bored.

Properly irritated now, Eliot was desperate to use the incident in the library against his older brother: *I've got a woman. A proper one. With bigger tits than your girlfriend. So there!* But he held it in, and the conversation lapsed into silence…until the driver revved the engine.

'Look, I've gotta go,' Michael said.

Again, Eliot glanced towards the house. 'Is David in?'

'He's next door, at Rob's.'

'For a change,' Eliot sneered: Rob was David's best friend. His father was an engineer and spent a lot of time away. Rob had all the latest toys and gadgets. He had gotten a ZX81 for Christmas. His mum, Ruth, was their mum's best friend and had known each other for years.

'Eliot, I have to go.'

He nodded.

Michael glanced at the house one last time. 'So what are you up to tomorrow?'

'Dunno," Eliot said. 'What's it to you, anyway?'

Michael took another deep breath, but his tone was conciliatory. 'I was just asking.'

'Sorry,' Eliot muttered.

'No, it's okay. I understand,' Michael replied.

'No you don't!' Eliot shouted.

For a second, Michael just stared at his brother, open-mouthed.

'But you don't,' Eliot mumbled, kicking at the ground.

'What the fuck's got into you lately?' Michael demanded. 'Well?'

Eliot was about to say something when the driver revved the engine again, only louder this time.

Michael ducked down and spoke to the driver of the car. 'I'm coming!' he hissed. Straightening back up, Michael tried to hide his embarrassment with a smile. 'Look, I'm popping back tomorrow,' he said. 'We'll talk then.'

'Sure you will.'

Michael let that pass, but his tone was a little sterner when he said, 'Tomorrow, *yeah*?'

Seeing Eliot step back from the car as though he expected it to leap off right that second, it was Michael's turn to hesitate. But then with a sigh he reluctantly got into the car. The driver gunned the engine loudly and the Mini pulled away from the kerb.

Eliot watched as the vehicle reached the top of the road. It turned left and was gone.

'So, how was your day?'

Startled, he looked up from the fridge door. His mum was standing by the cooker, clasping a green glass ashtray between her hands.

He shrugged.

His mum nodded, as though considering this response, and took a drag on her cigarette.

'We're out of cheese,' he said after a moment.

'Are you hungry?'

'No, I was just saying.'

'Because your tea's in the oven.'

'I'm not really hungry, Mum. Sorry.'

She nodded as though she understood. 'It might be a bit dry.'

He shook his head. 'It's not that. I'm just…I'm fine, honestly.'

His mum began clicking her wedding ring against the side of the ashtray.

'Okay then.' She took another drag on her cigarette. 'Your dad's been round.'

'Yes, I know, Mum.'

'Are you sure you're not hungry?'

He shook his head.

'Okay then.'

Swinging the fridge door between his hands, he waited whilst his mum finished her cigarette.

'It's the Easter holidays soon.'

Not knowing whether his mum was asking or telling him, he nodded and said, 'I suppose.'

After what seemed another long while she muttered, 'Gawd, will you look at this floor.'

'You could use this,' he suggested, pulling out the self-wringing mop from down the side of the fridge. He placed it between the two of them. The head was tightly wrapped in clear plastic. It had a lever mounted on the side of the handle which, when pushed down, brought together the dual sponge pads, wringing them dry. The man at the market had said it would revolutionise cleaning. 'Your mum won't know herself,' he promised.

She took another drag on her cigarette as though it might help her work things through. Then she shook her head. 'I don't think so, son.'

Frustrated, he said, 'But how come?'

His mum gave the mop another look, but he suspected it was just for show, and this was confirmed when she coughed and said, 'No, it'll get ruined,' stubbing out her cigarette in the ashtray.

He threw the mop back down the side of the fridge. 'I'm going upstairs.'

'Okay then, son,' she answered quietly, her eyes still focused on the floor.

As he moved down the narrow, dimly lit hallway, he heard his mum mutter, 'Will you look at the state of this floor.'

As usual, the heavy drape was pulled across the front door, blocking out the light. It was secured by a draft excluder in the shape of a long brown sausage dog, which held it tight against the base of the door and helped keep out the cold.

Passing his mum's bedroom, he glanced in. Boxes and black bin liners stuffed with clothing and various items could be seen piled high against the wall. He did not need to stick his head around the corner to know that other bags were piled on the bed. He supposed it was the reason why she now slept in the armchair most nights: his dad's armchair, now hers.

Eliot was on his knees between his and Michael's bed, the microscope down on the floor in front of him, examining the stains on the tissue which had been discarded by the woman from the library.

The tissue the woman had discarded was spotted with stains, whose translucent quality reminded him of chip oil deposited on kitchen roll. Ensuring that he got a good stain sample, he cut off a piece of tissue and prepared a glass slide. Excited, he rotated the objective lens array to 450x and slowly brought the image into sharp focus.

As always, he felt like he was looking down through the glass bottom of a boat, only tonight the world beneath his eyes was mostly white: a white sea, broken up by a faint latticework of grey lines. Specks of black spotted the sample, like dead things caught in a net, lying on a grey-white seabed. It was a place where nothing moved.

After a long while of careful examination, he concluded that he would learn nothing new tonight, nothing that would make sense of things as they stood. Disappointed, he sat back on his heels and allowed himself a moment to adjust his eyes.

Affixing a sticky white label to the slide, he took up his black felt pen. Worried, as always, about prying eyes, he hesitated before writing, '*13/2/82—Tissue*', then added it to his collection, which he kept in a long, narrow box lined with oasis. Slotting it home, he ran his fingers over the tops of the other plates all lined up like dominos: '*25/02/79—Salt;*' '*03/4/79—Sugar;*' '*17/07/79—Soil;*' and moving forward, '*13/01/80—String;*' '*11/02/80—iron filing;*' '*23/03/80—Bread;*' and also, '*24/05/80—Paint;*' '*21/08/80'—Wallpaper;*' '*19/09/81—Cigarette Ash;*' '*08/10/81—Dust;*' '*21/10/81—Dirt from Hoover;*' '*26/10/81—Tear drop;*' '*10/11/81—Lager;*' '*19/11/81—Daddy Longlegs Wing;*' '*05/12/81—Fingernail;*' '*07/01/82—Blood;*' '*06/02/82—Spit.*'

And now, '*13/2/82—Tissue.*'

Who was she? Would she come back?

There was only one way to find out.

Closing the lid, he packed everything away and got ready for bed.

He stared at himself in the bathroom mirror as the cold water from the tap seethed through his fingertips. For some time now, spots had started to colonise his face. First one, then a second, then two more, then millions of them, concentrated mostly around his chin and mouth.

There was this boy in his class, Humphrey Beswick, whose spots were so rampant across his face it was difficult to make out a clear bit of skin. With a first name like Humphrey, he had no real chance from the start, and the spots just heaped on the misery. The other kids labelled him "Acne Boy" and "Leper Kid," and at first he had felt secretly pleased that Humphrey was taking the flak that most likely would have been directed at him.

But Humphrey had taken the laughter and name-calling with detached calm, like he knew things beyond the understanding of the other children. Finally, Eliot was forced to concede that he appeared quite noble and superior, and somehow untouchable. Over time, his classmates realised it too, and the taunting gradually died down. Envy and curiosity had led him to try and get to know Humphrey, and one biology class he had sat down next to him.

'Fuck off, gay boy,' the boy hissed. 'How much more do you think I can take?' Stunned and hurt, he slunk off the chair, hoping no one else had heard. As Eliot grabbed his books off the desk, Humphrey leant forward and warned, 'Don't look at me, talk to me, or come anywhere near me...you hear? *Ever!*' Eliot nodded and quickly returned to his usual place at the back of the class, burying his head in his textbook, just about managing to hold back his tears.

Eliot brought his face up close to the mirror. A current spot, a particularly large one, had formed on the left corner of his mouth. He resisted the temptation to touch the large, angry pustule. The massive yellow head told him that it was full of puss again, only now there must be pints of it. Every day it grew noticeably larger, and he was sure it leaked puss in the night, which then dried to a crust, forming a new layer, like a brooding volcano. Layer upon layer.

As he stared at the spot, his thoughts went over the events at the library. He closed his eyes and an image of her breast surfaced in his mind; perched on the edge of the toilet seat he masturbated quickly, the dry, stabbing climax sending a tremor along his spine.

Later that night, he woke to the sound of David moving around in the dark. Sitting up on his elbow he called out to his younger brother, 'What time is it?'

David sighed and then answered, 'About twelve. Why?'

'*Twelve?*'

'I was round at Rob's,' David replied, sounding bored.

'Did you get told off?'

'By who?'

'Mum.'

'Being at Rob's doesn't count.'

'Did Mum say that?'

'When does Mum say anything?'
'That doesn't mean it's okay.'
'What's it to you, anyway?'
'Sorry. Just asking.'

He heard David climb into bed. A sudden movement told him his brother had rolled onto his side to face the wall.

Eliot stared at the ceiling until sleep took him some time later.

2 Sunday, 14 February 1982

Sunday was Eliot's best day of the week. No school. No computer lessons. No kids.

Across the room, David was fast asleep.

His mum had left his "casuals" on the end of his bed—of late, he had started to wonder just when she did this—and he quickly dressed, grateful that, for once, it was not a mismatch of Michael's cast-offs.

Oversized and worn in numerous places, Michael's clothes made him look like a gyppo.

He found his mum curled up in the armchair beneath a blanket which, during the day, she stowed out of sight down the side of the sofa. The television was on and her cigarettes and lighter sat in the green ashtray on the side table. Several empty cans of Tennent's Pilsner lay on the floor beside the chair. Through a gap in the curtains, a blade of light cut across her pale face.

He sat on the sofa and placed his cereal bowl on his lap, but instead of eating his breakfast he just held up the spoon, as though he was trying to remember what it was for, and stared at the man on the television, who was dressed in a suit and tie and was talking about God. No cartoons this morning. No *Tiswas*.

It was Sunday. Serious stuff.

God stuff.

Eliot had had a problem with God for some time now. Once upon a time he had believed in him without question, but now...now it was becoming increasingly obvious to him that God was either not listening, did not care, or simply did not exist. He let his nan die, for one, then his grandad.

And there was other stuff too.

He looked across at his mum.

She'd have him back tomorrow. That was what Michael had said only a few months back. *She still loves him, despite what he's done.*

At the time, he had wanted to know what their dad had done, but seeing David nod knowingly at Michael's comment he had kept quiet, having no doubts that David would use his ignorance against him at some later date—during a fight over a missing piece of Lego or a dispute over the ownership of a specific comic; something like that, anyway. *You don't know what Dad's done so how can you even care about Mum?* That was the kind of thing David would say, regardless of its relevance to the argument.

He took the green ashtray and emptied it into the plastic bag hanging over the door handle in the kitchen, then put it back where he found it. Next, very quietly, he took away the empty beer cans. Finally, he washed out his cereal bowl and turned it face down on the draining board.

As he turned the latch on the front door, a small part of him hoped his mum would wake and notice that he had tidied up.

Eliot, you're a good boy. The best son.

But she never did.

He let the front gate swing shut and began to run.

Finding golf balls was a skill; you had to have talent. He was the very best there was, and for the best part of a year now he had been fine-tuning his abilities. Each Sunday he would spend hours trawling the ditches, rummaging through the undergrowth or searching amongst the trees, looking for balls. He could get 30p for a good golf ball, a £1 for five. Titleist, Top Flite, Pinnacle—these were the good ones, the ones that sold.

Eliot stopped when he reached the end of the narrow, tree-lined footpath leading onto the golf course. His gaze skipped from the pond, which lay between the first and eighteenth fairways, and then on to the woods the far side of the course. This was where he needed to get to.

Beneath the canopy of those trees ran all manner of secret pathways that brought you out unseen at any number of spots around the course; time held little meaning, and school seemed like just another bad idea in a long list of bad, grown-up ideas.

Glancing to his left, he could see that the first tee was clear, so he shot across to the pond, skirted around the lip, then crossed over into the woods, the sound of the trees stirring in the breeze welcoming him in.

He began his search at the tricky par three, tenth. It was protected on three sides by trees. To make matters worse for golfers, those who over-clubbed lost their ball to the deep ditch that ran around the back of the green.

This was where he would begin. It was as good a place as anywhere.

Eliot jumped down, legs straddling the lateral water hazard, and in a swaying motion moved along the ditch, eyes searching for the tell-tale flash of white.

The ditch gave up three balls; a Dunlop and two Titleists. The Dunlop was an inferior brand but it was almost new. Of the two Titleists, only one was in very good condition, the other had numerous scuffmarks on it. But all in all, it was a good start to the day. He dropped the balls inside the plastic carrier bag he had brought with him and disappeared back inside the woods.

The fourteenth was a long, difficult par four; tee to green, the woods ran the entire length of the hole. Having found a suitable stick, he spent about half an hour swishing it through the tall grasses which grew up beneath the first line of trees.

So far, this strategy had come up short; however, and with the morning now almost gone, his total for the day remained at three golf balls. Slightly irritated, he stopped and stretched, for a moment letting his mind wander. He imagined the stick was a sword; he held it out and gave it a swish.

Zorro!

Instantly, the enemy swordsman materialised in front of him. Grinning, he turned side-on, locked his left hand to his left hip and raised his sword in salute.

En garde.

The masked enemy, who was dressed all in white, displayed no such gallantry and immediately lunged for his heart, but Eliot was expecting this and parried it easily.

The enemy was tall and quick with the blade, and his counterthrusts were almost deadly. But Eliot was quicker; his hands fast, his footwork nimble, his blade work scintillating.

After a series of furious exchanges Eliot stepped back, eyes narrowing. He feinted, then lunged forward. The enemy managed to block the attack, but only just. Eliot flashed him a smile.

Back and forth they went, the clash of steel ringing out amongst the trees. Feint, parry, riposte…feint, parry, riposte.

Finally, Eliot sensed the enemy tiring.

A shuffle, a flick of the blade, a flash of blood on the cheek, the lips…and the enemy knew his days were numbered.

The killing thrust was fast, to the heart, clean. Vanquished, the enemy dropped to his knees before him, bowed his head, and died.

Raising his arms, Eliot stood a little taller, turned and turned, acknowledging the shivering leaves and the swaying branches with a diffident nod.

For a moment, he stood like this, a part of him regretting the end, killing off the enemy so early. When he next looked down, his sword had converted back into a stick. Feeling slightly foolish, he tossed it away.

It was time he got back to the serious issue of finding golf balls.

A £1.50 day: better than average. It was late afternoon. A boy with money had choices; he could make things happen. *Money makes the world go round,* his dad often said. Hand in pocket, he rasped two coins together and stared into the heart of the pond that lay between the first and eighteenth fairways. Like a great mouth it gulped down the ball of the poor golfer not accurate enough with his shot. The water was dark brown. Black reeds grew around the rim. There were golf balls down there, he thought. Hundreds of them. Like maybe, a hundred pounds' worth. More even.

From out of his plastic bag, he took out the two ruined balls he had been unable to sell. Giving them a final once-over he then threw them, one after the other, into the water...luck for his next visit.

The water took the balls down, down. Ripples in the pond. Then it was done. Another Sunday over.

School tomorrow.

He hated school.

Eliot turned into the cemetery, a shortcut home. A network of paths threaded their way through the numerous rows of worn and crooked headstones, very few of which stood perfectly erect but leaned one way or another, mostly in the direction of the chapel, which stood dead centre of the cemetery grounds. It had been closed for some years. Except for the windows, which were mostly smashed or missing, the stone building remained stubbornly whole, the gothic steeple rising black against the white sky.

Wherever he looked he saw beer and Coke cans, wine bottles, McDonald's cartons, sweet wrappers, and cigarette packets being taken down by the green fire of tall grasses. Eyeing an empty beer can in the nearest plot, his vicious grin was nevertheless ambiguous; it seemed like a terrible way to die, even for a beer can.

Keeping his head down, he hurried past the chapel and exited the grounds via the south gate.

It was stood by the front door like a first tooth. He stopped and stared at Michael's white bedside cabinet, the one that *belonged* between his and his older brother's bed.

Hearing laughter, he charged into the living room. Michael and his girlfriend, Sharon, were sitting on the sofa, chatting to his mum, who was sitting in her armchair. The television was on but the volume had been turned down. The curtains had been drawn back and the room was considerably lighter for it.

On the low table in front of Michael and Sharon sat three mugs of coffee. Two were empty, but the contents of the third remained untouched and its pale, sickly corona told Eliot it was cold.

'What's your cabinet doing in the hallway?' Eliot demanded, feeling like he had a right to ask.

'All right, little brother?' Michael said.

The use of the word *little* irritated him, and when Sharon flashed him a smile he ignored her, as though his brother's use of it had been all her doing. Folding his arms he looked to his mum, whom, he noticed, had gotten dressed and was wearing jeans and a pale-green jumper. She had also done something with her hair.

'So what's it doing there? Is it broken? *Mum?*'

His mum looked up but a fit of coughing prevented her from answering him immediately, so Michael jumped in. 'Well, I have to have somewhere to put my things,' he said, taking hold of Sharon's hand and giving it a squeeze. Eliot did not like the return smile Sharon gave his brother; it looked timid and false.

According to David, Michael and Sharon were getting serious. Sharon was a nurse and had her own flat, which explained why his older brother was hardly ever at home. Sharon looked like she had stepped right out of *Dynasty* or *Dallas*: She was tall, and wore a short blue skirt over tight black leggings. Her hair was blond and full, and glittered when she turned her head. The padded shoulders of her yellow cardigan made her seem even less real to him, more like a doll.

'Things? What things?' Eliot demanded. 'I don't know what you mean.' Even though he did.

'*Ooh*,' Sharon suddenly exclaimed, deflating the energy of his outburst. 'What have you got there?' She leant forward, like a greedy person.

Quickly, he stuck the bag of cough candy twist, which he had bought from the newsagents with his golf ball money, behind his back, but it was too late; Michael held out his hand. 'Come on. You can't bring those into the house without sharing. You know the rule.'

'What rule?' he protested. 'That's not a rule.'

Michael clicked his fingers. 'Just hand them over.' Not wanting to appear selfish and greedy (like Sharon), he surrendered up the bag of sweets to his older brother. But he glared at Sharon as he did so. 'And sit down, will you?' Michael complained, as usual acting, in Eliot's opinion, all superior. 'You're making the place look untidy.'

He threw himself down in the other armchair, brooding as Michael offered Sharon the bag of candy twist.

'Ooh, go on then,' said Sharon impishly, taking a sweet. Only when the cough candy was halfway to her mouth did she glance at him and ask, 'You don't mind, do you?'

Yeah, I do, you big, fat glitter-pig.

But it was too late to refuse her—and she knew it. *False.*

And he had let it happen. He shook his head.

'What about you, Mary?' Sharon offered, and he watched on helplessly as she held out the bag of sweets for his mum. 'Would you like one?'

He was relieved to see his mum decline with a shake of the head, and felt no guilt that he did. 'No, that's all right, love,' she said, reaching for her cigarettes. 'I'm not very hungry.'

'Had your piece of toast for the day then, Mum?' Michael said quietly. His mum laughed, and Sharon was about to laugh too, but she caught the sidelong glance Michael gave her and popped the stolen sweet into her mouth and handed the bag back to Eliot.

Hah! he thought, snatching back his sweets. *Serves you right.* He stuffed the bag of candy twist between his legs, thinking it would have been better if he had just gone straight upstairs.

Michael was a good talker, and he soon had the two women laughing out loud at his jokes or producing thoughtful murmurs at his political observations. At one point during the conversation, Michael accused the last Labour government of wrecking the country. 'Rubbish not collected, the dead left unburied, everyone out on strikes. We'd have no soddin' country left if Thatcher hadn't got in'.

Sharon nodded and so did his mum, even though she had heard it all from Dad, mostly at the dinner table.

He took a closer look at his brother. He had gotten tall, he realised, and the wispy down on Michael's chin had been replaced by a dark shadow, which crept along his jawline and smudged his upper lip. It was clear his brother was trying to grow a moustache. Eliot hated moustaches.

Their mum lit another Lambert & Butler. When she handed Michael the packet, Eliot grabbed the sides of the armchair, eyes widening.

What was this? Wait until he told his Dad!

But he glanced at his mum, and knew that he would be saying nothing.

Michael took out a cigarette and offered the packet to Sharon, who took one with a soft smile. His brother handled the cigarette with a casualness that unsettled Eliot. And he had skills with the lighter, too.

He watched his older brother take a drag on the cigarette, talk through the exhalation of thick, blue smoke—just like their dad did. He even picked at his teeth in the same way as their dad.

Eliot tried to recall how Michael had looked in his school uniform—it was suddenly important. But no matter how hard he tried he was unable to do so, and he glared at Sharon as though this was also her fault.

In fact, he found himself glancing at his older brother's girlfriend quite a bit, and he hated himself for it. But there was just something about the way Sharon's breasts swelled the woollen fabric of the yellow cardigan that made him want to shout out loud, or run away—or both. Oddly, it made him desperate to add something clever or profound to the conversation—if only to show Sharon how clever and profound he was—but he had nothing.

A couple of times, Michael caught him staring at his girlfriend's breasts, but instead of shouting at him, he just gave him an odd smile, which made his ears burn and, for some horrible reason, pushed him further outside the community of the others.

To combat this, Eliot tried to think about the woman from the library. *His* woman. But all the while, he found himself slowly drifting away from the other three, as though his armchair (now a boat) had been cut loose from the shoreline and was being pulled out to sea by an unstoppable undercurrent.

He was searching for an excuse to leave when David stuck his head around the corner.

Michael looked up. 'All right, mate?'

David flicked his head in the direction of the bedside cabinet out in the hallway. 'Moving out then, Mikey?' he asked, flashing Sharon a grin.

Michael gave an awkward laugh. 'Well, we'll see.' Sharon dug her elbow into his ribcage. 'Ouch! Maybe.' Another dig in the ribs. 'Hey, enough,' he said, surrendering to her with a laugh. 'Yes, yes. That's the idea.'

'And don't you forget it, mister,' she said, glaring at Michael, who held up his hands in mock submission.

'Hah!' laughed David, pointing a finger at Eliot. 'Told you.'

He shrugged, 'Big deal.'

David's expression took on a crafty look. 'So, Mike,' he said, picking at something on the door handle. 'What, erm...what's going to happen about your bed?'

'You're not having it!' Eliot shouted, launching forward.

'It's not up to you!' David yelled.

'Nor you!' he said. 'Mike, tell him. Tell him I'm second oldest.'

But Michael refused to answer; he just crossed his arms. Eliot sensed that his older brother's outward display of calm was just for Sharon, and he confirmed it when, with a roll of his eyes, he gave her a despairing little smile, which angered him greatly. Who did he think he was?

Sergeant arsehole...that was who, he thought, pinching one of grandad's favourite sayings, who had kept it in reserve for those who had especially annoyed him—typically, the clerks at the post office.

'It's not about who's oldest, stupid!' David shouted.

'You're stupid!' Eliot shouted back. 'You're not going by the window!'

'Mum,' David complained. 'Tell Eliot he's not having Michael's bed.'

'Hah!' Eliot spat. 'I don't want his bed. I never said I *wanted* Mike's bed.' Unable to stop himself, he glanced at Sharon before adding, 'I just said *you* can't have it, so there!'

David ignored him. 'Mum, tell him. Tell him he's not going by the window.'

But before their mother could answer, Michael broke his silence. 'No one's getting my bloody bed!' he shouted. 'So pack it in, the pair of you!'

The two brothers glared at one another, both quietly assessing the risk of shooting off one last comment.

Their mum gave Sharon a weak smile. 'See what I have to put up with?' she said. Sharon tittered. 'They'll be carting me off to the loony bin before long, you'll see.'

After a moment of awkward silence, the conversation started back up. David took a seat on the arm of the sofa next to Michael. Occasionally he would shoot Eliot a sneering, superior grin, as though he had won something, which was clearly not the case, as far as Eliot was concerned.

Michael started talking about his job; he was up for promotion at the supermarket; section supervisor. Eliot listened for a while longer, but when the talk next paused so that the three smokers could light up more cigarettes, he stood up and crossed the room.

Michael looked up. 'You off, buddy?'

Eliot glanced at the bedside cabinet in the hallway and then back at his brother. 'What's it to you? You don't live here anymore.'

With a glance at Sharon, his older brother laughed but gave Eliot a very direct look. 'No need to be like *that*, little brother.'

'Like what?' Eliot replied with an exaggerated shrug. Pointedly ignoring everyone, especially David, whom he sensed was desperate to get in one last dig, he left the room and went upstairs.

He stopped the moment he entered the bedroom and stared at the ugly space between his and Michael's bed, which the removal of the bedside cabinet had created. Now the room looked wrong, he thought, and kicked the end of David's bed.

Stupid girls.

Taking out his grandad's set of binoculars from beneath his bed and then his diary, which he kept hidden under his mattress, Eliot climbed onto Michael's bed and turned the binoculars on the street.

'*Don't stare, Eliot. It's rude,*' his nan had said on more than one occasion. He was certain that this was not staring but learning, finding things out, which he felt sure was important and would help him close the gap on Michael, which he was now, more than ever, determined to do.

He turned the binoculars on Old Man Vic at No. 20, who was about a million years old. Most nights, Eliot would find him pacing his living room, chanting. On such occasions he would often stop abruptly and whirl around, as though someone had called out his name.

On other occasions, mostly during the day, he would stand by the window, opening and closing his curtains, often breaking out into song—not an old one, but a popular tune current in the charts—so loud he could be heard in the street.

At other times, Old Man Vic would stand around the side of the house and bang the dustbin lid against the bin, which would make a great deal of noise, but no one seemed to mind; no one went around to tell him off. In fact, no one ever came around to see him at all. He would bang it repeatedly, *bang, bang, bang,* as though he was a teacher on the playground declaring lunch break over.

Tonight, however, he was just standing in the middle of his living room with his hands behind his back, swaying like a poplar tree, left to right, right to left, as though he could not make up his mind which way to go. Michael claimed that Old Man Vic suffered from dementia, which meant, according to David, that he was possessed like the girl in the *Exorcist*—which showed just how stupid David was.

The man at No. 18 lived alone, but he had a lot of male friends who would visit him at odd hours. He liked to wear tracksuits and from what Eliot could see, he kept a tidy house, much like his mum did. Well… except for her bedroom.

The couple at No. 16 were sharing the sofa in the living room, watching television. They had just had a baby and it kept them up at nights. The woman always looked slightly dishevelled and bewildered, like she had lost something important and was worried she might never find it. Sometimes the man, no doubt tired from work, would lean over the cot upstairs and would shout and shout and shout at the baby, clutching the milk bottle like it was a hand grenade.

And yet there were other times when the man would just sit on his bed, hand draped over the cot, his expression altogether different, and one that Eliot often found himself drawn to, without understanding why.

As usual, the man at No. 14, whom he guessed was no older than his dad, was sat at his desk, tapping away at his typewriter. There was no end to his typing; Eliot believed the man must have started his story on an impulse and had no idea how to end it. Cigarette smoke poured upwards from an ashtray which sat on top of a deep pile of papers.

He had never seen a Mrs No. 14, but from conversations he had overheard between his mum and Ruth next door, he knew the man was married. So, in his diary he had written, *'Had a wife but she left him. Probably because he couldn't finish his story.'* A later entry dated October 24 predicted, *'If he finishes his book by Christmas, maybe his wife will come back.'*

Putting down his binoculars, he wrote, *'February 14. Still at his typewriter. Maybe he should write a letter to Jim'll Fix It.'*

Taking up his binoculars again, he watched Typewriter Man reach for his cigarette in the ashtray. He took a long drag, blew out the smoke, and then hunched himself back over the typewriter. He looked dead intelligent, but not in a teacher sort of way.

Not for the first time, Eliot wondered if he could sit there writing day after day, lost in a world of words; lost in a world of his own words, in a world of his own making (like Earthsea, Narnia, or Middle Earth); the radio playing something intelligent, like the symphony music his music teacher was always playing in class. The more he thought about it, the more he kind of liked the idea.

Hi, I'm Eliot Thomas, I'm a writer. I write stories. I don't go to school.

He was just about to climb down off Michael's bed when movement at the top of the road stopped him. The woman that came into view was pushing a pram. She was on the opposite side of the road, walking very slowly, body leaning slightly forward against the pram. The look on the woman's face left him with the strong impression that she had been pushing that pram for some time and was somehow unable to stop, and so was likely to continue pushing it for some time to come. Maybe forever. It was a look that strongly reminded him of the look his mum often had on her face when he caught her staring out of the window between the gap in the curtains, which was most days.

As she drew level with the house opposite, he found himself hoping to see a door open, a smiling face inviting her in.

Come in. Come in. The Sunday roast is about ready.

It was suddenly very important that someone did. He waited, but no one came out. When the woman reached the top of the road, she turned the corner and was gone.

Michael and Sharon left at around five o'clock. Eliot and David ate their tea on trays in the living room; fish fingers, chips, and beans. Their mum did not eat, and seemed content watching television and smoking.

David bolted down his food so he could get around to Rob's before the start of *The Incredible Hulk*. Just before he left his mum shouted through to him, reminding him to scrape his plate and leave it on the draining board. For once, Eliot held back from reminding their mum that, technically, Sunday night was a school night.

At around seven o'clock he also left the house, and headed for the park.

Climbing into the bushes, he settled down to wait for the woman to make an appearance. Time passed, and traffic and other town noises slowly receded...

'Your mum got a call from your teacher last week, I hear,' his dad said in a quiet voice. 'That Leeds chap. Mr Wilson, isn't it?' As always, his dad looked for confirmation not from Eliot, but from Michael, who was watching his younger brother closely.

The three of them were gathered in the back room, by the door leading to the kitchen. His mum was standing by the window, behind the ironing board, folding clothes into the laundry basket.

'He says you show some promise.' His dad's expression suggested he thought this quite unlikely, but he continued. 'So…you like computers then?'

'I like the games,' he mumbled.

'Life isn't about games,' his father snapped. 'You're at big school now, remember?'

'So what do you reckon, Dad?' Michael asked, folding his arms.

'Well…computers are the future, no doubt about that,' he said, looking at Eliot as though he still thought a mistake had been made. 'They're already stealing people's bloody jobs. Look at the car industry…Right, Mary?'

'I have enough trouble with the video recorder,' she said. It was an old joke, but Eliot knew what his mum was trying to do, and it made him feel a bit better.

His dad, however, considered her comment for a moment before dismissing it. 'So, when are these lessons?'

'Saturday mornings, I think.'

'You think? Or they are?'

'They are.'

'Now…Saturday mornings? I didn't know the school was open on a Saturday.'

Fixing his eyes on his shoelaces, Eliot shook his head.

'What's that? Speak up, boy!'

'Mr Wilson has it all set up at his home,' Michael explained. 'Isn't that right, Eliot?'

He nodded.

'I see? So how much does it cost?'

Eliot shook his head.

'What on earth does that mean?' Throwing up his hands, he looked over at Mary. 'Is there something wrong with him? Is that it?'

Hugging the school jumper she had just finished ironing close to her chest, his mum kept silent, her lips so tightly pressed together they were hardly visible.

'It's free, Dad,' Michael said quickly. 'That's what you meant, isn't it, Eliot? It's free?'

'Is that right?' his dad asked in a stern voice. He had thick, black eyebrows that made him look like he was permanently angry, and it was no different now as he used them against Eliot. 'Is it free?'

He nodded.

'Well, you could show a bit more gratitude then, don't you think?'

Not trusting his reply, he opened his mouth, then shut it.

'Damn it, speak up!'

'B-but it's on the weekend,' he replied. Knowing this answer would not be enough, he added, 'And football's at weekends, Dad.'

His dad laughed. 'You don't play football, Eliot. David plays in a team. Michael played in a team. But you don't. What team do you play in?'

He had no answer to that.

'Very well, then,' his dad sighed. 'Make sure you behave yourself, you hear? It'd be just like you to mess things up.' He looked at Mary as though he had already "messed it up" and it was all her fault.

As he shuffled down the hallway, he heard Michael asking their dad if he was going to stay for tea.

After about an hour, he realised she was not going to show. Disappointed, and feeling oddly betrayed, he backed out of the bushes and made his way across the park. On his way home he made a list of things that might have kept her away, but most of them occurred during the day; Sunday roast, a visit to the pier, going to church—did she even have a nan and grandad?

As he rounded the corner into his road he almost knocked over a girl, sending the tennis ball she had been holding bouncing across the road.

She was about his age, he reckoned.

'Sorry,' he said hurriedly.

The girl looked him up and down for a second, smiled, and then went and retrieved the ball. Not knowing what else to do, he waited until she returned with it in her hand.

'I'm Claudine,' she declared brightly.

He shrugged.

The girl bounced the tennis ball on the ground in front of her and caught it. 'So what do they call you?'

'You mean my name?' he said, shoving his hands into his pockets.

'You must have one,' she giggled, then bounced and caught the ball again.

'Yeah…course,' he sneered, trying to act nonchalant.

'I mean, it's quite important you have one,' she said, sounding quite serious.

'I suppose,' he said, having no idea what to make of this girl, only that she spoke funny, she was playing in his road, and she was standing in his way. She wore jeans and big, black bovver boots, like Doc Martens, only for girls. Her green woollen jumper looked at least three sizes too big for her so that it fell straight down, flat against her chest. Her hair, which was black, was cut quite short, more like a boy's.

'I've got to go,' he said, and tried to walk around her. But she stepped in front of him and held up the tennis ball. 'Do you want a game of kerby?'

He shook his head. 'I can't,' he said, adding, 'I'm sorry.' Not that he was.

Claudine's large, green eyes regarded him solemnly as she considered his reply.

Feeling like he had done something wrong, he scratched his arm and shifted his weight from one foot to the other.

Eventually, Claudine shrugged and said, 'Okay then.'

But when he tried to walk around her, she again blocked his path. Finally irritated, he gave her a look that demanded she get out of his way.

But she laughed instead. 'Tell me your name first,' she insisted with a crooked little smile. 'Then you can pass.'

'Why do you want to know my name?' he demanded, hating that his voice sounded quite shrill.

'Just because,' she said with a shrug.

Frustrated, he glared at her for a moment before conceding. 'Eliot,' he snapped. 'You happy now?'

'Eliot!' Claudine beamed out loud. 'It's a nice name.'

Not expecting this, he shrugged. 'I don't know, I suppose.'

'It is,' Claudine declared, and stepped to one side to let him go. 'Maybe we can play kerby sometime, *Eliot*.'

He nodded. 'Maybe,' he said, having no intention of doing so. Ever.

'Bye, then,' she called out after him. 'Bye, Eliot!'

'Yes, bye,' he muttered.

As he walked the short distance to his house, he could feel her eyes on him. He purposefully did not look back down the road at her as he opened the side gate and went down the alley.

He found his mum smoking a cigarette and watching television, *That's Life*. An open can of Tennent's Pilsner sat on the side table.

'Where's David?' he asked from the doorway.

'Next door,' his mum murmured, taking a drag on her cigarette.

'Still?' he complained. 'But it's Sunday.'

'He's not staying over. I've told him that.' His mum picked up the can of lager and took a sip. 'Maybe I should call Ruth,' she said, although he could tell she had no intention of doing so.

On the television, Esther Rantzen finished talking and handed over to a small balding man, sitting in a huge chair that seemed to drown him.

'Mum?' he said slowly, quietly, like he did not really want to be heard.

'Mmm?'

'Is Michael really moving out? For real?'

Stubbing out her cigarette in the near-full ashtray, she reached for another one. Lighting the cigarette, she went to place the ashtray on her lap but stopped when she saw Eliot still standing there.

'What's that, son?' she asked, exhaling so that a thick cloud of blue smoke formed between them.

'Forget it,' he said, turning away from her. 'Doesn't matter.'

As he climbed the stairs, he heard the television audience applaud.

He knelt on Michael's bed to close the curtains and spotted the girl. She was still standing at the top of the road. What was her name again?

'Claudine,' he answered out loud, purposefully making her name sound dangerous, and therefore something to be avoided. She was bouncing her tennis ball on the pavement, eyeing the other side of the road. With a flick of her hand she threw the ball and at the same time stepped out onto the road. The ball struck the opposing kerb and bounced back, low to the ground, difficult to catch.

But she did catch it, securely, in two hands. She stepped back onto the pavement and prepared herself for another throw.

Lucky, he thought, and waited to see what she would do next.

She threw again and stepped out into the road. This time the ball's rebounding trajectory was a high one, and he was sure she would miss it. Expecting the ball to fly overhead he was astonished when, at the last minute, the girl hopped high and caught it one-handed. Grudgingly, he conceded that she had some skills.

And so the game went on and he settled down to watch, determined to stick with her until she made that one clumsy, girly mistake and dropped the ball. But she never did.

She looked even more like a boy from this distance, he noted, as she caught another rebound. It was only the subtler movements, the lightness in her step, the way she covered the ground, like her feet were hardly touching the road, which suggested otherwise.

And then, abruptly, the game was over. Catching the last rebound, Claudine stepped back on the pavement and held up the ball in two hands and did not move. In fact, she did not move for so long that he found himself fidgeting, unable for some reason to bear her stillness. There was just something so permanent about the way she was standing that, for a moment, she appeared more solid and real than everything else around her; the road, the houses, the parked cars.

Finally, and with a sigh and shake of her head, Claudine did move— and she was suddenly at the top of the road, then disappearing around the corner.

For a while longer his eyes lingered on the top of the road, as though he was half-expecting to see her reappear.

But she was gone.

'Stupid girls,' he eventually muttered, with a shake of his head.

In front of the bathroom mirror a little later, he was glaring at his spots.

So what do they call you? Claudine had wanted to know. He had asked himself the very same question numerous times.

'Eliot Thomas, Spot Boy,' he said out loud, and then waited, like he expected a response.

But when none was forthcoming, he said in an even louder voice, 'Who *are you?*'

But this time he did not wait for an answer and left the bathroom.

Still no sign of David. Eliot stared over at his younger brother's bed. He thought about going downstairs to remind his mum to call Ruth; or better still, go next door and fetch him home herself. But he knew this would cause a fight.

Pulling a book from his bookshelf, *Dragons of Autumn Twilight*, he opened it to a favourite passage and started to read; he would give his younger brother a little longer.

Finally, David came in around eleven o'clock.

'What time do you call this?' Eliot quizzed, but his brother ignored him. 'Did Mum call Ruth? Did she? *David?*'

'Piss off,' his younger brother muttered wearily and got into his pyjamas.

In no mood for a fight, Eliot tossed his book to one side, but was surprised when he heard a *thump*. Looking down, he saw it lying on the floor, where Michael's bedside cabinet had once stood.

Stupid cabinet.

'You going to turn off the light then?' David asked, not really asking.

Eliot got up and turned off the light.

3

Monday, 15 February 1982

'Any trouble, don't come looking for me,' Michael had said on Eliot's first day of big school, September before last. Eliot had already watched David leave with Rob for primary school, and he had desperately wanted to follow.

The two of them were standing by the front door. Michael drew back the drape, making to leave, but stopped when he saw his brother's face. 'You'll be fine, Eliot. Besides, I'll be around if you do get into trouble.'

Eliot smiled.

'But!' Michael added, with a playful thump to his brother's arm, 'That doesn't mean you can hang round with me, right?'

Feeling slightly better nevertheless, he nodded.

Satisfied, Michael said, 'Good,' and then left.

Catching hold of the door, he watched as his older brother climbed into the waiting Mini outside, resentment momentarily overcoming his first-day-at-big-school nerves: if it had not been for his new girlfriend, Sharon, Michael would be getting the bus with him.

Arms folded, his mum had watched this exchange from the kitchen, smoking a cigarette. As Eliot was about to follow his older brother out the door, she stopped him and placed something in his hand. 'Lunch money,' she said, and backed up.

He stared at the few coins (50p in total), which would now replace his packed lunches. Without understanding why, he sensed that this was an important moment for them both, and he should say something grown-up.

The expectation grew in him but it was his mum who finally broke the silence, murmuring, 'Right then, first day at big school it is.'

Taking another drag on her cigarette, she continued to stare at the money as though she had something else to add, but she remained silent.

Finally, he asked, 'Mum, where's Dad been for the last two nights?'

But he had left it just a second too late, and his mum had already turned away.

School.

Stupid school.

Crossing the seafront road, he walked slowly along the esplanade towards the bus stop. To his left the windbreaks rattled loudly in the morning breeze.

At the end of October each year a council flatbed truck, stacked high with wooden fence panels, would appear on the esplanade. Starting at the eastern end of the beach, the men in overcoats would begin tying off the panels to the wrought iron railings. Progressing in a slow westward arc, they would affix each panel in place in a methodical, paternally brusque manner, moving down the esplanade until they reached the concrete storm wall beneath the pavilion.

By the end of the day, the half-mile segmented windbreak would be securely in place. Finished, the men would gather around the flatbed truck and reflect silently on their work, satisfied each had done their bit, given the tools at their disposal, to batten down the seafront as best they could in preparation for the winter.

Only time would tell. Each year brought something new.

But of course, despite their best efforts, Eliot knew that when the winds came, the sand would find a way through.

And as the days progressed into weeks, into months, and the cold fingers of winter insinuated themselves into the heart of autumn, inexorably, drifts of tiny particles would begin to appear on window ledges, at the base of buildings, along the roadside kerbs, and would get onto the clothes, into the eyes, stick to the lips—and so find a way into the mouth; and very little could be done about it.

Sand dunes would form beneath the seats of the Victorian shelters and the ground beneath the feet would become rough like sandpaper, just like it was now, squealing under Eliot's school shoes. Wind-crafted sand shapes would writhe across the wide esplanade, disintegrating, only to reform farther along; or would be whipped up into a gritty suspension and be cast over the town.

On stormy winter evenings when the winds really picked up, and the sea muscled and clapped under fat, black skies, the panels would begin to rattle violently as though, as Eliot had always thought, some mad, rough beast was testing the perimeters of its confinement.

Kicking out a pebble, Eliot dug his hands into his pockets.

Stupid school.

The usual group of kids were gathered to catch the bus. Most of them stood outside the bus shelter, smoking and discussing the events of the weekend. Eliot sat inside, watching the traffic through a missing panel in the shelter, like he was watching television. Beside him sat the really tall boy with long hair, his denim jacket covered in badges. He always stunk of petunia oil. The girl and boy at the far end preferred to stand. Thin and pale-faced, and dressed all in black, they had black hair, and painted black fingernails. As they talked quietly between themselves, their silver crosses and jewellery sparkled. His dad had seen "their sort" hanging around and disapproved immensely. *Everything black! What's wrong with them?* was the kind of thing he used to say at the tea table after a bad day at work. *And what possesses a boy to wear jewellery, for Christ's sake? Can anyone tell me that?*

Everyone at the table knew it was best not to try and answer.

To pass the time whilst he waited for the bus, he read the graffiti scrawled on the painted wood panels opposite. Generations of kids had taken to the shelter to leave their mark. Words overlaying symbols overlaying images overlaying words covered whole areas of the blue interior, mostly sexual or violent in nature. He did not even know what some of the words meant, but they still provoked an excited shock each time he read them: '*Liverpool rules ok,*' '*Michael Foot's a fucking gypo,*' '*Ken Dodd's mum got fucked by a rabbit,*' '*Tracey Luvs Rob,*' and '*Greenham Common women eat box.*'

Several phone numbers invited the boy to pick up the phone—they were just numbers, but they still managed to unsettle him.

'*Ossie Ardiles eats shit.*' '*Thatcher's a lezza.*'

Varying in size and colour, several swastikas had been drawn; there was also a Union Jack and a Star of David.

'Mods are wankers.' 'Capri drivers are gay.' 'The Bee Gees take it up the arse.' *'CND'* was scrawled over, *'Nuke the Commies.'*

'Join the KKK.' 'Bad Company are ace.'

And then there was *'Cunt.'*

'Cunt.' The word had always frightened and amazed him. It broke the rules. It was bigger than a word, than all the rest; like the bully in a playground of words.

His mum hated the word. His teachers found its use appalling and unacceptable. He had never heard it spoken on television. Four letters but grown-ups, it seemed, were helpless against it.

See. You. En. Tea. Broken down in his head, it was harmless enough. But said all together, out loud!

Which often had him wondering; was it the word or the sound it made?

'Cunt,' he mouthed, looking around, terrified that the author of that word would appear at any minute and get him—though another part of him kind of wondered just what that someone would look like.

'Cunt.' He hung the word up in front of him, let the lips of his mind roll over it as though he was trying to smooth it down, soften the edges, tame it. But it remained hard-edged and kicked-out. *'Cunt.'*

Frightened and excited, he imagined saying it out loud; at the tea table, in the classroom, standing up in church. *Dad, you cunt, pass me the red sauce. Teacher, you're a cunt, and this is a cunt lesson.* He licked his lips and grinned. In church he would wait until people had their heads bowed in prayer and then he would say it…just once, out loud. Loud! *CUNT!*

The outrage and fear in people's eyes!

Brilliant.

Teacher, you're a cunt.

Deep inside the town, the church bell rang out a series of solemn notes. The familiar flat, green face of the double-decker bus appeared, looming over the top of the other traffic. Standing, he took his place at the back of the line. Once on board, he took a seat on the lower deck, hoping he would not have to share it later in the journey.

As the bus started forward, he looked out the window to take in what the sea was doing.

It was not long before the pier came into view.

From the bus, he could just make out the top of the cantilever roof. It was not as big as some of the piers he had seen on television, and who cared if it looked a bit run-down? It was his pier.

Eliot kept his head pressed against the window as the bus rumbled on, bringing the pier ever closer.

Having learnt that the winner of the Press the Button competition had been published, he had bought the local newspaper after school and, purposefully not looking at it, had carried it all the way home—then up to his bedroom—before braving a look.

The article, when he had found it, was small, hidden in the middle sections of the newspaper, beneath a small piece on something called AIDS.

Be me. Be me, he had prayed as he sat on his bed, his eyes skimming over the article, seeking the name of the winner.

Be me. Be me.

But it was not him at all, and he had read on in stunned disbelief. Two girls from Birmingham had won the right to blow up the pier. From Birmingham! *His* pier. Then and there, he vowed he would never, ever, visit this stupid Birmingham place—wherever it was. Scrunching up the newspaper, he had thrown it out of the window.

Shortly after the winners had been announced the pier was declared unsafe, and it was finally closed to the public back in January.

The condemned structure was now as large as it was going to get, and as Eliot continued to stare up at it, his head pressed hard against the window, the school bus slowly swung around to the right before taking him farther and farther away from his pier—but closer to school.

It was the lesson before lunch break and Mr Snider, the geography teacher, was explaining the process of longshore drift to the class.

'A spit is formed by longshore drift,' he was saying. 'This is the process responsible for moving significant amounts of sediment, such as stones and pebbles, along the coast, resulting from waves meeting the shore at an oblique or...anyone?' Mr Snider paused. 'No? Oblique or *diagonal* angle.'

With the aid of the chalkboard, the teacher continued with his explanation. The chalk squealed loudly as he drew a crude representation of an imagined beachhead. 'Waves carry sand and pebbles up the beach at an angle of approximately 45°. The backwash, however...the backwash carries the material back down the beach at a 90° angle. So, we can see that the sediment has moved up and across, then down. Yes?'

Without waiting for a response from the class, Mr Snider continued. 'The next wave carries this same material back up the beach at the same 45° angle...and the backwash brings it back down the beach. Then the next wave comes in...up, then down. Up, then down...and so on and so forth. Can we all see the sideways movement of sediment?'

Again, without waiting for a response, Mr Snider went on. 'In this way, sediment is transported along the beach until it runs out of coastline and is deposited. Over millions of years, pebble after pebble is deposited at the headland, creating layer upon layer of sediment, building outward until a...until a what is formed?'

For whatever reason, this time, Mr Snider decided he wanted an answer. 'Come on...anyone?'

Eliot tightened his grip on his textbook and remained very still. He had quickly discovered that, unlike primary school, the classroom at big school was more a place of conflict than it was a place of learning—child against child, child against teacher, teacher against child—a place where it was best if a child was *not* seen and *not* heard.

'A what is formed...someone? Anyone? Thomas, how about you?'

Pretending he had not heard his teacher, Eliot stared fiercely at the illustrations in his textbook and refused to lift his head.

'Eliot *Thomas*?'

Go away. Ask someone else. Please.

'What was that?' Mr Snider demanded impatiently. 'Cat got your tongue?'

Seeing no way out, Eliot mumbled something into his textbook.

'Speak up now. What's wrong with you?'

Not looking up, he repeated his answer, but in a slightly louder voice, 'A spit, sir.'

Mr Snider nodded. 'A spit is formed...yes, good. Now...'

'*A spit, sir,*' mocked a voice directly behind Eliot. '*Blow me, sir. Ooohh, blow me, sir.*'

Stiffening, he tried to shut out the voice.

'*Oi, gay boy? Oi!*'

The pen struck him on the back of his head, point first, just behind his left ear. Blinking back tears, he stared at the missile on the floor beside his desk, not knowing what to do.

The voice came again, '*Give it back or I'll fucking kill you.*'

'Is there a problem, Mr O'Neal?' Mr Snider barked.

Eliot quickly bent and, without looking up, handed the pen back to O'Neal, who snatched it out of his hand.

'Well?'

'No, sir. Just dropped me pen, that's all.'

'Well don't drop it again, you hear? Unless you want detention.'

'Yes, sir. No, sir.'

'Very good,' Mr Snider said, and continued with his lesson.

A little later and obviously bored, the voice came again, '*Oi! Gay boy!*'

Eliot had had a problem with O'Neal for a while now. O'Neal had no fear. If rumours were true, O'Neal skived more days than he attended, and had been slippered more than any other kid in the school. It was said that in his first year, during the middle of a lesson, he had asked the new female biology teacher if she "*fancied a shag.*" Apparently not prepared for this, the young biologist had just stared at the grinning boy for a second, then rushed out of the classroom to get help. She was never seen again.

'Sir?' another voice piped up.

'Yes, Dickenson?' the geography teacher asked in a tired voice.

'Miss Jones in RE said that the world was made in six days.'

'Well, what of it?'

'Well, you just said that a spit is made up over millions of years.'

'I can get out a spit in a few seconds,' chipped in O'Neal, exaggerating a hawking sound. The class laughed.

'I won't warn you again, O'Neal,' the geography teacher growled.

The kids sensed something was coming.

'What about Miss Jones, sir?' Dickenson persisted.

Kids grabbed pens and shifted in their seats, exchanging excited grins with friends at nearby desks.

The *something* was definitely on its way.

'It's best if you direct that question at her.'

'Why's that, sir?' asked Dickenson.

'Because Miss Jones is talking bollocks,' O'Neal intoned loudly.

'*Out!*' roared Mr Snider. '*Get out, O'Neal.*' Despite the geography teacher's fury, the class erupted into hysterics. 'To the principal's office, *now!*'

Eliot risked a glance up. O'Neal had grabbed his school bag and was swaggering towards the door.

'Quicker, O'Neal. I haven't got all day. And the rest of you, *quiet!*' O'Neal slowly opened the door, then slammed it shut.

No fear.

'And you'll be next, Dickenson,' the teacher warned.

'But I haven't said anything, sir.'

'And keep it that way.'

Eliot rubbed the back of his head as Mr Snider resumed his class. It was French Studies next.

Monday over with, he leant against the wall and stole a glance in the direction of the bus stop. It was packed with children. Most of the older lads had already stripped away their uniforms and were smoking cigarettes. Older girls had loosened their ties and were glancing at the boys with unguarded admiration. Some of the juniors had joined the congregation and were aping the seniors. O'Neal was there. He had bummed a cigarette and was grinning viciously at anyone who dared look in his direction.

O'Neal may have been in Eliot's year, but to look at him, he could have passed for a lad of seventeen, eighteen even, and there were not many kids, of any age, who dared challenge O'Neal's claim that he had bought beer at an off-licence—not once, but on *millions* of occasions. He had a crew cut and had rolled up the sleeves of his school shirt so that his tattoos—'*Madness*' on his right wrist, and the lion of Chelsea F. C. on his left—were openly on display, contrary to the rules. His scruffy bomber jacket was tied around his waist.

A beat-up car stopped at the bus stop. The passenger window was down and the song 'That's Entertainment' by *The Jam* was playing on the radio, loud. A tall, blond girl stepped out from the crowd of kids and with a self-conscious flick of her hair, got into the car.

'Mods are wankers!' O'Neal screamed at the car, at the unseen driver. A few of the kids standing next to O'Neal tittered; others looked a little shocked. Everyone waited to see what the driver would do; hungry, Eliot knew, for a bit of violent entertainment of their own.

But the car pulled away with a sputter from the exhaust and O'Neal laughed out loud. This time more kids joined in the laughter; laughing at the departing car, at the driver who was too chicken to offer up a response.

O'Neal looked around imperiously and took a hard drag on his cigarette.

No fear.

Eliot hated him; hated that he wanted to be like him.

O'Neal caught Eliot staring at him. The big lad laughed and nudged the girl next to him. She reminded him of a wolf. With big, brown eyes she peered at Eliot between the spiked strands of her blond hair, which had been streaked with black. It was cruel hair, he decided, unable to look away. Without taking her eyes off him, the she-wolf nudged the boy next to her, Dickenson; Dickenson of the spit question, who had even more spots than him. He was quite possibly the spottiest kid in the world—except for Humphrey Beswick. The difference was, Dickenson did not care. He was too mean to care.

Together, the three of them stared at him, sharing some laughter at his expense. Afraid and red-faced, he looked away, which only prompted more laughter.

Just then the bus arrived.

O'Neal pushed past the smaller kids so he could get onto the bus first and take his place amongst the seniors on the top deck. It was why Eliot always sat on the lower deck, up front, in the seats behind the driver.

As Eliot approached the house, he saw a man in a suit with a briefcase talking to a short, large woman out on the pavement; Ruth, his mum's best friend. The man made several exaggerated gestures, to which Ruth shook her head. The animated conversation continued until they spotted Eliot. Quickly, Ruth said something to the man, who nodded. Then they shook hands, and the man got into his red Audi and drove away. With a nod in his direction, Ruth hurried back inside her house and slammed the front door shut.

He found his mum in the living room, chin in her hand, staring out of the window through a chink in the curtains, the television on but ignored. Briefly he thought about the woman with the pram from the other night.

'Mum, who was that man talking to Ruth?' he asked.

Lighting a cigarette, she said, 'A solicitor, honey; nothing to worry about.'

He nodded, even though he had further questions on the matter. 'Where's David?'

'I think he's having tea next door tonight,' she murmured through a cloud of smoke. 'Yes, that's it.'

'On a *Monday*?'

'Uh huh,' she replied, turning her narrowed gaze back on the street.

'I see,' he said, and stomped upstairs.

Later, he communicated his disapproval by having his tea (sausage, chips, and beans) at the dining room table in the back room. It meant him missing out on his TV programmes, *Harold Lloyd* and *Roobarb*, of course, but this was important. David was spending way too much time over at Rob's. A stand had to be made.

He was hungry but strangely, he could not translate that feeling into any kind of action, and his knife and fork remained unused to one side of his plate as a dark-red crust slowly formed over the beans.

For a moment, he let himself believe that this room and the kitchen were separate from the rest of the house, like it was his own flat—like Sharon had her flat where she kept Michael. That made him think of the woman from the library. He was certain she would be there tonight. He wondered what she would make of his flat. He looked around the room. He would have to fix the place up a bit, he concluded. The old brown sofa could stay but the tall, white display cabinet might have to go.

Reaching the ceiling and running the entire length of the partition wall shared with the kitchen, it had always been too big for the room. Books and albums and numerous other items, untouched and mostly ignored, were cramped up in ordered rows on the many open display shelves.

He ran his fingers through the thick dust on the dining room table, spelling out his name. Then, for no good reason, he said it out loud, but softly, slowly.

'Eliot…Eliot Thomas.' Spoken like this, his name sounded like someone else's name and he was hearing it for the first time. He discovered that he did not like the name, nor, he suspected, would he like the boy who possessed such a name. *Eliot Thomas.* It sounded made-up, pretend. When he glanced at the portable television perched on the end of the display cabinet, all he saw, looking sick and distorted, was his own expressionless reflection staring back at him.

Maybe if he turned it on?

Suddenly, Ruth shot past the back room door and bustled on up the hallway.

'Heart attack,' he heard Ruth declare, out of breath.

'Yes, I saw the ambulance,' his mum said, coming out to meet her friend. 'Do we know who?'

'Mr Finny at number 36.'

'You'd better come through.'

They moved into the living room. The volume on the television was turned down.

Eliot abandoned his tea and raced upstairs. On his way up he heard Ruth say, 'Well, he was a no-good sort anyway.'

'It's complicated, I heard,' his mum said.

'You can't make excuses for him, Mary,' Ruth replied in a scolding tone that he did not care for. Then in an altogether different voice she asked, 'So how are you, anyway?'

'It's difficult. I don't know what to say.'

'You'll have to talk to him?'

'Yes.'

And then one of them, Ruth, he suspected, closed the living room door.

The drama seemed well and truly over by the time he clambered onto Michael's bed. His binoculars had never been of any use against No. 36; the distance made the angle inaccessible, so he knew nothing of Mr Finny. When the ambulance doors were shut and it pulled away, he felt as though he had been denied the opportunity to feel bad and sorry for the man at No. 36, and the ambulance—no lights, no sirens—seemed all the more dispassionate for it.

He took down a book and waited until it was time to go out.

She made her appearance sometime after nine. Dressed all in black, she looked like no other woman he had ever seen; flawless, frightening. A miracle.

'So, what will it be…Ron?' she said. 'It was Ron, wasn't it?'

The man resembled a troll, a fat troll with a crew cut, and a tatty jacket and scuffed shoes. But his words—'I need it all, babe. Fucking all of it'—Eliot liked his words.

'It's twenty. Up front.'

After the exchange of money had taken place, the woman backed up against the wall, slid off her panties, and hitched her skirt up to her waist, keeping it high up there like a Hula Hoop.

'Well?' the woman said in a low, husky voice. 'I haven't got all night.'

He took it out. Its vicious, curved height seemed impossible, and Eliot grabbed hold of the branches either side of him. He wanted to look away but the secret truth of it was that he thought he might want Ron to stick it into her a bit.

As the man moved in, the woman widened herself.

The man's grunt was an ugly sound, but Eliot sensed that he had got deep into her. The woman lifted her hands above her head and made some encouraging murmuring noises…Eliot was sure he had been waiting all his life to hear those kinds of noises.

'Yeah, Ron, that's good,' she moaned.

Ron's savage rhythm was appallingly exact.

'Harder, Ron, do me,' she whispered, her head jolting.

Eliot plucked down a leaf from a nearby branch and crushed it down.

'Yeah, fucking yeah,' the man growled.

'Oh, stop! You are so good, Ron,' she said, her head slowly turning in the direction of the bushes. Staring back at her, Eliot plucked off another leaf and crushed it down to a wet pulp.

'Yes, Ron, yes.' But her words were toneless, like she was delivering an RE lesson.

And then Eliot had it! She was pretending. Ron meant nothing to her. Exulting, he sneered at Ron's dumb ignorance.

'Fuck!' Ron yelled, and his rhythm faltered. His body started to convulse in an ugly way. 'Yes!' he shouted. 'Fucking God. Yeah!'

For a moment after, there was silence. Silence filled the courtyard.

Then Ron coughed.

No longer able to look at the man, Eliot averted his gaze as Ron put himself away.

'So, what do you call yourself?' Ron said finally.

'Call myself?' The woman looked puzzled.

'Yeah, your name. What's your name?'

'Is that important?'

The man shrugged. 'Not to me, I suppose.'

'Then we're agreed, it's not important.'

But it was. Eliot wanted a name. It *was* important. He watched Ron depart, then the woman a few minutes later. Once they had gone, he hurried over to take up his place in the corner of the courtyard. He closed his eyes and called upon her image to join him there…*I need it all, babe*…and she came.

He touched her, touched her breast. Kissed the nipple.

'Yes...bloody...fuck,' he said out loud—and then blinked. He *liked* these words in their new environment.

Eliot tried out some other combinations: 'Fuck yeah...God...do it.'

Touching her; touching her breast; kissing the nipple...

'Bitch, come on...fuck...yeah...'

And when the dry stabbing pleasure doubled him up, he shouted, 'You fucker...God you...*fuck...*'

Finished, Eliot looked down at his hand.

Nothing. But he sensed that things were changing.

Lying on his bed later, he tried to recall the walk home but he was unable to do so. Consequently, the events in the courtyard remained very immediate, as though he had been transported from the library to his bedroom in an instant. His memories often behaved like this; sometimes it seemed like his whole life was just a series of isolated moments, intense, little bubbles...bubbles in a glass, rising and popping, and rising and popping—nothing outside of the bubbles, outside of the glass.

Downstairs he heard the familiar sound of the ironing board being collapsed, then the click of his mother's slippers moving down the hallway. She coughed loudly a few times and then the fridge door opened. He heard her move back down the hall. Seconds later...*Fzzt*, the sound of a ring pull. Then the volume on the television was turned up.

Twenty pounds. At first, his mind rejected the idea as stupid. But the more he thought about it, the more he thought...was it possible?

Of course, he thought he heard her reply.

Who are you? What's your name?

I'm here, waiting for you.

He slid off the bed. Kneeling beside his bookshelf, he peeled back the corner edge of the frayed carpet and pulled up the loose section of floorboard. Removing the small metal tin from its secret hiding place, he quickly counted out his money.

£1.73. It was a start.

As he returned the tin to its hiding place, he checked over his other secret stuff, just in case—the habit of a boy with brothers; a packet of Durex he had found at the railway station; a rusty penknife; a letter to Father Christmas he had written when he was eight or nine but had never sent—it listed a bike, which he got anyway; his dad's fountain pen, which had gone missing two years ago; his grandad's pocket watch; a baby tooth, one that had fallen out when he was eight, and he had purposefully rolled up in some tissue paper and hidden—to see if the tooth fairy would collect it anyway, which, of course, she had not.

His gaze came to rest on the small, black book and he pulled it out. Holding the spine in his palm, he ran his index finger along the block of red-coloured page-ends sandwiched between the covers. He had bought it at the summer jumble sale in his last year of primary school. It was the unusual combination of the red-ended pages and the black cover boards that had attracted his hungry little eyes in the first place, and he had snatched it up before anyone else could buy it. Greedily he had turned it over in his hand under the watchful gaze of the old woman behind the trestle table, thinking that perhaps it was maybe an old spell book or some other rare and fantastic work. He was surprised and disappointed when he discovered it was just a Bible.

'Are you going to buy it then?' the woman had said, her tone clearly suggesting that she expected him to buy it now he had picked it up. 'It's ten pence.'

At that point, he felt like he had no choice and so grudgingly, he had handed over the money.

Replacing the book, Eliot closed up his hiding place and went into the bathroom.

As he finished cleaning his teeth, he noticed the green stain on his fingertips. He brought his hand up close to his face and marvelled at how ingrained the leaf pigment appeared. He shot a quick look at the reflection in the mirror.

So what do they call you?

Eliot Thomas, Green Boy.

He picked up a cloth and began scrubbing his fingers.

4
Friday, 19 February 1982

£1.73

It was soon clear to Eliot that the woman's appearances were mostly random. He was certain of only two things; on Sundays and when it rained, she stayed at home, wherever home was. He knew this because on Wednesday night, when it had rained, he had waited in the bushes until he was soaked through before he could accept that she was not going to turn up.

Increasingly, the idea of her began to dominate his thoughts. Where did she live? What was her name? Where did she get all these men from? Did it somehow work like the Avon lady? Would she take anyone? Why the back of the library?

She would intrude upon his concentration during school lessons, disrupt his reading time, and generally impose herself upon him during moments of quiet. When he was watching television, something would occur that would make him think of her. And then his imagination would call her out.

I want to play! And the television was forgotten.

No place or space, it seemed, could be entirely free of her.

Twenty pounds.

It was not long before he was worrying about the end of the month. On the last Sunday of March the clocks would go forward, and he had gotten it into his head that she would abandon the park when the hours of daylight grew longer and the kids returned to play.

He was thinking about this very concern as he hurried down the school corridor. It was Friday, towards the end of morning break. As he rounded the corner, he slammed into a group of kids and his school books went flying. He staggered backwards, but the words of his apology died in his mouth when he saw who it was he had bumped into...

O'Neal.

He was with Dickenson and the girl from the bus stop, the she-wolf with the cruel hair. Grinning, O'Neal passed his bag to the girl and used his forearm to push Eliot up against the corridor wall, digging it into his neck so that he could hardly breathe.

'Well, well, if it isn't the teacher's pet.' His breath stank of cola cubes and cigarettes.

O'Neal applied more pressure to his forearm and Eliot's face started to redden.

'Give us your money, shithead.' O'Neal had a look about him that promised violence whether he handed over his lunch money or not, but he fumbled to find his lunch money anyway.

'Money, money, money!' the she-wolf demanded in a high-pitched voice, and laughed. Dickenson laughed. All three kids were soon laughing.

Then O'Neal stopped abruptly, his small, black eyes staring at him. 'Hand it over or you're dead.'

A tall shadow was suddenly looming over O'Neal and a hand thumped down on his shoulder. 'What the fuck?' O'Neal snarled and whipped around, ready to beat the hell out of the person who had dared lay a hand on him.

'Is there a problem here?' It was Eliot's tutor and maths teacher, Mr Wilson, who also ran the newly formed computer club, which was held after school on the Monday and Wednesday of each week. Eliot no longer attended the club. He used to, but not anymore. Not that he had told his mum or dad this.

But so what? He did his computer lessons on a Saturday. What more did they want?

Eliot could tell from O'Neal's expression that he was considering challenging Mr Wilson.

No fear.

But in the end, O'Neal shook his head, and the other two kids took that as a sign to back off.

'Good,' Mr Wilson said. 'Well, don't let me keep you, O'Neal.'

Eliot looked out from behind his teacher's back as O'Neal and his two friends retreated down the corridor. O'Neal pointed a finger at him and mouthed his usual threat, *'After, gay boy.'*

Eliot looked up at his teacher, grateful for the intervention but hating him for interfering.

'Can you get to your next class all right?'

'Yes, sir,' Eliot replied.

He made to go but Mr Wilson stopped him. 'Oh, and Eliot.'

'Sir?'

'You did well in your last maths test. Well done.'

'Thank you, sir,' Eliot replied, wishing his teacher had said, *'Your last test was shit. Get out of my sight. I don't want to see you again, you...you fucking spanner.'*

Eliot Thomas, Teacher's Pet.

Eliot did not see O'Neal for the rest of the day. Thinking he had bunked off school to help his dad, who, it was said, did a bit of labouring work on the side, despite being on the dole, Eliot decided it was safe to catch the bus.

The decision turned out to be a mistake.

O'Neal was at the bus stop, smoking and laughing. Close by stood the she-wolf with the cruel hair and, of course, Dickenson. Eliot's first instinct was to run. But that might alert O'Neal to his presence and excite the bigger lad into doing something for the sake of impressing the senior boys present. By staying, however, he risked O'Neal catching sight of him and starting in on him anyway.

Eliot hung back against the wall, positioning himself in such a way that a group of older, taller kids were in O'Neal's direct line of sight. He need not have worried, however, because a mock fight suddenly broke out between two seniors. O'Neal watched for a few moments and then quickly, faster than it ought to have been possible for a boy his size, darted in and got both boys in a headlock, one under each arm. The crowd laughed, but it was the kind of laugh that made Eliot nervous and short of breath—a starving laugh, one that needed violence to feed it.

A small space opened. The helpless seniors tried to make light of their predicament, but Eliot could tell by their clipped, awkward laughs that they were embarrassed and afraid, and each in their turn, lips hardly moving so the crowd would not see, muttered wheedling things up at O'Neal trying to get him to let them go. But the crowd knew; the crowd saw everything. And the seniors knew this, and it completed their deep humiliation.

O'Neal had no mercy in him. Loving the moment, the big lad spun them around and around, shouting out to the crowd. The crowd jeered and whooped, but always there was this hungry undercurrent, the crowd wanting more, and Eliot's heart beat a little faster. He, too, wanted to see more, and it sickened him.

Around and around O'Neal spun them, laughing and laughing. And then, with a final roar, he released the two seniors, much to the disappointment of the crowd.

Red-faced, the two boys stood back, trying to act as if nothing had happened, but they failed utterly. They had been taken and shamed by a kid in a lower year; they knew it, the crowd knew it, and O'Neal knew it.

Anger simmered in the eyes of the taller of the two seniors, a lad with short, brown hair who wore a fishtail parka with lots of badges on it. Eliot could see that he was thinking about making a move against O'Neal. Silently, Eliot urged him to strike. But in the end he, like his shorter friend, backed up and let the crowd swallow him up.

The bus pulled up shortly after this incident and cigarettes were expertly tossed away as a queue hurriedly formed. The doors slid open and kids started boarding, briefly flashing their passes at the driver. Eliot's hand tightened around the pass in his pocket as he took up his position at the back of the rapidly diminishing line. The engine running, the tall, green flanks of the bus trembled as it gorged on children. As he neared the vehicle, the smell of diesel excited his stomach and made him feel a bit queasy.

Grabbing the handrail, Eliot pulled himself up onto the high step. As he did so, he felt something large and flat strike his chest. He stared down at the huge open hand and then slowly up at its owner.

O'Neal. He grinned at Eliot. 'Do you think so, Joey Deacon?'

Eliot held onto the metal handrail as hard as he could and looked to the bus driver, who he hoped would intervene. The pressure on his chest suddenly eased, only to be increased tenfold seconds later. The violent shove made him lose his grip on the handrail and sent him tumbling backwards out of the bus. As he fell, the only thing that mattered in life was to stay on his feet, but the ground seemed to kick up at him and he skipped and stumbled backwards, his arms flapping madly.

With a jolt that hurt his teeth, Eliot fell on his backside. He got up quickly. But it was too late. Everyone had witnessed the fall. Bombs of laughter dropped from the top deck. He looked up. The girl who had been standing with O'Neal and Dickenson had slid open one of the small top windows and had thrust out her angled head as far as it would go. 'Gay boy!' she shouted. Other windows slid open, and Eliot knew that the whole of the top deck had rushed over to the kerb side of the bus, eager not to miss out on the fun.

Eliot stared at the bus driver but the bus driver, a long-haired, lean-framed man with a wispy moustache, gave him a tired, dispossessing look and jammed his vehicle into gear. The door hissed at Eliot before it collapsed shut.

The bus growled into life and slowly heaved forward. On the bottom deck, rows of white faces turned in his direction, grinning, smirking, laughing out loud.

He heard a shout from above and as he looked up, a gob of spit landed on the shoulder of his duffle coat. Seconds later, O'Neal's face disappeared back inside the slow-moving bus. The gears of the bus let out a meaty crunch and by halting increments it picked up speed, lengthening the gap between it and Eliot. O'Neal's face reappeared amongst the many laughing faces pressed up against the top rear window.

Eliot glanced at his shoulder. The thick, green gob slowly began its descent down the left side of his coat. When Eliot lifted his head, he found himself looking straight into O'Neal's eyes. The bigger lad made a shuttling gesture with his clenched fist, *wanker*.

He suddenly hated O'Neal with a deep hatred. He hated Dickenson. He hated the girl. He hated his computer lessons. He hated his mum and dad fighting all the time. He hated the fact that his nan and grandad were dead. He hated that they were going to blow up the pier, his pier. He hated that Michael was now living with Sharon. He hated his house. He hated living in his house, with his mum smoking and drinking all the time. He hated Rob. He hated that he was chicken and never said anything to anyone, about anything. But mostly, he hated God.

God, he hated. He did not listen. He did not exist.

Eliot wished he was more like Michael, or even Ron. *I need it all, babe. Fucking all of it.*

And then he did it without thinking, without consideration of the consequences.

Raising his right hand, he jabbed his middle finger in the direction of his larger classmate. The laughter on O'Neal's face turned to one of shocked outrage. He pointed a vicious, stubby finger at Eliot and mouthed words Eliot had no trouble translating, '*You're fucking dead, gay boy.*'

As the bus rumbled out of sight, Eliot stared at O'Neal's large, white face and he knew the big lad would make good on his promise.

When he got home from school, he found his mum sitting in her armchair. She was in her dressing gown, feet tucked up behind her, staring out of the window, chin in hand.

'Good day at school, son?' she asked. Eliot glanced at the television: the Australian soap *The Sullivans* was showing. Right then he wished he were in Australia and the other side of the world.

O'Neal was going to kill him.

'Yeah…okay, I suppose,' he shrugged.
'Learn much?'
'Some.'
'That's good,' she murmured.
'I'm going to read for a bit.'
'Okay then.'
'When's tea?'

Eliot waited but she did not reply. Not thinking the question was important enough to further distract her from the television, he went upstairs without another word.

What had he done? Unable to move or think properly, Eliot lay on his bed, staring up at the ceiling, the scene at the bus stop replaying in his head, over and over—his finger rising, unable to stop it, like someone else was in control of it—the look on O'Neal's face, his deadly promise…

O'Neal was going to kill him. It was just a matter of time.

He felt sick.

But who was he going to tell?

His dad? *No.*

Michael? *Just as bad.*

One of his teachers? *No way.*

And what could he say? O'Neal had not done anything yet.

Besides, if he did snitch, he might as well end his life at the same time.

To take his mind off things, he took out his binoculars and diary and climbed onto Michael's bed. Lifting the binoculars, he turned them on the street, like he was looking for answers, looking for someone to blame.

O'Neal was going to kill him.

Old Man Vic was turning the living room light on and off at the switch, chanting to himself. The man at No. 18 was sorting through his post. *'February 19,'* Eliot wrote in his diary, *'No. 18 is going through his bills but he doesn't look worried. I wish we lived over there.'*

No. 14 was at his typewriter but he had his elbows on the desk, his hands pressed together making a steeple. '*Typewriter Man could be praying. But it won't help. God doesn't write stories.*'

O'Neal was going to kill him.

Just as he was about to slide off Michael's bed, Eliot caught sight of his brother coming down the road. Rob was with him. They were deep in conversation, school bags tossed over their shoulders. He watched the boys cross the road and stop outside Rob's house.

Curiosity getting the better of him, Eliot carefully turned the handle on the window and pushed it open, just a little bit.

'….well if you don't want to, I'd fuck her,' David was saying.

Rob laughed. 'Maybe I already have.'

'No way!'

'Way,' Rob insisted.

'Have you really?'

'Nah…only joking,' Rob admitted. 'But she let me finger her.'

'Really? Where was her dad?'

'Downstairs. But I could have taken him. He's a wimp.'

'Yeah…says who?' David asked.

'My dad.'

David seemed impressed by this answer. 'So, what was it like?'

'Sweet. But she was really hairy and made my fingers stink.'

'Urgh!' David laughed, then asked in a low voice, 'Did you lick your fingers after?'

Rob smirked. 'What do you think?'

'Argghh, that's wrong!' David cried. Then he stopped dead and grabbed hold of his friend's arm. 'Hey, Rob?' he said, looking serious suddenly. 'I know what your mum's making us for tea tonight.'

Falling for it, Rob asked, 'What?'

David stuck his finger under Rob's nose. 'Fish fingers and chips?' The two of them made cringing noises and started laughing.

Shocked, Eliot realised he would have to rethink the matter of Rob. He had always considered him to be a bit of an idiot. He had jug ears and was a bit fat. But it was clear he knew some stuff.

'Give me a sec then,' David said, leaving his school bag on the pavement. 'I'll just see if it's okay with Mum.'

Eliot heard the front door open downstairs. He heard David and his mum talking for a while. Then the front door opened and closed and David reappeared outside. Jumping over the low wall he said to Rob, 'Yeah, Mum says it's cool.'

So, he was having tea next door, again!

'Look!' Rob suddenly hissed, grabbing hold of David's arm and pointing to something down the road. 'There's that Draper girl.'

Eliot turned his head. He could see Claudine at the top of the road. Once again, she was playing kerby all by herself.

'So what?' David looked bored.

'She's been with loads of boys, I've heard.'

David looked dubious. 'She can't be any older than us.'

'The year above, I think,' Rob said, his voice low, almost conspiratorial. 'First year of comp. My mate, Iggy, from football, says she'll blow you for a packet of cigarettes.'

'Shit!' David said, but he looked interested now, and took a good look down the road.

'Believe it. I've heard she's had two cocks in her mouth at once!'

'That's too much!' David shouted. 'What a slapper!' Grinning, his look turned sly. 'Would you?'

Rob pulled a face. 'Get lost. Look at her! I like a girl with...you know?'

'Go on.'

'With big, massive tits.'

'Yes,' David nodded, his voice catching.

'I've heard her bra left her.'

'Left her?' David asked. 'What? Why?'

'Because it was leading an empty life.'

The two boys roared with laughter.

Eliot shook his head. This was impossible.

Grinning, Rob went on, 'Anyway,' he said more seriously, 'she's really fucked-up, I've heard.'

'Tell me.'

'Her dad committed suicide. She found him hanging in the bathroom.'

'That's a lie!' David cried, although he clearly wanted to believe it, which Eliot thought was mean and horrible—though a bit of him was oddly excited by the idea of her tragedy, and wanted it to be true.

Rob nodded solemnly. 'Scout's honour; Mum told me.'

'Better stay away from the psycho then.'

Rob nodded again. 'What do you think she's doing, anyway?'

David shrugged. 'Beats me.' Then he laughed. 'Maybe she's gasping for a smoke.'

Rob laughed. And then David laughed, even though it was his joke.

'Let's get inside before she sees us.' Pretending to be frightened, Rob opened his front door and the two of them disappeared inside, still laughing.

A little shaken, Eliot closed the window. His mum needed to do something about David staying over at Rob's.

What was she thinking?

Eliot knew what his father would say about it all…

So, where the hell are they?

Out.

Out? Out?

Michael's eighteen, for Christ's sake, Donald!

And what about Davey?

He's at Rob's.

I don't care if he's in the fucking shed. It's a school night.

God, listen to you! It's a bit late to be going for Father of the Year.

Don't start that shit again. You knew I was coming round. They should be here.

It's going to take time, Donald. Give it time. This is new to everyone—perhaps you should have thought about that when…

Eliot glanced at the girl down the road. She was bouncing the ball in front of her and eyeing up the far kerb for a throw. He tried to picture this small, strange girl on her knees, mouth open, two men standing in front of her, grinning evilly to one another as they thrust out their hips; but for some reason his mind rebelled and the image collapsed. A part of him was quite glad about that.

When Claudine next bounced the ball, it hit the toe of her ridiculously large boots and shot out across the road. She gave a stamp of her foot and then chased after it. As Claudine stooped to pick up the ball, she turned her frowning face in his direction, slowly straightening up.

Alarmed, Eliot pushed back from the window. There was no way she could know that he was looking at her, was there? But he still found himself breathing heavily.

What was she doing in his road, anyway?

Cautiously, he took another peep out of the window.

But she was gone.

Given what he had just heard, his disappointment surprised him.

Eliot made a new entry in his diary: *'Disturbing news. A strange girl has started appearing at the top of my road. Rob says she does things for cigarettes and is messed-up because her father killed himself. Michael says Rob is spoilt and full of shit. But could it be true?*

Lean-framed and curving, the man nodded, his long hair veiling his eyes in a greasy black curtain. But it was the wispy moustache, barely established, that really troubled Eliot. It made him look mean and... sly. But he wasted no time in handing over the money.

The woman got down on her knees and took him out.

He had a small one, the smallest so far, and it was all over very quickly. His reverent gibberish rushed out like a hurried prayer, like he had never had a woman, like he was scared.

The woman, Eliot noted, *his* woman, kept her contempt to a minimum, like she felt pity for him.

Once the man and then the woman had gone, Eliot stepped out of the bushes.

He imagined himself taking a seat next to her on the steps beneath the security light. *They talk. He makes brilliant observations, political and social. Knowing his brothers and Rob have hidden themselves in the bushes—he can hear them fidgeting around noisily —he leans in quickly and gives her a long, hard kiss, using his tongue in an expert way that astonishes her, astonishes those he knows are watching.*

Eliot glanced around the courtyard.

Twenty pounds.

He needed to get to the golf course, but tomorrow was Saturday.

Stupid computer lessons.

Twenty pounds.

That was all he could think about on the way home.

His mum was asleep in her armchair. Several beer cans lay on the floor. *Cagney and Lacey* was closing out. The curtains, as usual, were ever so slightly parted. Sometimes he would imagine himself standing outside on the pavement staring back in at her, waving, trying to get her attention. *I'm here, right here, Mum!* But he could never get her to look directly at him. Or if she did, it always seemed that she was looking right through him, as though he was not there, her eyes fixed instead on something coming up behind him.

O'Neal was going to kill him.

5 Saturday, 20 February 1982

£1.73

Saturday morning. He could have quite happily stayed under the blanket, letting the world think he had gone missing: *'Child mysteriously disappears whilst still in bed,'* the caption would read. *'Police baffled, family devastated.'* Knowing what his dad would say if he missed his computer lesson Eliot sighed, threw back the blankets, and got dressed. *'Child hoax! Missing boy found hiding upstairs in his own bedroom.'*

He was surprised to find Michael in the living room. He was sitting forward on the very edge of the sofa, clasping a mug of coffee in his hands and talking quietly to their mum. She looked tired and pale, as though she had not slept well.

'You can't ignore this,' his brother was saying in a low voice. 'You have to talk to Dad.'

But when Eliot entered the living room the conversation immediately died, which angered him immensely.

Noticing the full black bin liner on the sofa, Eliot sneered, 'Sharon refusing to do your washing?'

'It's not washing,' Michael snapped. It looked like he was going to say something else but he glanced at their mum and fell silent.

'No, so what's in the bag, then?'

Michael seemed determined not to respond, which niggled Eliot.

'Well? *Tell me!*'

'Damn it, Eliot!' Michael shouted. And then in a much calmer voice he said, 'It's some of my old clothes, if you must know. Sharon's doing a car boot sale on Sunday.' Michael glanced at their mum. 'To raise a little extra cash.'

'You can't take those,' Eliot blurted, before he could stop himself.

'No?' It was Michael's turn to sneer, though he looked a bit surprised also. 'This from the boy who hates hand-me-downs.'

'You don't know what you're talking about,' Eliot bit back, slamming his hands into his jean pockets.

'Then what is it?' Michael demanded. 'Why don't you explain yourself...*for once*?'

'Leave it, Michael,' their mum said in a quiet voice. She started to cough, but it broke down and turned into a wheeze that seemed to go on for an age, like someone was letting all the air out of her. When it eventually subsided, she reached for the ashtray and her cigarettes.

'You need to give up smoking!' Michael complained, his eyes pinched.

'You can talk,' she said with a tired smile.

'You should both give up smoking, actually,' Eliot sniffed.

Michael, who, as far as he was concerned, was acting uncharacteristically moody this morning, glared at him.

'When I finally get rid of you lot, I might,' their mum said, and coughed again. A little redness exploded into her cheeks.

Michael gave her an odd little smile. 'I'm working on it, aren't I?'

Arching her thin eyebrows, she said, 'You mean Sharon is.'

Pretending to sound hurt, Michael said, 'Arrr, don't you love us anymore, Mum?'

'Huh, you'll be the death of me, the lot of you,' she complained. 'Particularly that bloody father of yours.'

Michael hid his face behind his mug of coffee.

'Bastard,' she muttered, turning to look out of the window as though she expected to see him pull up in his car right then.

Eliot suddenly wished that he too had a mug of coffee. 'I'm going to get some breakfast,' he said.

Michael nodded to reassure him things were still okay between them, but Eliot ignored him.

Eliot was sitting at the dining room table in the back room, his breakfast bowl in front of him. His mum and Michael were still talking in the front room. It was ten o'clock. Mr Wilson usually picked him up around eleven. Sometimes he got there a little earlier.

'In a tragic traffic accident earlier today, a maths teacher from a local comprehensive school lost his life when his vehicle collided with another car on the seafront. Although it is not known how the accident occurred, it is understood that travelling in the second vehicle were two girls from Birmingham, who were set to blow up...'

Eliot just wanted to be on the golf course. As always, his thoughts turned to his lady.

Twenty pounds.

Acting on an impulse, Eliot spent ten minutes rummaging down the back of the old brown sofa. By the time he was finished, he held in his hands several dirty coins, a bus ticket, a toy car, and a blue lighter, which he flicked to see if it still worked. It did. Putting the other items to one side for a moment, he sifted through the coins. One was an old penny-farthing. Another was a French franc. He stared at this coin for a moment. When had they gone to France? Discarding these, he counted the rest. Twenty-two pence! Hurrying upstairs, he went to his secret hiding place.

£1.95.

He sat on the end of his bed with the tin on his lap.

He was on his way.

'Local boy, thought missing, runs off with beautiful mystery woman.'

By ten thirty, his older brother was ready to leave. Astonished, Eliot watched from the doorstep as Michael walked up to the Ford Cortina parked outside and dumped the black bin liner in the boot.

'That's not yours, is it?' Eliot shouted.

Nodding, Michael opened the driver's side door. 'Got it a few months back, you idiot!' he yelled. 'Jesus, Eliot, join in, will you!'

Watching his brother casually start up the engine was a frightening moment. Where had Michael gone? He glanced at his mum, half-expecting to see her rush to the door and demand that Michael stop being silly and get away from the car, but she just reached for her cigarettes and stared out the window.

Eliot watched as the car disappeared down the road. Finally, on tiptoes, he willed it not to turn the corner, as though he was worried that if it did, he might not see his brother again. But it was soon gone.

'Don't forget the drape,' his mum called out from her armchair.

'It's not really that cold, Mum,' he said, but did as he was told anyway.

Something about *"the traffic"* and it being *"rush hour"* was the explanation Mr Wilson always gave, but he never dropped him back at home. The man on the car radio had just finished discussing Prince Charles and Princess Diana (who were expecting a baby) and Bucks Fizz's 'Land of Make Believe' *had begun to play* when the car pulled up outside the school. Thanking his teacher (which he always hated doing), he got out of the car and watched it pull away.

Ten minutes later and Eliot found himself leaning against the esplanade railings, staring down onto the beach. A couple were walking on the dark, wet apron of the sand, deep in conversation. The man was making some exaggerated hand gestures and the woman threw back her head and laughed. Seizing his moment, the man caught her around the waist and pulled her close.

It could be him soon, Eliot thought. He pictured himself down by the water's edge...

Shoes in hand, the woman from the library was walking beside him, laughing at his jokes. They were brilliant jokes that made her eyes shine. Then he told her a story, using many elaborate hand and body gestures to astonish and amuse her.

Later that day they go back to his place, and sit on the old brown sofa. He's thinking of getting rid of it but she insists that it stay. She loves that old sofa. After setting up the projector, they settle in to watch slides of their most cherished and intimate moments together...their holiday in Rhyl; their wedding; the summer days on the pier—the authorities having decided at the last moment that they would not blow it up, but restore it to its former glory—even a slide of the two of them back in the courtyard holding hands, commemorating the moment when he had first appeared before her and offered her some money, which she had refused, loving him from the start, promising him they would stay together, forever.

*Crack, crack, crack...*The sharp sound brought him back to the present. On the esplanade, only a few yards from him stood a big, black crow. It had a shell in its beak and it was beating it against the concrete. Eliot did not know if the shell was empty, but as the crow lifted it to the sun, he feared the worst.

Crack, crack, crack.

Against the sun, the crow's body was dark and shining. It was almost too real. It did not belong here, and Eliot let himself believe that the gulls were aware of its presence but dared not approach it. The crow continued to beat on the shell.

Crack, crack, crack.

And then suddenly, as though the crow sensed it was being observed, the bird spread its wings, stuck out its chest, and with a loud, mocking squawk, turned and turned. To Eliot it was an act of defiance, a declaration to the world, *Touch me if you dare!*

The crow turned some more. Then, without warning, it let out a piercing shriek and lifted its dark, shining body into the air, the partially smashed shell still in its murderous beak, not quite finished with it.

Like a sudden shout, Eliot felt his stomach swell with envy and admiration: to be a crow. To be *that* crow.

But no.

Sighing, Eliot pushed himself away from the railings. It was getting late. The seafront had emptied of people and the traffic seemed heavier. To the east, inside the closed amusement arcade, he could see the flickering lights of the machines. The odd shadow moved around inside; the maintenance guys fixing things up, repairing or replacing old amusements.

It had been a long winter.

Things broke down.

For a second he turned his eyes on the pier, then hung his head and turned for home.

The argument that was taking place in the living room sounded like it had been going on for a while. With one eye on the living room door, Eliot crept along the hallway and took the stairs two steps at a time, praying he was not heard.

Punishment for interrupting one of these "grown-up conversations," was...*comprehensive*.

He found David and Rob in the bedroom. They stood very still, as though they were playing a game of musical statues and the music had stopped. David was clutching his *Wombles* bag and Rob was beside him, his wide eyes never leaving his friend's. Eliot stopped where he was and grabbed the door handle.

Like that, the three boys listened intently to the argument coming up through the floor.

'It's just a pair of school shoes for God's sake, Donald.'

'Christ alive, Mary; how many times do we have to go through this? I'm just a bit short this month.'

Eliot glanced over at Rob, angry and ashamed by his presence.

'Look, this is doing no one any good, Mary, especially *you*.'

'Don't you *dare use that!*'

'Damn it, there's no talking to you sometimes.'

'Talk? When do we ever talk? When have we *ever* talked?'

'Come on, that's not fair.'

'So I'm just meant to forget everything...including *her*, I suppose?'

'Oh for God's sake, Mary, will you give it a rest?'

'*Rest!* Do you know how hard it is, Donald? Do you know how hard it has *been?*'

'I do. Of course I fucking do. But what can I do when I'm out of work?'

'Oh, God! Like there was a difference when you were *in* work.'

'Mary, please.'

'No! *NO!* School shoes, Donald. They're practically falling off him.'

There was another pause during which David pointed his finger at Eliot. '*You*,' he mouthed accusingly. Eliot wanted to protest, but with Rob there he felt that all he could do was shake his head.

Instead, he glanced down at his school shoes. They were indeed scuffed and natty—and he suddenly felt guilty and greatly ashamed.

'There *is* something...a job. But it's out of the area.'

'Bored of her are we, Donald?'

'What? No! I mean—'

'Well I can't say I feel sorry for her.'

'I'm going. I'm sorry...I can't do this right now. Call me when you're ready to talk sensibly.'

'No, wait...Donald?'

Eliot turned the door handle in his tightening grip. *She'd have him back tomorrow.*

'No!' his dad yelled. 'Enough's enough, Mary. I came here to talk. There are things we need to talk about. I mean, Jesus Christ! We have to talk about *this*.'

'Don't you think I know that, Donald?'

'Do you? I mean do you really?'

'No, wait...Donald, please.'

'Not when you're like this.'

'Don—' She started to cough, which gave his dad time to escape. The front door slammed shut.

After a moment, David and Rob started moving, as though the music had started back up.

Rob blew out his cheeks. 'Wow.'

'*What do you mean, wow?*' was what Eliot wanted to say but instead he ignored Rob and looked over at David.

'Do you think that had anything to do with that man coming round the other day?'

'What man?' David asked, hugging his *Wombles* bag.

'You know,' he said, 'the solicitor.'

David shrugged. 'Dunno anything about a solicitor.'

Any other time, Eliot would have used his brother's ignorance against him, but not tonight. Instead, he glanced at his brother's bag and asked, 'You're staying out again?'

'Yeah, so?' David answered.

'Nothing.'

'What are you, his mum?' Rob sneered, then turning to David he said, 'Come on, let's go.'

As the two of them stomped down the stairs, Eliot heard Rob say, 'Hey, Dave, why are Pakis shit at football?'

There was a pause.

'Because every time they have a corner, they build a shop on it.'

David groaned loudly. 'God, that's so *old*.'

After counting his money again (he still only had £1.95) Eliot read until tea, which he ate in the back room—bangers and mash with gravy. At a quarter to nine Eliot grabbed his coat from behind the front door. As he turned the latch on the lock, he half-hoped to hear his mum shout, '*Where the hell do yer think you're goin'?*' But all he heard was her coughing. Yanking open the door he waited, giving her a second chance, but when her coughing fit eventually subsided she lit up a cigarette, muttered a curse at the television, then fell silent, which Eliot took personally.

Deliberately, he slammed the door shut and broke into a run, heading for the park and the library and the woman waiting for him there.

Twenty pounds. That was all she wanted from him.

He was tall and had a narrow face, dark eyes and thick, black eyebrows. He looked like a man who spent most of his time angry. To Eliot he seemed unworthy of her, but he was powerless to stop her from giving the man what he wanted, which maddened him.

When the man was finished Eliot watched him depart, hating his dismissive manner...the absence of gratitude in his expression, behaving as though he had some kind of right to her.

When Eliot stepped out of the bushes...

...her sad expression turns to one of surprise. 'Eliot, my name's Eliot,' he says. She nods and they sit on the steps beneath the security light and he tells her his story. She listens, her surprise turning to anger...and then tears... and finally... finally love. She can see that he is no ordinary child; not a child at all. He is brave and incredible, she sees that...and clearly there is something special between them.

Quite alone, Eliot took his place in the corner, amongst the shadows.

Later that evening he was kneeling on Michael's bed, his elbows on the windowsill. Sighing, he peered into the streetlight outside until the light glowed more brightly, expanded, then poured back towards him until he felt like he was submerged in yellow.

He breathed heavily and repeatedly onto the window until a heavy condensation formed. Then he wrote 'Help me' into the breath-cloud.

He stared at these two words for a moment, wondering if it would help if he said them out loud. But before he could decide, the condensation receded and the words faded.

Sighing, he slid off the bed.

Who was going to help anyway?

Pulling up the sleeve of his pyjamas, Eliot slowly dragged the edge of the protractor (which he had sharpened on a brick) down the top of his arm. He hissed through gritted teeth and let the pain spike deeply into him. He increased the pressure…deeper and deeper…until there was only the pain, white in his head, burning out every other thought.

'Is there something wrong with him? Is that it?'

After a long while but with a reluctant gasp, Eliot pulled the protractor away. He stared at the line of blood running down his arm, the deep throb inside warming his stomach.

Placing the glass plate under the microscope, he peered through the lens expecting to see something terrible and sick, but the sample looked no different to the ones he had studied in biology class. He held his breath and really strained his eyes, but detecting nothing hideous—no black blood cells or strange mutations manifesting his fundamental wrongness—he shook his head and sat back on his heels, close to tears.

Then why him? Why?

Hesitating for just a second, he labelled the sample '20/02/82—Blood' and packed away his microscope.

Thirsty, he went downstairs. The television was on in the front room but the armchair was empty. He looked down the hallway and caught sight of his mother in the kitchen. Wooden brush in her hand, bucket by her side, she was scrubbing the vinyl floor.

Of course she was; his dad had been around.

Unnoticed, he watched his mum go at the vinyl, muttering to herself. The rapid flow of words seemed complicated and out of step with her deliberate lunges and heaves. Turning away, he spotted his school shoes sitting behind the front door and glared at them for a moment, as though they were the source of all his problems, before retreating upstairs.

School shoes, Donald.

Grabbing the hand basin he stared into the mirror. The spot by his mouth had grown larger, was expanding at a hideous, nightly rate. He was already mindful of its crispy presence between his lips when he spoke, making talking an uncomfortable experience, and he wondered if one morning he might wake to find his mouth sealed shut.

Eliot Thomas, Dumb Boy.

Do something! raged the boy in the mirror.

He waited until his mum had retired to the living room before creeping downstairs, returning a few minutes later with his school shoes, the shoe polish kit, and his dad's Super Glue, which he had found hidden beneath the cutlery tray in the kitchen drawer. He had never been allowed anywhere near the Super Glue: *'It'll stick your fingers together, it will,'* his dad had once warned him, catching Eliot with the tube in his hand. *'And if it gets on your lips or in your eyes, you'll be in big trouble...you won't be able to see or speak. Is that what you want? Not being able to speak?'*

Well, if his dad had wanted the glue, he should have taken it with him.

Eliot examined the shoes like he was a doctor, the shoes the patient.

It was his right shoe that was the real problem; specifically, the outer sole around the perforated toe. It had come away from the shoe upper so that when he walked, the sole slapped against the toe cap.

'This shoe has a lisp,' Doctor Eliot pronounced to the surrounding students. 'It needs gluing.' Embarrassed, the students nodded and took down notes on their clipboards. They should have seen this. 'And the shoelaces need replacing...in both shoes,' he added with a sad, thoughtful shake of his head.

Sitting on the floor, he laid out the shoe polish kit and took up the right shoe. Applying a goodly amount of the glue to the relevant parts, he then fastened a large fold-back clip over the front of the shoe to keep everything in place.

Eliot went over and sat on Michael's bed and waited for the glue to dry. He spotted movement up the road. A group of girls staggered into view. He could hear the clatter of their heels striking the pavement. Pushing the window open carefully, he leant forward and listened.

Swaying and swinging their bags wildly, they giggled stupidly and laughed high, startling laughs. Their language was uncompromising and frightening; 'fucking cow this,' and 'the silly bitch that,' and 'I fancied the fuck out of him.' They broke into song and their singing echoed all the way down the street.

It was difficult to imagine himself ever being ready for that kind of woman, he realised—or wanting to be ready.

And a part of him hated them for that.

As they drew level with the house, Eliot closed the window and slid off his brother's bed.

'Leather needs feeding,' his grandad used to say. Sticking his hand in the left shoe, he lifted it up and applied a thick amount of black shoe polish to the scuffed toe cap area. He let it dry for a moment, and then…three quick strokes. Pause. Then three more strokes—a solid, dependable rhythm, just as his grandad had shown him.

This done, he took out the cloth and buffed the shoe for a further 10 minutes until the toe and sides had a good shine. Done, he turned his attention to the right shoe.

Leather needs feeding.

Discarding the clip, he treated the badly scuffed toe with generous amounts of black polish.

Three strokes. Pause. Three strokes. Repeat. Repeat. Then buff and polish to a shine.

Leather needs feeding.

He gave the pair of shoes two further coats. Finally satisfied, Eliot replaced the laces in both shoes with a set taken from a pair of Michael's old school shoes he had found at the bottom of the wardrobe.

Finished, he held up his shoes.

School shoes, Donald…

'Fuck 'im,' he said out loud, believing he was almost ready to say it to his dad's face.

He just needed some more time with his woman.

6

Sunday, 21 February 1982

£1.95

The sun was high and yellow, and there was some blue in the sky. Clouds moved lazily in a westerly direction. Eliot stood at the top of the tree-lined path and inspected the course.

Green. Green course. Green space. But he was happiest in the woods, with the shadows. Under the apron of those trees he moved along light-fractured paths, letting his imagination play freely as he searched for balls; one moment he was a Roman general leading the fight against the Visigoths, the next minute he was on Moonbase Alpha fighting an alien incursion. It was brilliant, and he was brilliant, and capable of anything. Everything he did amazed the world.

He stood behind a large tree midway down the thirteenth fairway watching the slow progress of four golfers, all men. It was late afternoon. Three of the golfers had taken their second shots and were now waiting for the fourth member of their group, who had hit the longest drive, to take his approach shot into the green. The man, in grey trousers and a blue, diamond-patterned jumper, drew back his club, held it at the top of his back swing for a fraction of a second, and then swung. The clubface struck through the ball and sent it fizzing sharply to the right, towards Eliot, low to the ground.

A shank!

The ball clattered into the trees no more than fifteen yards from Eliot's position.

The man fell into a rage. 'Cunt!' he screamed, smashing the club on the ground. 'Fucking ball, stupid fucking wank bastard shitty game!'

Eliot stared at him in disbelief. The three other men started laughing, however, which shocked him even more. 'Stupid fucking shitty cunting game.'

Here was that word again, 'Cunt.' It seemed to be everywhere. The golf commentator on the television never said it; 'Well, Nick Faldo, that was a cunt shot. Really shitty.'

Eliot said the word out loud, slowly, dragging out each consonant and vowel, *'See-You-En-Tea*...CUNT.'

He immediately felt tougher.

The man hurled his club up the fairway. The steel shaft flashed brilliantly in the sun as it helicoptered away from the golfer, whose continued spew of vile words echoed around the entire golf course.

Eliot withdrew into the woods and got himself out of there, not wanting to be caught anywhere near the errant ball when the man came looking for it. Otherwise he might be called a 'cunt' too, and a thieving one. It was time to go anyhow. He could feel it on his skin. The temperature had started to drop, and the life noises of the woods had subtly altered, dulled, and hardened as the chill of evening slowly crept up on the afternoon.

The dark water took each ball, three in total, with a crowning plop that nudged out a sequence of oily ripples.

Heaving a sigh, he stuffed the empty plastic bag into his pocket and trudged off the golf course.

£1.70: a good day.

Eliot Thomas, Hunter Boy.

Eliot heard the shout as he exited the golf course. At the top of the road, still some distance from him, three kids sat on push bikes pointing in his direction. One boy was very large and had short hair. He wore a black bomber jacket.

O'Neal.

No doubt the two kids next to him were Dickenson and the girl, the she-wolf.

This was it. He was dead.

O'Neal said something to them and they pushed their bikes forward. Eliot turned and started to run. He was a good runner. The best.

'If you get chased, never run home,' Michael had said one night. *'That's the last thing you should do, right?'*

Michael was at a big school, so he knew stuff like this. David and Eliot listened enthusiastically, grinning at one another, feeling pride that their older brother thought they were ready to receive his wisdom.

'Why?' David had asked.

'Because then they'll know where you live, yer spanner.'

David's face reddened, and Eliot was suddenly glad his younger brother had asked the question before he could. When David next looked over at him, Eliot shook his head as if to say, 'Yer divvy, don't you know anything?'

Houses flew past in a blur. Road followed road. The slapping of his trainers echoed on ahead, faster than him, so that he wished he could alight the echoes of his own flight.

Gradually, however, the sound of pursuit faded, their yells growing fainter and more desperate. A nervous giggle escaped his lips.

When Eliot came to the crossroads, he risked a glance over his shoulder and seeing no one, he came to an abrupt halt. His breathing ragged, he sent his mind out; when it returned, he knew that the streets were empty. Everyone was inside. Only he, Eliot Thomas, had dared to stand up to the bad people.

He opened his shoulders and bared his chest north, east, south, and west, turning and turning.

And where *were* they now?

Was there no one left to challenge him?

Suddenly, his three pursuers came racing around the corner.

'There he is!' the girl screamed, pedalling faster.

He was not afraid of a girl.

'Kill 'im!' she yelled.

Eliot whirled around and started to run…

'Chicken!'

And then he was stumbling, falling.

He threw out his hands in front of him protectively, the heels of his palms shredding as they slid along the tarmac. It hurt terribly, but he ignored the pain.

'*Hah!* We've got the fucking weirdo now!' he heard Dickenson shout.

The sound of their sudden laughter was like a punch in his stomach.

Run.

In teary panic, Eliot staggered to his feet and started running again.

He shot into the cemetery. Now he had a chance.

But then he stopped, turned and turned, trying to decide which path to take.

'*Here!*' a voice called out.

Jumping in fright, Eliot whipped around.

It was her; Claudine Draper!

She was stood behind a headstone not twenty feet from him, waving him over. '*Quickly.*'

Shocked, Eliot hesitated, but the sound of his pursuers grew suddenly louder on the other side of the high sandstone wall; they were closing on the entrance, fast.

Whirling away, Claudine made for the far end of the cemetery, flitting from one headstone to another. She turned once, just to make sure Eliot was following—which of course he was; but only because his surprise had nullified his ability to come up with his own escape plan.

'Get down,' she whispered when he reached her. The urgency of the situation drove out any questions he had for this strange girl and he hunkered down next to her behind a large headstone.

Grinning, Claudine put her finger to her lips, warning him to remain quiet, and pointed.

Eliot spotted the three children as they entered the cemetery grounds through the north gate. He could hear them arguing. He took a peek. All three had dismounted their bikes and were pushing them along the path.

As they neared the chapel, the path split in two. Halting, the she-wolf shouted, 'You go round that way! We'll go this way!'

What was wrong with this girl?

Almost dragging his bike, O'Neal nodded his agreement and took the higher path, soon disappearing around the side of the building. Pushing their bikes, the girl and Dickenson remained in sight, circling the chapel by the lower path.

Claudine stirred beside him.

'What are you doing here?' he whispered, still breathing heavily from his recent exertions.

Eyes bright, she put her finger to her lips again and shook her head. Eliot could see that she was enjoying herself, which annoyed him. If O'Neal caught him, he was a dead man. Could she not see this?

O'Neal reappeared on the high side of the building, Dickenson and the girl soon joining him. The big boy shook his head. The she-wolf pointed towards the south gate. Wringing the handlebars on his bike, O'Neal's lighthouse gaze swept the cemetery. Eliot could almost feel the anger coming off him.

Claudine grabbed his shoulder and forced him back down behind the headstone. Breathing hard, the two of them waited, the girl still grinning stupidly.

Not to be shown up, Eliot shot her a grin of his own, though he was sure it probably looked more like a grimace.

A minute or so later, Eliot and Claudine lifted their heads.

They were gone.

Cautiously, the two children stepped out from behind the headstone.

'That was close,' Claudine breathed. Her tone suggested that victory had been achieved. She was wearing an overly large brown woolly jumper and a pair of jeans. And of course, her big, black boots.

'What are you doing here?' Eliot demanded.

'Walking,' she answered. 'I like it here.'

Her tone was so matter-of-fact that Eliot felt foolish for just asking the question, which proved what an irritation she could be.

'They're not very nice people, are they?' Claudine observed.

'Do you know them?' he asked, not taking his eyes off the south gate—in case his three pursuers re-entered the cemetery.

'I know their type,' she answered, her expression suggesting she really did. 'Bullies…nothing more. Nothing special.'

Eliot nodded, but he was now on high alert, remembering the conversation he had overheard between his brother and Rob. She did not sound like a psycho, but these things were hard to tell.

'Come on,' she said and moved off, heading in the direction of the central path. Following, he kept a wary eye on her as she weaved her way through the headstones. Occasionally she would slow, her eyes lingering on a nearby inscription, her expression sad and thoughtful.

When she reached the path, she stopped. 'Do you want to stay out and play?'

She said it so abruptly that he was caught off guard. 'Why?' he answered, a bit too quickly for his own liking.

Only then did he spot the tennis ball in her hand. Claudine bounced it off the path and caught it with one hand. 'They won't come back, if that's what you're worried about.'

'I'm not worried,' he said, puffing out his chest a little. 'What makes you think I'm worried?'

Claudine shrugged. 'No reason.'

'I'm not scared,' he insisted.

'Okay,' she said, eyeing the south gate. 'Come on, it should be clear by now.'

'They don't scare me, you know,' he said, falling in beside her. The path was just wide enough for them both.

'I only meant that there were three of them,' the girl sighed. 'I mean, anyone would be worried in a three-against-one situation.'

'Well, I'm not anyone,' he snapped.

'No,' she replied slowly, with the hint of a dimpled smile. 'I can see that.'

Not sure how to take that, he replied, 'Well, good then.'

He was devising ways of getting rid of this girl when he noticed something odd about the chapel. The padlock and chain, which usually secured the heavy wood doors, were missing, and the right door was ever-so-slightly ajar.

He stopped and looked around, expecting to see a groundsman somewhere nearby.

'What is it?' Claudine asked, following his gaze.

Claudine forgotten for the moment, he climbed the steps. He pushed on the right door. Creaking loudly, it opened inwards.

'What are you *doing?*' Claudine hissed.

'Come on,' he whispered, trying to ignore the edge to her voice.

But Claudine shook her head, stood her ground.

'What? *Why?*' he asked, a little hurt by her refusal. 'You chicken?'

He saw her eyes flash for a moment, but that was all.

'No,' she muttered.

Not even an explanation, he noted. 'Suit yourself, then,' he said. *Stupid girls.*

Disappointed, but knowing he was going to get nowhere with her, Eliot turned his back on Claudine and went inside.

'H-h-hello?' His voice echoed amongst the dark, arcing ribs of the roof. Shafts of light coming in through the arched windows seemed to hold the walls upright.

It seemed colder in here, colder than outside, and he shivered—for one strange moment not knowing whether he had entered the church, or the church had entered him. He advanced a little way down the dusty aisle, his fingertips lightly brushing the polished shoulder ends of the pews. A plain lectern stood in front of the altar, facing the rows of empty pews. An old piano stood to one side, a book of music open above the ivory keys.

The grainy suspension of the small interior had a peculiar effect on Eliot, and he suddenly imagined that he had been miniaturized, and in this form, had stepped beneath the lens array of his own microscope. Tilting back his head and holding out his hands, he turned and turned. And he would have kept on turning if it had not been for the shrill voice suddenly calling out his name, though it seemed very far away.

He tried to ignore it, but it came again.

'Eliot?'

Coming to a stop, his eyes came to rest on the cross hung on the wall directly behind the lectern.

'Eliot?'

He stared up at the cross. *Fuck off.*

'*Eliot?*' The voice now contained panic enough to bring him back to the present. Thinking maybe O'Neal and his friends had returned, and not wanting to get trapped inside the chapel, Eliot hurried down the aisle towards the entrance.

'What is it?' On high alert, his worried eyes scanned the cemetery for signs of trouble as he re-joined Claudine outside.

'What did you see?' she asked, her tone remarkably casual suddenly.

'*What?*' he exploded. 'Is that what you called me out here for?'

Claudine shrugged; a gesture which Eliot found almost as irritating as his older brother's superior tone.

'Are you kidding me? *Seriously?*'

Again, Claudine shrugged.

Eliot's eyes suddenly narrowed and his expression turned mean.

'So why didn't you want to come inside, anyway?' he asked.

She chose to ignore this, and instead pointed to his hand. 'You've cut yourself.'

Irritated, he nevertheless glanced down. The heels of both palms were heavily grazed from his fall earlier—in fact, they stung quite a bit. And the right hand *was* indeed bleeding. 'So?' he shrugged. 'Doesn't hurt.'

'You need to put some cream on it.'

'Maybe,' he said, not even inspecting the cut. 'Maybe not.'

'It'll get dirty.'

'*So?*'

'You can't just leave it,' the girl said crossly. 'It'll get infected.'

'I'm not leaving it!' he shouted, angry that she was suddenly angry. It was not even her cut. 'I never said I was going to *leave* it.'

'Well, good then,' Claudine muttered, bouncing her ball once again.

'Good to you, too.'

'Fine.'

'So why didn't you want to come into the chapel?'

'None of your business!' she snapped.

'Suit yourself,' Eliot sneered. 'Didn't want to know anyway.'

'Good. Wasn't going to tell you anyway.'
'Good then. Bye.'
'Bye, then,' the girl answered, and whirled away.
'Fine,' he muttered. 'Go! See if I *care!*'
As she exited the south gate he yelled, 'BYE THEN!'
And then she was gone.
'Stupid girls,' he mumbled in a much quieter voice, looking around. The cemetery appeared very empty suddenly. And much darker. He looked up, half-expecting to see the moon coming up. But the sun was still there, a pale, rusty coin dipping low in the west, like it was going home, but in no rush to get there.

Stupid girls.

Hearing voices in the living room, Eliot cautiously approached the open door. The tempo and tone of the conversation strongly suggested that this was no argument, which was a relief.

Standing very still, he peered around the door. Kneeling on the floor beside the armchair, Ruth had hold of one of his mum's hands and was patting her wrist, like she was tapping out a secret message in Morse code, her words just for show, pretend.

'Well we'll just have to get through this,' Ruth was saying. 'Together.'

When he reached for the handle, the door moved forward ever so slightly, making a loud creaking sound. Seeing him standing in the doorway, Ruth stood up quickly and said, 'Right, I'll be off then.'

His mum nodded, not taking her eyes off the ashtray on her lap.

Ruth leant forward and with one final squeeze of his mum's hand, she murmured, 'Perhaps we could get you out for a while, hmmm? What do you say?'

Eliot's mum nodded.

As she passed Eliot, Ruth jabbed a finger in his face. 'And you…' Eliot blinked and backed away from her finger. 'You could help round the house a bit more, you know.' In mock despair, she glanced at his mum and rolled her eyes with a smile, and then let herself out.

The front door closed.

Holding the edge of the curtain the way she would a cigarette, between her fingers, his mum peered out of the window as though she hoped Ruth might change her mind and come back inside. From the expression on her face, Eliot knew there was no point trying to talk to her, but he placed his hand on the back of the armchair anyway and was about to ask her if everything was okay. But she stopped him before he could get the words out.

'Do me a favour, son,' she murmured, not looking around. 'Pull the drape across the front door.'

Twenty pounds.

Eliot sat on the end of his bed with the tin on his knees. He had started with £1.73. The old sofa had given up 22p, and he had made £1.70 on the golf course today. That gave him £3.65. He was nearly a quarter of the way there, he realised, suddenly wishing he could be with her right now. But it was Sunday, so he would have to wait until Monday, maybe Tuesday, even, depending on the weather.

After counting his money again, he took out his microscope set.

He managed to peel off a good piece of skin from the heel of his palm for his sample, although it was painful and made his eyes water. Under the microscope, the skin resolved itself into a peculiar framework of irregular structures, cellular and hollow-looking, brittle. He had expected more from the sample. It was his skin, after all, the stuff that was supposed to protect him. It should look...well, tougher, he supposed, more defined, not flaky and full of ugly gaps that looked like something, anything, could get through.

Eliot Thomas, Hollow Boy.

Angry, he sat back on his heels. There was nothing new here.

Stupid microscope set.

With a scowl, he dated the sample, *'21/02/82—Skin,'* and packed everything away.

After cleaning his teeth, Eliot inspected the heels of his palms. They were quite shredded, and the cut on his right hand was quite nasty.

You need to get some cream on it.

Something his mum would say…used to say, like, *'Eliot, it's bath night.'*

He glanced down at the white bathtub; dirt rings ran around the inside, like growth rings on a tree. Lying on the bottom, bits of Lego, David's Rub-A-Dub Doggie, sponges and other toy pieces struck stiff and grimy little poses, like tragic shipwrecks. The bath tiles were chipped or cracked, and were held in place by stained and mouldy caulking.

He ran his hand under the cold-water tap, carefully washing the dirt and bits of grit from the graze. Looking in the bathroom cabinet he found all sorts of old medicines, but no antiseptic cream. Spotting the bottle of TCP, Eliot took it down and closed the cabinet door.

He stared at his spots; there were masses of them, led by the huge one spreading out from the corner of his mouth. Then he stared at the bottle of antiseptic.

The spotty, angry face in the bathroom mirror suddenly grinned nastily.

Go on. I dare you.

The heels of his palms throbbed.

Soaking a strip of toilet paper with the yellowish fluid, he began dabbing his spots with the TCP, viciously, and without mercy.

Die spots. Die!

It hurt horribly, and the smell of the antiseptic fluid was powerful and stung the inside of his nose, making his eyes water, but he persevered, trying to kill every spot by burning them in TCP.

Die!

Finished, he glared through watery eyes at the still grinning face in the mirror.

This kind of pain had to carry with it some kind of promise.

7

Thursday, 25 February 1982

£3.65

Monday and Tuesday passed quickly, if nervously. O'Neal was a no-show on both days, but Eliot kept to those corridors he knew were frequently patrolled by teachers, just to be on the safe side. He caught sight of O'Neal on Wednesday but managed to avoid him by ducking down low and moving with the prevailing tide of children and staff, even though it took him quite a bit out of his way, making him late for his next class.

He dared not venture outside the school premises, just in case he bumped into O'Neal at the sweet shop, and so each lunchtime he would get something from the tuck shop and take himself off to the empty gym hall to eat, where he would become a famous basketball player, a genius five-a-side football star, or a brilliant badminton player.

Lesson followed lesson, break time followed break time. Greatly daring, he skived the lessons he thought O'Neal might attend—something he had never, ever, done before, and would never, ever, have tried were his dad still at home.

After school, he chose to walk home rather than take the bus. In the evenings, he would settle into the bushes and wait for his woman. She made an appearance on Monday night, but it rained on Tuesday night and she was a no-show. She also failed to appear on Wednesday night, even though it had been a perfectly clear night, and he had spent the rest of that evening worrying about her, hoping she was okay.

Each night he would inspect his spot situation before he went to bed. It was clear that the TCP had not worked. If anything, his acne was getting worse, if that was at all possible; particularly the one on his mouth. It was hideously large, and he felt that it was only a matter of time before his whole mouth got infected and scabbed over.

David came home on Monday night, but stayed over at Rob's Tuesday and Wednesday, which was outrageous.

Clearly, the *'Not on a school night'* rule had gone the same way as Sunday bath night.

He stayed faithful to his diary each night, recording the goings-on in the street, often assuming the roles of the individuals he observed. And so, he would become the writer at No. 14 and he would finish the story, and it would be an amazing story; a story people would read over and over. The children at school would learn about it and they would feel jealous, though they would also be desperate to get to know him, befriend him, love him. It would be a story that would have strangers in the street exchanging whispers, '*Look, there's that brilliant boy; that brave boy…look how brave and amazing he is.*'

Or, as the man at No. 18, he would invite his woman from the library over for tea. They would share the sofa and watch *Bullseye* or *3-2-1* or *Happy Days*, or grow concerned watching the news: *Russia was playing up in West Germany*. And following the instructions in the government-issued pamphlet, they would draw the curtains and hide beneath the table, waiting for the first nuclear bombs to strike.

As Old Man Vic, he would march on the seafront, protesting the destruction of the pier, banging together his bin lids…massively loudly. One, ten, then hundreds of people would fall in behind him, answering the call; the Pied Piper of the Pier, angrily demanding a reversal on the decision.

On Wednesday evening, Claudine made an appearance at the top of his road. Playing kerby, she had the air of someone who was expecting something rather specific to happen—which never occurred, as far as he could determine. He watched this strange girl, repeatedly throwing and catching the ball; one minute hoping she would drop it, the next willing it into her hand.

Nothing about her made sense.

Who hung out at a cemetery? It was a bit odd—even for a girl. It suddenly occurred to him that maybe her dad was buried in the cemetery; but then, why would that have stopped her going into the chapel?

When Claudine finally picked up her ball and left, he kept the binoculars trained on her for as long as he was able, only lowering them when he became fully aware that he was staring at an empty street corner, and had been for some minutes.

Stupid girls, he thought as he put the binoculars away.

Later, lying on his bed, Claudine finally forgotten, he thought about his lady from the library...

... Stepping out of the bushes, he is carrying his bag of money out in front of him. Displaying no sign of surprise, as though she has been waiting for him, she leads him into the darkened corner. Taking the bag of coins from him, she shakes her head with smiling eyes and sets it down on the ground to one side, forgotten. Then she takes him in the mouth. It is her best mouth work to date, her rhythm sensitive and brilliant.

'Fuck yes!' he shouts. 'Fuck damn it, yes!'

Hissing, Eliot cramped up. Moments later, and with a final shudder, he slowly relaxed.

After inspecting his hand, he let it drop: still nothing.

Taking down a book, he read for a while until sleep finally took him. He dreamt of golf balls and money—having lots of money, having lots of twenty pounds.

On Thursday, the lesson before break was general studies. Mr Hatton was talking about class and the distribution of wealth.

'So you see,' Mr Hatton was saying, his gaze sweeping the class, 'they would have you believe that for a capitalist society to work, it needs an underclass of poor. We can't all be rich, now, can we?'

'My mum says I'm middle class,' Sarah-Jane Patterson, a freckled, red-haired girl proudly declared. She gave the rest of the class a smile, including Eliot, but it came across as aloof and a bit smug.

When Eliot looked around, he realised that he was not alone in thinking this, which he found encouraging.

'How very nice for you, Miss Patterson.' Mr Hatton's smile seemed like it was under tremendous pressure. He was wearing a corduroy jacket with padded elbows, and jeans. Two badges gleamed on the lapel of his jacket; one of them was emblazoned with the initials CND; the other featured a black-and-white portrait of a man who had wild hair, a moustache and goatee, and circular spectacles. Eliot guessed it might be a picture of Mr Hatton's dad, though that seemed a bit weird.

'What can we say about the middle class?' The teacher took a deep breath, leant against the girl's desk and looked directly into her eyes. 'In truth, the middle class are simply the salaried poor, aren't they? They like to think they have power, but they don't! Their wealth is illusory and can be taken from them in a heartbeat. No job, and the mortgage payments aren't met; bills go unpaid; little Miss Patterson's piano lessons are cancelled…no more skiing holidays. Debt will follow; repossession; homelessness; one or both parents will turn to drink; divorce will follow, perhaps suicide.

'Your parents know this. And so they work and work and work, and sacrifice everything, including *you*, terrified it might all be taken away from them.'

The teacher pushed himself away from the girl's desk. Sneering, his gaze skipped from one child to the next.

'You have nothing. And your parents have nothing. And most of you will amount to nothing. It's a fact of life. And how you deal with that fact will define who you are for the rest of your lives.'

The children stared open-mouthed at the young teacher. Some looked worried, as though being poor was a new and immediate thing to fear, whilst others looked troubled, as though going home to confront their parents would now be a difficult thing to do—not least Patterson, who had taken up her pen and was digging the point deep into the desk.

Eliot was not immune to his teacher's preaching. His efforts with his school shoes suddenly appeared shabby and desperate, and he pulled in his feet under the chair, out of sight. It was not like his mum had noticed, anyway.

Oh, Eliot, you are such a good boy. It was not like she had said that.

He thought about her poverty and felt ashamed, but he was even angrier with his dad.

A sudden whack to the back of his head caused lights to spark in front of his eyes.

'Thomas,' his teacher snarled. 'Eyes up front, if you wouldn't mind.'

Eliot lifted his head, sat up.

'There's a good boy.'

The break time bell sounded. The teacher swiped his books from the desk and was out of the door before a single child had cleared their desk.

Eliot sighed, closed his book, and picked up his bag. Once outside, he was caught in the confluence of children pouring out of other classrooms. Unable to turn, stop, or even simply step to one side, he let himself be carried forward along the corridor and down the stairwell.

And then over the sound of the other children came a voice:

'Hey, dickhead!'

Eliot looked up and was shocked to see O'Neal hanging over the handrails up above him. To his left leered the she-wolf; to his right stood the grinning Dickenson. O'Neal jabbed a finger at Eliot and mouthed one word, *'You!'*

As one, the three children detached themselves from the handrails and began moving down the stairs, O'Neal leading, violently pushing other kids out of the way.

Ignoring the shouts and threats from disgruntled children, Eliot barged his way down the stairs. But the sheer mass of children on the stairs was too great, and their heavy flow forced him to the outside, against the wall—finally ejecting him on the first floor, a level early.

Stumbling into the corridor, he turned and turned. Risking a look back, he saw that O'Neal and his two friends were almost down the last flight of steps and were gleefully ploughing their way through children to get to him.

'Oi, gay boy!' O'Neal shouted through a forced grin. 'Come here a minute. I've got something to show you. Wait up. Don't be like that.'

Eliot set off down the unfamiliar section of corridor.

'Fucking dickhead.'

Where are all the teachers? Eliot wondered angrily as he ran.

Spotting an arched opening to his left, Eliot stumbled through it. Blinking, he skidded to an abrupt halt.

It was the school library. Michael had spoken about it, but Eliot had never managed to find it until now. *'Just the place for someone like you,'* his older brother had said, sounding like he believed it was a place most sane people would wish to avoid.

Compared to the corridor, the silence was almost physical. It was a huge room lined with rows and rows of tall bookshelves which almost reached the ceiling.

'May I help you?'

Behind the reception desk, a woman regarded him with unamused curiosity. She was about fifty, with a long, thin nose, arching eyebrows, and grey hair. She wore a pair of half-mooned spectacles.

Panting, Eliot struggled to answer her.

'Speak up, young man,' she demanded.

'I…I think I might be a b-bit lost, miss, that's all,' was his halting reply.

He heard a shout in the corridor: 'He went this way!' It was O'Neal.

Eliot glanced nervously over his shoulder. The librarian followed his gaze, lips pressed together. Just for a moment, Eliot feared she might eject him from the library.

There was another shout in the corridor—the girl, demanding answers.

'Where's he gone?'

This girl was seriously mental.

Eliot took a step towards the desk so he could not be so easily seen from the corridor.

Scowling, the librarian turned her spectacles back on him.

'These books need to go back on the shelves,' she said slowly, inclining her head towards the trolley parked in front of the reception desk. It reminded Eliot of his nan's tea trolley, the one she used to serve up tea and cakes on when she had visitors. Only this one was full of books.

Surprised and uncertain how he should proceed, Eliot just stared dumbly at the trolley until the librarian spoke again. 'Unless, of course, you'd like to leave, young man?'

He shook his head and grabbed hold of the trolley. The librarian watched him take a few hesitant steps before shaking her head and resuming her work.

Once he got the swing of things and familiarized himself with the numbering system, he rather enjoyed pushing the trolley up and down the aisles. That numbers would be used to organize a room full of books was a small revelation to him, one he found, for some reason, rather funny. It seemed just a little bit topsy-turvy.

Looking like he had managed to give O'Neal the slip, Eliot's mind soon drifted. Suddenly, he was the greatest library worker in the world: if asked, he could tell you where each book belonged just by glancing at the number on the spine. *'Let's see, 900s...that's the history section. Now, 300s...don't tell me, that's social sciences...'*

But even more astonishing was that this boy had read each and every book in the library, and was brilliant on every subject.

O'Neal and his friends were waiting for him beyond these bookshelves.

But for now, it did not matter.

In here...

He could not be touched in here.

Eliot Thomas, Book Boy.

8 Friday, 26 February 1982

£3.65

A few lazy clouds drifted across the wide, blue sky. As Eliot watched, a particularly fat one settled over the pier. It caught his attention because, for a second, it thinned and stretched upwards; and then another came up behind and seemed to dissolve into it, so he was not sure which was which.

It occurred to him then, that memories were a bit like clouds: they were not constant things, but had a habit of changing shape—even while you watched—remaining true for but a moment, before breaking up, or dissolving to nothing—never to be recalled.

Never to be recalled.

If only.

Eliot sighed, suddenly wishing he had control over such things.

…he was on the pier playing tag with his brothers, which involved a lot of laughing and dodging and running over the wooden decking, which popped hilariously under their feet as they ran and hid from each other.

When Eliot took his place in the bus shelter, his hand reached for his mouth, covering his spot—but in a casual way, like he was contemplating a particularly difficult puzzle or some other dead intelligent thing. He could properly feel it between his lips now, a rough, crusty thing, massive to the touch.

He sat reading the graffiti on the bus shelter wall and hoped no one was staring at him.

When the large, growling lorry, which had stopped in front of the bus shelter, pulled forward, he was amazed to see Claudine on the other side of the road. She was sitting on the green bench outside the newsagents, swinging her stringed PE bag between her legs. Her school uniform was not much different from his own, he noted; black blazer, grey jumper, white shirt; only her tie was different. Hers was yellow-striped, his, red-striped. He was a little shocked, however, to see her wearing trousers instead of a skirt. Girls were not allowed to wear trousers at his school. And she was wearing her big, black boots! It was clear that either her school was a lot less strict, or she was a rebel.

Eliot wondered if he would like it at her school.

Still, this was strange. He had never seen her up on the seafront before; what was she doing here? His first thought was that she must be following him. Maybe she *was* a psycho after all, and she was seeking revenge for the way he had spoken to her in the cemetery.

But set against the tall, white buildings rising behind her, he was struck by how…how small she appeared, and alone, and he decided that he did not want to believe what Rob had said, what anyone had said—which was a decision that was as sudden as it was unexpected.

The longer he stared at her, the more he found himself willing Claudine to look over in his direction, even though he was quite certain he would have no idea what to do if she had. Turn away, most likely, pretend he had not seen her.

But she looked deep in thought.

He felt the other children in the bus stop stir. The bus had been spotted. As he grabbed his bag he saw a boy, wearing a tie that matched her own, come up behind Claudine and tap her on the shoulder. Claudine turned and stood, a hint of relief accenting her sudden smile. The boy said something and Claudine laughed.

Eliot shot out of his seat, but before he could properly organise his thoughts on this development, the double-decker bus closed out the scene.

With a hiss, the bus door opened and Claudine's face was replaced with the surly face of the bus driver, looking down at him from his high seat.

Stupid girls. What did he care?

Later that afternoon he was sitting on Michael's bed, watching events in the street, when he saw Ruth come out of her house. She went to the end of her small front garden, opened the gate and stood on the pavement, arms crossed, waiting.

David and Rob soon appeared at the top of the road. She waited until they got close and then she pointed to the house, the door to which she had left open. Thinking Rob must be in trouble, Eliot was about to laugh, but then he saw Ruth hold out her right arm and stop David dead in his tracks. His younger brother tried to say something but she gave him a look and he lowered his head and followed his friend inside his house.

Who did she think she was?

Outraged, Eliot was in half a mind to go downstairs and demand that his mum facilitate the immediate rescue of his brother, but just then Ruth happened to glance in his direction and he pulled back from the window, his enthusiasm for the endeavour rapidly cooling. Now he just hoped she had not seen him spying on her.

He waited a moment, then risked another look; strangely, Ruth was still waiting by the kerbside. Frowning, he was just about to slide off the bed when the solicitor, the one who had visited his mum the other day, pulled up in his red Audi. He got out—suit, tie, jacket, looking just like his dad used to look—clutching his big, black briefcase in his hand like he was the boss of the world.

Ruth and the man talked outside on the pavement for a moment, then she took out a key and let herself and the solicitor into the house. *His* house! Who the hell did she think she was?

The solicitor spent over an hour talking to his mum in the living room with the door shut. At one point, Eliot had gone out onto the landing but, unable to hear anything, he had started down the stairs. When he got halfway down he heard the living room door open and there was Ruth, standing in the hallway, arms folded. With a curt gesture, she silently ordered him back upstairs.

Stomping loudly (loud enough to let his mum, the solicitor, and the world know how he felt), he made his way back up the stairs.

Why was she letting this woman boss him around? Why?

He had a right to know things, not her. With Michael spending all his time around at Sharon's flat, surely he was the man of the house now, being the second oldest?

But it was clear from the way his mum was behaving that she was not going to do anything to support his advancement; in fact, quite the opposite.

He was being betrayed at every turn.

Lying on his stomach on his bed, chin on the pillow, Eliot's eyes roamed the themed wallpaper in front of him—Barbapapa and his family, a singular image repeated in vague ceremony across the wall. Eliot picked at a scab of loose wallpaper, tore off a strip, rolled it into a tiny ball, popped it into his mouth, and chewed.

This was not the first length of wallpaper he had stripped from the wall—not by a long shot. And it was beginning to show. He frowned. The bare patch was quite noticeable.

He would have to be careful. David was a massive snitch. Like his dickhead friend, Rob.

Suddenly curious, he pulled back his pillow…and immediately swallowed the tiny ball of wallpaper!

The area of exposed plaster…well, Eliot could hardly believe it!

Sitting up, he quickly pulled back the end of the mattress—the damage ran down almost to the skirting board, and at its widest point was almost the width of the mattress! It looked like the stencil outline of a massive, sick flower.

When had he done all this?

Shuddering, he quickly replaced the pillow and tried to put the patch of exposed plaster out of his mind.

Rolling onto his back, Eliot stared up at the ceiling (not even feeling like reading) and waited to be called down for tea.

After that, he planned to go to the park to see his woman.

Twenty pounds. He had £3.65.

He was a short man with a mass of brown hair; he wore jeans and brown shoes, a chequered shirt, and a corduroy blazer with patches on the elbows. She made him hand over the money immediately, like he could not be trusted, was a possible runner. To Eliot, he looked timid and soft. His reluctance to hand over the money suggested he could not afford it, was poor. Eliot also suspected the man had a small one: what his nan used to call a *diddle*.

She would refuse Eliot's money, of course; he was now certain of this. She would love him from the start and they would run away together.

He would have to demonstrate that he had a plan, mind. After all, this was serious stuff.

The corduroy man coughed. He was behaving scared, Eliot observed, like he had done or said something wrong and was about to get slippered for his transgressions. He moved against her awkwardly, clumsily; like he needed it, but was too frightened to properly claim it. Eliot was also right about his thingy…he did indeed possess a small one.

Eliot would have laughed at his dumb timidity, his smallness, but he was now busy making plans.

Serious stuff.

Once they got their own flat, he decided, they would throw out the television and replace it with books; millions of books, which he would order just like in a library, much to the delight of his woman. And they would read late into the night, out loud to each other, sometimes stopping to discuss certain meaningful passages that needed their serious and immediate attention.

'Fuck! God!' the corduroy man suddenly shouted out. His legs locked and his back stiffened, his arms shook.

And then it was over.

Corduroy man, looking ashamed, reached for his jeans and left quickly.

Sounding like she had a bit of a sniffle, the woman fixed herself back up. As Eliot's gaze traced the line of her jaw from her ear to her chin, eyes lingering on the lips and the mouth, he imagined kissing her gently, and her returning his kiss just as passionately. Then she would sigh, rest her head on his shoulder and close her eyes.

It's over.
Yes. All over.
When the woman coughed out loud and sniffed some more, Eliot worried she might be getting a cold.

He hoped she went straight home to bed.

Backing slowly into the embrace of the shadows, Eliot stared out over the courtyard, inwards over a mindscape of pale flesh, large breasts, thigh, and nipple—

I love you.
I love you.
—breasts, thigh, and nipple.
It's over.
All over.
He brought his hand up. Nothing.

As Eliot went to turn the handle on the back door, he heard laughter. It was coming from the brick shed abutting the house. He pushed open the door and was shocked to see David and Rob sitting inside, smoking a cigarette by candlelight.

Sitting on a wooden crate, David had his back against the wall. When he saw Eliot, his eyes registered a moment of panic before his expression resolved itself into one of naked hostility. Slowly and deliberately, his gaze fixing on Eliot, David took a long drag on the cigarette, causing the end of it to glare a fierce orange. Disturbed, Eliot watched as a cloud of blue smoke filled up his younger brother's mouth. With a vicious inhalation, David took it down into his lungs, making Eliot blink in alarm.

David kept his eyes locked on Eliot as he passed the cigarette to Rob, who, with a cocky grin, took a slow, deep drag on the cigarette, clearly daring Eliot to say something.

David watched Rob smoke the cigarette, but his grin seemed forced and his cheeks twitched.

Taking another drag, Rob's gaze switched between the two brothers and his expression grew cunning. Producing a packet of cigarettes,

Lambert & Butler, from beneath his jumper, he glanced at David, seeking approval. After a moment's thought, David nodded.

Grinning, Rob turned the packet of cigarettes on Eliot.

When David spoke, his voice was oddly tight. 'Take one,' he said. It was clear that this meant something to his brother, but Eliot hesitated.

Rob rattled the box in front of Eliot. 'What are you waiting for?'

Eliot opened his mouth, then shut it again. The silver box gleamed in the candlelight, making it appear precious and mysterious.

'Try one,' David urged.

Hesitating, Eliot stared at his brother. This used to be *their* shed.

'What, you chicken?' Rob mocked.

His expression hardening, Eliot shook his head. 'I'm going in,' he said, knowing that things might have been different if Rob had not been there.

'Pussy,' Rob said, lowering the box of cigarettes.

'You can't say anything!' David warned, but his eyes were saying something else, *please don't say anything*.

'If you do, there'll be trouble,' Rob added.

Eliot looked to his brother, expecting him to say something in his defence, but David refused to look at him.

Their shed.

Rob grinned and took a long drag on his cigarette, inhaling deeply. Puckering his lips into an O-shape, he snapped his jaw repeatedly, punching out smoke rings in Eliot's direction.

'Show off,' said David, and snatched the cigarette out of his friend's hand. 'Here, let me have a go.'

As Eliot pushed the door closed, he heard Rob say, 'Gay boy.'

David laughed, and Eliot knew things had changed between them forever.

That night he dreamt that he was sitting on his bed, pasting strips of wallpaper to his naked body, feeling them harden, layer after hardened layer until he was covered head to foot; the legs, the tummy, the neck, the eyes, the mouth—especially the mouth—until the mummification was complete.

Eliot Thomas, Papier-mâché Boy. Eliot Thomas, The Mummy Boy.

9 Saturday, 27 February 1982

£3.65

David came into the bedroom around six thirty and announced that he was staying over at Rob's for tea.

'You spend too much time over at Rob's,' Eliot snapped, making a point of not looking at him. Instead, he fixed his stare on the ceiling.

'So? What's it to you?' David answered, pulling out a pile of comics from under his bed.

'I'm just saying.'

'Well, don't.'

'Stay over at Rob's then!' Eliot shouted suddenly, the incident in the shed now between them. He lifted himself up onto one elbow. 'Go and live there why don't you? See if I care.'

'Fuck off!' David shouted.

'You're not the oldest!'

'Neither are you, flid boy!'

'I am when Mikey's not here! And you're the flid, you spazza.'

'Grow up,' David muttered, and refused to be engaged further. Instead, he sat on his bed and sorted through his comics. Occasionally he would select an edition and put it to one side.

As the pile grew, so did Eliot's suspicion. 'You're not swapping those, are you?'

'No.'

'Because you know how Mum gets.'

'I said no. But if I want to swap them, I will. Mum wouldn't care. And you can't stop me.'

'That's what you think.'

'That's what I *know*.' David was suddenly angry. 'So shut up.'

'You shut up,' Eliot muttered, without much conviction. He watched as David stuffed the comics into his *Wombles* bag, which he had pulled out from beneath his bed, then his pyjamas. Finished, David zipped up the bag and went to leave the room.

In a sudden moment of panic, Eliot blurted. 'David.'

David hesitated.

'I won't say anything'—he said, eyeing the bag as though it was a very real and physical threat—'about you smoking in the shed. Ok? It's just that—'

Eliot expected something, but not laughter—but that was exactly what he got.

'I know you won't,' David laughed.

And it stung.

'You wouldn't dare.' Then he left the room.

'You'd better tidy this lot up!' Eliot shouted after him, staring at the pile of comics on David's bed. 'Or Mum'll kill you!'

He heard his brother laugh on the stairs, and then the front door open and slam closed. He had to stop himself from going to the window. Instead, he turned his attention to the pile of comics.

He desperately wanted his mum to come up the stairs and see the mess David had left behind. *Right, you little bastard,* she would say, dragging him out of next door. *Get home and clear up that bloody mess.*

Just for a second, Eliot considered going downstairs and telling on his younger brother.

Who did David think he was?

Slumping back down on his bed, he picked up a book and tried to read, but the messy pile of comics on David's bed kept nagging him, demanding his attention. After a while it was clear that David was not coming back, and the comics were not going to tidy themselves.

Obviously, his younger brother expected their mum to tidy them up.

It was now clear Rob was turning David evil. Something had to be done about it. And Michael was no longer around.

He tried to ignore the comics, he did; but eventually, it became too much, and he gathered up all the comics and slid them under David's bed, out of sight.

The act almost brought him to tears.

The man wore a shirt and tie; he was shorter than the woman and was a bit fat, with sticky-out ears. He carefully folded his jacket before laying it down on the steps beneath the fire exit, as though it was something special. He then handed over the money; two ten-pound notes.

Twenty pounds.

It was quick; the man was quick and pathetic, and he was done before Eliot could properly settle—like it was his first time ever and simply could not help himself. Eliot felt a moment of anger on behalf of his woman. He should have taken his time, ought to have shown her more respect. Could he not see how special she was?

The man stepped back from her, pulled up his dark trousers, wiped his mouth, and retrieved his suit jacket. After fixing himself up he lit a cigarette, his expression taking on a vague, worried appearance, as though he was trying to figure out how he had got there. When the woman looked like she was going to say something, he quickly held up his right hand and said, 'Not a word,' his tone curt and irritable. 'I didn't pay you for that.'

The woman started coughing, so whatever reply she had planned turned into a simple shrug, and coughing, she watched the man leave. Minutes later, she too left the courtyard.

More than ever Eliot wished he could go with her, leave and go far, far away.

Eliot was not sure what woke him. He rolled over.

The room lay in darkness. David was out. Was *staying* out, he reminded himself. Unable to get back to sleep, he took himself downstairs to fetch a glass of milk. The door to the living room was slightly ajar. As always, the curtains were drawn. Parts of his mum's armchair reflected light from the television set, making it appear incomplete; arm, shoulder, a portion of the base.

He nudged the door open a little wider, and fighting down the very curious feeling that he was violating a sacred space, he stepped into the room. Programmes had ended for the night and the television screen was displaying the test card, an image of a young girl dressed in red, wearing a red Alice band.

Cautiously, he put his hand on the back of the armchair and peered down at his mum's sleeping form. Something was happening to her face, he noticed; dark pouches had formed beneath her eyes, the corners of which were heavily wrinkled and looked like comet tails. Her cheekbones were more pronounced, and the top of her lip was scored at intervals, as though it was slowly folding in on itself. And there was muzzy stuff growing there too, like she was growing a moustache.

Eliot had always thought of old age as something you were, like being a girl or having blond hair. Until this moment, it had never occurred to him that old age was something that *happened* to you; was a process, like the tide coming in. But here was his mum, and it was clear change was coming in fast; it had her around the eyes, at the throat, around the ears, had taken her by the neck.

The feeling came upon him quickly and coldly.

Disgust.

The sight of his mother's face suddenly disgusted and sickened him to the stomach.

And there was no defence against this, because it was in his mind.

Averting his gaze, his eyes locked on the girl on the television test card. She was smiling, like it was funny, because it could never happen to her.

His mum stirred and murmured something in her sleep and he snatched his hand from the back of the armchair.

Eliot slowly backed out of the living room, turned, and retreated upstairs.

Anger, then confusion…finally shame. There *was* something wrong with him.

Feeling like he could not breathe, he shuffled into the bedroom and turned on the light. The sound caught his attention immediately. Inside the lampshade a moth flapped about wildly, its fat, dark body banging away at the inside of the shade. Eliot felt something of its panic, and wondered if it was being thrown back by the very heat and brightness it was trying to get at.

Feeling hideous and angry, he wondered what would happen if he suddenly turned off the light. Fooled, would the moth wrap its papery wings around the hot, black globe and burn?

He suddenly needed to burn something…needed to burn the moth.

And the temptation…it was too much.

The decision to murder something now decided, he allowed himself a second to savour the moment.

He waited for what seemed an age to allow the bulb to really heat up.

Then he suddenly flicked off the light switch, plunging the bedroom into darkness.

He grinned viciously. Was it burning now? Was it screaming silent moth screams? Eliot stood in the dark, feeling hideous, but suddenly powerful.

Fuck off, God.

10

Sunday 28th February 1982

£3.65

As Eliot approached his secret pathway onto the golf course, he spotted a girl sitting on the kerb.

He stopped dead.

It was the Claudine girl.

At first he thought she was there to have a go at him for the other day and he considered turning back. But at that very moment, Claudine lifted her head and looked in his direction.

And smiled.

Not wanting to look stupid, he resumed walking, head down.

What was she doing here? he fumed.

When he was still ten feet away from the girl she stood up, dusted down the back of her jeans and walked right up to him.

'You got here then?' she said, placing her hands on her hips.

Eliot thought it safer not to answer.

Although her thick, yellow woollen jumper looked at least three sizes too big for her, she cut quite a fierce figure standing there, feet slightly apart, her expression determined.

'You're going to the golf course, aren't you?'

Eliot blinked and stared into her large, green eyes, trying to think of something clever and deadly to say to her.

'*So?*'

'I'm coming,' she declared.

'No you're not,' he snapped, trying to step around her.

But Claudine took a step to the right and prevented him from doing so.

'Free country, isn't it?'

'Is this about the other day? Because—'

'Don't be silly,' she chided with a smile.

'Then *why?*'

She giggled. 'Just because.'

'I usually go alone.' Eliot stuffed his hands into his pockets and kicked out at a stone.

'No one likes you, do they?' She said it quite matter-of-factly, like it was the most ordinary thing to say in the world.

Ears and cheeks burning, and with no way of answering her, he dropped his head and stepped around her.

'Just leave me alone.'

But she did no such thing. Instead, Claudine fell in beside him, matching his footsteps. 'It's okay,' she said. 'I understand.'

Eliot quickened his pace. They entered the cut-way together, side by side.

'You'll be wasting your time,' he said. 'I'm only here for a bit.'

'And how long are your bits?' she asked, without a trace of smile.

'A *bit*!' he shouted. 'Just a bit.' God, she had an answer for everything. Who *was* this girl?

'Well, I don't mind,' she sniffed.

Trees and tall bushes to either side of the path, which was well trod and dry, formed a natural tunnel; when he came to the end of it, Eliot came to an abrupt halt.

Smiling, Claudine stopped also, but added nothing further. He was not sure which was worse, her silence or her talking.

The golf course lay out in front of them. He had to say something. It was now or never.

'I'm not playing or anything. I'm looking for golf balls.'

'I know.'

'What do you mean, you *know?*' Eliot demanded.

But Claudine just shrugged.

'It's really boring.'

'I don't mind.'

'*Why?*' he complained. 'Why do you want to come?'

'Because I like you, dummy,' she said.

'*What?* What do you mean?'

'Would you like a dictionary?' Her offer sounded infuriatingly sincere. She then smiled, although it was a fierce sort of smile, like she was daring him to say something.

'But...' he began, 'you can't *like* me!'

'Is that a rule?' she asked, quite serious.

Feeling his cheeks flush, he said, 'That doesn't explain why you want to come.'

'No,' she replied.

'Then why?'

'Just because,' she answered.

'Stop saying that!' he shouted. 'You sound...you sound like my brother.'

'What would you like me to say?' she asked, glancing over at the woods on the other side of the fairway.

Feeling wretched, he realised that he had no way of getting rid of her.

'Come then,' he said, eventually. 'See if I care.'

Claudine grinned.

'But,' he said, holding up a warning finger, 'you have to do what I say.'

'Of course,' she beamed.

'It's important.'

'I'm certain it is,' she answered. Her look suggested to Eliot that Claudine had never doubted the outcome of the situation.

Sighing, he turned to inspect the golf course. The first tee was unoccupied, he noted, and the eighteenth fairway was clear. In fact, the course looked relatively quiet for a Sunday.

'We're going over there,' he said, pointing across to the woods. The girl beside him nodded, acting like she already knew.

Eliot set off across the fairway at speed. Claudine kept up with him, humming to herself. Eliot groaned, certain his day was ruined. They rounded the pond and after a quick look left and right, he led Claudine across the eighteenth fairway. With a faint rustle, the two children crossed over the leafy threshold and entered the woods.

The day started off slowly. For the first hour she had stayed close by, which was okay, because he thought she might be trying to pick up a few tips on where best to look for balls. But as the morning passed, she slowly drifted off.

By noon he had only managed to find three golf balls—and one of them was in bad shape, cut and water-stained, and it would have to be discarded.

It was her fault, of course. She was bringing him bad luck. It was maddening.

Twenty pounds.

That was why he was here, after all, he reminded himself. But every time his thoughts started to drift in the direction of the library, the sound of Claudine singing nearby rudely brought him back to the present.

Singing!

But this was a golf course.

It was about three o'clock. The day had been a disastrous one; just four golf balls. He was just about ready to give up when he felt a tap on his shoulder. He looked up from the bush he was rummaging in to find Claudine standing over him. She was smiling and had her hands behind her back. Frowning, he stood.

'So, how did you get on?' she asked.

'Yeah, good,' he replied, stuffing his hands into his pockets. 'Real good, actually. You?'

Claudine pulled her hands out from behind her back.

Eliot's eyes widened in disbelief: there in her cupped hands were... one, two...five! Five, gleaming-white golf balls!

'Are they any good?' she asked, quite casually.

He took one out of her hand, but slowly, as though he did not trust himself.

It was a Titleist, practically new. Not a scratch on it. He put it back and picked up another ball, rolling it over in his hands; Top Flite, flawless. He picked up another one; Pinnacle, hardly a graze on it.

They could have been his, *should* have been his.

He shrugged. 'Yeah, pretty good, I suppose.'

'Well, go on then,' she grinned.

'What?'

'They're yours, take them.'

He stared at the nest of golf balls, but his hands would not move. They were worth a pound, maybe a pound fifty.

'Well?' she demanded with a smile. 'Are you going to take them?'

'Are you sure?'

Claudine rolled her eyes. 'They're just golf balls.'

Suspecting a trick, he slowly took out his plastic bag and opened it. He watched as she dropped them in, one by one, *plunk*, *plunk*, *plunk*... relishing the way the bag got heavier and heavier.

'Done,' she declared, dropping in the last one.

Eliot snapped the bag closed. Grinning, he looked up at her.

And then he hesitated, feeling suddenly bad, which surprised him.

'They're, errmm,' he said, licking his lips.

'Yes?'

'They're worth some money.'

'Oh? How much?' the girl asked.

'Fifty p...maybe a bit more.'

She gave him a big smile. 'Well then, you'd better say thank you.'

'Er, yes,' he said, suddenly too self-conscious to say it.

Claudine laughed, like she understood. 'You're welcome. Shall we try somewhere else?'

Without waiting for a reply, the strange girl whirled around and stomped off in the direction of the fifth hole. It was not a place he would have chosen to go looking for golf balls, but she had done okay... so far. Watching her clomp along the wooded path in her ridiculously large, black boots, he decided that there was nothing really wrong with her; she could even be a friend—if she had not been a girl.

And she liked him, he reminded himself.

What did that mean, exactly?

A £2.15 day! A record.

Once he had sold the last of the golf balls (four, to be exact) to an elderly couple playing nine holes, he counted out the money. Claudine was close by, investigating things in the undergrowth.

'A pound fifty,' he declared.

'Is that any good?' Claudine asked, joining him.

'About average,' he answered, slipping the money into his pocket.

'A pound fifty?' Claudine looked a bit chuffed with herself.

Seeing her reaction, Eliot hesitated. 'About that, yeah. I haven't properly counted it yet, of course. Might be a bit more.' *Why did he say that?*

The light was beginning to fade. Eliot guessed it was around five thirty. 'Come on,' he said.

'It's been fun,' Claudine said as the two children arrived at the spot in the woods where they had first entered.

'Yes,' he replied, content to stand at the edge of the woods and look out over the golf course.

'It's quiet in here,' Claudine added, looking back over her shoulder.

Understanding, Eliot nodded. 'Yes,' he said.

The glance they then exchanged caused something in his stomach to tighten, and he swallowed hard.

'Err…let's go,' he said.

The fairway was clear and they crossed over to the pond. With a hand, he stopped Claudine from going any farther and took out all the ruined golf balls he had found that day. One by one, he threw them into the water.

Side by side, the two children watched in silence as the dark water broke open, accepting each ball.

When the last golf ball had been thrown in, Eliot heaved a sigh, scrunched up the plastic bag, and stuffed it into his pocket.

'What did you do that for?' Claudine asked in a quiet voice, her eyes fixed on the water.

Eliot shrugged and said, 'Golfing gods.'

'Golfing gods?' Claudine exclaimed. 'Do we have to make a wish now?'

Detecting a note of amusement in her tone, he said, 'You wouldn't understand.'

This nettled her for some reason. 'Because I'm a girl?'

He felt like she was acting a bit superior. 'Well, you wouldn't.'

Secretly, however, he let himself entertain the idea. A wish? Now what would *he* wish for? Well, that was easy.

'Come on,' he said quietly. 'Let's go.'

Claudine nodded.

At the entrance to the golf course they came to a stop. There was an awkward moment of silence between the two of them, broken only when Eliot again offered Claudine a share of the money. She refused.

'But you can walk me home, if you like?'

Her tone was such that he was not quite sure if she was asking or telling him, but feeling the weight of the coins in his pocket, Eliot reluctantly agreed.

After a short time they came to a stop outside her house, a narrow detached house with three windows (two up, one down) and a green door. Claudine placed her hand on the small wrought-iron gate but instead of going in she just stood there, looking at him, which in turn made him feel suddenly awkward and nervous.

Finally, she said, 'Do you want to come in and meet my mum?'

He stuffed his hands into his pockets. 'Can't tonight. Got to be home.'

'Oh,' she said quietly, her smile disappearing.

Eliot was not sure how to deal with that and he felt a bit mean.

'Maybe next time, then?' she ventured, biting her lip.

Without thinking about it, he nodded.

'Good,' she declared, her smile broadening massively. 'It's a date.'

He nodded hesitantly. *A date?*

They stood for a few seconds in silence, Claudine swinging the gate back and forth, Eliot looking at the ground.

'You sure you don't want any of this money?' he asked finally.

She shook her head.

'It...It might be a bit more than a pound fifty. Could even be as much as a pound seventy.'

'It's okay,' she replied quietly.

'Well, bye then.'

'Yes, bye,' she said. 'I enjoyed today. I really did.'

'Okay.'

'*Okay?*'

'Yeah, okay!' Eliot held up his hands. '*What?* You know what I mean.'

'*Do I?*' she snapped. Then, without a backward glance Claudine stormed up to her front door, opened it, then slammed it shut.

Eliot blinked, and stayed put.

After a minute, he reminded himself that he was supposed to be walking.

Just as he was about to set off, Claudine's front door opened. 'But this doesn't mean you can get out of our date!' she yelled, poking her head out.

Before Eliot could reply, she again slammed the door shut.

This time it felt final.

But then, what did he know?

He waited for a moment (just in case), then started walking.

He was halfway down the street before he realised that the commotion he could see up in front was occurring outside his own house. A white van was parked outside with its back doors open. He slowed in surprise when he saw Michael coming out of the house with a large cardboard box. He placed it in the back of the van and then went back inside. Seconds later Ruth came out with a smaller box, followed by Sharon, who was carrying a lampshade. She dropped it into the back of the van and disappeared back inside. Puzzled, he quickened his pace.

By the time he reached the front door, which had been wedged open by the draft excluder, the feeling that he had purposefully been left out of things, *again,* had properly tightened in his stomach into a hard, little anger.

Upstairs he could hear voices and a lot of activity. Glancing into the living room he saw his mum sitting, watching television. Ignoring her, he went in search of David, and found him sitting in the back room reading a *Beano* annual. It looked new.

'What's happening upstairs?' he asked his younger brother.

'Michael's tidying Mum's bedroom,' David replied, not looking up.

'Why?'

David shrugged. 'Ask Michael.'

'I'm asking you. Don't you know?'

Irritated, David said, 'No, why should I know? I don't know everything.'

'I didn't say you did. But there must be a reason for it, David!'

'I'm trying to read.'

'Tell me!' yelled Eliot. '*David?*'

David laughed. 'Ask Mikey.'

Throwing up his hands, he left his younger brother to his stupid *Beano*.

He found Michael on the landing. Five cardboard boxes and several full black bin liners stood on the landing waiting to be taken downstairs. He could hear a lot of noise coming from their mum's bedroom.

'What's going on?' Eliot asked, hoping his tone strongly communicated his belief that he should have known about this.

Michael glanced at the bags and boxes and then gave his younger brother a look, like he was playing a game of Operation and Eliot was a particular bone he thought he might try and pluck.

'I'm sorting out Mum's room.' Michael said it slowly, carefully.

'What for?' Eliot demanded, missing the warning signs.

These days, it was not often that he saw Michael properly angry, but he saw it now. Just a flash of it, and it reminded Eliot of his father. 'What kind of question is that?' he demanded. 'Well? What kind?'

Eliot backed away from his anger. 'I was just asking.'

'Well don't. It's a stupid question.'

'Keep your hair on, Mikey!' he yelled.

But Michael was not finished with him yet. 'Do you want her sleeping downstairs in the armchair? *Do you?*'

'No, course not,' Eliot mumbled, looking down at his trainers.

'Then why don't you help out?'

Before he could reply, Ruth appeared out of his mum's bedroom carrying a large box. Eliot stepped into the bathroom to let her pass and watched as she carried it downstairs. He did not like the sideways look she gave his older brother, and liked even less Michael's return look. He sensed that there was more going on here than Michael was letting on. Worse, Ruth was in on it. Even worse, he suspected it had something to do with him.

Michael saw him watching Ruth and he said, 'Ruth very kindly offered to help.'

'And I suppose I'm here just because I do as I'm told?' Sharon said, appearing from the bedroom with a black bin liner.

'As did Sharon,' Michael amended with a smile. 'Because she's wonderful.'

Dropping the bin liner, she gave Michael a playful cuff around the head and said, 'And don't you forget it, mister.' Then she disappeared back inside the room.

Eliot backed up, feeling like he had no right to be there.

'Not so fast, Eliot,' Michael said.

Eliot froze.

'Make yourself useful and grab one of those boxes.'

Before he could protest, his older brother wearily added, 'David's already taken a turn helping.'

'Actually, I was going to offer,' he sniped, stepping forward. 'Shows how much you know.'

Seeing the look in Michael's eyes, however, he hurriedly picked up a box and carried it downstairs. But he made sure it was the smallest box.

When they were finished later that evening, Sharon treated everyone to fish and chips. Everyone seemed happy with the room—except his mum, Eliot noted, who had remained oddly detached from the entire process.

Before he went, Michael tried to engage her one last time. Sharon was already up and waiting by the front door, and Ruth had left half an hour earlier.

Kneeling beside her armchair, he said, 'So what do you reckon, Mum? About your bedroom? You won't know yourself after a good night's sleep, hey?'

'Take more than bloody that,' she muttered, but then she smiled and patted him on the cheek. 'Thanks, son,' she murmured. 'Now get on with you.'

'Yeah, we've gotta go,' he nodded, standing; but he looked like he did not want to go.

Later that night, Eliot heard his mum go into her bedroom. Dropping his book onto his lap, he listened to her move around the room…hesitant steps; like first-day-at-big-school steps.

It made for difficult listening and he shifted his reading position every time he heard the floorboards creak; first on his back, next onto his side, then onto his other side—even on his front, which was no way to read at all.

Settle. Please.

Finally, she gave up and retreated downstairs.

A part of him was glad that she had. Another part felt angry.

What was wrong with her?

Needing a drink later, he took himself downstairs. Passing the living room door, he saw his mum curled up in her armchair, the television still on, the curtains slightly parted. Edging in so as not to disturb her, he glanced down and noticed that she had already fallen asleep.

Quietly, he fetched her blanket. Unfolding it, he carefully covered her sleeping form, wondering many things as he did so, not least if this was all his dad's fault.

He leant across her and took hold of the curtain ends. The street outside was quiet; yellow streetlight floated in the puddles in the road, like waterlilies. Curtains were closed all the way down the street—even at No. 14, who never drew his curtains.

Eliot's hands began to tremble. It was like time had stopped; or the world had emptied of people and it was just him and his mum, and the sound of her rattling breathing…below him, above him, all around him.

He dared not look at her then, fearing something more permanent might occur. Releasing the curtains, he stepped back from the armchair, turned, and left the room.

11

Monday, 1 March 1982

£5.80

He needed a further £14.20 by the end of the month.

The task seemed impossible.

'Got you now, dickhead!'

Eliot was grabbed by the arm and spun around.

O'Neal!

Behind him stood Dickenson and the girl.

It was the end of the school day and hundreds of children were criss-crossing the playing fields.

'Give me the fucking finger, would yer,' snarled O'Neal.

A horrible, icy fear weakened Eliot's knees. 'I...I didn't mean it. I didn't.' Backing up, he was suddenly conscious that other kids were slowing down, looking in his and O'Neal's direction, sensing trouble.

'Do you wanna go?' O'Neal yelled, working himself up. 'Come on then.' Suddenly, the world became O'Neal's face; small, black, mad eyes; thin, black eyebrows, large nose.

'Please...I'm sorry...please.'

'*Please*,' O'Neal mocked him. '*I'm sorry.*' Dickenson laughed, whilst the girl shrieked with cruel-eyed indifference.

Lights. Pain.

Eliot stumbled backwards as O'Neal's fist smashed into his mouth.

Blood.

How the children could smell it. Pouring in from all areas of the playing fields, they speedily converged on the two boys, space and white sky and green field collapsing in a calamitous rush.

Dazed and his face throbbing with pain, he swayed on his legs. Almost absently he gazed around and discovered himself deep inside the core of a bristling ring of screaming faces.

'Fight, Fight, FIGHT!'

O'Neal grinned.

There was no escape.

'FIGHT! FIGHT! FIGHT!'

O'Neal's massive fist arced murderously. Eliot stumbled backwards. Somehow, he managed to stay on his feet. Another blow sent all the air whooshing out of his lungs and he doubled over. A knee came up against his nose and pain, pain detonated inside his head. Sparks of light flashed in front of his eyes. And then the world tilted. Seconds later, Eliot found himself lying on his back.

A cheer went up, followed by screaming. 'Kill him, fucking *KILL HIM!*'

They wanted a death. Grinning, O'Neal moved in.

A shiver ran through the crowd of children. They thought they might get it.

'Go on, do him!' screamed a desolate voice amongst the clamour.

Eliot rolled onto his side, screwing himself up into a ball. He could smell blood and soil and grass in his nose.

'Kick him in the fucking head!' urged another desperate child.

O'Neal responded to the need of the crowd and shifted his attack, landing kicks to Eliot's head, fast and hard. The blunt force of each blow shook the world and sent it spinning off in a kaleidoscope of colours. Eliot threw up his hands and scrunched up tighter, but a particularly vicious kick found its way through his defences.

With a sickening thud, he felt heat deep inside his head, as though a sudden rip had torn open his brain.

Strangely, after that he felt and heard very little. He was suddenly both curled up on the ground, terrified, and hovering over himself, calmly observing events as they unfolded, as though his consciousness had sheered along a predetermined fault line when the last kick had landed.

'Bullies are cowards!' Swaying slightly his father stood, feet planted dead centre of the living room. He appeared invincible, huge to the watching boys in their pyjamas.

'Hit 'em first, really get one in, and they'll think twice before they pick on you again.'

Eliot and his two brothers listened carefully from the sofa. Their mother watched from behind the ironing board, her top teeth trapping the corner part of her bottom lip.

'Come on,' their Dad motioned with his hands. 'Let me show you. Who's up?'

Michael glanced at his brothers and with some reluctance, rose from the sofa.

Later, their older brother had said, 'If you ever get into a fight just go down, curl up, and take your beats. They'll get bored soon enough. If you put up a fight it will just get them excited.'

David had replied in a quiet voice, 'I think I'd just run.'

'That's the worst thing you can do, dummy. Just take it.'

Worse than this?

The crowd wanted him dead, he realised quite calmly; like he was the reason they had school, homework, parents, rules.

Dead.

A foot connected with his head...*bumpff*...and it snapped to the left. Woozily, his eyes rolled skyward.

Dead...Maybe that would be a good thing.

'ENOUGH!' a woman suddenly shouted. 'Stop this. NOW!'

The crowd shivered, as though this interruption hurt them dearly, but they slowly quietened.

'YOU!' roared a powerful male voice. 'You stay exactly where you are, O'Neal. The rest of you...clear out!'

Forced withdrawal made the resentful crowd brave. Things were muttered, remarks made.

'You heard! MOVE! Unless you want to spend all of next term in detention!'

There were some mumblings and even a few sniggers, but Eliot sensed the crowd dispersing; a space opening around him; cool air replacing the heat of the recent clench of massed children.

He was vaguely aware of two people leaning over him.

'It's okay now,' the female teacher said, placing a reassuring hand on his shoulder.

'How is he?' the man asked.

'We need to get him to the matron.'

'I'll take him,' the man suggested. 'You deal with O'Neal.'

'O'NEAL!' the woman barked. 'Come with me.'

'How do you like it now, gay boy?' laughed O'Neal.

No fear.

'That's ENOUGH! My God, but you're in big, big trouble, mister.'

Eliot tried to lift himself up, but he was too weak. He opened his eyes. Everything was blurred, grey.

'Hey, take it easy,' the man said softly. 'You've taken quite a beating. We'll get you to the matron, and then I'll take you home.'

No, he wanted to say, I'm fine, but the world suddenly collapsed down into black nothingness.

'Shit! Look at your face!' David exclaimed, his tongue blue from a gobstopper he had been sucking on.

Eliot put his book down and shrugged, regarding his brother with his one good eye. He had a headache, and he found talking painful.

The silence that followed was like an actual thing, physical. David grabbed the book out of his hand and read out the title. *'The Phantom Tollbooth.'* David tossed it back to him. 'Sounds rubbish.' There was more silence. Eliot sensed David's awkwardness.

The shed incident was still between them.

'Hang on,' David said. Diving under his bed, he brought out his wooden box, the one with TOP SECRET scrawled on it in large, black letters.

Opening it, he took out a book and handed it to Eliot. 'Here,' he said. 'You should read this. Mike gave it to me.'

The Rats, James Herbert.

'Ave woove wead it?' was Eliot's garbled reply.

David sniggered, but immediately held up an apologetic hand. 'Sorry.'

There was a bit more silence, and then David once again dived into his box. This time he brought out a notebook and pencil and handed the items to his brother.

'Use these,' he suggested.

Eliot took the items he had been handed, genuinely grateful. 'Fanks,' he said, and scribbled something down in the notebook. Lifting it up, he showed it to David, who had come and sat on the edge of the bed.

Have you read it? Eliot held up the book *The Rats*.

'Yeah, course.' David said, and then smirked guiltily. 'Well no, not really. Just the sex parts.'

Eliot glanced at the book with renewed interest.

'There's loads of sex in all of Herbert's books,' his brother hurriedly added. 'I've earmarked all the pages, see?' David pointed out a few of the pages, whose corners had been folded back.

Eliot tried to grin, though he was sure his expression made him appear hideous.

Falling into silence, the two brothers stared at the book for a while.

'So who was it?' David finally asked.

O'Neal Eliot wrote down.

'Fuck,' gasped David, his eyes widening. 'Even I've heard of him. He's a psycho.'

Eliot nodded carefully.

'Did you get any shots in?'

Eliot nodded, not wanting to write that down in case it was used as evidence against him at a later date.

'Good one.' David sounded genuinely impressed.

Pleased, he nodded.

The awkward silence returned then, only this time it was twice as bad. And it went on and on.

Finally, just as he was beginning to believe that the silence would never end, David said, 'I don't hate you, you know.' He said it quietly. 'It's just that...well, you've changed, you know? Big school has changed you. You're always so moody now, and up yourself. And you never *talk*.'

Eliot wrote something down. *I know.*

'Well all right then,' David muttered, but he sounded relieved.

Eliot nodded.

'Anyway,' David said, standing up. 'I betta be off,' adding, with a grin, 'best let you die in peace.'

Eliot tried to laugh. Hastily he wrote something down on the pad and held it up.

You coming back later?

But David was gone.

Seconds later, he heard laughter from downstairs.

Rob.

Hearing that laughter, Eliot grabbed the notepad and stared at the words he had written, wondering if he should keep them for later.

12
Tuesday, 2 March 1982

£5.80

'Right, what happened?' his dad demanded the next day. It was late afternoon. Next to him stood his mum. His damaged eye had purpled and was closed shut, and he had been in the process of testing out his altered perspective on the road outside when he saw his dad's car pull up.

'A fight,' his mum answered for him. She was dressed in jeans and a dark-green, roll-neck jumper, which looked way too big for her—like she was wearing hand-me-downs. She looked paler than usual too; much paler, which made him feel even worse. It was clear that getting beat up was the last thing she needed right now.

'I can see that.' His dad stared at his son, a hint of disgust in his tone. For a long while he said nothing and then, 'So, was he bigger than you, this lad?'

Eliot nodded.

'Did you hit *him*?'

He stared at his dad for a long time before he shook his head.

'So he did all of this to you,' he gestured with his hands, his disgust clearly evident now, 'and you didn't even hit him back?'

Eliot shook his head again, fighting back tears.

'What's wrong with him?' Donald demanded of his mum. She did not answer immediately, so he rounded on Eliot again. 'What's wrong with you?'

'Donald, you don't know the other boy,' his mum said, folding her arms. 'O'Neal...he's an animal.'

'More reason to hit him. Sounds like he needs to be taught a lesson.'

His parents continued the argument with their eyes for a while. Eliot hated it when they did this, and wished they would do it someplace else.

'Anyway, he'll need the doctors,' his mum said finally, giving Eliot's face a critical once-over.

'For God's sake, Mary. It's a black eye and a few bumps and grazes. No need to mollycoddle him.'

'Just look at him, Donald. *Look!*'

'I am looking at him,' he muttered, clearly irritated.

'So, are you going to take him, or do I have to organize something with Ruth?'

'Jesus, why does that woman have to come into everything?'

'Because she's there when I need her!' Mary snapped, then started coughing. She lit up a cigarette.

'You know,' Donald said to her in a quieter voice, 'It wouldn't hurt you getting out for a while.'

'If you don't want to take him, just say so, Donald.'

'Damn it, Mary, that's not what I meant!' Donald shouted. 'You know I didn't mean it like that.'

Mary was quiet for a moment before saying; 'It's Doctor Hunter. You'll need—'

'I know who the fucking doctor is,' Donald snarled.

Mary blew out a heavy cloud of blue cigarette smoke, and then from behind it, she said, 'Well that's something, I suppose.'

Donald took an angry step towards her, his fists clenched. For an instant, it looked to Eliot like his dad was going to hit his mum—for real. But instead he just stared at her, silently. For a long time, silent. Then with an angry nod at Eliot, he left the bedroom.

Eliot glanced at his mum, who, looking like she was not quite finished with the argument, gave him a hesitant, almost apologetic smile, and then quickly left the bedroom.

Eliot picked up his book when they started up again, their angry words reaching him through the floor. But only for a little while, then things grew quiet, which he found even more unsettling. Lowering his book, he tried to make out what was being said, but it was no use. Later, much later, his dad departed; the door, for once, closing without sending a shudder through the house.

Sometime after that, he found himself in front of the bathroom mirror. Confronted with his damaged face, he felt raw and ashamed. The heavy bruising on the right side of his face made him look deformed. The eye on that side was swollen shut, the lids appearing like red, fat lips.

What would his woman say if she saw him like this? If she knew what had happened? How could he look her in the eye again?

For days afterwards, he refused to take another look at himself in the mirror.

Eliot Thomas, Elephant Boy.

13 Wednesday, 3 March 1982

£5.80

He had suffered a mild mandible fracture. Treatment included resting the jaw so the bone could heal. *No talking—unless it is absolutely necessary.* On top of this, the doctor had prescribed a liquid and soft-food diet, to avoid chewing.

The drive there and back was taken in silence. Eliot's dad did not have to be a talker for Eliot to sense his dad's heavy disappointment. The man on the car radio made things worse; unemployment was rising steadily. The prime minister was coming under pressure to do something about the jobless. Things sounded grim. Eliot sat in the back of the car, staring at the back of his dad's head, feeling trapped inside his own shame.

'Fucking benefit scroungers,' his dad muttered, changing radio stations.

Later that evening, he was on Michael's bed.

The streetlight outside poured yellow into the bedroom. Eliot breathed repeatedly until a heavy condensation formed on the window.

Twenty pounds. He wrote in the breath-cloud.

'Get me out of here,' he whispered, through closed teeth. 'Perwease.'

That night he dreamt that he was in a boat. In every direction, there was open sea. The wind picked up and the motion of the boat grew increasingly excited, churning his stomach, so that at one point he thought he might be sick. It began to rain, a drizzle at first, and then falling harder. The boat spun and rocked. The wind whipped the rain in every direction, striking his face painfully, bringing tears to his eyes. When a violent gust caught the sail it snapped taut; another gust, and it snapped taut again. Slowly the boat began to spin, faster and faster, until everything was a blur.

But then he was no longer in the boat but standing at the very edge of the high cliffs, watching the boy's increasingly desperate efforts to keep control of the spinning boat.

Great waves muscled and heaved and crashed down on the small craft...

Eliot wondered at his own indifference as the boat was slowly torn to pieces, no longer identifiable amongst the spray and thrash of the massive waves.

And the rain fell until the sky was almost black.

14 Friday, 5 March 1982

£5.80

It felt strange not having to go to school. It should have excited him but instead he felt puzzlingly agitated. Try as he might, Eliot found it difficult to settle. There was a constant buzzing in his head, and he felt lightheaded and fuzzy. His books would not let him in, even his favourite ones, which left him feeling bereft and a little edgy. The street outside remained quiet for long periods of the day so there was nothing to look at.

So, for great stretches of time he lay on his bed, his nerve endings feeling like they had withered and died, his thoughts languidly drifting from one imaginary space to the next.

At one point, he pictured himself as a patient in a hospital, nurses and doctors suddenly converging on his bed as he went into cardiac arrest.

'CLEAR!' a female nurse cried shrilly…and then *pumpff*, his body jolted as the paddles sent a powerful electric shock through him. 'CLEAR!' the nurse cried again. And then, *pumpff*.

But his body remained unresponsive.

'CLEAR!'

But mostly his thoughts turned, and returned, to his planned tryst with his lady from the library, though masturbation had lost its edge, and he spent a great deal of time worried that she would sense his absence and feel betrayed; worse, abandoned.

He needed to get out.

He needed money, a further £14.20 before the clocks went forward, but there was no way his mum was going to let him go to the golf course, he knew—no matter what argument he presented.

The fresh air will do me good. I need to get out. Why do you care? You don't care.
Boredom complete, he took to roaming the house.

On Thursday morning, his mum found him in the kitchen examining the unused mop he had bought her.

'Bed!' she chided wearily, predictably—though it was her, in Eliot's opinion, who needed the sleep. She looked tired and...and, *creased*.

'But I'm okay, Mum,' he said, his voice thick and his jaw clicking.

'You've got to give it time,' she said and turned away from him, conversation over.

Angry and frustrated, he watched her shuffle down the hallway and disappear into the living room. 'I'm not like you!' he wanted to yell, but he kept his mouth shut and did as he was told.

Retreating upstairs, he turned his binoculars on the street.

No. 18 was sitting watching television. The husband at No. 16 was out to work. Typewriter Man seemed preoccupied and unable to type. He just sat there smoking cigarette after cigarette, staring out of the window, as though the malaise affecting Eliot had slowly oozed out over the street and had finally ensnared the man. Then again, maybe it was the other way around, and No. 14's inability to write was somehow spreading out from him and was affecting Eliot in some strange way.

Whatever the cause, No. 14 looked like he wanted to be anywhere but at his typewriter. He kept snatching up pieces of work he had already written, his expression at once both bewildered and aggravated as he scanned his work; as though an unexpected element had been introduced into the story and he was not entirely in control of it.

Typewriter Man looks like he's met Claudine, his diary entry for that day suggested.

By Friday, Eliot's boredom had got so bad that he dragged himself in front of the bathroom mirror. There was more than a hint of desperation attached to the act, as though he was hoping the shock might anger him into confronting his mum. *I'm going out. You can't stop me. So there.*

His face appeared bloated, and the area around his eye was discoloured, yellow and dark purple. Where the eye was partially open, a whitish crust had gathered along the seam of the lower eyelid, like a dried glue. To make things worse, his spots were as bad as ever, particularly the one at the corner of his mouth. He had hoped that O'Neal might have smashed it so hard it had burst and totally emptied of pus, but even that had not gone in his favour and it was as large as ever, maybe larger. His jaw remained painful to the touch and continued to make a loud clicking sound in his head when he opened his mouth. A bottom front tooth, a baby one, he guessed, wobbled so significantly when he gave it a wiggle, he was sure it would be out sometime in the next week, if he spent enough time on it. And time was something he had bags of.

Twenty pounds. If only the tooth fairy were real.

David got home from school around three thirty, only to inform his mum that he was staying at Rob's—again! But Eliot was too tired to feel anger.

That evening, around six, the doorbell rang. Eliot was lying on his bed, working on his tooth.

The bell rang once, then twice, and then after a pause, a third time. Finally, his mum answered the door.

'Oh, hello,' he heard her say. Her tone brought Eliot out onto the landing.

'So how's the patient?' A male voice. One he recognised.

Eliot grabbed hold of the banisters.

'Battered and bruised, but he'll live,' his mum answered. Her matter-of-factness stung Eliot. 'It was kind of you to bring him home, Mr Wilson.'

'That's quite all right, Mrs Thomas,' the teacher replied. 'And I'm glad he's doing okay.'

'He is. He's fine.'

Eliot tightened his grip on the banisters. *Then let me out.*

'I'm not very happy about the whole incident, you understand,' his mum continued.

'Of course not, and perfectly understandable, I might add.'

She coughed.

'Well, yes. Good. I'm glad you see that.'

'Of course. Who wouldn't? But as regrettable as the incident was—and it *was*, Mrs Thomas, it really was—some good has come out of it.'

'I don't understand.'

'The decision was taken yesterday. The boy's been expelled.'

Eliot pushed himself away from the banisters. *O'Neal, expelled!* He could hardly believe it.

His mum coughed again, 'I see...it's probably for the best, of course.' She hesitated before continuing. 'But it's a shame, all the same—when a boy turns bad, I mean. It's hard not to ask questions of the parents, don't you think?'

Mr Wilson let out an ugly snort. 'For all the good it would do: I met his father once. Talk about the fruit not falling far from the tree.'

There was a pause in the conversation. Eliot guessed his mum was taking out a cigarette, lighting it as she thought about what Mr Wilson had just said.

Expelled! No more O'Neal.

'Will Eliot be well enough for his computer lesson tomorrow?' Mr Wilson enquired.

No! Eliot leant forward over the banisters. *I'm not allowed out!*

His mum sighed: 'Lord only knows he could do with getting out, but...well, I'm not sure it's a good idea. But he'll be back Monday, don't you worry about that.'

There was another pause. 'Quite right, of course. Let him rest up.'

'I must say, Mr Wilson; it's unusually kind of you taking an interest in Eliot's welfare.'

'Gordon...please. It's Gordon.'

No...a first name would only make things worse.

'Well, it's kind of you...Gordon. I am worried about him. You see, Eliot is...well, Eliot's a—'

'—a quiet boy.'

'Yes. Yes…that's him exactly.' Eliot heard his mum cough, like she was embarrassed.

Eliot gripped the banisters more tightly.

'Which reminds me,' Mr Wilson tutted. 'I've got something for him. Thought it might cheer him up.'

'Oh, you didn't have to do that.'

'Nonsense,' Mr Wilson laughed. 'No harm in spoiling one of my star pupils.'

'Star pupils?'

'Oh yes,' he replied. 'So…I'll just fetch it from the car then, shall I?'

There was a long pause and then he heard his mum exclaim, 'What's this?'

Eliot leant as far forward over the banisters as he dared.

'A loan. I hope you don't mind.'

'I don't know what to say.'

The teacher laughed. 'How about telling me where you want it?'

Where you want, what? What'd he brought around?

'Sorry, yes, of course. On the dining room table in the back room will do just fine. That way.'

'Right you are.'

'Goodness!' he heard his mum exclaim. 'Well, it all looks so expensive. And the school is fine with this?'

With what?

'Actually, it's mine, Mrs Thomas…' The voices trailed off down the hallway. Minutes later, Eliot heard the two of them moving back up the hallway.

'Well, I shan't keep you any longer, Mrs Thomas.'

'Right you are. And thank you…for everything, Mr Wilson.'

'Not at all. Well, do send him my regards, won't you? I hope he enjoys the games.'

'He might have to fight off his younger brother.'

'David! That's right, I almost forgot. Yes, I'll be having him next year, won't I?'

'Yes. I don't know where the time goes. Do you have kids, Mr Wilson?'

'No, but...well, why would I?' They both laughed at this. 'And I've told you, it's Gordon...please.'

'Well then...Gordon. Thank you. And you must call me Mary.'

No. No. NO!

'Well...I'll be off then.'

Once Mr Wilson had gone, Eliot stomped downstairs. He found his mum in the back room. When he saw the...the *thing* on the dining room table, he froze.

'It's a computer,' his mother declared, folding her arms.

Monitor. Keyboard. Cassette drive. Magazines. User Manual.

What would the kids at school say about this?

Eliot Thomas, Game Boy.

'Don't want it.' His jaw clicking, the words came out shrilly, like a kettle boiling over.

'Not now, Eliot,' she sighed.

But Eliot refused to listen. 'It's like having the school in the house,' he complained. As he shook his head, a bit of dribble escaped his lips and ran down his chin. His jaw was properly starting to ache.

'Honestly,' she sighed, reaching into her dressing gown for her cigarettes. 'Nothing's ever good enough, is it?' Lighting one, she regarded the computer through the smoke, her shoulders slightly raised.

'If the kids at school find out about this...' he mumbled. 'It's bad enough already...look at me,' he complained, pointing at his beaten-up face.

'That's not school, that's one boy. And he's been expelled.'

'You're not listening,' he mumbled.

'Look at it though,' his mum said, pointing at the computer. 'Just think how much smarter you'll be than everyone else.'

'Now you sound like Dad.' Unable to look at her anymore, Eliot shoved his hands into his jean pockets and fell into a miserable silence.

His mum smoked her cigarette, her expression suddenly thoughtful.

After some time, his mother sighed and shook her head. 'It looks very flash,' she muttered, leaning forward to stub out her cigarette in the small glass ashtray on the table. 'We never had anything like this in my day. We had to use our imagination.'

He would have said something to that, but a strange, worried expression had come over his mum's face suddenly, as though she was suddenly not quite sure whether this thing was here to replace her, so he turned and left the room.

Served her right.

Later that night, he was hunched over his microscope concentrating on the blood sample he had taken, when he heard his mum's bedroom door slowly creak open. He stopped and looked up to listen. There was nothing for a while, only the throb from the cut in the top of his arm sending a steady, pulsing beat to his ears.

Despite the efforts of everyone the week before, his mum had stubbornly refused to go anywhere near her bedroom, as though she was afraid of it. Which made no real sense. Instead, she chose to remain sleeping in the armchair downstairs. Not that he was unhappy about her decision, but it did seem a bit weird that no one had said anything to her; not David, not Michael (who had popped around a few times since then, once to check on him and the extent of his "war wounds"); not even Ruth.

The silence went on for an age, and just as he was beginning to get a little anxious himself, he heard his mum begin pacing the room; slowly at first, shuffling, muttering to herself, and coughing. Coughing a lot, the floorboards creaking loudly when she did.

After minutes of this, he gave up on the sample under the microscope and put everything away, his concentration ruined. He grabbed a book, intending to read for a while, but his mum's continued pacing proved too distracting so he gave up on that, too, flinging the book to the floor.

For a while he just lay on his back, opening and closing his mouth just so he could hear his jaw click inside his head. But it was much fainter now, producing in him a rather puzzling sense of loss. He kind of liked the sound of damage; it was tangible proof of hurt.

He played with his loose tooth for a while, discovering that if he twisted it in a certain way, he could get it to flare up with pain, but it was clear the baby tooth was not ready to come out and he sighed, letting his hand drop to his side.

Finally, when he thought things could not get any worse, he heard the small portable television going on, the one from the back room, which Michael had brought up for her. This seemed to settle his mum a bit and eventually her pacing ceased. Also, her coughing fits grew less frequent.

So now he had a new noise to contend with, and the needling thrum of television noise coming through the wall steadily bore into his brain. He stared up at the ceiling, arms flat by his sides until it became too much for him.

Swinging off his bed, Eliot took himself and his book downstairs. The curtains in the living room were drawn and the main light was off, but his mum had left the television on, the volume quite low, as though the armchair was a pet she did not want to leave alone in the dark.

Clutching his book, he sat on the arm of his mum's chair and glanced down at the seat cushion, surprised not to see a deep depression at the heart of it. There were a few rumples in the fabric, but overall there was no real evidence to suggest that his mum spent any length of time sitting there. Impulsively, he ran the palm of his open hand across the rough, green fabric. It was cold to the touch, and he was alarmed at how easily he managed to smooth out even those few rumples.

Troubled, he looked away, but as his eyes roamed the room every photograph, every ornament, every item of furniture he gazed upon only added to his deepening sense of disconnection—as he tried, and failed, to understand the significance of these things and what they should mean to him personally. Fighting back the isolation he felt creeping up on him, he started pacing the room. Occasionally he would stop to touch something (a picture, an ornament, an LP in the record player cabinet), hoping it would perhaps prompt a memory, but nothing worked.

The room just felt wrong somehow. And everything in it seemed completely alien to him. Even the television sounded wrong, more tinny than usual, as though the room had grown somehow larger.

Suddenly beset with an odd kind of panic, like he had lost his parents in a crowd, he backed out of the room and retreated down the hallway.

He wished Michael were home, or even David.

The light in the back room blew when he flicked the switch. Hesitating, he edged into the dark room and sat down on the old, brown sofa, the end nearest the door, the very end, so that he remained within the skirt of light from the kitchen.

His mum's bedroom was directly above him. Tilting his head, he searched for a sound (needing to hear something); the portable television, her coughing, the creak of the floorboards, but there was nothing.

He felt alone.

But that was no longer true.

There it was, a squat thing on the dining room table, a fat silhouette in the dark, black as a crow, a sliver of light caught on the screen of the monitor. He tried to ignore it, but the thing pulled on his eyes.

Why had his mum let it into the house? What would his dad say?

Eliot was suddenly afraid that if he stared at the computer monitor for too long it might sense his presence; turn on all by itself, words slowly appearing...

> *Shhh, Eliot...you are not alone... touch me here...*
> *yes, like that, just there...Now, let's play a game.*

Eliot got up and backed into the kitchen. He had nowhere else to go other than back upstairs. But that was defeat. It was dark outside, and the garden was hidden in shadows. He imagined himself standing at the backdoor, looking in...*It was a narrow kitchen, used...the boy was on his knees, scrubbing the kitchen floor...*

Leaning against the worktop, he put on the kettle; it was an act of defiance against the silence of the house and the darkness.

Listening to it whir, he suddenly wanted the doorbell to ring... Michael with his laundry; David after a fight with Rob; Dad, with flowers, saying sorry...the break time bell at primary school.

Things going back to the way they used to be.

PART TWO

15 Saturday, 6 March 1982

£5.80

The next morning, his mum called Eliot into her bedroom.

He entered reluctantly.

The curtains were closed, he noted.

She was propped up in bed, watching the portable television Michael had placed on the dresser. The news was on. An ashtray, a lighter, and several cans of lager sat on her bedside table.

'Can you fetch me some ciggies from the offie, hun?' she asked, grabbing her handbag, which lay beside her.

'After that, can I go out for a bit?'

She looked at him for a moment. 'But only for a while,' she muttered.

Eliot nodded, having no intention of staying out for just "a while."

'I don't know where it all goes,' she grumbled, staring into her purse.

He glanced at the cans of lager on the bedside table, but kept quiet when she handed him a five-pound note.

'It's your bastard father's fault.'

Eliot could understand her positon on this and nodded. As he turned to leave his mother said, 'Wait on, love.'

He did as he was told and waited as his mum took out a pad and pen from her handbag and wrote something down.

The note.

'Mum, I don't really need that anymore,' he complained. 'They know me.'

'Take it anyway,' she said, and held out the note. 'Just in case.'

'How's your mum?' the short, fat man behind the counter asked as he handed Eliot the packet of cigarettes. He was unshaven, and Eliot felt a moment of anger and shame that this scruffy man, with his tatty brown bomber jacket, felt that he could ask such a question.

'My mum said I shouldn't talk to strangers,' he said, feeling like he should defend his mum in her absence.

Much to his annoyance, the man just chuckled. 'Quite right, too,' he said. 'Well, send her my best anyway. Tell her we're all thinking of her.'

He did his very best to give the man one of his dad's looks as he took the change, then turned before the man could say anything else to him.

Two young lads were lounging against the low wall outside the shop, laughing and smoking. Holding up their cigarettes just a little higher than seemed natural, elbows cocked, they sucked on them quickly, then blew out in an exaggerated manner. Trying to act tough, their attempts only appeared obvious and foolish to Eliot, but he was careful not to provoke an incident.

When the taller of the two lads spotted the packet of cigarettes in Eliot's hand, he nodded approvingly and took another drag on his smoke.

This was a new development! Straightening a little, Eliot acknowledged the taller boy's approval with a cool wave of his mum's Lambert & Butler. He kept walking, but he slowed his pace a little, and added a bit of a swagger.

Feeling the moment warranted a little grown-up sophistication, Eliot made an elaborate show of unpeeling the clear plastic wrapper from the packet, sliding out a cigarette and setting it between his lips. He stopped and feigned looking for a lighter about his person, and then, pretending he had found one, moved on.

Once he got around the corner, Eliot hastily returned the cigarette to its packet, careful not to snap it. But he still felt absurdly pleased with himself, and as he walked the short distance home, he turned the shiny silver packet over and over in his hands, as though it was something newly found, and quite possibly valuable.

'I'm off out then,' Eliot announced when he handed her the cigarettes and change.

'Just for a while, then,' his mum reminded him, eyes on the portable television.

'When's tea?' he asked.

'Hmmm?' she murmured, not looking up.

'Doesn't matter,' he answered, just grateful to be escaping the house.

He stopped dead when he heard voices up ahead.

Whoever it was, they did not sound like golfers. So, slipping off the path, he came up on them quietly, through the bushes, circling around behind the green.

Laughing and joking, three large lads were standing behind a cluster of trees watching the tee, which was currently clear. Keeping low, Eliot tucked himself behind a tree and risked a glance in their direction.

They were large lads, maybe sixth formers. Relaxed and behaving as though they owned the course, they were smoking cigarettes and did not care how much noise they made. They were wearing jeans and polo shirts, the up-to-date brands; Fred Perry, Lacoste, Kappa. All three wore white trainers, and all three had long, curly hair cut short at the sides. One lad had blond hair, another brown, and the tallest lad in the group had black hair.

Eliot's attention was drawn to the swollen plastic bag sitting on the ground between them. He was certain it contained golf balls; twelve, maybe more, he guessed.

'See the Villa game the other night?' Black was asking his mates.

The other two nodded.

'Get that ref? What a wanker.' He took a drag on his cigarette. 'Least we got to beat the shit out of the Palace boys.'

The three of them laughed.

'Talking of wanking,' Brown asked. 'How did you get on with the girlfriend the other night?'

'Ooooh, there was none of that,' Black declared, taking a dramatic drag on his cigarette.

Grinning, Brown and Blond exchanged looks and stepped in a little closer.

'I nicked one of me dad's pornos and made her watch it.'

'Go on,' Brown grinned. Brown wanted to know more.

Sniffing, Black stretched. 'Then I fucked her, good style.'

'Who could blame you?' Brown laughed, nudging Blond.

Blond wanted details. 'Where did you *do* her?'

'On the sofa. She really wanted it, let me tell you.'

'Lucky her mum didn't come home,' Brown pointed out.

Black shrugged. 'If she had, I would have given her a slap and reamed her up the arse; made her squeal.'

'Oink! Oink!' Blond snorted. Brown laughed.

'Pig noises?' Black demanded. 'What's that? You're not at playschool, for fuck's sake.'

Brown stopped laughing.

'Slap 'em and ram 'em!' Black decreed. 'That's how you treat a woman. Anyone tell you different, they're bent.'

There was a silence. The three lads sucked on their cigarettes quickly, deep in thought. Blond and Brown shot their tall friend quick, awed glances. Clearly, Black was their leader.

Eliot felt drawn to this kind of talk. Maybe he and his lady friend could watch a porno, and she could take him in the mouth afterwards, and then she would beg him to fuck her. All night.

Of course, he had not visited her for a while, and that did worry him; but mostly, he was wondering where he could get hold of a porno film.

'Golfers on the tee,' Black suddenly hissed, motioning for his friends to back up behind the tree, out of sight.

Eliot glanced up the fairway. Two men had indeed arrived on the tee and were preparing to take their shots.

Blond peered out from behind the tree. 'First one's teeing off,' he reported back. A faint whack echoed amongst the trees. Seconds later, the ball landed on the green with a dull thud. The small, white ball rolled forward to within twenty feet of the pin.

'Lucky bastard,' Blond snarled.

The second golfer took his tee shot. It looked good to start with, but as the ball slowly climbed it began to veer to the golfer's right; seconds later, it was clattering in amongst the trees. The ball dropped down near where the three boys were standing. Black ran over, picked it up, and stuffed the ball in his pocket. Joining back up with the others, he flashed them a grin.

The two golfers approached quickly, as though sensing trouble. They were smartly dressed and their bags were large, expensive-looking. One of the golfers, the one who had lost his ball, wore yellow trousers; the other, red trousers. They found the three lads pretending to be looking for the ball. Occasionally one of the lads would kick out at a bush or a clump of long grass to demonstrate this.

Yellow Trousers stepped up to Black. 'Where did it go?' he demanded.

Black shrugged.

Eyeing up the three boys, Red Trousers glanced over at his partner. 'Hit another one, Pete.'

'No, Eddy,' Pete said, shaking his head. He was still clutching the club he had used to tee off with and he now pointed it at Black. 'These pricks know where it is.'

'Who are you calling a prick?' Black said in a quiet voice.

'Come on, Pete,' Eddy suggested, trying to keep his tone light; but his eyes never left the three lads.

'No!' Pete shouted, sounding more and more like David did when he thought a particularly serious injustice had occurred. 'I know they have it. Besides, they shouldn't even be on here.'

'It's a public course,' Blond jeered from behind Black. 'You can't stop us.'

'There's nothing bloody public about my membership fees!' he shouted, waving his club around. 'Layabouts...why don't you get a job and make something of yourselves?'

'What, and work for someone like you?' Black looked him up and down. 'Poncey twat.'

'Hand it over, you...you scoundrel,' Pete demanded, his face purpling to a beetroot colour.

'*Scoundrel?*' Black laughed; but then his voice dropped. 'Or do you mean thief?' Black stepped towards the unhappy golfer. 'Are you calling me a thief, mister? Is that what yer calling me?'

'Leave it, Pete,' urged Eddy. 'Come on.'

Pete shook his head, his lips suddenly very wet. 'It's a disgrace, that's what it is.'

'You best put that down, mister,' warned Black, eyeing Pete's club. 'You might do yourself some mischief.'

'Yeah, mister,' laughed Blond evilly. 'You don't wanna fall on it.'

'Or maybe he does, the bender!' Brown laughed. 'Look at him! He's dressed like a puff. What a bender.'

'This is *my* golf course!' Pete yelled, his eyes impossibly large and wild.

'*Your* golf course?' Black enquired, taking another step towards Pete. Black was smiling, but Eliot could tell he was ready; he was like a coil of wire.

Eliot's throat tightened just looking at him.

Black against O'Neal... He clicked his jaw... Now that would be a good fight.

Pete swung his trolley around and placed it between him and Black, who looked ready for anything. 'Go on, Eddy!' he cried over his shoulder, his voice suddenly shaky. 'Finish up. I'll pass this hole.'

But Eddy was already on the green, putter in hand. Without sizing up the putt, he stabbed at his ball. The little white ball rolled eight feet past the hole. A part of Eliot felt sorry for him. His tee shot had been a good one. To make par he would need to sink a tricky downhill return putt.

Eddy hurried over to his ball and stabbed at it again, missing. The ball pulled up only a foot from the hole. Tapping it in, Eddy quickly replaced the flag and walked off the green. Without returning his putter to his bag, he grabbed his trolley and headed for the next tee, not even looking to see if Pete was following.

'Look!' Blond mocked. 'Your bum-boy's leaving.'

Pete glanced over his shoulder; Eddy was, by now, some distance away. He licked his lips and then started moving. 'Should be banned, the lot of you!' he shouted as he hurried to catch up with his playing partner. 'The club president will hear about this, I can promise you that! Public course or no public course!'

'Well, so long as the president doesn't order a nuclear strike on us, that's fine by me,' Black laughed. Blond and Brown laughed, too.

'My God!' Pete screamed, slowing down. 'There's another one, Eddy! *Eddy?*'

It took Eliot a second to realise that Pete was talking about him. Somehow he had managed to drift out from the safety of the tree line.

'They're bloody everywhere!' Pete complained shrilly. 'Christ, what the hell's this place turning into? A playground?'

'See ya, fuckhead!' Black shouted to Pete, but his keen eyes were now fixed on Eliot, interested.

Blond and Brown were also staring at him.

Keeping his eyes on Black, Eliot slowly backed up, careful not to make any sudden movements that might agitate the situation.

'Hey, where are you going?' Blond shouted, glancing at Black for instructions.

'Leave him,' Black said, still staring intently at Eliot. 'He's just a kid.'

'You sure?' Brown sounded disappointed. 'He might 'ave some golf balls on him.'

Eliot tightened his grip on his own bag of golf balls.

Black shook his head. 'Nah! Besides, looks like someone's fucked him over already.'

Despite the situation, Eliot felt his cheeks redden. Black knew things; he had no desire to appear weak in front of him.

Back beneath the tree line now, he wheeled about and fled deep into the woods, just in case Black changed his mind and ordered the chase.

Eliot took himself to the far side of the golf course. Just to be on the safe side. Hunting in unfamiliar territory, he found several golf balls over the next two hours, but his search was continually distracted having to maintain a constant vigil for other strangers. Frustrated, he was about to give up for the day when a ball suddenly clattered in the trees above him. It landed with a soft thud on the path in front of him.

Thinking of Black, he stared at the ball for a long while, the palms of his hands itching.

Golf ball hunting was a skill, he reminded himself. A *skill*. You had to have talent.

'It came in about here!' he heard a man shout.

Eliot stared at the ball for a moment longer—what would Black do? *Twenty pounds...*

Moments later a short, fat golfer came into view, club in hand. He was wearing thick-rimmed glasses. The unlucky player began his search for his golf ball, using his club to stab and swish at the heavy foliage.

Eliot grinned. The man was never going to find his ball.

The golfer, however, made no effort to widen his search, and if anything looked bored and disinterested, which Eliot found mystifying.

The short, fat man spent only a few more minutes stabbing his club at the undergrowth before glancing over at his playing companions, who were standing by their bags out on the fairway, quietly talking to one another.

It was done so quickly that Eliot almost missed it.

The golfer made a brief show of bending down, but as he did so, he took something out of his pocket. Another golf ball! Then he was suddenly standing up, waving to his playing companions, indicating that he had *found* his ball!

But that was impossible! Leaning back against the tree, Eliot took the man's ball from his pocket: a Maxfli, practically new. The man had made no effort to find it.

What a cheat!

The two golfers on the fairway nodded and motioned for him to hit his shot. The golfer whacked the ball out onto the fairway and acknowledged the murmured appreciation of his playing partners with a casual wave of his hand, like he was special or something.

As he re-joined the other players, Eliot felt only anger towards the fat little man.

What a cheat! What a horrible cheat. Shoving the Maxfli back in his pocket, he continued with his search, though his heart was no longer in it.

On his way off the golf course he stopped at the pond, where he wrestled with his conscience for a minute or two.

It had been a £1.40 day, which was okay. That made it £7.20.

But he still needed £12.80.

No time for bad luck. The risk was too great; he had to give it up. Taking out the stolen Maxfli, he threw it out over the pond. The dark-brown waters took it down greedily.

When he got home, he found David and Rob sitting at the dining room table in the back room. They had set up the computer and were playing a shoot-'em-up game. Rob was furiously banging away at the computer keyboard trying to annihilate a series of cascading alien invaders.

'Who said you could play on that computer?' Eliot shouted from the doorway, his jaw protesting with a loud click.

David turned, his face flushed with excitement. 'This is totally ace. And the school lent this to you?' He shook his head, clearly believing it was unfair.

'Get off it!' Eliot yelled, advancing into the room.

'How about a thanks for setting it up?' David said, keeping one eye on how Rob was doing.

'Yeah,' Rob chipped in, banging away at the keyboard. 'Where's our thanks?'

'I didn't ask you to set it up,' Eliot said, glaring at his brother. 'Who said you could set it up?'

'Mum did.'

'*Mum did?*'

'What's your problem? It's not like you're playing on it!' David snapped.

'So? That's up to me.'

'What's the big deal?'

'It's not yours!' Eliot shouted.

'It's not *yours* either, Rocky,' Rob quipped.

David laughed. 'Hah, *Rocky*...good one.'

Eliot's hand went up to his face. 'You're just jealous coz it's better than yours!' he shouted, hating himself the instant he said it.

'Am not,' Rob retorted with a sneer. 'And it isn't.'

'Well, it is a bit,' David conceded quietly, with an apologetic shrug to his friend.

Rob let him know just what he thought about that before turning his attention back to the game.

'So what are you doing here, anyway?' Eliot asked his brother.

'He lives here, dickhead,' Rob interjected, and glanced at David. The two of them burst out laughing.

Helpless before their laughter, Eliot turned to leave before things deteriorated further.

'Dad's been round, by the way!' David shouted.

Eliot stopped by the door, slowly turning. 'Dad?'

'Yep.'

Too late, Eliot shrugged; tried to act casual. 'So,' he said.

David grinned, his eyes narrowing. 'He's coming round tomorrow.'

'What for?'

David affected his usual superior tone. 'You'll just have to wait and see.'

'You mean you don't know,' Eliot sneered.

'Do.'

'Do not.'

'*Do!*'

'So prove it,' Eliot spat. 'What's he coming round for?'

From the cunning expression on his face, Eliot knew that Rob was looking for an opening to jump in.

'Not telling.'

Eliot suddenly had a thought. 'Did, er…Dad did see the computer?'

'Why?'

Eliot picked at the door handle. 'No reason…so, did he?'

'What do you think?' David replied, sounding bored now.

'So, what did he say about it?'

'Who?'

'*Dad!*' Eliot shouted, finally losing it.

David shrugged. 'Nothing.'

'Nothing?' Eliot demanded. 'He wouldn't have said nothing.'

'Who cares?' David snorted, his eye on the computer monitor. Rob had started up a new game. 'Why do you care?'

'I don't,' Eliot replied hurriedly. 'Just thought he might be interested, that's all.'

David blew out his cheeks, wanting very much to get back into the game. 'If you must know, he just wanted to know how much it cost.'

'What did you say?'

'Said the school lent it to you, stupid,' David snapped.

'And what did he say to that?'

'Nothing. Why would he?'

'Nothing…no reason.' Eliot turned to leave once more.

'Oh, he did say one thing,' David said, leaning back in his chair, head thrown back so he was almost looking at Eliot upside down.

'What's that?'

'He said he'd better not catch you using it to play games.'

Rob and David looked at each and burst out laughing.

'Go back to playschool!' Eliot yelled. 'You…you *benders.*'

As he rushed down the hallway, he heard David and Rob start up a chorus of the *Rocky* theme music.

To make himself feel better, Eliot spent a little bit of time catching up with events in the street.

Old Man Vic was pacing up and down in his living room, occasionally stopping to remonstrate with the carpet.

No. 14 was absent from his typewriter. Maybe he had gone off to see his wife. Maybe the story was just getting too much for him and he could no longer trust himself being in the same room as the typewriter.

Why doesn't Typewriter Man give up? Write something else? Eliot enquired of his diary. It had occurred to Eliot that maybe writing the story was not entirely Typewriter Man's idea; maybe it had been given to him, like homework. *Maybe he's not allowed to write anything else, not until he's finished with the story he was on.* Maybe that was a writing rule. Did writing have rules?

No. 18 was entertaining a friend. The two men were sitting on the sofa watching television, sitting quite close. A bottle of red wine and two glasses sat on the low coffee table in front of them. Their talk was interspersed with soft laughter.

He lowered the binoculars, suddenly quite jealous of all these people with their own places; never having to worry about school, family, being told when they could and could not go out.

If he had his own place he would do whatever he pleased, whenever he pleased. And the only visitors he would allow were people he liked, like his lady.

Downstairs, Rob laughed out loud. It was a horrible laugh.

Rob he would never let in; Rob could fuck off.

A bit later Ruth brought around a casserole, which meant that Rob got to stay for tea, which angered him.

Go home. You have a mum.

At least David and Rob stayed in the back room, leaving him in control of the television. His mum had taken herself upstairs. '*There's nothing much on anyway, love,*' she had said before going up—which meant he could watch whatever he pleased. In the past, on the rare occasions he had found himself in control of the television he had, if only for a while, put something grown-up on, like the news, or the weather, or *The Waltons*, hoping that someone would enter the room and see how grown-up he truly was. But no one ever did, and he would quickly turn to a program more to his liking, like *Scooby-Doo* or *Danger Mouse*. Which was probably not such a bad thing: Eliot had never understood why grown-ups would want to watch *The Waltons*—*The Waltons* was shit.

Finished with tea, Eliot gathered together the ashtray and the empty beer can his mum had left on her side table and dumped both items on to his empty plate.

He also picked up what he thought was an empty packet of cigarettes; but as lifted it, something inside made a rattling sound. Putting down his plate, he looked inside. It was a single cigarette. He stared at it long and hard, recalling the recent incident in the shed with David and his stupid friend. It was not like his mum to leave one in the pack; better not leave this lying around for them, he thought, dropping the packet onto his plate.

As Eliot entered the kitchen, he heard Rob in the back room roar, 'Fire! Fire, you idiot!'

'I am. I am!' David laughed back.

He felt such anger for his little brother at that moment that he saw himself storming into the room, ripping the wires out of the computer and smashing the monitor. But of course, he remained motionless, his feet refusing to take a single step into the room. *I'll show you*, he vowed, frustrated, though silently determined to one day get his own back on the pair of them.

As quietly as possible, Eliot entered the kitchen. Into the plastic bag hanging over the back door, he swept the beer can and the contents of the ashtray.

But not quietly enough; and he was quickly subject to another chorus of the *Rocky* theme as he slunk back down the hallway.

Bastards.

The man slapped her across the face and she staggered back against the wall.

No! Leave her alone. Please leave her alone.

Wearing a tatty brown bomber jacket he was a short, fat man with banks of hair sticking out from the sides of his large, balding head.

He raised his hand to strike her again.

Stop it! Eliot mouthed, grabbing a fistful of leaves. *Call the police. Do something! Why don't you do something?*

The man raised his hand to strike her again.

'No, that's enough!' the woman protested loudly, pushing her attacker away.

The man said nothing in reply, he just stepped in, grinned, and backhanded her.

'You bastard,' she growled, wiping her lips.

'Yeah, that's right, you goddamn bitch,' the man laughed, and undid his belt.

For a moment, he thought the man was going to use it against her. But instead the man dropped his trousers and pants, and took it out.

Eliot stared at it. It was a small thing, but *fat*.

He sobbed out loud, knowing it was going to do so much damage.

The man swung around. 'What was that?'

Eliot held his breath.

'What?' the woman demanded.

'I thought I heard something.'

'Just get on with it, you bastard,' the woman snapped.

The man eyed the bushes suspiciously before returning his attention to the woman he now had backed into the corner.

Eliot breathed out. *Thank you.*

He spun her around, bent her over and kicked her legs apart. Fumbling only a bit, the man got himself in. And then, with one hand grabbing her hip, the other placed on her lower back, he began. His technique was atrocious...a slow, measured withdrawal and then... bam! A fast, hard, upward thrust.

Eliot watched his lady brace herself against the wall; she took it all silently, without complaint, her head turned in his direction. She looked calm, not even frightened.

I'd scream, he told himself, over and over. *I would. I would scream so loudly the world would hear it.*

Eliot quickly sensed that the man was struggling to get there...the stretch of his neck, the whitening of his knuckles...lifting onto his toes. He slapped her across the backside and then grabbed a handful of her red blouse. Eliot heard the tear of the material quite clearly, the courtyard amplifying the sound as though it, too, wanted the world to hear it.

Stop it! Stop it! Eliot clung to the branches as though a fierce wind was trying to rip him away.

Finish it.

'Say something, bitch,' the man strained.

She murmured, 'Ooh yes, that's good,' staring deep into the bushes. 'I'm almost there. Come on.'

Eliot thought he detected a note of amusement in her voice. *Hah!*

The man slapped her again, a good one, loud across the buttocks. Eliot felt an unexpected tingle in his stomach. '*Finish it,*' he mouthed. Or was it, '*Hit her again.*'

And the man *did* hit her again. Hard. Then his legs locked up, and his body locked up, and the courtyard swelled with the sound of his angry hisses.

Silence for a moment. Just the sound of the short, fat man panting. Then he stepped back, wiped his hand across his mouth and slowly pulled up his pants and trousers.

Call the police.

'What about the fucking blouse?' the woman snarled.

The man hesitated, then dipped his hand into his pocket and brought out a couple of crumpled notes. 'God, you must need it bad,' the man said, his voice full of disgust.

'Keep your opinion to yourself.' Sniffing, she took the money quickly, without looking at him.

'It's your body,' the man shrugged, and left the courtyard without another word.

Bristling, Eliot watched the man leave.

Who did he think he was? Concerned, his gaze returned to his woman. She looked a little dishevelled and tired. Sniffing, she fixed herself up and then with a sigh, she also left the courtyard.

Soon now. I'll take you away from this, he promised her silently. *I'll get the money.*

Eliot watched her leave and then stepped out of the bushes. Sitting on the steps beneath the entrance to the library, he pulled out the packet of Lambert & Butler from beneath his jumper. Taking out the one remaining cigarette, he held it between his index finger and thumb and rolled it back and forth for a while, nervous, before lifting it to his nose. The tobacco smelt sweet, woody, almost *vanillary*.

Digging his hand into his jeans pocket, he pulled out the blue lighter he had found down the back of the old brown sofa. He knew the moment was big as he put the cigarette to his lips: this was no longer pretend stuff.

He was closing the gap on Michael…maybe even his dad.

This'll show them.

With a rasp, he drew a flame from the lighter. It seemed to echo around the courtyard. He stared into the orange flame as though it contained the secret to life, school, family, growing up.

He lit the cigarette, dragging on it quickly to get the red end going, momentarily alarmed at the glowing heat inches from his nose and mouth. Smoke stung his eyes

Then he did it: he took a long drag on the cigarette.

For a moment he held the smoke in his mouth, cheeks blown out like a puffer fish. The smoke felt oddly coarse against the inside of his cheeks. Heat started filling his mouth, burning.

Inhale. Inhale.

Feeling his heart thump in his chest, Eliot took a sharp intake of breath, sucking the smoke deep down into him.

For a second he could not breathe…pins and needles prickled his scalp…sparks of light fizzed across his eyes. A bubble of hot air expanded rapidly in his throat; his mouth began to fill with saliva. Panicked and feeling sick, he exhaled quickly. He started coughing and his throat burnt. Eyes watering, he paced the courtyard trying to distract himself as the urge to vomit steadily increased.

Breathe in.

He imagined the look on his brothers' faces and he liked what he came up with… amazement, envy, respect.

The feeling of nausea quickly receded, and was soon replaced with one of wonder. *He was doing it. Smoking.* Now…finally; he felt like he had been waiting all his life to feel this massive.

The second drag of the cigarette was not as bad. His mouth felt like it was full of ash but he only coughed a couple of times.

Strutting back and forth across the small courtyard, he took a couple more quick drags on the cigarette, sucking the smoke down fast and hard to avoid further coughing. With half the cigarette gone, the urge to cough or retch had faded completely.

'Fuck off,' he said out loud, feeling powerful and unstoppable. 'Look at me,' he declared, pumping up his chest, feeling deadly. *Where the fuck was O'Neal now? Or the she-bitch?*

He took another fierce drag of his cigarette and found himself thinking of his woman. He saw himself taking her up against the library wall.

'Yeah, you cow. Take me…suck my fucking crayon.' The words, the way they sounded in the small courtyard, made thrilling sense. He took another drag on his cigarette and thought back to what Black had said to his mates, 'Come on, bitch…or…or I'll *slap* you.'

Finished with the cigarette, he flung the butt away from him. Sparks blazed as the burning end broke apart.

Breathing hard, he stepped into the shadows of the courtyard and finished himself off quickly. It was a big one and it doubled him up.

Breathing hard, he straightened up and stared into the sky, anticipating a sudden change in the world order.

'I'm Spartacus!' he yelled.

Zipping back up, he suddenly desired another cigarette.

Eliot Thomas, Smoker Boy.

When he arrived home, he was surprised to find Michael and David talking in the kitchen. Michael had a mug of coffee in his hand and David was sitting on the washing machine.

'What are you doing here?' he said to Michael, closing the back door.

'Do I need a reason to come visit?' he asked, but he smiled.

'Well, no,' Eliot conceded. 'Not really.'

Michael stroked the top of his lip where his moustache was developing quickly. If he was trying to look all grown up, he failed. To Eliot, he just looked foolish and self-important.

'Out late, aren't you?'

Eliot shrugged. 'Golfie, looking for balls.'

'In the dark?'

'So?'

'G-y-p-o,' David said in a low voice.

'Shut up,' Eliot snapped. 'Least I've got money.'

'You shut up!' David yelled. 'And I don't need money.'

'Where's your bummer friend, anyway? Was it his bedtime?'

Michael sighed. 'Come on, you two.'

'Mum'll kill you if she sees you sitting on the washing machine,' Eliot warned in a quieter voice.

'She won't,' David replied, trying to sound like he was bored. 'Not unless you tell her, she won't.'

'So, where is she?' Eliot demanded, making out as though he was going to go and get her. 'In the living room?'

'Knock it off, will you!' Michael suddenly shouted, dumping his coffee mug on the work surface, spilling it. 'Jesus Christ, no wonder Mum's knackered,' he said. 'Who wouldn't be, with you two going at it all the time?'

Stung by the comment, but angry also, Eliot snapped, 'He started it.' Who did Michael think he was?

'Did not,' David retorted.

'I don't care who started it,' said Michael in a tired voice. 'But he's right, David. You shouldn't be sitting on the washing machine. You know how Mum gets.'

David went red in the cheeks and shouted, 'You never had a problem with it until he showed up!'

Knowing it would infuriate his younger brother, Eliot grinned... hard.

It worked. 'Shut up, you divvy!' David yelled.

'Didn't say anything,' he jeered.

Michael sighed. 'David, down...*please?*'

David stuck out his chin. 'You gonna make me, Mikey?' But he slid off the washing machine.

Michael shook his head. 'Salty bastard,' he muttered, but he was suddenly grinning.

Annoyed, Eliot glared at Michael. 'So what are you doing here, anyway? You never said.'

Michael stroked his moustache. 'Sharon's got late shifts over the next few nights, so I'm at a bit of a loose end.'

He could tell that Michael was keeping something back; he glanced at David, but his younger brother was staring down at the vinyl floor, humming a tune.

'So? It's not like Sharon hasn't had late shifts before,' he pointed out, which seemed to annoy Michael for some reason—not that he cared. 'But it's not though.'

'Your face is looking better,' Michael finally replied, making it clear that the conversation was at an end.

'Like you care.'

Still looking down, David laughed, and his tuneless hum became the theme tune to *Rocky*, only quietly, to avoid provoking Michael.

Later that evening, a band of lads entered the street. They were making a lot of noise. Eliot climbed out of bed and went to the window. They walked tall, and with swagger, shoulders forced back, jacket sleeves rolled up over the elbow joints as though they were heading for a prearranged fight. A few wore their footballs tops.

Like O'Neal, they had no fear.

Eliot could see this. It was in the way they shouted to one another. They did not care that people might not want to hear them; did not give a damn that people might be sleeping. They sang, exchanged challenges, mock fights broke out. *Hooligan scum,* his dad would say of these lads. *If they wanna fight, they should join the army.*

Their ugly laughter banged off bricks and windows. One lad dragged out the bin from No. 16, kicked it over so the contents spewed out into the road; cereal boxes, baked bean cans, newspaper, leftover food and nappies.

A cheer went up. But no one came out to challenge them.

Another lad disappeared down the side alley between No. 14 and No. 12. Eliot watched as the hot arc of piss splashed up against the wall. It collected in a puddle at the lad's feet, rivered down the path, cut across the pavement like a knife and gushed over the kerb.

Still no one came out to challenge them.

And Eliot watched on with envious eyes.

Unstoppable, invincible, he imagined himself their leader, and they would fear and love him. The tallest and strongest amongst them, he would smoke cigarettes and order them to do his bidding. They were his to command…and so he had them…

...*marching to war...marching on a rival gang...marching on O'Neal and his two friends...marching on the school...marching on his two brothers, who, terrified, pleaded to be spared, begged to join him...marching, finally, on the council to stop the destruction of the pier.*

The lad taking a pee suddenly yelled out and a terrified cat shot out of the side alley and across the road.

Another cheer went up.

Zipping himself up, the lad re-joined his friends out in the road.

Eliot watched them for a while longer. Finally, the group made it to the top of the road and disappeared.

He stared at the book in his hand; perhaps he should be looking at changing his reading material. Tossing *The Lion, the Witch and the Wardrobe* to one side, he picked up *The Rats* and started leafing through the pages in search of...of something.

16 Sunday, 7 March 1982

£7.20

The argument in the hallway had been going on for some time.

David had answered the front door before Eliot had time to escape upstairs.

Trapped in the living room, he leant over the armchair and tested the latch on the window. It was stuck stiff. The golf course was calling, but it was clear to him that, for the moment at least, he was going nowhere.

Across the road he could see that several gulls had gathered along the gutter of No. 16. He stared at them for a moment, wondering what they would think if they saw him leap out the window.

Golf balls. *Money*.

That was all that mattered now.

£7.20. That was all he had. Something needed to happen.

The argument in the hallway started to build.

David had gone next door to Rob's, which Eliot thought was unfair, given he had let their dad in.

Chicken. And where was Michael? Only he was brave enough to stay. Make sure their mum was okay.

Then he saw it.

His dad's wallet.

It was wedged down between the armrest and the seat cushion. Tufts of bank notes poked out the top.

He had it in his hand before he had time to think things through. It was large and heavy, made of brown leather, a veined patina of yellow whorls running across the shiny surface.

Across the road, more gulls gathered. He hesitated.

Just then his father's rising voice yelled something about *Fucking Ruth...*

The muscles around his face twitched and tightened.

He stroked the tops of the bank notes with his thumb. There must have been at least twenty, thirty pounds in there. Impulsively, he took a sniff. The money had an odd, greasy odour to it, lovely. He gently massaged two notes between his fingertips and thumb, his heart beginning to pound in his chest.

Miraculously, when he looked down, two one-pound notes were suddenly out of the wallet and in his hand!

Served him right.

He glanced at the door. His mum was yelling something the other side of it. Stuffing the liberated pound notes into his back pocket, he put the wallet back in the exact same place and quickly sat down in the other armchair, waiting it out.

Things had gone quiet in the hallway; Eliot's eyes darted to the door, worried that his dad and mum somehow knew what he had done. Fixing his eyes on the door handle, he half-expected to see it turn viciously, then his parents charging into the room.

Hand them over, you thief!

Aren't things bad enough?

He started to shake. What had he done?

Put it back.

Put it back.

Seconds passed, feeling like minutes, hours, forever.

An itch developed in the centre of his back. He tried to scratch it out, but maddeningly, the itch kept migrating.

Worse, his bum began to ache, and no matter what position he tried, he could not get comfortable.

A further minute or two passed. He gave his baby tooth a vicious twist. Pain! Flaring outwards from deep within his gum.

His dad would know. Of course he would. *You're in deep shit. Do something...Do something...*

He pushed himself up.

But at that moment, the door opened and his mother and father entered the room.

His dad was scowling and his mum's cheeks were flushed.

Hastily, Eliot sat back down.

Spotting his wallet when he swiped up his jacket, his father leant forward and grabbed it.

Neither of his parents had said a word since entering the room.

Eliot tensed, watching his dad turn the wallet over and over in his hand as though he did not recognise it.

Then he opened it.

It was me. I took it. Sorry....sorry....sorry...don't...

Scowling, Donald's fingers sifted through the contents of the wallet; Eliot was certain he was counting the notes.

It was me.

'This is the new address,' his dad finally said, producing a small piece of paper.

New address?

Eliot watched his mum take it, turning it over in her hand. 'Why do I need this?' she said, sounding genuinely confused.

'Mary! *Please.*'

She handed him back the piece of paper. 'Really, I don't need this.'

There was a pause.

His dad appeared fidgety; and for once, oddly defenceless against her.

His curiosity got the better of his fear. Something was going on here. Something important. He wanted to be the first to know about it.

'Mary...I have to take the job. It's a good job.'

'Give my regards to what's her name...I'm sure you'll both be very happy living in Manchester.'

Without another word, his dad left.

His mum gave Eliot a faint smile and then disappeared into the kitchen. Seconds later, he heard the cupboard doors open and close.

Then water from the tap filling the bucket...

Manchester. Where was Manchester?

A little later, Eliot was sitting on his bed with his money tin on his lap. Taking out the two stolen one-pound notes, he held each one up to the light, like he was checking to make sure they were not forgeries— though a part of him hoped they were, because surely that would mean his crime did not count.

He now had £9.20.

But he needed more. More.

Returning the tin to its hiding place, he got ready to go out.

It was soon clear that Claudine was not taking things seriously.

In a repeat of last Sunday, he had found Claudine sitting on the pavement opposite the path leading onto the golf course, only this time she had brought *sandwiches!*

'What?' she had replied to his complaint. 'I got hungry last time. Anyway, what happened to your face?'

'Nothing,' he had mumbled, realising any attempt to get rid of her would prove no more successful than last time.

'Doesn't look too bad,' she had remarked, giving his discoloured face a quick once-over. 'It's an improvement, actually.'

'Didn't hurt, if that's what you think,' he had said as she stood up and fell in beside him.

'I'm almost certain it didn't,' was her reply, with a perfectly straight face.

For some reason, this really needled Eliot.

The morning had got no better. Where was she now, anyway? Eliot looked around and saw her bending over what looked like a large clump of tall weeds. Claudine happened to look up just at that moment and smiling, she raised her hand.

Frowning, he waved her over.

'I don't think you're taking this seriously,' he said when she reached his position.

'What do you mean?' she said. 'I am. Very.'

'So what's that?' he asked, pointing to what she had in her hand.

'It's a flower!'

The flower had small white petals and a dark centre.

'Exactly,' he said. 'That's not a golf ball.'

'No,' she said, nodding her agreement, 'it really isn't.'

He opened his mouth. Shut it. Opened it again. 'Anyway,' he said eventually, 'it's a weed, not a flower.'

Claudine looked surprised. 'It's only a weed if it's in your garden. Out here, it's a flower.' She gave him a smile and offered it to him. 'Pretty, isn't it?'

He should have known: clearly, the first time had been all luck. Now it was too late.

He took a deep breath. 'To find golf balls,' he began slowly, 'you really need to look, concentrate.' Bending down, he made an exaggerated show of searching in the tall grass in front of him to demonstrate how she should look. 'You really need to get in there, look around. It's the only way.'

Lifting the flower to her nose, Claudine nodded.

'And look!' Eliot cried, reaching down. He came up with a golf ball. His expression, however, quickly changed as he examined it. 'No,' he muttered, with a disappointed shake of his head. 'It's no good. But do you see now?' he insisted. 'See how easy it is to find them when you really look?'

Claudine nodded.

'That ball was quite hidden.'

'Yes, I see that.' Claudine nodded, her expression grave.

'I can find balls that are a lot more hidden than that one.'

'I think you can.'

'Really, I can!'

'I believe you. I would have missed that one.'

'It's hard work. And takes skill.'

Claudine nodded. 'Can we go and eat now?'

'What?' Just when he thought he was getting somewhere.

'Maybe if I ate something, I'd find a lot more.'

'*More?*' he cried, wishing he could forget that she had made sandwiches. *Sandwiches!* 'But you haven't found *any* yet!'

'You see the problem then?' she observed sadly.

Eliot wanted to scream.

This girl was…was impossible, infuriating.

He took another deep breath. '*Then* will you help me look for some golf balls?' he demanded, refusing to look at her.

'Of course.'

'*Properly* look, I mean!'

She nodded.

Eliot sighed, 'Fine then.'

Claudine beamed. 'I know a place,' she said, and skipped off without another word.

Sighing, he followed after her. This was not fair. Then he stopped. And what did she mean by, *I know a place?*

He sat down and crossed his legs, waiting patiently as Claudine organised the sandwiches. Grudgingly, Eliot conceded that the spot Claudine had picked was sort of okay.

She had led him deep into the woods. So deep, in fact, that he was just starting to suspect she had gotten herself lost but was too embarrassed to say anything when the glade seemed to open out in front of them, as though by magic.

She stopped so abruptly he bumped into the back of her, which irritated him.

'Sorry,' he said, not truly meaning it.

Unperturbed, Claudine breathed in deeply and looked around. 'Here we are then,' she beamed.

They were sitting beneath a cherry blossom tree. He could just make out the buds on the thin, dark branches starting to crack open, exposing just a sliver of the pink inside. To most people this was a sure sign that winter had been beaten and spring was upon them, and the promise of better things to come.

Eliot had his own thoughts on the matter.

But here…right at that moment…well, the place was okay. The sun was out and tossed down her yellows, warming his face. Sweet grass fragrances mingled with other earth smells and lifted out of the ground…soil, bark, and fallen leaf scents filled his nose. Rising out of the grass, stiff-stemmed dandelions appeared to stand gossiping to one another in tight clusters, an occasional yellow head nodding soberly. Birdsong filled the glade, and flying insects buzzed about without haste or menace.

And not a wasp in sight.

The air was clean. He felt *clean*, lighter; like a layer had been lifted from him.

He looked around. Yes, quite okay.

Not that he would ever admit that to Claudine. He glanced over at the strange, annoying girl who seemed determined to wiggle her way into his life.

Look at her, with her huge, silly boots. Nothing seemed to bother this girl.

Humming to herself, she placed a white cloth napkin on the grass and ordered the sandwiches, which were cut into squares, according to their fillings. Two little stacks quickly appeared.

They could have been anywhere, in any world, two weary adventurers taking a rest from the rigours of a secret, deadly quest. Smiling, Claudine handed him a sandwich. He took a bite. It was lemon curd. Discovering that in fact he really was quite hungry, he finished the sandwich in three bites.

Claudine nodded approvingly and took a nibble on her own sandwich.

He ate the next sandwich with a bit more restraint.

Cheese and ham this time.

Unfortunately, a bit of it went down the wrong way and he was suddenly choking. His eyes watered and he started coughing uncontrollably. Seemingly unconcerned that he might be dying,

Claudine threw a piece of crust at him. 'That will teach you to bolt down your food,' she said with a grin.

Eliot gasped some more.

'Goodness me!' Claudine acknowledged, giggling. 'What a funny colour you've turned!'

Somehow, he managed to get his coughing fit under control. 'I was choking!' he protested, wiping his watery eyes. 'I could have died.'

'*Died?*' It was Claudine's turn to choke...with laughter.

Eliot threw the remainder of his sandwich at her. The missile hit her square on the nose. The sight of her blinking in shock as his half-eaten sandwich struck home and separated into two pieces was too much for him, and he barked out a laugh, which, although a bit sharp and vengeful at first, quickly resolved into genuine laugh-out-loud amusement.

Eliot's contorted face was a source of fresh amusement for Claudine and she threw herself back onto the grass. Before long the two of them were laying on their backs, clutching their stomachs, the sound of their laughter ringing around the glade.

Finally, their mirth subsided. Breathing hard, the two children lay next to each other, elbows almost touching, staring up at the circle of blue sky. Eliot decided he quite liked this arrangement; there was something quite grown-up about it.

Giving in to the moment, he felt his body relax, lighten. The shiver of leaves and the creaking sway of the branches, and the occasional cloud arcing overhead, made it seem like the woodland glade had transformed into some sort of open-top vessel and was gliding over the top of the world.

The question was out before he had time to really think about what he was asking. 'Do you believe in God?'

'I have to,' Claudine answered in a quiet voice. 'My dad's dead.'

'Oh,' he said after a moment. 'I suppose you do, then.'

With uncharacteristic seriousness, Claudine nodded.

'I mean,' he added, 'I'm sorry.'

'That's okay,' she said.

A sudden gust of wind shook the tops of the encircling trees.

He bit his lip. *Stupid question. Stupid God.* Now he had to know more; had to be sure that what David and Rob had said about her, about her dad, was not true. Because if it was…

Yes? What then?

Did he really care?

But it was Claudine who spoke next. 'I have a picture of him,' she said quietly. 'Do you want to have a look?'

'Well…okay then,' he said, sitting up.

Claudine produced a small photograph from her back pocket. It was wrapped in cling film. Eliot took the photograph and held it carefully between his finger and thumb. The man in the picture had short, dark hair and a dark moustache. The tightly knotted yellow tie he wore matched the carnation pinned to the lapel of his grey suit. He looked quite alone, standing at the top of some steps, framed by a stone archway that loomed up behind him, but he was smiling.

'I miss him,' Claudine whispered in a voice that sounded like it had travelled a long way just to get there for this moment.

Then she smiled.

The effect it had on him was surprising: to Eliot, it was a smile that said her sadness belonged only to her. His stomach began to fill with a peculiar kind of envy.

Well go on then, cry! If you're really sad, let me see you cry.

'He was kind,' she added with another one of those smiles. 'My mum loved him very much.'

It was upon him before he could control it, an angry desire to own a part of her loss. And in his mind it was now he who had lost his dad, not Claudine. And people were gathering at his house. Michael and David were nowhere to be seen; it had all been too much for them; but he…he was sitting dead centre of the living room surrounded by solemn-faced, but sympathetic grown-ups.

Look! a voice in the room declares out loud. *Look at this boy. Look how sad he is. Can anyone feel any sadder? He is the saddest boy in the world.* And everyone looks and sees that it is true and is amazed. *But how brave he is,* someone else proclaims. *What a heroic boy. What courage. How brilliant.* And it makes him feel a little better, if only for a little while.

'Eliot? *Eliot?*'

Claudine's voice brought him back. Realising he had drifted off, he shook his head.

'Is something wrong?'

He shook his head.

'You look like there is.'

Wondering just how long she was going to make him hold the photograph, he said, 'My dad's going away.' It sounded weak next to her story, and he said it more harshly than he intended, but Claudine appeared not to mind.

'Where?' she asked, her eyes kind and sad.

'Manchester,' he mumbled.

'When?'

'I don't even know that.'

'I'm sorry,' she said.

And he knew that she meant it, which made him feel even worse that he had tried to steal her sadness. He handed back the photograph.

'It's not nice when you lose someone you really care about,' Claudine muttered.

'No,' Eliot agreed, and the two of them lapsed into silence.

Finally, Claudine heaved up a massive sigh, and then she was smiling again.

'Here,' she said, handing him a packet of crisps from the plastic bag. 'They're salt and vinegar, I'm afraid.'

'That's okay,' he said. 'I like salt and vinegar.'

'Well that's good then.'

With both hands he squeezed the packet until it burst with a soft *pop*.

Claudine smiled.

Looking to change the subject, Eliot, through a mouthful of crisps, said, 'They're going to blow up the pier. Have you heard?'

Taking out a packet for herself, Claudine nodded. 'It's such a shame.'

'It is, isn't it?' he nodded, genuinely pleased she felt this way.

Claudine placed her packet of crisps between her palms and tried to copy Eliot's little trick and pop it open, but it just swelled with air, refusing to burst. 'My mum and dad used to take me there when I was little,' she gasped, squeezing the crisp packet some more.

'Mine too,' he said, eyes narrowing as the thin plastic packet got fatter and fatter.

'They say it's ugly,' she wheezed, red-faced. 'I don't think it is.'

'It isn't, is it?' he said, bracing himself.

Holding her breath, Claudine gave the packet an almighty two-handed squeeze... and then it popped, really loudly, and crisps gushed out the top like a spewing volcano.

They both laughed.

'I'm sorry about your dad,' he finally said, and chomped down on a crisp.

'That's kind,' Claudine said.

And everything was all right again.

'She won't bite,' Claudine reassured him, pushing open the gate, her crooked smile more incontestable than ever.

Eliot shoved his hands into his pockets. 'Never said she would,' he muttered.

'Well then?' she said, swinging the gate back and forth.

He stared at the front door, furiously trying to think of some way to get out of this.

But so far, he had nothing. The problem was, she had an air about her...maddening...like David.

The day had finished well: £1.40 in total. Which managed to make her behaviour worse.

More troubling by far, however, was the realization by Eliot that the afternoon could have been a lot more profitable. But the constant need to know what Claudine was doing—to make sure she was taking things seriously—had slowly eroded his sense of purpose, and he had wasted a great deal of the afternoon wrestling to keep his mind on the job.

Annoyingly, when he had located her, he immediately looked away, feeling like *he* had done something wrong!

He felt a gentle tug on his jumper.

'What?' he said, blinking.

'So, are you coming in?'

'Ermmm.' His hand reached for his face.

'Oh, stop it,' Claudine clucked. 'It's hardly noticeable. *Honestly!*'

There was no mat. That was the first thing he noticed. The second thing that struck him about the house was its warmth. It was overly warm, just like his grandparents' house used to be. He found it an effort just to breathe.

Claudine's mum was sitting on the sofa in the living room, watching television, her legs curled up beneath her. On the low coffee table in front of the sofa a large, clear-glass ashtray brimmed over with thin, brown cigarette butts.

Claudine left him standing on the dark-green rug that occupied the centre of the small room and went around the back of the sofa to stand behind her mum.

'Well, hello there,' the mother said, plucking a long, thin More from between her thin, red lips. She made no effort to turn down the volume on the television.

Eliot suspected it was a tactic to make him speak up.

She had dark hair and large, piercing green eyes, which regarded him with keen curiosity as he tried not to fidget.

Or run.

She stood up slowly. She was wearing a large, woolly jumper of many coloured squares and circles, and jeans. A large ABBA badge was pinned above her right breast, which, he could tell, was quite sizeable.

'And who's this handsome young man?' Her voice was deep and earthy.

'Mum, this is Eliot,' Claudine grinned, though what she found funny was beyond Eliot.

'Eliot,' her mum repeated, offering him her hand. 'It's a nice name. Very…*literary.*'

He stepped forward and took her hand, which felt a bit dry, and surprisingly light.

'It's Susan,' she said. Eliot nodded, uncertain what he should do with her hand now he had it.

So, it was with some relief when she took it back.

Resisting the urge to stick his hands into his pockets, he stood on the rug and let mother and daughter look him over. After what seemed an age, Claudine said, 'I'll be back in a tic. Do you want something to drink, Eliot?'

Eliot shook his head. 'N-n-no thanks,' he said, his voice dry and scratchy.

'So where do you go to school?' Susan asked.

Seeing Claudine leave the room added an element of panic to his answer. 'Er, Mill Lane.'

Susan took a long drag on her cigarette and nodded, as though that one piece of information revealed everything she needed to know about him.

He felt like he was being tested, and wished this was the sort of thing you could spend time revising for.

She took another drag on her More. Mesmerised, he had no answer to the steady column of blue smoke streaming from her lips as she exhaled.

Scratching his thigh, his gaze sought refuge amongst the ornaments and numerous family photographs hung around the room, but always there was the feeling that Claudine's mum was watching him intently through a haze of cigarette smoke.

He discovered that he did not like being watched; not one bit.

Where was Claudine?

A small, wooden-framed photograph sitting on the television caught his attention. The three family members, mum, dad, and Claudine between them, stood with their backs against a wooden railing. The sea served as a backdrop. It was a windy day and they were all wrapped up in coats and scarves, mum and daughter laughing hard, hair flaming all around them.

With a spike of jealousy, Eliot was certain the photograph had been taken at the pier. *His* pier.

His gaze moved on.

There was a large bookshelf set against the wall behind the sofa and he was scanning the shelves for any book that had a familiar look about it when he heard Claudine's mum say, 'Shit.' Out loud.

Eliot pretended not to hear.

'It's all shit,' she said in a louder voice, clearly determined she was heard. 'I don't know why I have it on.'

Relieved, he realised she was talking about the television.

The news presenter was talking about Margaret Thatcher, and something called the 'Right to Buy Scheme.'

'The Milk Snatcher's at it again,' Susan remarked. She gave Eliot a critical once-over and then shook her head. 'I suppose you're too old.'

Eliot still had no idea what she was talking about, but he liked the idea of being too old for something.

As though she could read his mind, she said, 'Thatcher. She scrapped free milk at primary schools. Now she's after our houses.' Susan took a drag on her More. 'Bitch.'

Eliot gave her a terrified smile.

'And where are the poor going to live if they sell off all the council houses?' she demanded. 'Tell me that.'

'Err, hotels?' he replied, wishing he were someplace else.

Susan's laugh was throaty. 'Funny. Claudine said you were funny.'

Feeling a bit sick, he smiled. It never occurred to him that he might be the subject of conversation in someone else's house. It was a horrible thought.

Grabbing the remote, she turned off the television. 'It's social cleansing of traditional communities, that's what it is.'

'*Mum!*' Claudine complained, coming up behind him. Eliot turned, almost tripping over his own feet. Without her boots on she looked tiny.

'What?' her mum replied. 'I was just saying. Besides, Eliot doesn't mind a bit of politics, do you, Eliot?' She winked at him. 'Smart boy like you.'

Eliot was not sure if he should nod or shake his head, so he just nodded, hoping it was the smart response.

'You sure you don't want a drink?' Claudine asked.

He shook his head. 'No thanks.'

'A sandwich, perhaps?' Susan suggested.

What was it with these two and sandwiches?

Eliot felt caught between the two of them. The room…it was too hot.

'Gotta get back,' he croaked.

Claudine's smile disappeared. 'Oh,' she said. 'Really?'

'Sorry,' he said. 'Promised my mum.'

'Then you best get off,' Susan murmured.

'I'll see you out then,' Claudine said, her tone flat. Puzzled, Eliot nodded.

'Bye, handsome,' Susan waved.

'I had a nice time,' Claudine said to him at the door, making it sound like an accusation. 'Today, I mean.'

Confused, he nodded. 'Yes.'

'*Yes?*' Claudine demanded, her hand on the door, as though she could not wait to close it on him. 'Just, *yes?*'

Angry with himself, he kicked out at a stone.

Both children watched it bobble and skip down the short path until it came to a stop by the gate.

Fighting down a ridiculous impulse to go and fetch it (so he could kick it again), he desperately tried to think of something else to say.

'Well…bye then,' he managed, after a furious few seconds in thought.

'Fine,' she said, and closed the door on him.

Heaving up a sigh, he started down the path. When he reached the stone, he gave it an almighty hoof and it shot out under the gate into the road.

Later that night, Eliot lay on his bed trying to list the things he did not like about Claudine, but he found that there were none. For some reason that irritated him. He tore off a strip of wallpaper, rolled it up into a ball and stuffed it into his mouth.

He heard laughter from downstairs; Rob laughing, then David joining in.

Stupid computer.

His thoughts turned briefly to his lady from the library.

It was not a betrayal, he reminded himself for the umpteenth time. This internal debate had started on his walk home. Besides, she would probably like Claudine. It was not like she was a normal girl, after all.

It was David's turn to laugh out loud.

Their mum was in the living room watching television. He wondered how she could even think with all that racket going on in the back room. She should go in there and tell them to shut up.

If it had been him, he would have.

17
Monday, 8 March 1982

£10.60

Easter was fast approaching. Wherever he looked it was evident the town was preparing itself for the opening of the season. Council workers had already taken down the wood windbreak panels; they were sitting in piles along the esplanade, waiting to be collected. The flowerbeds in the large, raised, brick planters had been turned over and men were planting plugs in the dark soil. On the beach beneath the pavilion, diggers and trucks were dredging sand and transporting it to areas of the beach where winter tide erosion had taken its toll.

In the distance, he could see the maintenance crews scrambling over the seafront statue, scrubbing it clean of bird mess and other winter stains. Scaffolding encased several seafront buildings. Inside these hollow and delicate-looking structures, men were busy repairing and painting the white vaulting frontages.

Turning, his eyes sought out the shoreline. It was clear, to Eliot at least, that the sea was making a calm but watchful retreat from the beach in response.

Leaping over the esplanade railing he landed compactly, the pebbles letting out a satisfying *crunch*. The smells of the beach excited him as he trudged down to the water's edge. There he stood for a moment, the widening bay out in front of him, land opening out behind. He raised his arms, imagining himself the dead centre of a giant hourglass.

So what do they call you?

Eliot Thomas, Hourglass Boy.

Reaching down he picked up a pebble, turning it over and over in his small hand as he gazed out to sea. He found it hard to believe that out there, just over the horizon, there were other countries, other towns, just like his. Maybe there was a boy just like him looking back over the horizon in his direction, thinking the same things as him and seeing no way out other than to wait until he got older.

A single bird troubled the sky. A gull. As he watched it flinch and snap and rise on the invisible currents, the gull's cry reached his ears, faint and filled with a bleakness that struck a chord within Eliot.

He turned his thoughts on the sea, probing beneath the surface, keen to know more of her quality. He submersed his mind, willing it deeper and deeper. Childish fancy gave him access to a subterranean world where mermaids lived and strange creatures blinked, trotted, and scuttled over the murky sediment below. Just for a moment, he felt his mind brush up against the sea's massive preternatural presence and sensed, very briefly, something of her weight and mood. And he knew that she waited, heavy and calm, but capable of rising in anger and smashing the town to bits. Increasingly of late, he wished that she would do just that, so the council would be forced to start again, rebuilding the entire town, including the pier.

Viewed from where he stood, the pier could be seen running out into the bay on her rickety criss-crossing wood piles, quite noticeably breaking up the gentle curve of the bay. Eliot knew from the local newspaper that this was one of the principle reasons why some people wanted it gone; they did not want some old, broken structure ruining their view of the bay.

As if to add insult to this, a block of modern flats (all glass and metal and gleaming white) were rapidly going up across the road opposite the pier, making it seem just that extra bit older and unwanted.

He turned the pebble over in his hand. *Stupid flats.*

The date set for the destruction of the pier was April 12, the Easter Bank Holiday Monday.

It could not be stopped.

This much was clear.

With a nod, he turned his back on the old structure, trudged back up the beach and took his place in the bus shelter, losing himself in the graffiti until the bus arrived.

Pakis and Niggers fuck off home.

Eliot stared at the word *Niggers*. It was like the word "cunt," horrible and violent, only this one he heard being spoken quite often, particularly at school.

You don't see blacks in seaside towns, his dad had once said. But that was not true. Eliot had seen one on the beach last summer: a family of them, in fact. The people close by behaved as though the black family was something to fear, which Eliot thought was mean and stupid—given that everyone on the beach was desperately trying to darken their skin colour. But for a long while after that, he wished he could be black. He would walk down the beach with a swagger, huge and beautiful, glaring at any grown-up that dared look his way. *Fuck off, I'm black!* he would shout, sending their stupid, mean kids screaming down the beach.

Eliot Thomas, Black Boy.

There was no hero's welcome. Just for a moment that morning, as he got himself dressed, he had let himself believe that when he got to school he would find all the kids and teachers lining the corridors, clapping and cheering: *That's the boy who got O'Neal expelled!* overawed, overwhelmed, loving him. *That's the boy that beat up O'Neal!*

But no one made mention of the incident. No one spoke to him at all, despite his face still evidencing a hint of discolouration from the bruising; faint yellows and blues, particularly below his right eye.

There was the occasional glance in his direction, whispered conversations amongst the other kids, looks from huddled groups, but that was not entirely new.

Of course, Mr Wilson had made a bit of a fuss in tutorial before classes started, which prompted the usual sniggers and comments under the breath, but for the most part, it turned out to be no different from any other day at school.

So much so, in fact, that he started believing that perhaps Mr Wilson had made a mistake, and Eliot had spent a lot of the day looking over his shoulder, half-expecting to catch sight of O'Neal's massive presence bowling down on him in some distant corridor where his cries would not be heard.

After school he took the bus home. Dickenson and the evil she-wolf girl were present at the bus stop, but they paid him no real attention. On the one occasion Dickenson did look over in his direction, he had an expression of pure disgust on his face; but even this act signalled the promise of progress, because Eliot sensed it was absent of any real desire to inflict physical retribution, now or any time soon.

This was something, at least, and the revelation rather emboldened him. And when he climbed up into the bus, he gave the driver a superior sneer, feeling like the man deserved it. At the very least, it made him feel better.

As he sat, it began to rain. He heard an older kid nearer the back declare, 'Oh well, here comes summer.' Someone laughed. As the bus pulled away from the kerb, he thought, *not yet, please,* as he stared out the window.

'Mum gave *you* the money?' Eliot felt as though something had slipped. Still in their school uniforms, David and Rob were in the back room on the computer.

'Invaders!' David warned.

'I see them,' Rob said, eyes fixed on the screen in deadly concentration.

David turned and seemed irritated that he was still standing there: 'Me and Rob are going later. What's the big deal?'

'But I usually get the fish and chips,' Eliot protested. He hated getting the fish and chips but that was not the point.

'Fine, you go then,' David snapped, impatient to get back to the game.

'I will,' Eliot snapped. 'Where is Mum, anyway?'

'Upstairs, watching TV.'

Out of nowhere a spaceship shot across the screen, all angles, swift and deadly.

'Bonus ship!' David cried.

'I see it!' Rob shouted. 'I see it!'

Columns of invaders moved across the screen, dropped down, moved back the other way, increasing in speed. The computer beat out a dull, synchronous pulse in keeping with the invaders' advance... *dum...dum...dum...dum.* The large defender-ship at the bottom sent a continuous volley of missiles into the descending host. The four bases, which were ranged across the bottom of the screen and which the defender could hide behind, were slowly disintegrating, pulverised by enemy fire. Soon there would be nowhere for the defender to hide.

'They're getting lower!' David shouted. 'Get the ones on the bottom row!'

The main body of invaders dropped down another line, sped up... *dum – dum – dum – dum.*

Rob's finger pounded the space bar.

'They're too fast!'

Eliot stepped forward to get a better view.

'They're too low!' Rob cried again. 'Too fast!'

'Keep firing!' David yelled, choking back a laugh.

'The game looks...okay.' Eliot said quietly.

David looked at his brother as though he had forgotten he was there. '*Okay?* It's brill,' he said.

Ron disagreed. 'It's a rip-off of *Space Invaders,*' he said, smashing the "fire" button. 'And the graphics are pretty shit.'

The bases had been completely destroyed. There was nowhere to hide.

'Get that one!' David suddenly yelled, indicating an invader right at the bottom.

'Got it,' Rob gasped.

'Now that one!' David warned.

'It's too fast!' It was true, and Rob kept missing the ship. Soon, the enemy ship was no more than a line or two away from landing... *dum-dum-dum-dum.*

Unconsciously, Eliot put his hand on the back of David's chair; the speed of the invaders was now mesmerising.

'I can't hit it!' Rob shouted.

'Oh my God!' David shrieked. 'Do something, Rob!' David laughed.

The invader had one last line to go and then...

Rob fired and fired, but he kept missing.

'I can't...stop it. *Stop it. Please.*' But he was laughing hopelessly.

'Too late!' David cried...*dumdumdumdum.*

The invader dropped to the bottom line, raced across and smashed into the defender. There was a loud crashing sound.

"Game Over" the computer declared.

'Fuck!' David shouted.

Rob sighed. 'Better than a wank.'

The two boys fell against each other, laughing.

'Brilliant,' David choked. Noticing his brother standing behind him, he said, 'I thought you were going to the chippy?'

'Don't really care,' Eliot answered, snatching back his hand and stepping away from David's chair.

'I wish you'd make your bloody mind up,' David sighed, indicating to Rob that he should reload the game. 'Fine,' he said. 'We'll go.'

'I'm going upstairs, then,' Eliot said, trying to make it sound like a threat.

'You do that,' David retorted.

'I will.'

Disgusted and angry, he stomped upstairs.

And why was Rob getting chips, anyway? *Fuck off home, Mum can't afford it*; David should say that.

Well, he just hoped Ruth was paying.

She should. In fact, she should come and get Rob, really. After all, it was a school night.

Jug-eared turd.

He was just about to climb down off Michael's bed when he spotted Claudine coming down the road. She was still dressed in her school uniform and had a determined look about her.

This was exactly the problem with the days getting longer…kids staying out to play. Panicked, he flung his binoculars on the bed and rushed downstairs.

David and Rob were making a lot of noise in the back room and he managed to open the front door without alerting them. Grabbing his coat off the hook, he slipped out of the house.

He met her as she drew level with the front gate.

'What are you doing here?' he demanded.

His sudden appearance startled her, but she quickly regained her composure.

'I didn't realise I had to get your permission to use this street?' Her expression was decidedly flinty.

'Well, no,' Eliot flushed. 'I thought—'

'Is that a new rule? *Eliot's Rule?*'

'What I meant is—'

Claudine laughed suddenly. 'I'm joking.'

Detecting an edge to her amusement, he smiled weakly and glanced over his shoulder. The door was ajar and he could hear David and Rob laughing in the back room, faintly but still within earshot.

If they came out now!

'Actually I *was* coming to see you,' she admitted. 'But I wish I hadn't bothered now—if this is how you're going to treat me.'

'I'm sorry,' he said quickly.

Up close, he was surprised by how…well, how nice she looked in her school uniform. She still wore her big, black bovver boots, but they seemed to compliment her scruffy black blazer (which had holes in the elbows), and he kind of admired the way she wore her tie, loose, and the knot dead tight. She looked…rebellious.

He particularly liked her red Alice band because it kept her hair out of her face; *and* the way her white shirt stuck to her slight frame, accentuating the curve of her small breasts (which were a revelation all by themselves), and had him wondering if she would end up with breasts the size of her mother's. The thought disgusted and excited him all at the same time. Mostly, it excited him.

'Want to come out?' she asked, interrupting his thoughts.

'Out?' he asked, glancing over his shoulder.

'Yes,' Claudine sighed. *'To play.'*

Eliot ignored the barb. 'To do what?'

'Does it matter?'

Again, he glanced over his shoulder before shrugging, 'Suppose not.'

Claudine put her hands on her hips. 'The door can come too, if it'll make you feel better!'

Before Eliot could answer, Claudine let out an exasperated growl and started down the road in the direction of the seafront. 'You coming?' she shouted over her shoulder.

He quickly closed the front door, then, red-faced, hurried to catch up with her.

Leaning against the esplanade railings, Eliot and Claudine surveyed the beach. Ominously, the concession huts had begun to appear: blue-and-white-and-red-striped, they arced back into the east like carriages on a train lumbering into a sandy terminal.

Down on the flats, a few dog walkers were making the most of things. Soon they would not be allowed on the beach with their pets and they would have to go someplace else to walk them.

Two beach control men, wearing cream jumpers and navy blue tracksuit bottoms, eyed the dog walkers as though they wanted them off the beach right that minute. Spotting Claudine leaning over the railing, the taller of the two men, who was blond-haired and had a blond beard, smiled up at her. She smiled back, her cheeks flushing a little, Eliot noted.

The two men finished erecting the last of the beach safety signs: *'Caution, there is no lifeguard service in operation,'* the sign warned, tall white letters on a big red board. Other than the dog walkers, however, the beach was empty, and to Eliot these men just looked boastful, their roles absurd.

'Let's go,' Eliot snapped.

Claudine nodded and pushed off from the railings—but not before giving the tall beach control man one last smile.

'Hurry up,' Eliot said.

'All right, keep your hair on,' Claudine replied. And then she smirked, 'Do you need the toilet?'

'That's not funny. You're not funny.'

Claudine just laughed.

Why did she have to joke about everything?

They walked in silence for a while before stopping at a point on the esplanade which afforded the best view of the sand sculptor's enclosure below. Beneath the partially hooded arena, Egyptian figures had started to take shape in the sand.

The sculptor's wide, swaying back faced the esplanade so that the two children could not see his face. Hunched forward, the sculptor moved fluidly about the enclosure. Occasionally he would stop at a particular sand shape, reaching down. Starting at the base, his hands would then rise in a wavy motion, caressing the sides of the mysterious structure as though he was a magician, and not a sculptor at all, and was summoning his creations, lifting them up out of the sand.

Eliot leant over the railing. 'Look at all that money,' he said, pointing to the silver and copper coins lying on a large sheet of blue tarpaulin. 'There must be about twenty or thirty pounds down there,' he whispered.

'It's like the bottom of a wishing well,' Claudine observed.

'Yes,' he muttered, his eyes on the money. 'I suppose.'

'Make a wish,' Claudine grinned.

Automatically, Eliot's gaze drifted down the beach towards the pier. After a moment, however, he shook his head. 'Ner.'

'Oh, go on,' she said. 'Don't be such a spoilsport.'

'I'm not.' Why did she have to say things like that? 'Besides, you can't make a wish unless you put some money in. Everyone knows that.'

'Fine.'

Before Eliot could stop her, Claudine fished a coin out of her blazer pocket and threw it into the enclosure.

'Happy now?" Closing her eyes, Claudine made her wish, her lips moving rapidly.

Finished, she opened her eyes. 'There!' Claudine declared, in Eliot's opinion, somewhat smugly. 'All done.' Without another word, she breezed past him and set off down the esplanade.

'So, what did you wish for?' he asked, falling in beside her.

'Oh no,' she said, waggling a finger at him. 'I don't think so, mister. Why should I tell you, when you couldn't even be bothered to make one?'

'Suit yourself,' he shrugged. 'Didn't want to know anyway.'

When she refused to bite, he added, 'Besides, wishes don't come true. Everyone knows that.'

'That's not the point,' she said airily.

'Stop trying to sound so…so mysterious,' was his response.

'Can if I want; will when I can,' she chimed.

Eliot had nothing left. What did she know?

They walked on in silence for a while. Wrapped up snugly, people were walking along the esplanade, staring out to sea as though they were looking for a sign to reassure them the sun was on its way.

The Tea Cabin was now open and a handful of people sat outside, but eating chips rather than ice creams, drinking tea or coffee rather than milkshakes or pop.

The noise of their conversations reached Claudine and Eliot as a jumbled murmur, like the sound of a noisy classroom heard from next door.

Brave stall owners stood behind their trestle tables trying to entice day-trippers into making a last-minute purchase; a caricature portrait, an item of glass jewellery, a Union Jack mug.

They walked on for a little while longer. When the pier came into view, Eliot slowed.

'When did you say it was getting blown up?' Claudine asked, following his gaze.

'Easter Monday,' he replied after a moment, his eyes tracing its grey outline.

'Did you enter the competition?' Claudine asked quietly.

He nodded.

'You *did!* Why?'

The tone of her voice held no hint of accusation, but he suddenly felt guilty for having entered the competition. That was her fault.

'Because,' he snapped.

'That's not a real answer,' Claudine gently reproached.

She was standing quite close to him. He could sense her scrutinising him. Shifting his weight, he shrugged again.

'*Just* because.'

Claudine said no more, but he knew her eyes had not left him.

'Come on,' he said, trying to keep the irritation from his voice. 'It's getting late, and it's a school night.'

'A school night!' Claudine choked. 'Did you say a, *school night*?' And then she was laughing, hard.

He picked up his pace to get away from her stupid, girly childishness. She always had to ruin things.

'Oh, come on, Eliot,' she called after him. 'Look, I'm sorry!'

But she was lying. And she proved it moments later when she declared, '*A school night!*' And though she said it more to herself, she was still laughing. He could hear her.

They walked for a while in silence, Eliot fuming, Claudine still chuckling to herself. As they rounded a corner into a new road, Eliot noticed several lads up ahead and he instinctively slowed, noticing that Claudine did, too. The lads were smoking cigarettes, laughing and shouting. Their chopper pushbikes were propped against the brick wall behind them.

Not long after the film *The Wanderers* had premiered at the box office, gangs had started appearing all over town. Many months after the film had showed, kids could still be heard in the school corridor, shouting, '*Don't fuck with the Baldies!*' *It was a pronouncement that augured violence*. No doubt these boys were part of such a gang—though it mattered little to whichever one, The Red, The Baseballers, The Black, or The Bowly, they still presented a significant and immediate threat.

Inevitably, the lads spotted Claudine and Eliot and they ceased their chatter, turning as one—hunters appraising a potential quarry.

Eliot greatly wished he and Claudine had been walking on the other side of the road.

Claudine slowed up significantly and suddenly stepped behind him. This one movement was enough to provoke a series of grins and nudges amongst the lads. Eliot knew they were in trouble now, but strangely, Claudine's actions made him feel a little less scared.

She believed he could protect her!

Albeit nervously, he accepted the lead.

'You okay?' he called over his shoulder.

'Yes,' Claudine said, an edge to her voice. 'Why wouldn't I be?'

Before he could reply, two more boys, older boys, pulled up on motorbikes. The younger lads gathered admiringly around the bikes; there was much murmuring and touching.

Under different circumstances, Eliot would have sneered: *what suck-ups, easily impressed.* And the bikers, well, they were just show-offs.

Wrenching down on the throttles, the newcomers made their bikes roar tremendously loud.

See. Show-offs.

A cheer went up from the younger boys.

Eliot did not hesitate. Using the distraction, he grabbed hold of Claudine's hand and pulled her across the road.

Detecting the sudden movement, however, the group slowly turned their heads, fixing their greedy, dark eyes on him and Claudine.

As they drew level with the gang, the taller of the two new arrivals, a thickset lad with long, dark hair, started making loud sucking noises. The other boys burst into laughter.

Eliot went red and started to shake. Claudine pressed up against him so she was shielded from the gang's direct line of sight. The movement made him feel suddenly exposed.

The laughter eventually subsided. But not to be outdone, one of the younger lads stepped up to the kerb and started jabbing his fist towards his mouth, whilst ballooning his cheek with his tongue.

Eliot's felt the small hand, which was still in his, tighten considerably.

'How about a blow job?' the long-haired older boy cried.

This set the other lads off again.

Pretending not to have heard a thing, Eliot stared down at the ground and kept moving forward, pulling Claudine along with him.

'Here, I've got a packet of smokes,' another boy jeered. 'Will Marlboro do?'

'I've heard a rollup's enough.'

This was too much for the gang, and the laughter was louder and longer than ever before.

Claudine snatched her hand back from Eliot. Crossing her arms, she dropped her head and picked up her pace. Eliot found it difficult to keep up with her without looking like he was running.

He suddenly understood. They were laughing at *her*. Not him.

He should have felt bad for her; but what he truly felt was relief.

Eliot risked a glance over his shoulder. Bored, the younger lads had gathered around the tall biker, listening to what he had to say, touching his bike.

Eliot glanced to his left. Claudine's face had lost all colour and she had bitten into her bottom lip, drawing a spot of blood.

'Idiots, aren't they?' he said quietly, not knowing what else to say.

Claudine gave him a weak smile. 'Mum's always told me to stay away from boys like that.' She laughed a little. 'Well, from all boys, really.'

'Good advice,' he said, but his mind was churning over and over.

Were the rumours true, then?

She lifted her head and stared him right in the eyes, her chin stuck out defiantly, as though she knew what he was thinking and was daring him to say something. Her eyes were green. Large. It was the first time he had properly noticed their colour. They were green…like the sea. A very familiar green.

He knew then, without really knowing a thing.

'Come on,' he said. 'Fuck 'em.'

Claudine gasped '*Eliot Thomas!* Wash your mouth out.' But her eyes shone.

Wash your mouth out. It was something his nan would have said. He let out a little laugh.

And then Claudine laughed. Only quietly, so the group of lads up the road did not hear.

As they walked, her small hand found his. It should have panicked him. And he knew with some certainty that tomorrow he would see this differently. But for now, it was okay.

A few minutes passed, and then, trying to keep his voice casual, he asked, 'So, ermm…so what did you wish for?'

'Oh *no!*' she said, shaking her head. 'On your bike, mister!'

They looked at each other and laughed.

More seriously then, and thinking it important, he said, 'I don't want to see it blown up, if that's what you think.' He coughed. 'That's not why I entered the competition.'

'So, why did you?' Her tone…well, she sounded just like the school matron as she was fixing him up after his fight with O'Neal.

He suddenly discovered that he wanted to talk to someone about the pier, properly talk about it.

Why did everyone want to see it blown up? It was wrong. Plain and simple.

Maybe he had finally found someone who would agree with him. Would, at the very least, listen.

He took a deep breath and as they walked, he tried his hardest to explain something he did not fully understand himself.

18 Sunday, 22 November 1981

They were told the news once they arrived at the hospital. Michael and David left the room quickly, his older brother choking back sobs, David crying openly. But not him. Seeing his younger brother being led out by the nurse made Eliot more determined to stay.

If he had not been told, he could have pretended his grandad was just asleep. His naked arms lay outside the blankets, resting close by his sides. The hospital tag on his right wrist looked overly large and reminded Eliot of his microscope collection: *22/11/81—Grandad*.

There was a big liver spot on the back of his grandad's veiny hand. It was like a dark, oddly shaped wafer, something that would dissolve on the tongue. Light coming in through the window appeared to be dissolving his grandad before his eyes, beaming him up to somewhere else.

Staring at the liver spot, he had a thought, *I don't even know what this means. If Grandad's "not coming back," then where's he not coming back from?*

Nothing made sense, and it was a struggle not to prod the body to see if it would move. In fact, the only reason he had not given in to temptation was the presence of his mum and dad sitting in silence behind him.

Why were they watching him? *Was this a test?*

He started to worry about how he was (and how he should be) feeling. He was certain he felt sad (and was going to miss his grandad loads), but no one emotion was yet to assert itself, take control.

You're glad he's dead, so leave.

No, that was not true. He shook his head.

Yes, you are. You don't feel a thing.

Not true.

You're not even crying!

Suddenly angry about being forced to look at his dead grandad, he felt like turning around and shouting at his mum and dad, 'What are you doing? Why is this necessary? Get me out of here!'

He tried to make himself feel better by arguing that perhaps death was not such a big deal after all, but then he thought about Michael and David's reaction and concluded that it *was*, and therefore there must be something wrong with him.

And then there was the television: look how people reacted to death on there!

Of course, all of this made no sense. Because if there was a God, and therefore a heaven, why was everyone so miserable?

But it was a thought that only served to heap on the guilt and shame, and confuse him further.

Clenching his fists together, he gave the body his most intense stare, determined never to forget his grandad, nor any of his many stories.

I won't forget you. I promise.

19

Wednesday, 10 March 1982

£10.60

Eliot stopped halfway down the hallway, loosening his school tie. There was a man standing by the front door. He was tall and had a big, black briefcase. At first he did not recognise him, but then he remembered him from the other day.

It was his mum's solicitor.

The man looked down the hallway at Eliot, his smile something of an effort. He had eyebrows like his father's, thick and black.

'I'll be seeing you soon then, Mrs Thomas,' he called over his shoulder, without taking his eyes off Eliot.

Eliot shoved his hands into his pockets and did not move.

'Okay then,' he heard his mum reply.

Satisfied, the man nodded, but he was no longer smiling. And when he twisted the latch on the front door with a snap of his wrist, to Eliot it felt like a threat, or the prediction of a hurt.

'What's the solicitor man doing here?' he asked his mum once the man had gone off in his red Audi.

'Just here to sort some things out, love,' she said. 'Nothing for you to worry about.'

'You said that the last time,' he accused. 'And Dad's going to Manchester; so what's to sort out?'

He had a right to know. And it suddenly occurred to him: now that Michael was gone, he was the oldest.

'It's complicated, Eliot,' she sighed.

'Complicated?'

According to his nan, "complicated" was an adult's way of saying, "Mind your own business."

She nodded and reached for her cigarettes.

He took that as a sign he should go.

In the back room, David was suddenly screaming at Rob to, '*Fire! Fire! Fire!*' Rob shouted back that he was *trying*, then burst out laughing.

Not wanting to ask David if he knew anything about the solicitor man and what was going on, particularly with Rob there, Eliot stomped upstairs.

Angry, he stared at himself in the bathroom mirror. Here at least he was making some progress. Evidence of his recent beating had all but disappeared and his spots seemed to be receding, particularly the large one at the corner of his mouth. The massive whitehead had been replaced by a scab of reddish black, and surrounding it, newer, pink skin could be seen emerging where the surface was heavily flaked.

Finding no reason to move, his gaze bore into the green eyes in the mirror until he felt only numbness, no curiosity beyond the action itself.

Who are you? Really? Tell me that.

Eliot stood by the lamppost and scanned the leafy perimeter. The park was empty but he frowned nevertheless. The shadows were losing their hold, receding like black glaciers melting under a fierce and unstoppable sun. It was an unwelcome reminder that when the clocks went forward in just under three weeks' time, light would fill this place, and the children would return.

And he would lose her.

He needed a further £9.40.

Eliot took his place in the bushes.

He was dark-haired, balding, with a large nose, thin lips, and thick, black eyebrows. Tall. He looked like a man without humour, without kindness; one of those adults that seemed to occupy a large amount of space but did nothing kind with it.

Her mouth work had only just begun when he was suddenly shouting out, shouting to God; his legs locking up, his arms grabbing a mass of her hair, an angry exclamation spitting through his clamped teeth.

Then it was over, and the tall man was mumbling his thanks and leaving.

As he watched his lady fix herself up, it became increasingly clear to him that the courtyard was also losing its fight against the light; the darkness like a tree uprooting, preparing to leave.

Soon there would be no need for the security light.

He imagined the courtyard at the height of summer, bathed in sunlight, without mystery, and he felt afraid.

His lady was taking a bit longer than usual to fix herself up, so he took his time moving his eyes over the curves and angles of her landscape; face, body, legs—noting as he did, the bruising up and down her arms; no doubt, he thought angrily, damage inflicted on her by the man from the other night. Adding to his concern was her cold, which she had still not managed to throw off and was sniffing quite a bit.

I love you, she says, when he closes his eyes.
I'm ready if you are, he replies.

Before he went to bed, he counted his money again.

£10.60. It was nowhere near enough.

He needed a miracle. But miracles did not happen to someone like him, if at all.

He took a book down and climbed into bed, but instead of reading it, he just rested the open book on his chest and closed his eyes. Next door his mum was coughing quite a bit, and the sound of the portable television was loud and sounded asthmatic coming through the walls. Such distractions continually disturbed his efforts to summon an image of his lady's breast. Finally, he gave up.

Throwing back his hands, he peeled off a scab of wallpaper and stuffed it into his mouth. Chewing, he stared up at the ceiling.

When sleep eventually took him, he dreamt that he was being chased down the street by a giant clock. Shrilly it called out his name, promising him terrible punishment if he were caught. *Eliot! ELIOT!*

And Eliot ran and ran; he was a good runner, the best.

But to his horror, he realised could not get away from the clock.

20 Friday, 12 March 1982

£11.10

The sound of Punch split the air, loud and nasal. Twenty or so cross-legged children were seated in a semicircle on the sand before the tall, brightly coloured Punch and Judy booth.

The show was just beginning, and Punch was swinging from side to side, his big nose grotesque and comic.

Judy appeared. An excited exchange occurred between the two puppets and then Punch disappeared, only to reappear with a club. He clobbered Judy. Judy staggered back.

One or two of the faces in the small gathering of children sought reassurance from their parents, who were stood on the esplanade high above them. And they found them laughing. Laughing hard when Punch hit Judy again, his voice shrill and relentless.

Encouraged, first one child giggled—albeit nervously—then another. Then another.

A bigger lad sitting right next to Eliot chortled, 'Go on, hit her harder.'

Soon all the children were laughing.

Like their parents.

Everyone laughing.

Except Eliot. 'Hit him!' he suddenly yelled. 'Hit him back!' But his words were ripped out of his mouth by a sudden gust of wind.

And Punch continued to beat Judy.

All around, mums and dads were leaning over the rails, one or two taking the steps down onto the beach to get a closer look; closing in as the creature clobbered away.

Eliot stood beside a stack of deck chairs and stared down onto the beach. School was over for another day.

He had spotted the little red-and-white-striped booth the minute he'd gotten off the bus—Punch and Judy, returned for another year. When he was younger, the show used to frighten him, but his nan and grandad had still insisted on taking him and his brothers to watch it. The older he got, the less he liked the big-nosed, evil Punch, but that never seemed to matter to his nan. 'Oh, stop being silly,' she would chide. 'It's not the seaside without Punch and Judy!'

He caught the smell of something familiar. Fish and chips. His stomach once again let him know how it felt about his new strategy... Keeping back his lunch money.

With today's 50p, he now had £11.10.

His stomach growled again. *I'm hungry...hungry,* it seemed to be saying.

A hand on his shoulder startled Eliot. Fearing O'Neal had found him, he spun around.

'On yer own, kid?' The man was tall and thin, his lean frame curving high over Eliot. He wore a dark jumper that had lost its shape and was full of holes. Eliot stared inside one of the larger holes and saw bare flesh. The man smelt bad and his teeth were crooked and yellow.

He tried to look anywhere but at the man.

'How 'bout ten pence for a cup of tea?' he asked, giving Eliot's shoulder a squeeze.

Eliot tried to walk around him but the man took a step to his left, blocking any possible way forward. *'Never speak to strangers,'* his mum had always warned him.

But what did you do if they spoke to you?

She had never said anything about that.

'Come on, kid,' the man said, once again placing his hand on Eliot's shoulder. 'Ten pence? It's not much. I know you got it.'

Reluctantly, Eliot dipped his hand into his pocket and pulled out a cluster of coins; his unspent lunch money.

The man sniffed a few times, licked his lips, and picked out two fat ten-pence pieces. 'That's all right, isn't it, kid?'

Eliot nodded.

Now you're back to £10.90, a snide voice in his head pointed out.

This is what happens when you starve yourself, his stomach added.

Eliot expected the man to move on, but no; he remained where he was, blocking out the light.

His stink was becoming too much, and Eliot looked around for help.

'Yerra good boy, I can see that,' the man said, eyeing the other coins in Eliot's hand. 'A real good kid.'

'*What* are you doing?' a fierce voice suddenly demanded.

Startled, the man glanced over his shoulder, his fright quickly replaced by a look of surprise.

Claudine bore down on the man, her school tie flapping about madly.

'Nothin', my lovely,' he drawled. 'Just havin' a chat with my friend here.'

'You're not his friend,' Claudine insisted, coming to stand by Eliot. He gave her a bewildered nod, which she acknowledged with a despairing roll of her eyes before switching her attention back to the man. 'Why would he be your friend? *I'm* his friend, not you. He doesn't know you.'

'Whoa, now, take it easy there, girlie,' the man laughed, though he quickly cast an anxious look around.

'I won't,' Claudine bristled. 'And don't you "*girlie*" me. If my mum was here she'd punch you in the mouth.'

'Now that's no way for a young lady to talk.' Struggling to know just how to take Claudine, Eliot felt a moment of sympathy for the dirty beggar man—if only for the briefest of seconds. After all, Claudine could be quite impossible. Still, he was dead impressed by her fierceness, though he wondered just how much of this was to make up for the other night. And then there was the embarrassment of her coming to his rescue. It was not like he had asked her to. Or even needed her to. But he was certain she would not see it that way.

'I'm no lady!' Claudine declared shrilly.

Licking his lips, the man looked around again.

'My dad's a policeman,' she warned. 'And if you don't go away right this instant, I'll scream and scream, and then you'll be in serious trouble. I can, and I will. Just try me.'

Claudine thumped her hands onto her hips and looked the man up and down; a gesture clearly designed to convey her displeasure that he had not yet scarpered.

'Keep your hair on, missy,' he complained, holding up his dirty hands. 'I meant no harm.'

And he quickly shuffled off.

Eliot could hardly believe what he was seeing.

'I don't care what you *meant!*' Claudine shouted after him. 'And don't call me *missy!*'

Frowning, she then turned to Eliot. 'You should stay away from people like that.'

'Yes,' he said. 'I think you're right.'

Claudine sniffed. 'Of course I'm right, silly.' But then she grinned at him.

'Anyway, what are you doing here?' he asked.

'You know, you ask that question quite a bit.'

'Really?'

'Yes,' she said, quite matter-of-factly.

Muttering something, he shoved his hands into his pockets.

With a despairing look, she linked her arm around his. 'Come on,' she said, suddenly excited. 'I've got something to show you.'

'What?'

'Now that would be telling.'

'And *you* never answer anything,' he complained, though he let her drag him forward.

'Why thank you,' she remarked with a straight face.

'I wasn't trying to be nice,' he fumed.

This girl was just about the most irritating person... *Ever!*

'We can't go in there,' he said, trying not to sound nervous. She had dragged him halfway across town (through parts he had never explored; not even with his mum or dad) until he found himself standing in an alleyway facing a large, blue door, the paint heavily flaking.

It was the side door to the old cinema.

He had overheard kids at school say that drug-users used this place, and that boys and girls would go there to drink and smoke. There was other talk of drugs, and of old men doing dirty, horrible things to boys, and boys doing things to *other* boys, all of which he could not think about without feeling properly sick.

'Really?' she said. 'Where's the sign that says that?' Rather annoyingly, she then made a show of looking for the non-existent sign.

'That's not the point,' he snapped.

'Oh, but it is,' she grinned, and pushed on the large, blue door. It swung inwards with a loud creak. 'And *look*! It's not even locked.'

He felt something splash on his cheek. He looked up. Another splash.

Rain.

'And just in time, too,' Claudine beamed.

Without another word, she went in.

Reluctantly, Eliot followed.

Another splash. Even the weather was against him.

There was a heavy smell of damp in the air. Cans and bottles and cigarette butts littered the aisles. The two children took a seat on the back row and were staring up at the old cinema screen. It had a great gash in it, like someone had taken a giant knife to it. There was a stage below the screen, painted black.

Light poured in through three ornate windows high above them. All but one of the windows had lost their dark burgundy drapes, and that one hung in filthy tatters.

'It used to be a theatre first,' Claudine said in a quiet voice. 'That's why there's a stage. But people stopped coming, so they turned it into a cinema. That's what my nan says anyway.'

'Bit small for a cinema,' Eliot observed quietly, though he quite liked the look of the place. It was not what he had expected. There was a kind of ancient, almost magical feel to the place.

He imagined the two of them exploring backstage, where they would find a large wardrobe filled with costumes. But on further examination they would discover it doubled as a magical portal to another world, where animals talked and where a war had been raging for centuries. The land would need a brave warrior to fight the evil lord, whose merciless grip had killed all joy and hope in the world.

Claudine continued to demonstrate her knowledge of local history. 'They used to show films from the olden days,' she was saying. 'Not the new ones, which are *boring*.'

'Like black-and-white films, you mean?'

Claudine nodded. 'Yes. And some early colour ones, too, like *Gone with the Wind*.'

'Gone where?' he asked absently, his gaze roaming the interior.

With a sigh, Claudine chose to ignore this remark. 'My nan and grandad used to come here all the time. But they closed it anyway.'

Thinking of the pier, he said, 'Grown-ups...they don't understand things.'

Claudine nodded. 'My mum says the country's falling apart.'

'I blame the last government,' Eliot nodded, hoping he sounded political.

There was a break in the conversation.

The loud, dull rhythm of the rain drumming on the roof above filled the old cinema.

'What are your favourite sweets?'

It was an odd question and he hesitated before answering, 'Er, cough candy twist.'

Claudine did not seem at all interested in this answer, but she nodded anyway. 'Yes, they're nice.'

For a while she said nothing more, content, it seemed, to pick at the green upholstery in front of her. She seemed distracted.

'Do you like the Tories?' she then asked.

Wishing Claudine's conversation would not jump around quite so much, Eliot shrugged, 'Never listened to them. Are they in the charts now?'

'Funny,' Claudine remarked, though more to herself. 'You are funny.'

She picked at the seat some more, not looking at him.

'Er, yeah,' Eliot laughed; only it was a nervous laugh. Claudine's behaviour was making him a little edgy. He sensed she was waiting for him to say or do something.

But then it always came down to that, he suddenly realized. In the end, it was always about someone, somewhere, waiting for him to say or do something.

'These seats are a bit ruined,' Claudine observed.

'Er, yes,' Eliot agreed, noting how heavily water-stained they were.

But then, the whole place was in a poor state, really. Scratching the top of his arm, he turned his attention to the wall beside him. The lower sections of the walls consisted of wood panelling, which at one time or another had been covered in gold-leaf patterned wallpaper. But it was now torn or was peeling away from the walls or had been blackened by damp. Graffiti covered some sections, none of it nice. Recessed in ornate sconces, fancy light fixtures had come away from the walls, bulbs missing or smashed.

He felt her fidget beside him.

What was wrong with her?

When she next spoke, which was after a good while, she did so in a quiet voice. 'I know what people say about me.'

Eliot shifted his bum. 'Okay,' he said, his eyes automatically seeking the location of a door, a fire exit, a way out.

'It's not true,' she said, keeping her eyes on the stage, 'what they say. It isn't. None of it is.' Then she turned her big, green eyes on him and gave him a look that demanded he say something.

'What do they say?' he asked, trying to sound casual. 'I haven't heard anything.'

But when he looked at her, he could tell that Claudine knew he was lying.

He took a deep breath, suddenly worried: if she told him things, would he have to tell her things back?

'W...wh...why do you think they say those things?' he asked, hoping she would refuse to answer.

Claudine screwed up her nose and thought about that for a moment. Then she shrugged. 'I played kiss chase once.' Her laugh sounded awkward.

Eliot laughed too, although he was not quite sure he liked the idea of her kissing other boys.

Not that he wanted her to kiss *him*.

She sighed, 'People can be mean.'

'Like O'Neal,' Eliot muttered, understanding this at least.

'The one that beat you up?'

'Well,' he stammered, 'he got in a few lucky shots.'

Claudine arched her eyebrows.

'Yes,' he said, feeling his cheeks warm. 'Yes, the one that beat me up.'

The two of them lapsed into silence.

The rain was still coming down hard against the roof.

And then: 'My dad was a soldier,' Claudine murmured. 'Northern Ireland.'

'I thought your dad was a policeman,' Eliot said.

Claudine rolled her eyes.

Hurriedly he added, 'Anyway, I don't care what other people say.'

She gave him a smile. 'Well, that's good, then.'

Eliot stared at the stage, suddenly overwhelmed with a desire to get up there and demand answers from an audience he imagined into being.

We don't need you. It's all your fault. What's wrong with you?

'What do you want to be when you grow up?' Claudine asked, interrupting his thoughts.

The question took him by surprise. Worse, he felt a sudden pressure to have an answer.

'A writer,' he said, hoping she would not laugh. It was suddenly important to him that she did not laugh.

A writer? Said out loud, it sounded silly and impossible.

But Claudine looked interested. 'What do you want to write?'

He shrugged. 'Stories.'

Claudine rolled her eyes. 'Really? And here was me thinking you wanted to write bus timetables.'

Smirking, she gave him a nudge.

Eliot grinned. 'What about you?'

'A nurse—like my mum.'

'That's good then,' he answered.

'Hey, I've got an idea,' Claudine gasped, suddenly excited. 'Maybe you could write a story for here!'

'Perhaps,' he said cautiously, thinking maybe this was one of her teases. After all, he was having difficulty keeping up with her today.

'*Perhaps?*' Claudine cried. 'How about, *Yes, yes! Absolutely*!'

She stood and started waving her hands in the direction of the stage. 'And you and me can play the main characters.'

'Okay,' he grinned.

Claudine clapped her hands together.

'Does it have a happy ending?' Eliot asked, thoroughly caught up in the idea now.

Claudine thought about that for a moment. 'Hmm, probably not.'

Understanding, he nodded.

'Best if it didn't have an ending at all, I suppose,' Claudine mused. 'Good or bad.'

'But there should be a journey,' he insisted, in his mind already at his imaginary typewriter.

'Of course,' she snorted. 'What's a story without a journey?'

'Well, it's practically not a story,' Eliot agreed.

'Precisely.'

'What about a dragon? It should definitely have a dragon.'

Claudine groaned. '*Boys!*'

'What?'

'And I suppose you'd have to rescue me?' she complained.

He grinned. 'Maybe. If you're lucky.'

Claudine scowled. 'Do I look like bloody Cinderella?'

'Errr...' Eliot was not sure how to answer this. 'Erm, I suppose not,' he ventured, hoping it was the right answer.

Claudine's nod suggested it was. 'I'd be rescuing *you*, more like,' she pointed out.

'Me?' he objected. 'I wouldn't need rescuing.'

Claudine said nothing, just used her eyebrows against him.

Eliot went red and mumbled something.

They exchanged a look, then burst out laughing.

Laughter filled the old theatre.

'But I must warn you,' he said after a bit, suddenly looking worried he might ruin the whole project. 'I can't act.'

'Bah, anyone can act,' Claudine said with a dismissive flick of her hand. 'It's just pretending. You've played pretend before, haven't you?'

He gave her a cautious nod.

'There you are then.'

Relieved, Eliot let out a laugh. 'I'll need to get writing then.'

'Yes, you will,' agreed Claudine.

'All right then.'

'Just *finish* it.'

Eliot nodded, giving her a look that said, *Yeah, of course.*

But where could he get a typewriter? Perhaps he could knock on No. 14's house; *do you have a spare typewriter? I want to be like you. Well, mostly. You're old. And I wouldn't smoke.*

The two of them fell silent. But it was a comfortable silence.

The rain, which had intensified over the last few minutes, slowly began to ease, now no more than a scattered titter-tatter above them.

Claudine glanced up. 'Sounds like the rain is giving us an applause,' she murmured with a wistful smile.

'So it should,' Eliot murmured.

But he felt it too.

It was time to go.

Eliot walked Claudine home. When they reached her front gate, Claudine stopped, abruptly swung around, and stared at him quite fiercely. He thought her eyes looked overly bright; mad-bright. In fact, he was sure Claudine was about to tell him off for something he had or had not done (or said).

But instead she suddenly lunged forward, without warning, without even asking, and planted a kiss on his cheek.

'There!' she grinned a little breathlessly. 'Now we're engaged.'

He blinked. *Engaged!*

With a laugh, Claudine whirled away. Before he could say anything (not that he knew *what* to say) she was at her front door: 'Bye then!' she shouted, and the door closed.

Eliot just stood there for a moment, his fingertips touching the side of his face. When he realised he was grinning, he coughed out loud, took a self-conscious look around, and quickly started for home.

His brisk pace soon turned into a run.

By the time he reached the cemetery, his thoughts had become slightly more confused, and he slowed to a walk.

What was happening? This was not the way it was supposed to be.

Kicking at a loose stone on the pavement, he entered the cemetery grounds.

He was a few yards along the path when something lying just off the verge caught his eye. At first glance he thought it was just a crumpled piece of coloured paper. But there was something familiar about the colour and pattern. His hands were shaking as he reached down for it.

It couldn't be...

Snatching it up, he stared at the folded piece of paper in disbelief. It was a five-pound note! A whole, real, five-pound note! Carefully, he unfolded the damp bank note, then smoothed out the creases. Pressing it against his chest, he quickly scanned the cemetery grounds, half-expecting to see its outraged owner come charging down the path towards him, demanding their money back. But the grounds were empty. Eliot held up the bank note to marvel at it some more, his hands still shaking. A whole five-pound note! It was massive in his small hands, stained and greasy and wrinkled, but the most precious thing ever.

Quickly, he folded up the money, slipped it into his front pocket, and started walking, head down.

After only two steps he stopped, dipped his hand into his pocket and touched the bank note, just to be sure it was still there. Shaking his head, he resumed walking.

Only he had to stop again, after another two or three steps—to be certain it had not slipped out when he had withdrawn his hand. And then again, shortly after—to be certain he had not dislodged it when he was checking to make sure it had not slipped out.

Finally, not being able to trust his himself whatsoever, he thrust his hand in his pocket, closed his fingers around the bank note, and vowed he would not release it until he got back to his bedroom.

Now he was at £15.90.

Eliot shut his tin. Well, at least he did not have to starve himself now. He shivered, recalling the episode on the esplanade.

I'd rescue you.

Claudine. She had kissed him. It was just a peck on the cheek, nothing more.

But still…

He shook his head.

Three Sundays remained in the month.

He had to remain focused.

She understood him. They shared a secret.

Claudine was just a girl. And she complicated things.

As he returned the tin to its secret hiding place beneath the floorboards, his eyes caught sight of the black Bible and he frowned. Finding the five-pound note had been a miracle gift. That much was true. Maybe God was saying sorry. Maybe God intended for him to go off with his lady. Maybe that was his plan all along.

He shook his head, not wanting that to be true.

To kill time before his visit to the park, Eliot went over to the window to catch up on what was happening in the street.

No. 14 was back at his typewriter, smoking, a more focused look on his face—like he was running a long-distance race and was determined to finish it. *Looks like Typewriter Man has decided he has no choice but to finish what he started.* Why he would want to write a story that would prove so painful and difficult was something Eliot could not quite appreciate. Maybe one day he would. Though he hoped that would not prove the case.

The couple at No. 16 seemed to be enjoying a quiet evening in by the television. No. 18 had a friend around. A tall, blond man with numerous earrings—Eliot knew what his father would say about that.

Old Man Vic was turning his living room lights on, then off, on, then off. '*He's pretending to be a lighthouse,*' he wrote in his diary. Thinking about that, he then wrote, '*He's bound to fuck up a few ships.*'

Eliot giggled when he read the entry back. It was the first time he had used a swear word in his diary. It looked good, like it belonged there, he decided, recognising that the words he had been using thus far were soft, tame.

Not grown-up.

Grown-ups swore, used the heavy stuff; the *good shit*.

Just as he had got himself settled into the bushes it began to rain again. He waited for a while, hoping it might ease up. To pass the time, he fiddled with his baby tooth, which appeared no looser—and if anything felt a little stiffer, like the gum was repossessing it, healing back up.

The rain fell with increasing heaviness, and all he could do was stare out from his hiding place, the pattering sound of water striking leaves filling his ears.

It was clear she was not going to show tonight. He gave his tooth one last sharp tug, but it refused to budge, and he climbed out of the bushes.

When he got home, he found his mum in the living room. She was watching the news. She looked tired and pale and was coughing a lot.

Clearly, she was getting no more sleep being up in her bedroom.

'There's not much on,' she murmured, meaning the telly, stubbing out her cigarette.

The news presenter was talking about a place called the Falkland Islands. They were British territories, it seemed, though the Argentinian government seemed very unhappy with this fact for some reason. Eliot had no idea where the Falklands were, although he thought it likely they were located somewhere in the Channel.

'I suppose not,' he said.

He heard Rob and David in the back room, laughing and arguing over the computer. It was getting late. Rob should be getting home to his own house. *Go home.*

His mum sighed and opened a can of Tennent's Pilsner. He counted the empty cans by the armchair. It was her third.

'Don't you like it upstairs?' he asked.

'It's a bit early for you to be sending me to bed,' she observed drily.

'I didn't mean it like that,' he blurted, feeling bad.

'I wasn't being serious, son,' she said with a smile; it was a smile that came out of nowhere, as startling as a sudden shout in a quiet place.

'Your tea's in the oven, love. It's not much, I'm afraid.' She started coughing again. 'There's not much in.'

Eliot put his hand on the back of her armchair and said, 'If you want to go to the shops tomorrow, I could come and help.'

'We'll see.' She began reaching for her cigarettes on the side table; they always seemed to help ease the coughing. 'But I think Ruth said she'd go for me.'

'Oh, okay then,' he muttered.

Ruth. It was always Ruth.

'Mum?'

'Hmm?'

'I don't want to go to my computer lesson tomorrow.'

His mum sighed, lighting the cigarette. 'How many times must we talk about this, Eliot? You need to talk to your dad.'

'But he's going to Manchester.'

His mum gave him a long look, but she remained silent.

Eliot's hand dropped to his side. 'Doesn't matter,' he mumbled.

Slowly, his mum's eyes started drifting back to the television and there was nothing Eliot could do to stop it from happening.

Later that night, the sound of David coming to bed woke him. He was talking in quiet whispers to someone close by. It took a few seconds before it registered that Rob must be staying over and had taken Michael's bed. Angered, but pretending to be asleep, he listened to their whispered conversation for a while, which was interspersed with annoying giggles, before throwing back his blankets.

'You awake then?' he heard his brother say. Rob snorted a laugh.

'No thanks to you,' Eliot snapped, and without another word he dragged his blanket off the bed. As he left the room he heard stifled laughter.

Eliot was about to settle in his mum's armchair in front of the TV but, for some reason, he could not bring himself to do it. In fact, the idea made him shudder, which was unexpected. Throwing himself on the sofa instead, he tried to get back to sleep. It took a long time. The rain had returned and it was even heavier than earlier, sounding like one hundred people tapping on the window, all wanting in.

21 Saturday, 13 March 1982

£15.90

Eliot woke to the sound of laughter next door. It was clear that David and Rob had come down early and had booted up the computer. Eliot groaned and wrapped the blanket around his head and tried to get back to sleep. It took about a minute for him to realise it was not going to work.

He was awake now.

Angry, he glanced at the old clock above the gas fire: nine o'clock—not long before Mr Wilson picked him up for his computer lesson.

Just as he was getting breakfast, Michael made an appearance.

'What are you doing here?' Eliot asked as his older brother entered the kitchen.

'Come to see Mum, of course,' Michael replied, switching on the kettle.

'She's upstairs.'

'Good.' He took down two mugs from the cupboard. 'What the fuck's up with you, anyway?'

'Nothing.'

'He's just pissed off coz he slept on the sofa last night,' David grinned, appearing at the doorway to the back room.

'Fuck off,' Eliot snapped.

'*Whoa*,' Michael laughed. 'Steady there, tough man.'

'But Rob slept in your bed last night!' Eliot shouted, pointing an accusing finger at David. 'He did.'

David shrugged. 'Big fucking deal.'

'Cut it out, David,' Michael warned.

Eliot laughed.

'And *you!*' his older brother growled, pointing a finger at him. 'It's just a bed, for Christ's sake. Grow up.'

This stung. Worse, David had a triumphant grin smeared all over his face.

He suddenly found himself wishing Claudine were there, with her smart mouth—she would sort his brothers out. He was certain.

'So what are you up to, Mikey?' David asked after a moment. 'Can't see your laundry bag anywhere.'

'Funny,' Michael said.

'Has Sharon learnt to use a washing machine, then?'

'Cheeky bastard!' Michael yelled, chasing him into the back room.

As Eliot made good his escape with his breakfast bowl, he heard David yelp.

'Get off, Mikey!' he cried, laughing through the pain his brother was obviously inflicting upon him.

Smash him one, Eliot thought, though he knew Michael would do no such thing.

Turning on the television, he watched some cartoons. *Wait Till Your Father Gets Home* was on. He hated this cartoon. His favourite was *Danger Mouse*, but that was only shown during weekdays.

After breakfast, he went upstairs to read for a while.

Just as he was settling down with *The White Dragon*, he heard Michael enter their mum's bedroom. The murmured conversation that followed interrupted his concentration so he took himself back downstairs.

Mr Wilson dropped him off at school at around five o'clock. When he got home, he discovered Rob and David in the back room playing on the computer. *Again!*

Wishing to avoid a fight he ignored the two of them, although his greatest desire in the world was to destroy the computer. Get shot of it.

Mum was nowhere to be seen and she had forgotten to make tea. Rather than ask David what was going on, he decided to make a cheese sandwich. Finished, he tidied up after himself. He then cleared the draining board of dishes, glasses, and mugs. He performed this activity loudly, and when David shouted through, demanding to know what all the noise was about, Eliot shouted back, 'I'm sorting things! Things need sorting!'

When he got a laugh from David, he yelled back, 'You just don't care!'

This remark was met by another round of laughter from the back room.

Go on, laugh. See if I care, he sneered, stomping upstairs. *Play on the fucking computer.* He had his lady. David and Rob had nothing like her.

What did they have?

Piss off, she would say to them with a laugh. *You're just kids. What do you know? Stop wasting my time; go fiddle with your little twinkles.*

They would start crying.

And it would be his turn to laugh; laughing so hard the bushes would shake. Laughing so hard the leaves would fall.

All the leaves in the world, falling.

David crying. Like the baby he was.

Goblin-man was back. But he was drunk and clumsy, and it took him some time. Eliot was not even sure if he managed to finish off properly. She appeared embarrassed for him and even helped him pull up his trousers, like he was a kid at primary school.

Once he had gone, she fixed up herself up. Her black ankle boots gleamed and flashed as she moved, and he hungered after her breasts; but they were concealed, which made him want them even more.

'I took money from my dad for you,' he whispered, ripping off a leaf and squashing it down.

She looked over in his direction, but said nothing. As he watched her powder her nose he noted a small, red blotch had appeared at the corner of her mouth; a small thing, but enough to worry him, what with her cold, also.

I'd rescue you.

Finished, she slipped her compact back into her small, black bag. She made a move to leave, then stopped. Frowning, she slowly turned her head. She sniffed, looked skyward, then sniffed again.

She could smell it, he realised: the death of winter; time was running out.

Soon now, he promised. *Soon.*

The woman nodded and left the courtyard.

When he got home he went straight upstairs and took out his money tin.

£4.10: that was all he needed.

He was certain he could do it.

Hesitantly, he lifted out the five-pound note he had found in the cemetery and examined it closely.

It made little sense. Why would God give him money? Was this his way of saying sorry?

But if that were the case, why did he let bad things happen in the first place?

Because God doesn't listen, he reminded himself, shutting the tin lid. *That's why.*

Stupid fucking computer lessons.

Returning the tin to its hiding place, he lifted out the little black Bible, then replaced the loose floorboard and covered it back over with the carpet.

Sitting on the end of his bed, he turned the book over in his hand, thinking, thinking. Then he stood, decision made. 'One last chance,' he declared out loud. 'But that's it.'

Taking a red felt-tipped pen out of his pencil case, he opened the Bible. Noting the page, 179, he then placed the pen in the valley of the pages and closed the book on it.

Kneeling beside his bed, he whispered, 'This is it; this is your last chance. Please understand, God, if you don't show me a sign after this, I can't believe in you. How can I? And…I'll hate you.' He slipped the Bible under his pillow and went into the bathroom to clean his teeth and inspect his spots, which were getting better by the day.

Later that night, he woke. Without opening his eyes, he listened. First, he heard the crackling static from the portable television next door. It sounded like a hundred tiny worms gnawing at the walls. A thousand maybe. And then across the room he heard his brother snoring, loud—enviously so.

Slowly rolling over, he opened his eyes and caught sight of the dark shadow on Michael's bed.

Rob! Rob was staying over again!

Fully awake now, Eliot sat up in bed.

Was David doing it on purpose?

Slipping out of bed, he went into the bathroom for a pee. Finished, he suddenly grabbed the edges of the bathroom sink and glared into the mirror, demanding answers.

But none were forthcoming.

Too angry to sleep, Eliot took himself downstairs with his blanket and curled up on the sofa.

22 Sunday, 14 March 1982

£15.90

He was suddenly nervous.

Put it back, a warning voice urged. *Don't even look at it. You're just being silly anyway.*

Finished with his breakfast, he had waited until his brother and Rob had risen and left the bedroom. When he heard the computer go on in the back room, Eliot had gone back upstairs and grabbed the Bible from beneath his pillow.

Put it back. That voice; he was sick of it inside his head.

There won't be anything there, stupid. You're just being stupid.

Eliot Thomas, Stupid Boy.

But he had to know.

Clutching the Bible to his chest, he dropped to his knees. It was time he looked. No excuses. He gave the Bible another squeeze, however, knowing that once he looked, there was no going back.

He would know for sure, one way or the other.

It was time. Taking a deep breath, he opened the book.

Ignoring the felt-tipped pen, which slipped out as soon as he opened it up, he scanned the pages, excitedly looking for the "sign" he believed might be there.

Nothing.

His eyes frantically scanned the centre pages.

Hah! Told-you-fucking-so!

Nothing! Not a single mark or sign, just blocks and blocks of small, printed words he had no desire to read, now or *ever again*. Embarrassed and angry in equal measures, he took up the red felt-tipped pen and stared at it for a moment, even checking the nib against his index finger to be certain it had not dried up.

'I hate you!' he shouted out loud, and his words filled the bedroom. 'I don't believe in you!'

When he caught sight of his microscope set, the corner of which was just peeking out from under his bed, he grabbed it.

Maybe. Maybe this was all just a test.

Why make it obvious, after all? he reasoned. Otherwise, everyone would be demanding a sign.

He tore out page 179, then took up a pair of scissors. He hesitated.

Deciding from where on the page he should take a sample proved more difficult than he would have thought: where, on a page, in a Bible, would God leave a secret, invisible sign?

And then he had it: between the lines, of course. Surely God, he reasoned, would have the sense to avoid leaving a secret, invisible sign where it could be confused with the printed words on the page. Certain he was right, Eliot made a careful incision between the lines of two sentences and cut out a neat, blank square.

Kneeling, he placed the little strip of paper on a glass slide, then set it beneath the objective lens. Taking a deep breath, he leant forward and peered through the lens.

Please be there. Something. Anything.

Nothing.

But what looked like empty cells, one after the other, in rows—laid out like fat, hollow bricks in a wall.

Stupid sample; stupid Bible; stupid idea…stupid microscope.

He clambered to his feet.

Stupid, stupid *him*.

Hollow bricks in a stupid hollow wall.

He snatched up the Bible, climbed onto Michael's bed and opened the window.

For a second only, he hesitated.

You sure? the voice asked.

Fuck off.

Taking a deep breath, Eliot hurled the little black book out of the window.

I hate you.

It travelled quite some distance, arcing though the air, the pages roaring and flaying like a startled bird.

'Cunt!' Eliot shouted.

The book snapped shut and dropped out of the sky as though the sun had shot it down.

It landed dead centre of the road.

Good. Now the world would get to see how fake it was. Quickly, he scanned the road left and right, searching for possible witnesses to this act of blasphemy. But the road was clear. Eliot slammed the window shut, hoping the wind and the rain and the sun would utterly destroy the thing.

For a while he lay on his bed, staring up at his ceiling, chewing on what was left of page 179.

I'm not going to go and get it. I'm not. No way.

He swallowed hard, silently hoping he would shit out page 179 later.

'The little fucker went that way!' the golfer shouted.

Eliot ducked down behind the bush, heart thumping.

'I just can't believe the shit ran out onto the fairway and actually stole your fucking ball!' another golfer exclaimed. 'I mean...*the fairway!* What's the world coming to?'

Eliot had no idea why he had done it.

What was wrong with him?

He had not found a single golf ball all day, so when the ball had landed on the fairway with a soft thump, he had found himself staring at it for longer than was normal. And it had been right there, in front of him, not four yards from where he had stood...white and gleaming. And the golfers had not left the tee...were *miles* away. He was a good runner, was he not? The best. And he knew the woods.

'I tell you, something has to be done about it,' the first golfer promised; he was somewhere to Eliot's right. 'It's getting worse. I mean, where the hell are the course marshals?'

'They need to put a fence around the whole place,' complained his playing partner.

'That won't stop them,' the first golfer gloomily predicted. There was silence for a moment, then he snarled, 'Fuck it! I'll hit another ball. *But*,' he vowed, 'if I ever catch that shit, I'll hang him up by his fucking balls, so help me God, I will.'

As the two men moved away, Eliot stepped out from behind the bush. He stared down at the ball in his hand. It was not even a very good one; an inferior brand of low quality that would fetch very little money.

He was done for. He could see it now; the gathering army of course marshals by the clubhouse; a meticulous skirmish line forming, ready to scour the woods with sticks and dogs to flush out the golf ball thief.

He looked along the woodland trail. He would have to leave. He could not stay here.

Eliot Thomas, Prey Boy.

As the stolen golf ball hit the water, it made a splash and sent up a fountain of brown water. 'Sorry!' Eliot cried out loud, staring into the heart of the pond. Thinking back to that morning, he was suddenly, unexpectedly, and horribly conflicted as to which act he was referring. 'I am.'

Confused and feeling miserable, he crossed the first fairway and left the golf course, thinking he might never see it again.

When he got home, David and Rob were in the back room playing on the computer. He risked sticking his head around the corner. Rob was reading instructions from a magazine, which David was inputting into the computer. 'Is that it?' he asked Rob.

David said, 'Yeah, but it's still not working.'

'Is there a problem?' Eliot asked, not caring, but hoping the computer was broken.

David shook his head, but his cheeks were red. 'No, we're just typing in a new game from this magazine.' He held it up, *Your Computer.* 'Nothing for you to worry about.'

'Yeah, nothing,' Rob added with a sneer.

'Doesn't look like nothing.'

Neither boy had a reply to Eliot's vicious grin.

Hah.

Eliot climbed onto Michael's bed and breathed on the window until a cloud of condensation formed. With his finger, he wrote, £15.90.

That was all he was going to get from the golf course.

He would have to keep his lunch money back after all, starve himself; could he do it?

He went to breathe on the window again but instead, he found himself looking down at the spot where the Bible had landed, though it was now clear.

He sighed and glanced down the road.

But there was no one there, he noted with some disappointment.

Sitting bare-chested on his bed, he slowly dragged the edge of the protractor down his arm. The pain lifted him up and up and up until he felt lighter than a leaf, a fly, a mote of dust—a particle within the dust.

Fingers trembling, he increased the pressure until there was only the pain, white in his head, drowning out any noise; burning out every other thought, tears blinding him.

Is there something wrong with him? Is that it?

He pulled the protractor away with a gasp. Each deep pulse emptied out the pain, brought him down, until he felt the burden of his body once again, all around him, heavy and numbing. Wiping his eyes, he stared at the top of his arm, disgusted, and yet viciously satisfied with how much blood he had drawn.

No need for the microscope.

Given recent events, he knew he was changing, was being altered in some dark, internal way, turning bad.

No, no need for the microscope.

Using his fingers, he smeared the blood down the length of his arm.

Eliot Thomas, Blood Boy.

Downstairs, David and Rob had obviously got the game to work or had loaded up a proper one, and the sound of their stupid laughing and shouting further maddened Eliot.

Laughing and laughing.

He had to do something about that stupid computer. As for Rob....

He's not staying here again. No way...

Bare-chested, still bleeding, he was suddenly tearing the blankets from Michael's bed, flinging them behind him, then the pillows. Finally, the base sheet, until there was a great heap of bed linen behind him.

Fuck off. Go home.

He stared in shocked revulsion at the horrible brown stains in the centre of the mattress, not wanting to believe that it was Michael's mattress. *Michael's.* Altogether, the stains formed a shape which resembled a poppy, like the ones his grandad used to wear once a year, only a sick one. Jagged rings of fading yellows surged out concentrically, like the growth rings of a tree, until they broke against a darker, implacable, outer-edged ring. No doubt the stains had seeped down into the mattress like the killing roots of an evil disease.

His sudden anger made his head spin and, feeling sick, he had to look away. But no matter how hard he tried, his gaze kept returning to it. At one point, he sat at the very end of Michael's bed, fighting down the impulse to touch the stain. Was this really Michael's bed? Could he have done this? Maybe it was Rob? Yes, that could be it.

The dirty bastard.

But the stains looked old, and he knew the truth of it.

All Michael's advice...pretending to be grown-up, like he was the boss...acting like their dad. And look at it...

With his mother's expert eye, he knew the stains were never coming out. As he grabbed a spare sheet from the bottom of the wardrobe, the asthmatic crackle of the portable television next door was suddenly overlaid with the sound of his mum coughing, and coughing.

Is everything sick in this house? he thought, throwing the sheet over his brother's mattress.

But the coughing continued. Coughing like she did not care...only cared about herself.

Dad was leaving.

This was his mum's fault.

The need to get out came upon him like a dark thing. Throwing on his jumper he hurried downstairs, took his coat off the peg from behind the door and left the house.

He started to run. It was Sunday, and he knew she would not make an appearance, but he needed to see her.

The park was quiet, but it was like someone had shined a torch full of daylight on it. He looked around, amazed. It was so much greener than he remembered it, and smaller. Absent of a single shadow, everywhere he looked there was detail, colour, signs of returning life.

A gentle breeze tugged at his coat, reminding him why he was there. Quickly, he settled into his hiding place and stared out into the courtyard. Closing out everything, he let the silence eat up everything in his head; scenes, images, noises…never to be recalled or remembered ever again.

When he opened his eyes…

…she is there in front of him. They are beneath the security light, laughing and talking. Their conversation is clever, mature, sophisticated. She is wearing a light summer dress, he a jacket and a hat. He is smoking a cigarette.

She gives him a look. A needing look. It is like a shout from the eyes. Flinging his cigarette away he pushes her into the corner, slaps her once, then twice, and then takes her then and there. She gasps and makes some sex noises and shouts out his name. She loves him. 'Let's run away,' she pleads.

He does not answer her for a moment, but when he does, he asks her, 'What's your name?'

But she does not answer him.

Suddenly it is the most important question in the world. 'Answer me. Answer me. Tell me your name.'

But she remains silent.

He slaps her across the face, hard. 'Tell me!'

She smiles instead.

'Please,' he sobs, trying to fight back his tears.

As he rounded the corner into his road, he bumped into Claudine.

'Wow! What's the hurry?' she cried.

'Claudine!'

'That's my name, don't wear it out,' she grinned. 'Game of kerby?'

Eliot shook his head, but thought it best to keep an eye on the tennis ball she had in her hand.

'What are you doing out on a Sunday?' he demanded.

Her eyes narrowed. 'Is that your way of telling me it's bath time? Are you saying I smell?'

In no mood for her teasing, but feeling his ears go red anyway, he shook his head. 'That's not what I meant. I meant it's late, that's all.'

She scowled. 'I'm not nine.'

'Didn't say you were. I'm just saying…it's *late*, dark out.'

'And girls shouldn't be out after dark. Is that it?'

'*What?* No!'

'Anyway,' she sniffed, 'it's not that dark.'

Which was true.

Claudine bounced the tennis ball, hard. The rebound was very high, and Eliot watched it climb. As it began its descent, she snatched it deftly out of the air. 'Besides, my mum lets me do what I want. She trusts me.'

'So does mine.'

'Didn't say she didn't.' Her look turned suspicious. 'But you never know.'

'What do you mean by that?' he demanded.

'Maybe you sneaked out, *escaped*.'

'Escaped?'

She shrugged. 'Maybe.'

'You think I *escaped*?'

'What I think isn't important. It's the truth that matters.'

'Yeah?' Eliot yelled.

'Yeah.'

'Well the truth is, I can stay out *when* I want, for as *long* as I want.'

'Is that right?' Claudine looked impressed.

'Don't even have to go home.'

'And you can go *wherever* you want?'

Eliot nodded.

'Prove it then,' she said, her expression suddenly cunning.

Too late, he realized that he was being maneuvered.

His response was cautious. 'Prove what?'

Claudine bounced her ball. A soft bounce, calculated. 'I have an idea...if you *dare*. If you're not afraid.'

He knew he was playing into her hands, but he still got angry. 'I'm not afraid of *anything!*'

'Well then,' she said, stepping in closer, her smile widening significantly.

Despite his anger, Eliot was suddenly reminded of her kiss and his cheeks warmed, thinking it would be okay if she leant in some more, got even closer.

'I have an idea,' she said, her lips close to his left ear, making it itch a bit. 'What do you think about this...?'

He listened to her big idea, silently determined to find fault with it...but the more he listened, the more he realised it had...possibilities.

In fact, he wished he had thought of it first.

23 Monday, 15 March 1982

£15.90

Lunch break. Eliot was sitting on the wall outside the newsagents, stomach growling. His gaze drifted over to the newsagents.

Hungry.

Yes, he was. But if he kept back his lunch money, it was another 50p saved. And how else was he going to raise the money?

By now there would be "Wanted" posters up on every tree on the golf course.

He was a thief, wanted.

Eliot Thomas, Wanted Boy.

£15.90…He shoved his hand in his pocket…well, £16.40, if he could last the day. Inexorably, his gaze turned towards the newsagents… and the many coloured enticements on display in the window…

Sweets. Sweets. Sweets.

A sudden buzzing sound interrupted his thoughts. On the wall beside him, there was a discarded Coca-Cola can. Immediately he spotted the wasp, which was fussing around the top of the can, dipping and rising, its wings fizzing at about a million flaps per second. Frightened of wasps, Eliot's usual response would have been to leap away. But not today. He was too worried about other things to be frightened.

The wasp dipped and rose some more until finally, decision made, it settled on the lip of the can. Its tiny hooped abdomen seemed to pulse.

Spot Boy. Green Boy. Game Boy. Smoker Boy. Thief Boy. Prey Boy. Blood Boy. Wanted Boy. Starving Boy.

As Eliot watched on, the insect scuttled over the aluminium surface—he fancied he could hear the faint *click…click…click* of the wasp's tiny feet as it did so.

It stopped when it reached the dark, keyhole-shaped opening.

Sensing something important was going to happen, Eliot grabbed the wall behind him with both hands.

The wasp scuttled over the rim and plunged in.

Quick as a flash, Eliot lunged for the can, picked it up and shook it vigorously.

And then he heard it…the echoes of tiny panic, faint, frantic—atomic out of the mouth of the black chamber.

And then silence.

He imagined the wasp drowned…exhausted…lifeless on a black and fizzless sea.

The pleasure Eliot had derived from this act of murder was immediate, and immediately over. Now he felt only guilt and shame.

But it's only a wasp!

It made no difference. He felt bad. Hideous.

And it was biology class next. He had no right to go.

He was a fake. Fake Boy.

Fake Boy *turned* monster, he amended, staring at the empty can.

What was wrong with him?

Hungry, Eliot slipped off the wall, wishing he had all the money in the world saved up, suddenly wanting things done and finished with.

Eliot Thomas, Monster Boy.

Michael appeared around six o'clock.

'What are you doing here?' Eliot asked, coming downstairs.

'Fish and chips,' Michael declared, holding up a bulging plastic bag which was giving off some mouth-watering aromas.

'How come?' Eliot demanded.

Michael closed the front door and pulled the drape across. 'How come what?' he replied irritably, taking the chips through to the kitchen.

Eliot followed. 'Why isn't Mum making something?'

'Hi ya, Mike!' David shouted through from the back room.

'Why isn't Mum making things?' Eliot repeated. Getting an answer from his brother was suddenly very important to him. It was like they were all just helping to keep her up there, like they did not care. *'Michael?'*

'She's just a bit tired, Eliot,' Michael explained, getting the condiments from the cupboard; vinegar, salt, tomato sauce. 'And so am I,' he added. *'I'm* tired!' He slammed the cupboard door shut.

Eliot was not entirely satisfied with that answer but he let it go; not because his older brother was getting annoyed, but because he had a more pressing question for his brother. In a voice he kept very low, he asked, 'You didn't get Rob any, did you?'

'What didn't I get Rob?' Michael sighed.

'You *know*...fish and chips.'

Michael looked less than pleased with Eliot's question. 'If you must know, it was Ruth who asked me to go to the chippie.'

'Ruth?' *Fucking Ruth...always fucking Ruth.*

'She phoned me.'

'Why would she phone you?'

'Why's that important?' Michael growled.

'You know,' Eliot hissed. 'It's *Rob!* He shouldn't get any. He should go home.'

With a finger, Michael beckoned Eliot closer.

'Ruth's paying for it,' his older brother hissed. Opening another cupboard, Michael took down a pile of plates. Sounding more bored now than angry, he said, 'Christ, what the hell's wrong with you, Eliot?'

Stung, Eliot intended to use the stained mattress against his older brother, but the jibe got stuck in his throat. The words refused to come out. Finally, and with a clarity that hurt, he realized that Michael had changed and he could no longer accurately predict how his older brother would react. If he used the mattress against Michael now, he could well choose to ignore the comment; then again, he might get properly angry. Or worse, it could well end things between them, *forever.* It was just impossible to know for sure.

'Nothing's the matter with me!' Eliot instead yelled.

'Then shut the fuck up.'

Eliot stormed out of the kitchen. *Michael was not the boss of him.*

24
Wednesday, 17 March 1982

£16.90

Eliot managed to keep his lunch money on Monday and Tuesday, but by Wednesday he relented and set off for the newsagents as soon as the break bell sounded. After all, he told himself, he did not want to end up starving like that poor prisoner Bobby Sands had done last year. There must have been a very serious reason behind him doing something like that he decided as he sat on the wall outside the shop, his stomach gratefully receiving its first cola bottle in *ages*.

Starving himself was not the answer.

But what else could he do?

Twenty fucking pounds.

He spotted Claudine the moment he entered his road.

She was sitting on the pavement outside his house.

Worse, Michael's car was parked in the road. *No. No. No. NO! Not wanting Claudine to see his panic, he broke into a kind of trotting run-walk, which made him feel foolish; he felt like a spazza chicken with the runs.*

'Claudine?' he gasped when he reached her.

The girl stood, smiling. She was dressed in her school uniform and he wondered if she had been home yet. She had her tennis ball in her hand.

'Hi,' she said. 'Want to come out for a bit?'

He glanced in the direction of the house. He shook his head. 'No,' he said, 'I can't. I have to…I have to help my mum move some stuff tonight. Right now, actually. My brother's already here. That's his car. He's here to help.'

'Oh, okay then,' she said. No teasing. No silly grinning.

She just bounced her tennis ball in front of her. More evidence that she just confused things.

Eliot said, 'You, err…I mean, who answered the door?'

'Oh, I didn't try the door.' She bounced the ball again. 'Why?'

Scratching the top of his arm, he replied, 'No reason.'

Snatching her ball out of the air she said, 'You know, I haven't met any of your brothers.'

Eliot suddenly wished that he had a ball to bounce. Putting himself between Claudine and the door, he said, 'Maybe you can sometime.'

She glanced at the front door and nodded slowly.

He blew out his cheeks. 'Well, I have to go now,' he said. 'Bye then.'

He was surprised when she just sighed. 'Just don't forget Friday night.' No sarcastic remarks. No fight. 'You did promise, after all.'

'Yeah, I know,' he said. *Stupid promise.*

'Unless of course, you're *scared!*'

'Of course I'm not scared,' he snapped, wishing he had never agreed to anything.

'Good then.'

'Good.' Keeping an eye on her ball he said, 'Bye then.'

'Okay, bye.'

Hurrying down the path, he took out his keys. Turning the latch, he pushed on the door which, as usual, got caught up in the drape. Red-faced, he glanced over at Claudine, but she was already walking in the direction of her home.

Feeling sorry for her and a little bit mean, he slammed the door shut harder than he intended.

Stupid girls.

His mum, dressed in her blue nightgown, was sitting in the living room. She was with Michael. More from a deep-rooted sense of obligation than any sense of desire to do so, he popped his head around the corner. Grabbing the door handle as though he needed support, he nodded at his mum, who gave him a weak smile back. She looked red around the eyes. Like she had been crying. *Crying?* But that was impossible. His mum never cried. *Mums didn't cry, did they? Well, maybe other mums did...but not his.*

He gave Michael a questioning look but his brother just shook his head and indicated that Eliot should leave.

There followed a moment of awkward silence as he considered staying put. *Who did Michael think he was?* But Michael frowned sternly and with an airy, *I-don't-care* shrug, Eliot left them to it. She was probably just tired anyway. That was it. Just tired.

Having to listen to Michael, he could understand this.

The absence of noise coming from the back room gave him cause to hesitate on the stairs. Surrendering to his curiosity, he reversed down the stairs and checked the back room, but he found it empty.

Good. Well, this was something anyway.

He glowered at the computer. He could not recall his mum and Mr Wilson discussing the issue of it going back, so he knew it would be down to him to bring the matter up. Rapidly opening and closing his mouth, he confirmed that his jaw had finally stopped clicking. He was better. There was no need for the computer to be here any longer.

But Michael was in with their mum now so he would have to leave it, pick his moment.

Of course, he could always throw it out of the back window. He would get into massive trouble, but seeing the look on David's face would be worth it.

He grinned viciously and went upstairs.

25 Thursday, 18 March 1982

£16.90

The school day passed without incident, although he regretted slipping up again and buying lunch. When he got home he found Michael (home, *again*) in the kitchen, talking to Ruth. They were drinking coffee.

Ruth's presence was unexpected and made him feel uncomfortable, as though he had entered the wrong kitchen. He heard Rob and David laughing next door.

'Mike?' he said, looking directly at his brother as he closed the back door. 'What are you doing here?'

Michael shook his head. 'Really? Every time?' But he smiled and said, 'I needed to pack some things up for the flat.'

'You mean Sharon's flat,' he said.

Ruth intervened before Michael could reply. 'So how are you, Eliot?'

Suspicious, he kept his response to a cautious shrug. 'Okay I suppose.'

'You've grown,' she remarked, her gaze unrelentingly upon him. 'I hadn't really noticed it before. But yes…quite the young man these days. Hasn't he grown, Michael?'

Ruth and Michael exchanged a look before Michael nodded. 'He'll be just fine,' he said quietly.

Mum's friend or not, he felt she had no right to look at him in this way. It felt like he was being touched.

She said, 'You'll be needing some new clothes soon, mind.'

Eliot looked to his older brother. 'Where's Mum?'

'Upstairs,' he replied. 'Why?'

'No reason,' he said.

He had the feeling they were going to talk about him some more once he left the kitchen. Who cared?

'I'm going upstairs to change,' was the explanation he gave to excuse himself; though it was more for his own benefit.

He spent a bit of time with his binoculars and diary.

The upstairs light went on over at No. 16. The man appeared with a bottle. From his expression, Eliot sensed the infant had been crying for some time. *'He doesn't even know how to shut it up,'* he wrote in his diary. *'What kind of dad is he?'* Eliot read this entry back and then quickly scrubbed it out.

No. 14 was hunched over his typewriter, his hands moving quickly, but his expression remained oddly at variance with this activity; distant, elsewhere. *Typewriter Man has that look Mum gets when she's staring out of the window.* Eliot regarded him for a moment longer before concluding that Typewriter Man must have decided that some things were more important than a story. Would his wife come back if he stopped writing? Taking one last look at him, Eliot decided his wife would not. To look at, he had always been a right miserable bastard.

No. 20 suddenly appeared at the side of his house and was banging his bin lid against the wall, chanting something loudly. *'Old Man Vic's doing his "dinner's ready" thing again. Someone should take his bin lids away; that would shut him up.'*

Tea was fish fingers and chips. Michael cooked it, which was a big surprise to both Eliot and David.

'Is Sharon making you take cooking lessons or something?' David teased.

'Funny,' Michael said, closing the oven door. 'Anyway, I've told you, she's got late shifts on at the minute,'

Plates on their laps, the three boys sat in the living room, David on the sofa and Michael, Eliot quickly noted, taking their mum's armchair, like he was the boss. Eliot took his seat across the room, the heat of the plate on his thighs working up an itch. Ruth had taken Rob home half an hour earlier, which Rob had not been happy about.

Hah!

Watching television, the brothers ate quickly, and for the most part in silence. When Michael finished, he pulled out a packet of Lambert & Butler and lit up a cigarette.

The early evening news was on.

Margaret Thatcher was making a speech in Parliament, then it switched to a shot of her standing outside her house, addressing several journalists who were trying to crowd in on her, shoving microphones in her face.

'Trouble's brewing,' Michael predicted, expelling a vast cloud of blue smoke.

'What trouble?' David asked excitedly.

'The Falkland Islands.'

'What are they?'

'Please tell me you're joking,' Michael said. 'You know, the Falklands Islands.'

David blinked.

'The Falkland Islands?' Michael repeated in a louder voice.

Their dad did this, Eliot noted: if you failed to answer a question the first time, he would simply repeat it, again and again, as though he believed repetition (varied only by increments of increasing volume) would eventually force out the right answer from the person being asked the question. The worst thing was, he would abbreviate the question each time he asked it, like a countdown, which put you under more pressure.

'The *Falklands*!'

Like that.

Maybe it was a smoker's thing?

'Yeah,' Eliot jeered. 'The Falklands.'

'You don't know!' David shouted.

Eliot shrugged. 'Do.'

'So, what are they?'

Eliot sighed. 'Tell him, Mike.'

Michael gave him a long look, but answered anyway.

'They're British islands, but near Argentina. Argentina claim they're theirs, and want them back. Christ, don't you know anything?'

Eliot was quick to laugh at his younger brother's embarrassment.

'You didn't know that,' David spat.

'Did.'

'Bullshit.'

'*David!*' Michael warned.

'Then tell him, Mikey. He didn't know where the Falklands were.'

'I so did,' Eliot said, pretending to sound bored.

'You liar!' David shouted. 'You're a liar...Ellie.'

'Don't call me Ellie!' he shouted back.

'Why not...*Ellie*?'

'I'm warning you.'

David stuck his face forward. 'Ellie, Ellie, Ellie,' he trilled.

'Michael,' he complained. 'Tell David to stop calling me Ellie.'

'*Stop it!*' Michael yelled, spinning out of the armchair. Tall and lean, head almost touching the light shade, he stood dead centre of the room and glared at his two brothers. 'The pair of you...just fucking stop it.'

Eliot and David stared at their brother in shocked silence.

Explosion over, Eliot sensed the anger leaving his older brother, and an awkward silence took hold in the room. Swiping the ashtray from the side table Michael sat back down, turned his gaze on the television, and finished his cigarette.

Their own dispute forgotten, David and Eliot exchanged nervous grins.

'God, is there no end to your arguing?' Michael grumbled, not looking around. He was suddenly stabbing his cigarette into the ashtray on his lap, repeatedly, until the stub had utterly disintegrated between his finger and thumb. Immediately, he grabbed another cigarette out of the packet and lit it. 'I mean, Christ *alive!*'

As Michael lit his cigarette, Eliot noticed that his brother's hand was trembling.

David grabbed his plate and stood up. 'I'm going to play on the computer.'

'You do that,' Michael snapped, still refusing to look around.

David flicked up a finger behind his older brother's back and left the room.

'God help me,' Michael continued, more to himself. 'I'm surprised Mum's not in a loony bin.'

Eliot felt it best not to say anything.

About ten minutes went by before Michael felt calm enough to swing around in the armchair. He took a very deep breath and said, 'So, what are you up to tonight?'

'Probably out for a bit,' Eliot answered cautiously.

Behaving as though this bit of information was important, Michael pursed his lips. 'Don't be late then,' he said after a moment.

Eliot surprised himself by nodding. Grabbing his plate, he followed David's example and hurried out of the living room.

You're not the boss of me.

His lady appeared that night. Accompanying her was a rather tall, wiry, nondescript man. He had the walk of a man who believed he was in charge of things, but when he got down to it, he demanded very little of her, like he was a beginner. She performed some of her mouth work on him and it was over within minutes and without incident.

Eliot took up his position in the corner once his lady had departed, but his thoughts were on other things tonight and nothing worked for him. He walked home with the pace and uncertainty of someone who suspected things were slipping.

The ordinariness of the encounter left him feeling strangely unmoved, and later, as he lay on his bed and stared up at the ceiling, he conceded that the thing most dominating his thoughts was the promise he had made to Claudine.

You're excited about it. Admit it. He gave his loose tooth a vicious tug; it refused to budge.

Which proved what a nuisance she truly was.

26

Friday, 19 March 1982

£16.90

'What happens if we get caught?' Claudine whispered.

'This was your idea,' he hissed back. He was still having a hard time believing they were doing this. If she had changed her mind, called it off, at any stage during the walk up to the seafront, he would have quickly agreed—but now...now that they were here...

She gave him a look. 'I'm just saying.' She was wrapped up in a big green duffle coat with a fur-lined hood, like they were going on an epic journey to the North Pole.

He was surprised she had not brought along a picnic.

'Well, don't,' he snapped. But he immediately regretted using that tone with her. 'I mean,' he amended, 'there's nothing to worry about.'

Claudine gave him a stiff little nod.

The two children stood side by side, staring at the sign hanging from the thick rope barring their way:

'Unsafe structure: Do not enter.'

He mouthed the words, finding it impossible to believe they were man-made, written. They did not even seem like words, but something else entirely. Words were used to write stories. These things, and the warning they carried, felt like a fact, something that *was*, had always been, and would therefore remain so for all time.

Glancing at Claudine, he could see that she felt it too, or something similar.

The urge to test himself against that fact came upon him quickly and without compromise, but when he took a step toward the sign, Claudine remained where she was standing.

'Well?'

Claudine eyed up the rope as though it was a snake. 'I thought we were just going to take a look, that's all.'

'You chicken?' he teased.

Claudine's eyes flashed with anger. 'Of course not.'

'So, let's go then.'

Checking first that they were not being watched, he ducked under the rope and held it up for Claudine. The girl still hesitated.

'Come on,' he urged. 'What are you waiting for?'

Trying to mask her reluctance, Claudine ducked low under the rope, careful it did not come in contact with her, which he found both amusing and, for some reason, irritating.

Turning, the two of them stood the other side of the cordon, staring in awe, first at the back of the sign (which was blank) and then at each other, as though by their actions they had the erased its words and had henceforth altered the order of the universe so that anything was possible from this point forward.

Eliot broke the silence first. 'Well, this isn't too bad,' he said, noticing that he sounded a little breathless.

'We haven't gone anywhere yet,' Claudine muttered. 'I mean, the pier's down there.' She pointed to the distant unlit structure at the far end of the promenade.

'I know,' he said, also feeling nervous.

'We'll just have to go down there then. Yes?'

'This was your idea,' Eliot reminded her.

'Yes,' she replied. '"Yes, it was.'

Keeping close to the sides, they walked slowly over the decking. He ran his hand over the smooth wooden railing. It felt cold to the touch, but he fancied he could detect a faint pulse of life beneath his palms. The darkness between the gaps in the decking and the repetitive sound of waves rushing up the shoreline and breaking somewhere behind him produced in Eliot a strong feeling that the pier was not connected to anything, but had broken away from the world and was floating out towards an as yet undiscovered country.

His excitement started to grow. *They were really doing this.*

The decking underneath their feet grew increasingly uneven, and despite their cautious passage, the wooden planking occasionally—and often alarmingly—groaned or creaked.

He caught Claudine frequently looking over her shoulder. The possibility that she might relent suddenly and turn for home worried and angered him, because he knew there would be nothing he could do about it.

He shot her a look that said, *You're spoiling it. Don't spoil it.*

But he need not have worried. Her smile was faltering but resolute, and slowly the entrance to the arcade grew larger as they approached it.

Facing two sets of large double doors, both padlocked, it seemed impossible that they could go any further. Like sentries, two coin-fed rides stood either side of the structure; to their left, a horse, and a butterfly ride to the right.

'Do you think this still works?' Claudine wondered aloud, casting a speculative eye over the coin-operated horse ride.

'What's that?' Eliot murmured, inspecting the padlock.

'This ride! *Eliot?*'

'What?'

'Do you think it still works?' Claudine murmured, stroking the side of the horse.

An irritated glance at the machine suggested to him it would not; the metal base plate was sitting in a dark bleed of rust, and several nuts were missing. The power cable, sticking out of the back like a tail, was unattached, and the plug was missing. 'It's broken,' he said to her.

'What about this one?' Claudine said, crossing over to the butterfly ride.

'Probably not,' he predicted impatiently. 'But what about the doors? We have to get in somehow.'

Claudine acted as though she had not heard him and without warning, she hauled herself up into the seat.

'What are you *doing?*'

'Nothing,' Claudine grinned. 'Why don't you get up on that one?' she suggested, indicating the horse ride.

'No!' he said, shaking his head. 'No way. Anyway, we're not here to play.'

'Oh, go on,' she said in a wheedling tone. 'No one's going to see you, if that's what you're worried about.'

'I'm not worried about anything,' he answered. 'Only about trying to get inside here.'

'Then get up.'

'But why?' he complained.

Claudine patted the side of the butterfly. 'There doesn't have to be a reason. It's just a bit of fun. Oh, go on,' she pouted. 'Just for a second?'

With an angry sigh, he climbed up and plonked himself in the saddle of the horse. 'Now what?' he demanded flatly.

Claudine giggled. 'I don't know. But who cares?'

'This is stupid,' he said, feeling stupid.

But Claudine had already closed her eyes and was gently rocking in the seat, humming a tune. Watching her, he suddenly felt torn. Looking around, he knew there had been a time when the world would have looked different from up here, magical.

He tried to close his eyes, but it was no use.

'Can I get down now?' he said, fighting down the feeling that he had lost something forever.

'You're too serious by half,' Claudine chided, opening her eyes.

He gave the side of the horse a petulant kick. 'Giddy up,' he said. 'You see? It's not working.'

'You're such a spoilsport.' Scowling, she got down from the ride.

Regretting his actions, he quickly climbed down from the ride. 'Sorry,' he mumbled, thinking his behaviour may well have called an end to the night's adventure.

And he could tell she was thinking about it.

'Stupid boys,' she muttered, but she gave him a weak smile. 'Forget it...doesn't matter. Now, what about these doors?'

With a relieved grin, he stepped over to the door, grabbed the padlock, which felt cold and heavy, and gave it a sharp tug. But it was securely attached to the chain looping through the two large door handles.

He released it and the padlock struck the door and made a loud, dull thump.

'Maybe there's another way in,' Claudine murmured, staring around thoughtfully.

'Maybe,' Eliot muttered, still staring at the padlock.

Moments later, Claudine was calling out to him: 'How about over here?'

When he looked up, he discovered that Claudine had wandered off and was now at the far-left end of the building, waving him over. As he approached her position, he saw that she was standing beside a window. It was smashed, and the decking was covered in fragments of glass which crunched beneath his feet as he neared her position.

Claudine ran her hand over the bottom inner frame. Resembling shark's teeth, numerous jagged shards of glass remained lodged in the frame.

'Careful,' he said.

Claudine just nodded and set about picking out the bits of glass from the frame. Following her lead, he grabbed a particularly large shard of glass and wobbled it free of its gum of rotting putty. To avoid making any noise, he carefully set the shard on the floor before grabbing another piece.

Side by side, the two of them worked in silence until the entire window appeared free of broken glass. Eliot stepped back. It would be a tight squeeze, he reckoned, but there was just enough room.

'This might be difficult for you,' he said to Claudine.

Tight-lipped, she gave him a little look of defiance and declared, 'I'll manage.' She sniffed, 'Besides, this was my idea.'

'Okay. But I'll go first?'

Nodding, Claudine wrapped her arms about her body and watched as Eliot stuck his head through the opening and lifted himself up. It was an effort, and the window frame dug into his stomach as he wriggled his body forward. But after a brief struggle, he managed to worm his way through. Controlling his fall with his hands, he was soon standing the other side and was sticking his head through. 'Okay,' he said, his face flushed. 'It's okay.'

Eyeing up the window, Claudine nodded.

Sensing her apprehension, he felt obliged to ask, 'Are you sure about this?' He suddenly needed her to acknowledge that she wanted to do this. Really wanted to do it.

Claudine nodded resolutely. Taking hold of the window frame, she lifted herself up on her hands, the gymnast on the mount. She held herself like this for a moment, the ridge of the frame digging into her palms. With a gasp, Claudine pivoted her hands around one hundred eighty degrees, her right hand clockwise, her left anti-clockwise, so that the heels of her palms were now pointing outwards, toward Eliot.

'That's it,' he said quietly.

For a moment she held herself perfectly still, not daring to move in case she disturbed the balance she had found for herself. And then, with a stifled little cry, she leant forward and stuck her head through the opening.

'You've got it.'

'Yes,' she said breathlessly, her face screwed up in concentration. Shifting her weight onto her right hand, the left hand snaked out, pawing at the inside panelling, looking for any kind of purchase to help heave herself through. She grimaced in pain as the pressure built rapidly on her wrist. Her right arm started to tremble.

He could tell that Claudine was fighting down the urge to throw herself backwards and end the pain, but despite the obvious discomfort she was experiencing, he sensed that it was important that she get through without his assistance, and so he did nothing to help, just watched her struggle, feeling both excited and cruel all at the same time.

'Rest your tummy on the edge,' he urged finally.

Teary-eyed, Claudine nodded and managed to drop her stomach onto the edge of the window frame.

'You've got it,' he murmured. 'Now shuffle forward.'

Again, she reached in with her left hand and searched for something to grab hold of. Finding the inside ledge beneath the window, she clasped it fiercely and pulled. A combination of feet-kicking and awkward wriggles saw her slowly progress her body forward, her tummy scraping over the thin lip of the window frame.

The frame was now digging into her...well, private area, and he caught himself wondering if it hurt her there, despite her having no sticky-out parts. It excited (and frightened him a bit) that he wanted it to—but just a small amount.

'That's it!' he gasped. 'Last bit...now pull...pull yourself forward.'

Claudine suddenly squealed in pain.

'What's wrong?' he said, panicked.

'Nothing,' Claudine said. 'My hand—I think I've cut it.'

'Which one?' he asked, glancing down at the hand gripping the inside ledge.

'Which one do you think?' She said it so fiercely he had to fight down a giggle.

'You're almost there,' he urged.

Angry now, Claudine took a deep breath and heaved herself forward. He could tell that her shifting body had reached some crisis point and, sensing the time was right, he reached out to grab her shoulders, but he was too late.

With a final cry, Claudine had managed to pull herself through and was suddenly falling. He tried to catch her but he missed and her head cracked against the floor.

Quickly kneeling, he asked, 'Are you all right?'

Her left hand was bleeding from a small cut.

Eliot was suddenly aware that his knees were trembling. 'Claudine?'

Claudine did not answer. Instead, she pushed him away and stood up. Refusing to look at him, she brushed herself down. He reached into his pocket and found some tissue. Claudine took the tissue and dabbed the cut on her hand. He fidgeted nervously, thinking she was going to hate him forever.

Finished with the tissue, Claudine handed it back to him. Eliot took it and stuffed it into his pocket and waited for Claudine to say something.

Once she had finished tidying herself up, Claudine looked up and gave him a dimpled little smile, which, relieved, he quickly returned.

Together they turned to face the dark interior of the arcade. This was a place forbidden to them, but they had dared to enter it regardless. Glancing sideways, he wondered if the anxious triumph he suddenly saw in Claudine's face was mirrored in his own.

Oddly, he now found himself reluctant to go any further; maybe having trespassed here was enough. Claudine took hold of his hand as though she felt it, too.

She whispered, 'What now?' But such was the hushed wonder in her voice, she might just as well have said, *'But what does this mean?'*

He shrugged and replied, 'I don't know.'

As he stood there, he felt an expectation growing inside of him, faint at first, and then more insistent, until he understood, with some certainty, that the choice to go on or retreat was now no longer available to them.

'We go on to the end,' he said quietly.

'Yes,' said Claudine. 'I suppose that's the right thing to do. After all, we won't get to do this again.'

'No,' he said.

Together, as though they were bound at the feet, partners in a three-legged race, they took a step forward.

The air was thick with dust and the place was a layered confusion of smells; salt, damp, oil, and a tang of metal that fizzed on the end of his tongue. Slowly, the ghostly silhouettes of the arcade machines, standing side by side and back to back, hardened into solemn definition, deepening in Eliot a feeling that he had stepped through a door into a place that contained his most precious memories.

It saddened and frightened him, and he felt no immediate comfort when Claudine edged closer to him, tightening her grip on his hand.

Sighing, he tried to imagine the arcade as it once was; a constellation of glittering lights, scales of colours, flashing bulbs, bells and sirens going off, the sound of machines pumping out coins, running feet, laughter, and shouting. And on the periphery of his imagination, the swirling smells...candy floss, hot chips and popcorn...whilst all around him, tinny music filled the air like bee noise.

He coughed. His throat was dry, as though the dusty silence had entered his body through his mouth and was filling up his stomach, making it heavy. There was a grainy quality to this now-muted environment that was strangely familiar; in the way the millions of airborne particles were adrift and visible in the many narrow shafts of light that beamed down though tiny holes and cracks in the roof.

'Phew, it smells,' Claudine declared, sniffing loudly. 'It really does.'

He laughed, which made him feel a bit better, lightened the burden of responsibility he felt he should carry for them both—without understanding why.

'We should keep going,' she said, glancing down at their interlocked hands with a shy smile.

Smiling, he decided that, for now, at least, it was probably best if he let her keep her hand in his.

Together they navigated their way through the arcade, their footsteps making very little sound on the floor as they passed, as though the dust was soaking up all the noise. They were confronted by another set of double doors the other side but, much to their relief, they were unlocked. And when he heaved on one of the doors it opened with a slow, creaking shudder. A sudden gust of cold wind took him and Claudine by surprise and when they took a bracing step back, their hands broke loose.

Acting like adventurers confronted with the grim certainty that, should they elect to press on, they were unlikely to return unscathed (if at all), both children glanced over their shoulder and then at each other, and then stepped outside.

The bandstand area was enclosed on all sides by a cantilever roof. He had forgotten how much it felt like being inside a theatre or miniature stadium.

'The ceremony for the destruction of the Pier Bandstand,' the council spokesman had said in the newspaper article, *'a symbol of the resort's holiday heyday in the 1950s and 1960s, will take place on the Easter Bank Holiday Monday, eleven o'clock. Whilst it remains a financially prudent course of action, the decision to destroy the pier was nevertheless a profoundly difficult one to make, and no doubt many will be sad to see it go. The pier has proven to be a very popular venue over the years, hosting band concerts, open-air dancing, roller skating, carol singing, and even wrestling and boxing.'*

Eliot and Claudine paused in front of the empty stage where the bands used to play. The dark surface was heavily worn, and cracked in places. In other areas, mostly where the stage sagged, rainwater had collected, forming still, dark pools. He found it difficult to believe that people had once performed here.

Slowly, he turned and turned and turned, and wherever he looked he saw signs of neglect and decay; flaking paint, wood panels split, decking lifting, sections of wrought-iron railing bent or missing, parts of the cantilever roof missing or collapsed, graffiti everywhere—all of it…unclean. Even the tall, white flagpole atop the arcade roof was missing its flag. The place felt antique, but without value; so old it seemed pointless to continue fighting off the inevitable. And this sense of futility was reinforced by the distant whoosh and rumble of breaking waves which, though faint, carried with it the ineluctability of change, impermanence.

'Sad, isn't it?' Claudine sighed.

He nodded. 'Yes. Yes, it really is.'

The two children moved off around the back of the stage, where they found two further sets of double doors. He pushed on the metal bar attached to the door nearest to him and it opened easily.

Sea smells reached him on the cool evening breeze as he walked towards the far end of the pier, which resembled the back of a ferryboat. Set out in an arc, a series of fixed wooden benches faced outwards.

'Look!' Claudine cried. 'A telescope.' She hurried forward before he could stop her.

It was mounted on a thick, blue cast-iron column, which in turn surmounted a boxed metal baseplate, a part of which formed the footplate.

A peculiar uneasiness slowed his own approach.

Excited, Claudine stepped up and grabbed the telescope; laughing, she turned it on Eliot as he drew nearer.

'Do you think it still works?' she asked, not sounding as though it mattered.

Stepping out of its line of sight, he regarded the stubby telescope for a moment before saying, 'I doubt it.'

Claudine pulled a face. 'How do *you* know?'

'Well I don't, I suppose.'

Bent slightly forward, Claudine turned the telescope one way, then the other, pretending she could see through it and was spying out various objects across the bay, on the seafront, inside the town. Hundreds of town lights illuminated the evening skyline. Like the innards of a great machine, traffic moved along the esplanade, a chain of red lights rubbing up against a chain of yellow, which moved in the opposite direction.

'I think we should try it,' Claudine declared, standing up. It sounded more like a dare.

'How much does it take, anyway?' he asked, eyeing up the machine like it was a thief.

Claudine quickly wiped away the dust and grime from the plaque above the coin slot.

'Ten pence,' she grinned.

He dug into his pocket and brought out some change. Handing her a ten-pence piece, he watched with curious foreboding as the girl rolled the coin into the money slot and peered through the telescope.

£16.80

'It works!' she declared with an excited shriek. 'It really works.'

She swung it around to the west end of the beach. 'Ohhh, I can see people by the ferry terminal...and look, there's the pavilion. And there are people outside the night clubs...do you like dancing?' She flung the telescope skyward. 'I can see a bit of the moon, too.'

Looking up, he saw that a faint half-moon hung over the bay.

After a minute or so of breathless commentary, punctuated by several delighted squeals which made mention of 'lights' and 'a ship' and something about not being able to see France, Claudine stepped down from the pedestal.

'Your turn,' she said, indicating the telescope.

He hesitated.

'Well?' she demanded. 'What are you waiting for? The time's running out.'

Reluctantly, he took his place on the pedestal and took hold of the telescope. It was cold in his hand and felt heavy. He was very conscious of Claudine watching him and his discomfort grew, as though she was about to watch him perform something private.

'Well?' she demanded.

Feeling like he had no choice, he sighed and peered through the scope. Darkness at first…then lights reflected in the sea beneath the storm wall by the pavilion, wet colours juggling in the water. Slowly, he swung the telescope full on the town.

To Eliot, the tall, white flanks of the seafront buildings appeared Lego-like, not real. Squinting and concentrating hard, he thought he saw the occasional shadow person flicker across a lighted window.

'Tell me!' Claudine's voice sounded faint but insistent, much like the sound of the waves whooshing and breaking down below.

'Tell you what?' he muttered, suddenly wishing he was alone.

'What do you see?'

Eliot ignored the question. He swung the telescope a little further to his right, tilted it ever so slightly….

There…

A street running off the seafront road. More streets…the rooftops of houses…rows and rows of them. A break in the houses, a main road…a dark space in the middle of the houses as though everything in that area had been swallowed up.

When the magnification of the telescope failed him, his imagination took over…

...a hedge; then a park; the light from a lamppost bathing the brick path in yellow light; a climbing frame; a miniature football pitch; a row of wild bushes...a courtyard. The courtyard.

And there in the courtyard, stands a female, quite alone. She looks tired and pale, with dark rings around the eyes. She has a cough, and bruises run up and down her arms.

Like the pier, she looks beaten and old.

Where is he? Eliot imagined he heard her whisper. *Has he abandoned me?*

He swung the telescope away from him and hurriedly stepped down. 'Rubbish,' he declared, backing away from it.

'What's wrong?' Claudine asked.

'Nothing. Let's go.' Not waiting for her, he headed back towards the pier bandstand area.

Confused and hurt, Claudine kept up with him as best she could.

'What happened?' Claudine asked at one point as they crossed the bandstand area. 'I don't understand.'

'Happened?' he demanded, stopping outside of the arcade. 'Nothing happened. What kind of stupid question is that?'

In a small voice, Claudine said, 'I don't understand?'

'It's just a stupid telescope.'

'Then why are we going?'

Eliot pushed open the door and went through into the arcade.

'*Eliot?*'

'Just because,' he said. 'I mean, we shouldn't even be here.' His voice was loud, and he felt like he was committing an act of violence upon the silent, grainy darkness.

'Eliot?' Claudine called. 'Will you stop a second? Eliot? What's *wrong?*'

Stopping beside the broken window he shouted, 'They're going to blow it up! Don't you understand anything?'

'No!' she shouted back. 'Because you never tell me anything. I have to find out everything for myself!'

'What's that meant to mean?'

He placed his hand on the window frame, eyeing her suspiciously.

Claudine bit her lip.

'What do you mean by that?' he yelled.

'Nothing!' she shouted. 'Just nothing...all right?'

Claudine pushed his hand away and took hold of the window frame. With an angry heave, she lifted herself up. He stepped back and refused to help her as she struggled to climb through, even when her arms started shaking with the effort. After a brief struggle she was through to the other side, landing on the decking with a loud thump; but she did not cry out, which angered him further.

Struggling to her feet she started walking back down the pier towards the sign, not looking back. Not looking like she was going to stop.

She was leaving him there, he realised.

Him! But what right did she have to do that? How dare she steal his anger.

Eliot stubbornly refused to call out to her, but he quickly lifted himself up onto the ledge of the window and heaved himself through. He made a bad landing the other side, and the heavy jolt shook his teeth and made his loose tooth flare with pain.

Scrabbling to his feet, he quickly hurried after Claudine, although he had no idea what he was going to say when he caught up with her. By now, he was more confused than angry. Something had slipped. Gone wrong.

The decking groaned and creaked as he flew over it.

Claudine, meanwhile, had passed beyond the roped cordon and was waiting for a space in the traffic so she could cross the seafront road.

By the time he had ducked clear of the cordon, Claudine was turning down a side street.

'Bye then!' he shouted, but the sound of a passing lorry ripped out his voice. *See if I care*.

But he did, he realised. He really did.

It took less than two minutes. The man, a scrawny creature with a moustache, threw back his head and let out a shout, but it was more like anger. Then the courtyard was silent.

Eliot wrinkled his nose.

The way things had ended between Claudine and him had left him confused and irritated, and he had intended to go straight home. But instead he had found himself walking in the direction of the park, like he had no choice, like it was no longer up to him and he was being made to do it, which he resented.

I should have gone home.

She looked paler tonight, and a bit haggard, and her continued scratching felt personal, like she was doing it on purpose, letting him know that she felt his betrayal on her like a physical thing. And her constant sniffing was just as bad, acting like there was a bad odour stalking her, and she was desperate to locate it.

Eliot had fixed his eyes on her breasts, the one thing that made sense. They remained lovely, and he longed to touch them, to crush his face against them.

He watched the tall, dark-haired man leave and then the woman shortly thereafter.

Soon, he promised her departing form.

She left coughing, like she did not believe him.

This will end soon.

As Eliot took his place in the corner of the courtyard, something strange occurred. Slowly, as he listened to the night sounds of the park, a peculiar kind of apathy seized him, a wearying disinclination to do anything; move, walk…talk.

It was like the darkness was slowly invading his body, gradually filling it up, making all the parts of his body heavy and unresponsive; finally producing in him a tired desire to just stay where he was, forever, have nothing more to do with anything, anyone—family, school, Claudine; even his woman. And the desire grew so strong in him that his head spun until he became nauseous.

The breeze was stiffening and the bushes rustled so loudly it sounded as though a large creature was moving about at the heart of the understory. He stared at the leaves, at the spaces between the leaves, deep into the shadows, and pictured himself crouched there, watching himself, and what he saw disgusted him.

His hand moved away from the zip on his jeans.

Feeling tired and suddenly very foolish, he stood there for a while listening to the evening sounds, but for once (and very strangely), all he desired was answers from the sun.

He found Rob and David in the back room. They were waiting for the computer to load up a game.

'Where have you been?' David asked.

Eliot's hand reached for the door handle. 'Out,' he answered, in no mood to talk.

'Where out?'

It was quick, but he saw it, a sly exchange between David and his friend. Still irritated, but now cautious, he said, 'Just out.'

'Yeah, but where?' David insisted.

It was clear from his tone that his younger brother knew something and was not going to let it go.

'If you must know, I've been down to the pier.'

'The pier?' David said, acting like he was surprised. He glanced over at Rob, who, tapping away at the computer, gave the slightest of nods. *I told you so.*

Feeling his cheeks warm, Eliot pointed at the computer and yelled, 'That's going back soon!'

'All right, keep your knickers on,' David smirked.

'Why don't you two fuck off next door!' Eliot shouted, leaving the room. 'And stay there while you're at it.'

He was halfway down the hallway when the sound of sucking noises stopped him dead in his tracks. He heard David burst out laughing. 'No *way!*'

'Way,' Rob snickered.

'I don't believe it,' his brother said. 'It just can't be true.'

Rob laughed, 'I'm telling you.'

'You don't think he's getting any, do you?'

There was a pause, and then Rob replied, 'Nah, he doesn't smoke!'

The two of them burst out laughing.

Slamming the side of his fist against the wall, Eliot stomped upstairs.

They know nothing, he kept telling himself. *Nothing.*

Mystified, he sat back on his heels and stared at the microscope.

But there was no escaping the fact; his and Claudine's blood samples were identical. This truth should have offended him. After all, she was a girl, and he...well, he was boy. There ought to have been some sort of discernible difference—though he had formed no real idea how he thought this might manifest itself.

But facts were facts.

Labelling the plate, *'19/03/82—Claudine's Blood,'* he slotted it home inside the narrow box and packed everything away, wondering in a moment of guilty unease what Claudine would think if she knew he had examined her blood without her permission. Knowing her, she would react badly. That at least gave him a certain amount of satisfaction. How dare she walk off on him!

And after letting her come to the pier, too. *His* pier.

He lay down on his bed. He would have to avoid Claudine. She... confused things. Every time he was with her, she confused him, gave him confusing things to think about.

Maybe she won't want to see you again.

Ignoring that, Eliot counted up his money in his head.

£16.80.

If he went without lunches next week, that would make...£19.30.

But it was hard...being hungry...

And it would still leave him short by 70p.

Eliot attempted to summon the image of his lady, her breasts, large before him, like moons (his tongue going to the nipples) but the sound of the television next door, rising and falling, like it was trying to break over his mum's coughing, was a constant distraction.

Swinging off the bed, he began pacing the room. Only two weeks ago he had wondered whether his mum was ever going to use her bedroom. Now he wondered if she would ever come out of it.

Later that night he woke up and, feeling thirsty, he went downstairs. The living room door was open and he poked his head around the corner. Someone was sleeping in the armchair. He edged in and peered down.

It was Michael!

The television was on and the test card girl was giving his older brother a crooked smile, like she knew all his secrets.

Asleep, his face was all smoothed out, and hints of the old Michael were present; the one before he had left school. The one before their mum and dad had split up—the one before Sharon had taken him.

An overwhelming desire to shake Michael took hold and he had to fight it down. *Hey, Mikey, do you wanna talk for a bit? How about a game of Mousetrap or Battleships?* But instead he took out the blanket from down the side of the sofa and gently draped it over his brother, careful not to wake him.

He took the ashtray, which was full, into the kitchen, and emptied it into the bag hanging over the handle of the back door.

As he passed out of the kitchen, he closed the door to the back room, and felt stronger for it.

David was asleep in his bed, snoring.

Rob had gone home.

Lying in bed, he guided his tongue over the top of his baby tooth and he welcomed the little flares of pain as it wobbled in the gum.

He just wanted it out. It was time for it to go.

27

Saturday, 20 March 1982

£16.80

'I don't know how she does it,' Michael commented, stretching in the armchair. 'God, I'm stiff.'

Clutching his cereal bowl, Eliot sat down on the sofa.

Dropping his arms, Michael grabbed his cigarettes off the side table. Looking around he said, 'Hey, where's the ashtray?'

'In the kitchen on the work top,' he answered, his mouth full of Weetabix.

Michael raised his eyebrows. 'Don't suppose you can fetch it for me, could you?'

Eliot nodded and went and got it. By the time he returned, the news was on. He ate his breakfast in silence for a while, his glance occasionally darting in Michael's direction, questions queuing up on the back of his tongue.

The news presenter was finishing up a piece about an ongoing dispute between the government and the miners. After that, he started talking about rising unemployment, a slowdown in manufacturing output, and a reduction in interest rates. As Michael picked a string of tobacco from his lip, Eliot wished he understood more of what was being said on the television so he could say something intelligent to engage his older brother.

'I can't wait to leave school,' was what he finally said, however.

'Don't be in such a hurry,' Michael cautioned, turning to look at him.

'Why? You've left, and you're doing okay.'

'Oh, is that right?'

'Yeah,' he insisted, disliking the tone Michael was assuming.

There was silence for a moment as the news switched to the deepening crisis over the Falkland Islands.

'Don't you like school, then?' Michael asked, taking a drag on his cigarette.

He shook his head.

'Any particular reason?'

Eliot filled his mouth with a spoonful of cereal, then shrugged.

'Going out to work's not all it's cracked up to be, you know,' Michael pointed out.

'Don't care.'

'You will,' Michael predicted, like he knew it all.

'So?' Eliot felt his frustration begin to get the better of him. The conversation was not going the way he had wanted it to. Michael was being all superior for no good reason.

Michael stubbed out his cigarette, turned right around in his chair and gave him a very direct look. 'Come on then, out with it.'

'Out with what?'

'What's really up?'

'Nothing. Nothing's up.'

Michael shook his head. 'Jesus Christ, Eliot.'

'That's all you ever say!' he complained loudly. 'You sound like Dad. Stop sounding like Dad.'

'So that's it?' Michael said.

'That's what?' he said, squeezing the sides of his cereal bowl.

'It's the computer lessons, isn't it?' his older brother demanded. 'You're still pissed with Dad for making you go?'

'You don't understand, Mike!' he yelled. 'You don't!' His brother was acting like a know-it-all, and he had no right. Despite his anger, he held back on the mattress.

'No,' Mike shook his head. 'No, I don't.'

'I hate them.'

'Because they're on Saturdays?' Michael sneered. 'Jesus, I have to work on Saturdays. *Every* Saturday!'

'It's not that,' he protested.

'Then what is it?'

Under the cool glare of his brother, he hesitated. 'No one...no one asked me,' he finally mumbled, nudging a chunk of Weetabix around the pool of milk in his breakfast bowl.

'Give it a rest!' Michael reached for his cigarettes. 'For fuck's sake, just give it a rest.' He lit his cigarette, inhaled, and blew out. 'Christ, you're like a cracked record,' he muttered. 'Try thinking about someone other than yourself—just for once.'

'What do you mean? I don't know what you *mean*.' Eliot stood up, breakfast bowl cupped in his hand. 'But for your information, I'm not going to my computer lesson today.'

'Really?' Michael sighed. 'We'll see.'

'Yeah, we will.' Michael was not even looking at him now. 'And... and I'm not going to Manchester...*Ever*! Manchester can fuck itself.'

Michael slowly turned his head. 'Well that just goes to show how much you know,' he said, acting, as far as Eliot was concerned, massively, intolerably superior.

'What's that meant to mean?'

'Dad isn't going to Manchester anymore...well, not for a while, at any rate.'

'That's not true!' he shouted. 'You're lying. He's got a job. I heard Mum and Dad talking about it. Why would he not take the job?'

School shoes.

'You don't know anything!' Eliot yelled.

'I know more than you, that's for damn sure,' Michael retorted, not looking too happy about the fact. 'A lot more.'

'Yeah, and then you keep it all to yourself so you can look...look all important!' he shouted. 'You never tell me or David anything.'

'Because you don't fucking listen, Eliot!' It was Michael's turn to shout. 'That's your problem. That's always been your problem. You never say anything, and you don't listen. You listen to fuck all. It's like you're on a different planet. A pod person…from the planet Mars. Eliot the Pod Boy.'

'Why are you being like this?' Eliot screamed.

'Like what?' Michael sounded bored, which made Eliot even more furious.

'You know, sitting there all…all'—Eliot flustered—'pretending like you know it all. Pretending to be grown-up. Like you're the boss. You're not the boss. You piss the bed.'

Michael opened his mouth, then shut it.

'I've seen your mattress. And the piss stains.'

Michael started laughing.

Eliot felt like hurling his breakfast bowl at his brother.

'Jesus, Eliot,' Michael laughed. 'Grow up.'

'I bet you tell Sharon everything!' Eliot shouted. 'Sharon, Sharon, stupid Sharon!'

Michael lunged out of his chair and was across the room in a heartbeat. 'One word!' he said through clenched teeth, jabbing his finger at him. 'Just one more word and I'll burst you, Sunny Jim.'

Eliot backed up. 'You're not the boss of me!' he yelled, and stormed out of the room.

He got as far as the kitchen when he heard Michael shout, 'Eliot! Come here. I'm sorry. I'm just tired, that's all. Crap. *Eliot, I'm sorry*. It's complicated, that's all. Eliot? It's complicated.'

'Twat!' Eliot shouted back, yanking open the back door.

Just then, he heard David's voice. 'Hey, Mikey,' he said. 'What's all the noise?'

Not waiting to hear Michael's reply, he left the house, not caring that he had forgotten his coat.

He had about an hour and a half before Mr Wilson showed up.

Complicated? Well, things were about to change.

They'd see.

It was a cool morning and the wind stung his face. By the time he reached the seafront his anger had cooled, but he was still upset with Michael.

He'd see. They'd all see. He'd show them "complicated."

The seafront was about ready for the start of the season. Repairs finished, the scaffolding had come down from the hotels and they now gleamed with fresh, white paint. Looping from streetlight to streetlight, multi-coloured bunting snapped and fluttered in the morning breeze. On the esplanade, numerous tables and chairs had been set out, although currently they stood empty beneath their coloured parasols.

Crossing the road, he wandered along the esplanade. There was a chill in the air, winter trying to hang on, and the sky was milky-white. Up ahead he saw that the amusement arcade was open and machine lights glittered and flashed, albeit weakly in the hard morning sun. Down on the beach the concession stalls were finally ready; even the miniature golf and the donkey ride and the trampolines were all set up, ready to go. And down by the shoreline, pedalos were all laid out like lines of ducks.

But there were no takers. *Hah!*

The town may have readied itself for business but to Eliot, it reminded him of a wounded animal waiting to be pounced on by a pack of starving creatures.

The sound of a boy crying made him turn his head. He saw a child and his father not twenty feet away. The child, a boy of three, maybe four, was facing the sea, both hands clutching the railings in front of him. Feet apart and his head thrown back, the boy was bawling. He bawled and bawled and the father, who was clutching the boy's woolly hat, could do nothing about it but hold onto the child.

Eliot held the child and his father in his gaze for a moment— particularly the father: *do something*—before moving on.

He'd show them all. All he needed was £3.20.

He could find that, he promised himself, turning to face the pier. Easy.

When he got back from his computer lesson, Michael had gone, and there was no sign of David or Rob.

Good.

His mum called out to him as he was going into his room. 'Eliot?'

Reluctantly, he backed up. His mum's bedroom door was closed.

'Eliot?' Her voice sounded weak, distant.

He put his hands on her door as though he was trying to prevent her from calling out for a third time. But when she did not call out, he pressed up his ear, close—a doctor listening for a pulse. All he could hear was the sound of her portable television, faint and wheezy. Eyes this close to the door, he noticed the numerous imperfections in the paint finish; ridges of white gloss standing out in sharp relief, like fat veins feeding paint to other smoother sections of wood.

His mum started to cough and he quickly pushed himself back from the door. Out of the corner of his eye he could see the figure reflected in the bathroom mirror looking across at him.

He raised his hand and waved. It was with some relief that the dark figure waved back at him. He stuck two fingers up at it. The figure mirrored the gesture. He jabbed a finger at it, and the figure returned the insult with a viciously complicated grin.

'Eliot, is that you?'

Instantly, the grin disappeared from his face.

'Eliot, can you come in here please, son?'

He slowly turned the handle and went in. His mum was sitting up in bed. She was no paler than usual, but she did appear a little thinner.

'Can you pass me the controls, Eliot?' She pointed to the remote, which had somehow found its way to the end of the bed.

The need to refuse her was sudden and powerful. He was sure that if she got out of bed and retrieved the controls for herself, things would immediately begin to get better.

Fuck him.

'Eliot?'

He handed her the controls. '*3-2-1* is on tonight,' he said.

His mum nodded with a weak smile.

'It would be better on the big telly downstairs.'

'I think you're right,' she said, reaching for her cigarettes. 'Is Michael back from work?'

He shook his head.

'Ruth's made a casserole. It's in the oven and needs heating up.'

'I can do it,' he offered.

Turning the controls over in her hand, she stared at him thoughtfully before shaking her head. 'Best let Michael do it, sunshine.'

'Yeah, sure, whatever,' he said.

'How was the computer lesson?'

Eliot shrugged.

'And how's Gor…Mr Wilson? How's he?'

'Yeah, fine,' he answered, jamming his hands into his pockets.

His mum regarded him quietly for a moment before sighing heavily. 'What am I going to do with you, Eliot?' she asked.

Fortunately, the local news came on, saving him from having to answer her.

'Look, they're talking about the pier,' he said.

A man in his late forties was doing a feature on the impending destruction of the pier. He stood on the beach beneath the condemned structure. It looked windy, and the sea behind him was grey and appeared agitated.

On the black-and-white portable, the pier seemed ancient.

'It's such a shame, isn't it?' his mum murmured.

He agreed. 'They obviously think it's anachronistic.' The word felt odd and hard angled in his mouth, but he was proud he had found a use for it, and in the presence of his mum, too. If only David had been there. Better yet, David and Michael!

He *was* closing the gap. The gap was almost closed.

The funny look his mum suddenly gave him was disconcerting and made Eliot feel as though he had done something wrong. 'That's a big word,' she said. 'You didn't get that from me.'

He took his hands out of his pockets and placed them behind his back. He shrugged.

'But that's not one of my words,' she insisted, her head coming off the pillow. She looked like she had just lost him in a crowd or something.

'Where'd you learn that?'

He could not understand this behaviour and he was helpless against the thing he saw in her eyes. He wished he had never used the stupid word now.

'At school,' he mumbled. 'English.'

She thought about that for a moment, then asked in a quiet voice, 'Do you know what it means?'

It felt like an accusation. Her tone was wrong, like she did not…

His thoughts trailed off. 'Dunno,' he lied. 'Forgot.'

Looking oddly pleased, she settled her head back into the pillow. 'It means,' she said, 'outdated.'

'Outdated,' he repeated. 'I'll remember that.'

Sighing, she reached for her cigarettes, a gesture that left Eliot feeling certain she would not be leaving her room anytime soon, Dusty Bin or no Dusty Bin.

Michael appeared around six o'clock and reheated the casserole in the oven. As he was doing this, David stuck his head out of the back room.

'Can me and Rob have our tea in the back room, Mikey?' he asked.

Michael nodded. 'But don't make a mess.'

Eliot, who was leaning against the fridge, brought his head up sharply, but said nothing. No mention had been made of the argument from that morning, and he wanted to avoid a possible flare-up.

Watching the TV, Eliot and Michael ate their tea in silence, Eliot as quickly as possible.

Michael was sitting in their mum's armchair. As usual.

You're not the boss of me.

When *3-2-1* came on, Eliot listened intently to the questions, desperate to answer one out loud, but they were beyond him and he grew increasingly frustrated.

'Mum wouldn't have let Davey eat his tea in the back room,' he suddenly blurted, before he could stop himself.

'Well, I'm not Mum,' Michael answered, and lit a cigarette.

'No,' he said as he stood, empty plate in his hand. 'No, you're not.' But he left it at that.

As he carried his plate into the kitchen, he heard Michael laugh at something on the television.

You're not the boss of me.

It started raining at around eight o'clock.

Heavy rain.

She would not come out tonight.

Stupid rain. Stupid God. Stupid computer. Stupid Dad. Stupid school. Stupid Michael. Stupid everything.

He made just the one entry in his diary later that evening: '*No. 14. The bottle is back. I'm not sure he's going to make it.*'

The streetlight outside was on. Elbows on the windowsill, he bore his eyes into the light until it glowed more brightly, expanded, then poured back towards him until he felt like he was submerged in yellow.

As the first pearls of rain materialised out of the dark, Eliot recalled a fragment of a car journey he had taken one night with…with someone; his grandad? His dad?

He could never recall the purpose of the journey, but he remembered staring out of the windscreen, the rain coming in hard against the shield wall of white the headlights threw up. Warm air from the vents filled the car. He had been in his pyjamas. Beyond that, he could not remember a single thing, other than a lingering impression of feeling snug, safe, of wanting the journey to go on forever.

Not like now.

Sharon turned up at about nine o'clock. Eliot was lying on his bed, struggling to concentrate on his book. He heard her and Michael go into his mum's bedroom. They were soon talking out loud, sometimes laughing—only it sounded forced and fake, particularly Sharon's laugh.

£16.80.

He wished he had more. A lot more. *Eliot's run away. It's all our fault. We've been mean to him. We've got to find him, say sorry.*

Eliot, we're sorry.

Gripping his book in both hands, he glared at the words on the page as though he was a diver preparing to throw himself off the diving board.

28 Sunday, 21 March 1982

£16.80

Eliot was sitting in the front room when the doorbell rang. Standing, he went out into the hallway and pulled back the drape. The frosted glass door panel distorted the identity of the diminutive figure.

Cautiously, he pulled open the door…and saw who it was.

'Claudine!' he said, quickly glancing down the hallway.

David and Rob were at the computer. He could hear them laughing.

Sighing, Claudine thumped her hands onto her hips. 'No, it's the Avon lady.'

'Well, what do you want?' Eliot had not forgotten that she had walked off on him the other night, even if she was pretending that nothing had happened.

'Charming as always,' she remarked. 'Actually, I thought you might want to go for a walk along the seafront.'

'Why?'

Claudine shrugged. 'Make a change from the golf course. You don't want to go there, do you?'

He thought about his recent theft. 'What, the golf course? Why do you say that? What is it?'

'Well, it's a big green place where posh little men amuse themselves by trying to get a little white ball down a little round hole.'

'That's not funny,' he said pointedly.

Claudine shrugged. 'No, it's not. Do you know how many millions of trees they had to cut down to build that golf course?'

'You're not funny, you know. You're not being funny.'

Claudine shrugged again. 'Suit yourself, grumpy. Anyway…shall we go?'

See! She was acting like nothing had happened at the pier.

He heard a snigger behind him. Too late he remembered…

He turned slowly. And there they were…David and Rob! Spying on him from the kitchen.

'*I told you,*' he heard Rob gloat.

'*Well, fuck me sideways,*' David declared under his breath.

Red-faced, Eliot hurried out onto the doorstep and pulled the door towards him—he could not close it, otherwise he would lock himself out. And he knew exactly what information David would try and extract from him to be let back in. Consequently, the conversation between his brother and his friend continued to pester his hearing, like a fly busy around his ear.

'*But it's Eliot?*' David muttered.

'*So? There's your proof.*'

'*No way; it's impossible.*'

'*She's standing outside your fucking house!*'

But what was impossible was the tone in his younger brother's voice—he thought he detected a hint of envy.

'Eliot? *Eliot?*' Claudine was staring at him. 'Is there something wrong with your neck?'

Eliot shook his head.

'Good, shall we go then?'

'Er, yeah, sure.'

'*No way. Just no way.*' There it was again. David, sounding like he was missing out on something!

'*What's the big deal?*' he heard Rob grumble.

The feeling came upon him suddenly, the same as before, with O'Neal at the bus stop, and he did it without thought, without thinking of the consequences.

He swung the door open, *wide*! So that David and Rob could see Claudine standing on the doorstep wearing her green duffle coat. She had the hood back and her red Alice band kept the hair out of her small, round face. She smiled at the two boys standing in the kitchen, who looked small suddenly. And a bit scared.

'I'm off out,' he declared, giving his brother a look that dared him to say something out loud.

And it felt good. He felt good about it, and…and secretly, a bit superior.

Claudine waved, though Eliot thought he detected a hint of defiance in the gesture. *What are you looking at?*

Rob ducked back out of sight. Timidly, David raised his hand, waved back.

Eliot liked what he saw on his stupid brother's face.

Hah!

David disappeared into the back room.

Grinning now, he said, 'One sec.' And then he raced upstairs to get some money. Hesitating for only a second, he grabbed a pound note (one of the two he had stolen from his dad). Replacing the tin, he then rushed back downstairs. He found Claudine standing *inside* the doorway, humming to herself. It made his stomach do an odd flip. Ignoring it, he grabbed his duffle coat off the peg. Smiling, Claudine stepped outside to wait for him.

As he closed the door, Rob made a loud sucking noise.

'Just load up the game, dickhead,' David ordered with irritation in his voice.

Yeah, go fuck yourself, dickhead. Hah!

They spent the morning roaming the seafront. Eliot marvelled at the inexhaustible range of subjects Claudine could talk about in detail—and at great length. She had just changed tack once again and was enthusiastically discussing her new favourite song in the charts when they came upon the pier. The two of them stopped, glanced at each other, then laughed. Nothing more was said on the subject.

The seafront was surprisingly busy; how different from the day before, Eliot wondered. It was like someone had turned on the tap and people had come rushing out. But Easter was still a few weeks away and the sun was high up behind a heavy veil of grey-white clouds. Not that it was cold. In fact, it was just about right; not too cold, not too warm, unnoticeable. His grandad used to call it "underpants weather," meaning, *you don't notice it until you start thinking about it.*

In the afternoon, he bought both himself and Claudine an ice cream, 99ers, with flakes.

Down to £16.06.

Shut up.

Even with next week's lunch money, all £2.50 of it, he could now only raise £18.56 before the clocks went forward—which would leave him short by...£1.44.

Shut up. Just shut up.

They were sitting up against the esplanade railing with their feet dangling over the edge and their elbows resting on the lower bar. He sank his teeth into the cold, creamy heart of his ice cream. His loose tooth blazed with pain.

Seeing his grimace, Claudine laughed.

'Loose tooth,' he explained, using the back of his hand to wipe the corner of his mouth where a melted spot of ice cream was threatening to go on the rampage down his chin.

Clucking in mock despair, Claudine batted away his hand and cleaned his face with the paper tissue that came with her ice cream.

Surprising himself, he let her do it, even turning his head and jutting out his chin so she could do it properly.

Finished, Claudine inspected her work. 'Well, don't forget to put it under your pillow,' she muttered, meaning his tooth. 'When it finally comes out.'

'You don't believe in the tooth fairy, do you?' he asked. 'Really?'

Claudine's expression was withering.

Despite his cynicism, Eliot felt somewhat envious of her—it seemed that she believed in *everything.*

The two children finished their ice creams in silence, content to watch the activity down on the beach.

At one point, a white Jeep drove down the wharf and onto the beach. They could see from the large trailer that it was delivering buckets and spades, inflatables and kites, and large net-bags full of plastic footballs to one of the striped concession huts.

Farther along, the donkeys had arrived, but currently there were no takers. It was the same with the trampoline man, presently wandering down the modest aisles of his unoccupied trampolines with a forlorn expression on his face.

'Maybe we should have a go?' Claudine said, giving him a nudge.

He shook his head. 'And have my ice cream come up?'

She screwed up her nose. 'Urggh, no thanks.'

A loud shout interrupted their laughter.

Both he and Claudine glanced down the esplanade as two young boys broke through a crowd of grown-ups. Laughing, they were chasing down an escaped blue balloon. With little wind, it was just out in front of them, and still no more than seven or eight feet off the ground.

They chased it down hard, but the balloon—in a series of tugs and jerks—remained just out of their reach, and slowly, inexorably, it lifted higher and higher.

Seemingly untroubled that the balloon had become an impossible thing to reach, the boys charged on, their expressions fiercely determined. Neither of them cared to look where they were going but it did not matter, and Eliot stopped and watched on enviously as the smiling crowds parted to let the two boys pass.

He held his breath, willing the balloon down, but it kept climbing.

He felt Claudine's hand take hold of his. Surprised, he glanced down at their interlocked hands then up at Claudine, who was blushing.

His voice cracked before anything could come out.

She smiled, understanding.

Together they turned to watch the blue balloon continue its climb, higher and higher…higher than the manufacturer had ever intended.

The boys neared his and Claudine's position at pace, no longer laughing, but apprehensive, expressions slightly desperate.

And still the balloon climbed.

'The clouds will get it soon,' Claudine murmured.

He felt it too. 'Yes,' he nodded.

The two boys came to a stop no more than ten feet away from where Eliot and Claudine were sitting. The balloon was now tiny in the massive, white sky, a tugging tadpole of a thing, dark and bereft.

Eliot was suddenly conscious of the connection the four of them now shared, watching as the balloon moved towards its inevitable conclusion.

The crowds of adults continued to move along the esplanade, not caring that the balloon would soon be lost forever. He was suddenly angry with them. This was important, more important than anything else.

He longed to see the balloon begin to descend, but he knew there was no way of stopping it now.

Beside him, Claudine shivered, as she, they—all four children—watched the balloon inseminate the dark clouds and disappear.

He could do nothing for the boys. Or for himself. The blue balloon was gone.

'Time to go,' he said in a quiet voice.

'Yes, I suppose so,' Claudine sighed.

But they sat for a while longer, in silence; each thinking about the balloon.

Finally, Eliot said, 'It's been nice.'

'Finally,' she declared with a laugh.

Evening shadow filled the room. His mum was downstairs with Michael and Sharon. There was no need to look outside to know that it was raining, had begun not long after he had lain down on his bed. Its soothing, drumming pitter-patter reminded him of his recent visit to the old theatre with Claudine.

Claudine of the dimples, of the fierce temper.

He pictured her beside him, lying on her side, her eyes staring into his, smiling.

Don't be silly. No one can see you. And if they could, who would care? It's natural. Everyone does it. Let me show you. Like this…see? You do it like this. There. Shall I do it some more?

With a small cry he cramped up, a tremor shaking his small body. It was a big one. When he looked down he was amazed to see a small amount of fluid between his fingertips. He peered it at closely. It was like a translucent gel, and it felt slick between his thumb and forefinger.

The semen dried quickly, forming a crispy film on his fingertips. Quickly, before it could disintegrate altogether, he jumped out of bed and took out his microscope set, careful with his fingers to avoid inadvertently brushing off the specimen.

After scraping a goodly sample of the crispy film onto a blank slide, and when everything else was ready, Eliot took a moment to calm himself.

This was it.

Finally, something *important*.

It felt a bit strange examining something that had come out of him, and he was a little bit nervous, which, the more he thought about it, was even stranger.

He took a deep breath and peered through the ocular lens.

Nothing! *Bloody nothing!*

Well, nothing revelatory anyway. Nothing of interest.

It was like examining an overcast sky up close. There were variations in the grey-white cloudscape, and black motes pitted the sample, like birds seen from a great distance.

But nothing moved. There were no wriggly things, no evidence of life here. He checked the microscope, but it was set at its maximum magnification.

Rubbing his eyes, he examined the sample again, but nothing had changed. If anything, the landscape before his eyes appeared more bleak than before.

There were no secrets here. None.

Is that fucking it?

When he finally sat back on his heels, he knew he should be upset, but instead a feeling of immense relief slowly overtook him. Clearly, his microscope could not provide him with the sorts of answers he was looking for. He now suspected there was not a microscope anywhere in existence powerful enough to give him that.

Labelling the sample '*21/03/82—Me,*' he packed everything away and slid his microscope set back under his bed.

Just for an instant, as his fingertips broke contact with the box, he felt a moment of acute loss, knowing that it was quite possible he might never return to his microscope set again. But when he pulled his hands free of the bed, and when he stood, something of the moment's significance entered him, and he let himself believe that he had properly, physically closed the gap on that which he most desired.

Only now, he was not entirely sure what that exactly was.

29 Monday, 22 March 1982

£16.06

As Eliot approached the house, he saw Michael and Ruth standing on the pavement, talking to the solicitor. It was windy and the front door was wide open, letting in the draft; this small detail irritated him more than it ought to.

As he approached, Michael waved to him, but then shook the solicitor's hand quickly, who then got into his big, red car and drove off. Ruth gave Michael a hug and then disappeared inside her own house.

A *hug*! Why would she do that? Why would he *let* her do that? What was wrong with him?

'How was school?' Michael asked when Eliot reached him.

'What was the solicitor doing here?'

Michael scratched his neck. 'He was passing this way and had some things Mum needed to sign.' Michael held up a folder full of documents and pamphlets.

'Shouldn't you be at work?' Eliot sniffed, staring at the folder as though his older brother had stolen it from his book collection.

'Day off,' Michael said.

Not listening, Eliot reached for the folder in his brother's hand. 'I'll take that up to Mum,' he said.

'No,' Michael snapped, putting the folder out of Eliot's reach. 'I mean…no, it's okay, I can do it.'

'No, it's all right,' Eliot insisted, keeping his hand out.

'It's not for you, Eliot.'

'And it's not for you, either!' Eliot shouted. 'You're not even meant to be here! I should be the one dealing with the solicitor!'

'You don't know what you're talking about,' Michael countered angrily.

Across the road, Old Man Vic was out in his garden singing 'I don't like Mondays.'

The brothers ignored him. Like everyone ignored him.

'Give it here,' Eliot insisted, holding out his hand. 'I'll take it up.'

'No!' Michael said sharply. 'Jesus, Eliot! What the hell's wrong with you?'

'Don't say that!' Eliot yelled.

'Then *grow up!*' Michael snapped.

'I am grown up.'

Michael took a deep breath, and in a more controlled tone said, 'Just leave it, Eliot, yeah? It's complicated.'

'Bed-pisser!' Eliot shouted, and stormed into the house.

This time, Michael did not call him back.

'March 22—Old Man Vic is pissing me off. Why doesn't someone come and take him away? Put him in a home or something? Why?

Simmering still, Eliot lowered his binoculars.

He glanced up the street. But there was no one there.

In the next room, the murmur of voices told Eliot that Michael was pretending to be all important with their mum.

Fuck the solicitor.

It began to rain. He felt quite relieved about that. He did not feel like going to the park tonight anyway. He had a bit of a headache.

It must be his tooth.

Lying on his bed, he played with it for a while, but the fucker would not come out.

Finally, sleep took him.

30 Wednesday, 24 March 1982

£17.06

It was about a week after his grandad's funeral. While his dad went off to retrieve the mail, or turn off the electricity, or do whatever it was they had gone there to do, Eliot waited in the darkened living room, trying to remember what it used to look like—what it was like when he used to visit; when his grandparents were alive.

But he could not. And the failure served only to reinforce the truth; the big, fat facts.

They were dead. And they were not coming back.

Why had his dad brought him here? Why him? It was usually Michael who got picked to do things…important things.

The decision arrived slowly, as his gaze drifted around the room…this bungalow, without his nan in the kitchen and his grandad watching the football from the sofa, sliding out the odd fart to outrage his nan; this place full of packed boxes, and with the curtains drawn like they were ashamed; this place with its cleared shelves and empty display cabinets, naked lamp stands and disconnected phone; this place with the white sheets thrown over the furniture; this place was not his grandparents' home anymore—and he was certain he wanted to be about a million miles from it. Maybe farther.

His dad was suddenly standing beside him, stuffing keys into his jacket pocket. When Eliot looked up, he saw something in his dad's expression he never thought he would see. And it made Eliot feel something towards his dad he thought he would never feel…it was sadness. He felt sorry for his dad. And it hurt him inside.

Without thinking of the consequences, Eliot reached up and took hold of his father's hand. Not looking at Eliot, his eyes fixed on something across the room only he could see, silently his dad gave Eliot's hand a gentle squeeze, then sighed.

Nothing more than that.

They stood like that, hand in hand, for such a long while that Eliot started to believe the two of them might never move again. And he was not sure what he thought about that.

Eliot turned away from the pier and took his place in the bus shelter.

Three days left before the clocks went forward.

And with another 50p (and another day without lunch), he was now up to £17.56.

£2.44 to find.

You're gonna be short.

Fuck off.

And you're hungry.

His eyes scanned the graffiti as though somewhere, in amongst all the scribbles and drawings, a way forward would reveal itself to him.

It was not long before the bus appeared, a massive, green thing looming over the tops of the other traffic. He was certain that one day, it would take him to school, but he would not come back.

After school, he found David and his dickhead friend, Rob, playing on the stupid computer. Michael was in the kitchen, preparing dinner… *again*, like he owned the place!

You're not the boss.

Go back to Sharon's.

As he passed his mum's bedroom, she called out to him. Hesitating for a moment, Eliot edged into the room.

'Be a love, hun,' she said, rifling through her bag. 'Can you fetch me a packet of ciggies from the offie?' She pulled out her purse.

Eliot nodded.

'You're a good boy.'

Eliot nodded as he took the five-pound note from her.

He gave the five pounds a long look.

When his mum started coughing, he creased up his face and said, 'I'll go now, then.'

When he returned a little later, he handed his mum her cigarettes and then volunteered to put the change back into her purse.

Lighting up a cigarette, his mum watched him perform the act hastily, clumsily. The coins went back into the purse, the purse back into the handbag.

'Thanks, Eliot,' his mum had murmured. 'You're a good boy, Eliot. Such a good boy.'

A coughing fit provided him with an opportunity to escape her bedroom before she uttered another word.

Escape with £1.50 from the change.

His mum's change.

Later that evening it rained, as it had Monday and Tuesday night. Michael stuck around for a long time after dinner. He spent it upstairs with their mum, like he cared, no doubt talking big things as he smoked *her* cigarettes.

Eliot stayed downstairs on purpose and played the television loud, hoping it would somehow send Michael a message.

Go home.

He was a bit shocked when the doorbell rang at around eight o'clock. Thinking it might be Claudine, he leapt up and hurried out into the hallway.

Michael was not ready for Claudine.

Glancing upstairs, he pulled back the drape and opened the door.

'Hello, son,' his dad said.

'Dad,' Eliot answered, hiding his shock.

His dad appeared...well, nervous.

This was new, and emboldened by his father's apparent weakened state, Eliot purposefully stood his ground, held the door close to his chest, preventing his dad from getting a proper look inside the house.

Fuck him. Fuck Mr School Shoes.

'I'm, er, here to see Mum,' his dad said, licking his lips.

Liking this new dynamic between them, Eliot pretended to consider his dad's words for a moment—for as long a moment as he dared—before nodding and stepping aside. He hoped his expression warned, *Well, don't be long up there, or there'll be trouble!*

Closing the door behind him, his dad hung up his coat on the coat stand.

An act which Eliot regarded with quiet hostility.

With an awkward nod, his dad disappeared upstairs.

Not wanting to push his luck, Eliot remained downstairs and tried to watch television, shutting out everything else. But after a couple of minutes, it suddenly occurred to him that Michael was not going to be sent downstairs, which was simply unfair. Michael was not a grown-up. He should warn someone. *Dad, Michael wets the bed. Don't tell him anything.*

Why was he allowed to be up there?

Next door he heard Rob and David laughing.

But David should be in the living room with him, discussing the outrageous behaviour of their older brother! Did David care about anything?

Standing beside his mum's armchair, he took out the coins from his pocket; £1.50.

David would care about this.

£1.50. Money he had stolen from their mum.

Such a good boy.

Feeling sick and guilty, Eliot stuffed the coins back into his pocket. It was too late to reverse things.

He pulled back the curtains and stared out into street. The rain was coming down hard.

Just don't rain on Saturday night. Please.

He now had £19.06. If he kept his lunch money tomorrow and Friday…well, that would be it! £20.06. He wanted it over with now, finished, self-disgust at his most recent theft ruining any excitement he might have otherwise felt.

Eliot Thomas, Such A Good Boy.

31
Friday, 26 March 1982

£20.06

Eliot went to school angry. That morning he had discovered Michael asleep in the armchair again, the ashtray full, and half a dozen empty cans of Tennent's Pilsner on the floor beside the side table.

Who does he think he is? Who?

And when he got back from school, Michael was still there.

He found him in the kitchen, talking to their mum. Seeing her downstairs came as a massive surprise.

'I don't care, Mum,' Michael was saying as he came through the back door. 'You shouldn't be down here.'

'Leave it, Michael,' his mum replied irritably.

'What's going on?' Eliot asked. The 50p in his pocket meant he had also gone without his lunch again, so he was hungry, and this fuelled his irritation. Still, it did mean one thing: £20.06.

Twenty pounds!

Michael raised a cautionary finger. 'Stay out of this, you.'

Eliot said, 'Actually, I was talking to Mum, not you.'

Their mum took a drag on her cigarette. 'Gawd, will you look at this floor,' she muttered, like she had not heard a thing Michael had said.

'Then *do* something about it,' Eliot demanded, upset.

'Not now, Eliot,' Michael warned, using his dad's eyebrows against him.

'There's nothing I can do?' their mum muttered, her eyes fixed on the floor.

'*Mum!*' Michael's unexpectedly stern rebuke surprised Eliot. 'Don't say that.'

And irritated him further.

'Leave her alone!' Eliot yelled, grabbing the unused mop from behind the fridge. 'Mum, use this!' he said, his eyes, for some reason, collecting water. But he did not care. Everything was topsy-turvy, all wrong. His mum was standing by the washing machine, a cigarette in her hand. Daylight poured into the kitchen through the back door, so that he could make out the dark outline of his mum's figure through her nightie, which fell from her shoulders like a curtain. She looked thin, without contours, her wrists and ankles like twigs. He gazed upon her in disgust, disgusting himself.

Despite his anger towards his older brother, he said, 'Michael, tell her to use this. *Tell her.*'

Michael scowled. 'Please, Eliot...not now.'

'But it'll help things, Mikey. It will.'

Ignoring him entirely, Michael said, 'Come on, Mum, let me help you back upstairs. I'll bring you up a mug of tea, yeah?'

'She doesn't need your help!' Eliot shouted. 'Do you, Mum? Leave her alone. Why don't you leave her alone, Mikey?'

'Hush now, Eliot,' his mum replied in a quiet voice, smiling. 'And Michael...I'm not an invalid, you know,' she said, patting him on the cheek.

'I know that, Mum,' Michael muttered, looking miserable. 'It's just...' But he could not finish the sentence.

'I know, son,' she said quietly, and shuffled past both boys.

Eliot and Michael watched as she moved down the hallway, her right hand brushing the wall, like she needed help from the house to find her way back upstairs.

When her footsteps were heard on the stairs, Michael suddenly lunged at Eliot, pushing him up against the fridge. 'What the hell is wrong with you?'

'Fuck off, leave me alone!' he yelled in a frightened voice. 'You don't even live here anymore.'

'Fuck off, is it?' Michael snarled. 'You a big, tough man now?'

'Shut, up! What do you know?' he howled. 'You don't know anything!'

'I don't know anything, yeah?' Michael sneered, his voice horribly quiet. 'Well, I know Mum's dying.'

Just as he said this, the back door opened. It was David and Rob.

Quietly, Eliot said, 'What?'

'She's got cancer,' Michael said, looking like it was all Eliot's fault.

'Cancer?' Eliot whispered, struggling to comprehend what this meant.

Letting go of Eliot, Michael stepped back. He looked like he had smashed something precious and of extreme value, and knew without being told that it could not be mended, nor replaced.

'Cancer? Who's got cancer?' David asked eagerly, letting his school bag slip to the floor. Rob kept quiet.

'Mum,' Eliot answered, keeping his eyes on Michael.

'Cancer?' David repeated in a much quieter voice. 'Is it contagious?'

'I'll come back later,' Rob suggested quietly, edging back toward the door.

Looking like he wanted to go with him, Michael nodded. 'Probably best, Rob,' he smiled. 'Tell Ruth I'll pop round later.'

'I will,' he promised, and left.

'Mum's got cancer?' Eliot's voice cracked. 'But when?'

'I shouldn't have said anything,' Michael said, more to himself. 'Shit.'

'Cancer,' David grinned, his eyes overly bright, his bottom lip suddenly twitching.

'You happy now?' Michael snarled, shoving Eliot back up against the fridge.

'*Me?*' he cried, afraid. 'What have I done?'

'Mikey?' David complained, tugging the sleeve of his older brother's jumper. 'Mikey, stop it. What are you saying? What does it mean?'

'Nothing good,' he whispered. Staring at the vinyl floor, his long, lean body suddenly shuddered. 'I shouldn't have said anything,' he repeated quietly, his head dropping, so that it looked to Eliot like he was saying a prayer.

'Not good?' David faltered, looking frightened and confused now. 'Then call the doctor, Mikey. Do it now.'

'That was the doctor, wasn't it?' Eliot said quietly, suddenly understanding. 'That man on Wednesday...he wasn't a solicitor, was he?'

Michael shook his head. 'She should be in the hospital, but she won't go.'

'Make her!' David shouted, close to tears. 'You have to.'

'She's frightened she won't come out,' Michael replied with a bitter smile.

His head whipped up. 'Don't you dare fucking say anything,' he said, jabbing a finger into Eliot's stomach. 'I'm warning you. Mum can't know you know.'

Eliot shook his head.

'Nor you, David.'

'But she should go to the hospital, then,' David protested. 'If it means she'll get better. She has to.'

'*David?*' Michael pressed.

'I promise,' he mumbled.

'It's her...' His voicing catching, Michael went over to the back door. Turning his back on his two brothers, he stared out of the window. 'She won't go to the hospital,' he said. 'It's her decision.'

Eliot stared intently at the spot deep between the ridges of his brother's clenched shoulder blades and he felt his stomach tighten. 'So what happens now?' he asked quietly, not wanting an answer.

'I don't know,' Michael murmured, keeping his back to his brothers. 'I'll talk to Dad again.'

'Dad knows?' David asked.

Michael nodded.

Eliot had another thought. 'How long have *you* known?'

Michael sighed. 'Does it really matter?'

'Why didn't you tell us?' he shouted at Michael's back.

'Dad knows?' David asked quietly. 'So why's he leaving?'

'He's not,' Michael answered. 'Not yet, anyway.'

'What do you mean?' David asked in a frightened voice. 'What do you mean, *not yet?*'

'You should have told us, Michael!' Eliot yelled.

Michael whirled around, his eyes red. 'And what difference would that have made?' he shouted. 'Good old chatterbox Eliot to the rescue, dispensing his great wisdom. Then off upstairs to his microscope and his binoculars and his fucking fairy books, where everything turns out happily ever after.' He lunged at Eliot again, pressing him up against the fridge. 'What difference has telling you *anything* ever achieved?' he demanded.

'Go on!' Eliot cried. 'Be Dad. Do it!'

Michael shook with anger. Leaning forward until his and Eliot's noses were almost touching, he said, 'You're full of shit, Eliot.'

Seeing the tears in his older brother's eyes, Eliot felt a moment of vicious glee.

Good. I hope you cry.

'Mikey,' David sniffed miserably. 'Stop it. Please, stop it now.'

'*I can't!*' Michael shouted. 'I can't *stop* it.' Releasing Eliot, he stormed out of the kitchen, opened the front door and was gone.

'What's happening, Ellie?' David asked in a small voice.

Eliot sneered at his younger brother, glad he was scared. 'Go round to Rob's, for fuck's sake. Go on. And not a word to Mum.' Staring at the front door, he muttered, 'He's not the boss of me. No one is the boss of me.'

Leaving David in the kitchen, he grabbed his coat off the coat stand and left the house.

It was raining.

Michael's car was gone.

And then he ran. Ran fast. Faster than he had ever run.

When he got to the park, he climbed into bushes and cried and cried and cried. And the rain came down hard, joining his tears, but making no difference.

Later, when he got home, he found Michael asleep on his own bed.

Rainwater dripping from his hair into his eyes he stood by the door, reluctant to enter the room in case he woke him. The sound of Michael's snoring comforted him for some reason. But it was a strange sight, seeing his brother asleep like this. If it had not been for his feet hanging over the bed, he could well have believed he had been granted his wish, and things had gone back to the way they used to be.

And that longing was suddenly massive and powerful and filled his stomach, made it ache.

Eliot tip-toed into the room and fished out a couple of old sheets from the bottom of the wardrobe and wrapped them around his older brother's long, lean body.

He shuffled downstairs. Taking the blanket from behind the sofa, he turned off the light. Making sure the curtains were completely drawn across, he curled up deep into his mother's armchair and threw the blanket over his head.

32 Saturday, 27 March 1982

£20.06

His walk to the park was taken at a slow pace. Having emptied the old Scrabble bag, it was now full of coins, and it felt heavy. On more than one occasion he caught himself wondering if, after tonight, he would ever go home again. Perhaps he should have packed a suitcase.

After all, what was there to go back to?

Earlier, when he had gotten home from his computer lesson, he had found Michael watching television in the front room.

'Hey,' Michael had said. 'How was your lesson?'

'Don't want to talk about it.'

'Look, I'm sorry about last night,' Michael had then said, sounding like he meant it. 'For losing my temper, I mean. You know I wouldn't have hit you.'

'Okay,' Eliot had mumbled back.

'I mean, you get that, right?'

Eliot had nodded.

'It's important you do.'

'Yeah.'

'Okay then,' Michael had said, lighting a cigarette. 'That's good.' Blowing out a stream of blue smoke he had then said, 'Fish and chips tonight…my treat.'

'Is Rob getting any?' Eliot had asked, but regretted it immediately.

Michael had taken a deep breath.

'I didn't mean that, Mike,' he had said, meaning it. 'Sorry.'

Pressing his lips together, his older brother had just nodded and turned his attention back on the television.

Tonight, he would meet his lady. Curiously, as he approached the park, he felt very little excitement at all, only a heaviness of mood, a dull and vague confusion, as though he had just woken from a deep sleep, only to discover that he was not where he should have been.

This was a night like no other; he had no idea what to expect, but something was coming to an end. He did not need a microscope to tell him that. He knew it, felt it. The uncertainty weighed in his stomach, withdrawing feeling from his body so that his legs felt heavy and not his own.

Rather than go straight to his hiding place in the bushes, he walked over to the centre of the miniature football pitch. Eliot glanced to the evening sky, which was clear and bright, and held no promise of showers later that evening. He could quite clearly see the sun and the moon holding position across from each other, as though one or both had forgotten what to do, rise or fall away. Both appeared pale and distant, and not very real, more like they had been crayoned or painted onto a curious, blue sky.

Standing in the depression that was the centre spot, he looked around and tried to imagine the place on a spring day. The evening was so much lighter now, it was not a difficult thing to do.

> *From the first touch, the other children marvel at his skill and brilliance. His teammates shout for him to put a cross into the penalty box, and so he does, finding his man effortlessly. And then he has the ball back again and he is sprinting down the wing, laughing, riding tackles, delighting in the sound of his opponents' swearing as he leaves them choking in the mud behind him. From the sidelines, the cluster of yellow-haired girls dressed in a variety of brightly coloured knee-length dresses clap and shout. Holding each*

other close, his mum and dad hold their breath while his brothers wonder at his talent.

But he has no time for any of them. There is a game to win—it is 1-1. Every time he touches the ball he does something unexpected, brilliant; his opponents are defeated.

Seconds to go. He rides two tackles, turns, goes past two more defenders, looks up, and shoots into the top right corner. GOAL! GOAL! His teammates rush in and despite his protests, lift him up.

'E L I O T! E L I O T!' they cry, hoisting him higher and higher.

One last time they pitch him up, and at the top of his arc he sees a small figure standing by the corner flag, hands behind her back, her big, black boots easily giving away her identity.

When his eyes opened, he was quite alone. In a few more days this place would begin to fill with children in the evening. Later and later they would stay, playing football, and capture the flag, and British bulldogs; telling jokes and laughing…making new friends, falling out with old friends, making up again. Giggles in hushed groups; girls pointing over at boys, who would puff out their chests and pretend they had no idea they were being talked about. Summer would push out spring and move in. And he would retreat, envious, afraid, waiting for the clocks to go back. Autumn. Winter.

What's wrong with you?

Sighing, he walked along the touchline towards the bushes, knowing that it was not excitement he was feeling, but confusion, sadness even. The bag of coins in his hand felt much heavier, but not in a good way.

Settling into the bushes, he waited.

The man reminded Eliot of the pier. She helped him with his trousers. When they were down around his ankles, she got to her knees.

Screwing up his nose, Eliot tried not to think of his grandad.

The old man's shins were like cuttlefish, the flesh behind them nibbled at by age until there was nothing much left, only thick, blue veins.

His penis was the one thing about him that appeared youthful, like a shiny new chess piece on a natty old board—though it seemed to vibrate with an odd, unsettling anger.

Your move.

His knees trembled as the woman set to work, her lips retreating over her teeth as her mouth consumed his thing, cheeks ballooning....

He threw back his head and sighed.

Her rhythm was always good.

The old man's breathing grew shorter, and he made sounds as though he was being throttled, and then...then he let out a horrible gagging sound, lifted onto his toes...and then...and then Eliot felt a prick of pain, short-lived but intense, as the tooth snapped free. Unaware that he had been playing with it, he stared at the bloodied white nugget in his hand, the dull throb from his gum filling his head, and wondered what he should do with it.

The clinking of a belt buckle reminded him of where he was. Smiling, the old man was hitching up his trousers, fastening his belt. Coughing, he bid the woman goodnight and departed the courtyard, walking a little taller, a little more erect, his expression distant and wondering, as though something lost in him had been restored.

As usual, his lady remained for a few moments longer, tidying herself up. She was sniffing and coughing a lot, and the dark rings under her eyes were quite noticeable tonight. She looked tired, and pale, and...and old.

She coughed some more. He knew that sound now.

The sight of her should have disgusted him, but instead he discovered only a deep mixture of sadness and gratitude. He held up the baby tooth in front of him. But that was okay. The mystery would continue, though he sensed it was ready to move on from here, to...to who knew where.

He ran his tongue over his bottom teeth and felt the gap where for so long the tooth had bothered and comforted him with pain.

The gap!

He missed playing with it, missed the pain. But on a night like this, it was right that he should have the tooth in his hand.

He tried to move, but found that he could not.

No...no, that was not true...

The truth was, he made no effort to move—not at all.

And he did not feel conflicted or bad about it.

Maybe he should tell Claudine about all of this. He could imagine her reaction: *Who did you think she was? Cinder-fucking-rella? I'll tell you this for nothing; if you tried to give me twenty pounds, I'd punch you in the mouth.*

Smiling, he closed his eyes. Well, he had the tone right at least.

When he opened his eyes, the woman was gone.

Guided not by instinct, but by some other impulse, he stepped out of the bushes and placed the tooth in the corner. *Make a wish.*

He smiled again, and made one.

If only he had two.

And then he left the library courtyard, walking slowly, and with purpose.

It felt right...and good. Comforting.

Like an act of faith. As though, just like the old man, something lost in him had been restored.

33
Wednesday, 7 April 1982

Five days to go.

Eliot and David waited in the kitchen whilst the doctor spoke to Ruth and Michael at the front door. At one point in the conversation, it looked to him as though Michael's legs were going to buckle, but his hand reached out for the wall and after a brief moment he straightened up.

Once the doctor departed, Ruth remained for a little while longer, speaking to Michael, who was at least a foot and a half taller than her. She spoke in a quiet, unhurried manner, her watchful eyes measuring his responses. At one point, she reached up and patted him on the cheek, her lips pressed together so tightly it looked like she was holding in a massive shout. When Ruth had finished she left, albeit reluctantly, and not without a glance up the hall at Eliot and David.

Having seen Ruth out, Michael slowly walked down the hallway into the kitchen, where they were waiting. As usual, David had taken up residence on the washing machine, but there was no real will in Eliot to issue a rebuke or voice his complaint to Michael. Shuffling nearer to the fridge, Eliot made space for his older brother, who turned and leant his back against the worktop.

Michael lit a cigarette and pulled the ashtray from behind him and clasped it in both hands, his gaze going to the chequered vinyl floor. Reluctant to be the one who broke the silence, Eliot glanced towards

David, but his younger brother was swinging his feet out in front of him and staring intently at the ends of his trainers, as though he were contemplating taking a run.

Eliot found the language of their silence comforting and familiar, reconnecting. It communicated without waste, without unnecessary other stuff, something he could hold onto. Most precious of all, the silence let him pretend, for a little while longer, that things had not changed, that everything was still okay.

But things were not okay.

At one point Michael's head dipped, as though his knees were still threatening to buckle, but he reached out a hand and found the edge of the worktop. Realising Eliot had noticed this moment of crisis, Michael gave him a weak smile and released his hand, using it instead to offer a gesture of reassurance to Eliot by squeezing his arm.

It was David who broke the silence first. 'I'm hungry.'

Chuckling, Michael shook his head. 'Of course you are,' he said.

Tentatively, David tried out a grin on his older brother. 'Well, I am,' he said.

For some reason, Michael found this hysterical, and his chuckles quickly became full-blown laughter. He nudged Eliot and gasped, 'He's hungry!'

If Eliot was a little confused at first, his confusion did not last long; the sight of his older brother laughing uncontrollably soon had him also chuckling.

David grinned and started laughing also.

All three were soon laughing without constraint.

'Who's cooking then?' Michael gasped, his eyes wet.

'Not Mum, that's for sure,' David chortled.

'That's a relief,' Eliot laughed. 'We'd probably get her Toad-in-the-hole!'

'More like Frog-on-an-embankment,' Michael choked. 'On a very hot day.'

This set the brothers off again and howls of laughter filled the kitchen. Michael's elbow caught the kettle behind him. Still laughing, he held it up. 'Do you remember the old one?' he said. 'The one that whistled?'

Giggling, David nodded. 'Dad said it sounded like a Clanger getting humped.'

More laughter followed. Big, fat laughter, filling the kitchen.

Finally, the hilarity subsided. 'Now get off the washing machine, David,' Michael sighed. 'Or I'll chuck you in it.'

David laughed and slid off the machine. As usual, set on the floor beside the washing machine there was a plastic bowl full of soapy water; socks in soap. And as David slid forward, his foot caught the side of the bowl and it tipped over.

Suddenly silent, the three boys stared at the white socks on the floor, the dirty water slowly feeling its way across the vinyl. Without saying a word, Eliot reached down the side of the fridge and pulled out the mop. He handed it to Michael.

'I got that for Mum,' he said in a quiet voice as he watched Michael peel away the clear plastic wrapping protecting the two parallel sponge pads.

'I remember,' Michael said quietly, nodding.

'Her birthday, wasn't it?' David said, staring at the mop as though it was something he should commit to memory.

Eliot nodded. 'Yes, her birthday.'

They watched their older brother take out their mum's old yellow bucket from beneath the sink. Setting it on the ground, Michael ran the mop through the spillage. The mop soaked up a good amount of water. Michael then held the mop head over the bucket and pumped the handle, bringing the two pads together, squeezing them tightly. Dirty water drained into the bucket.

Michael prepared to make another pass through the spillage. Eyes fixed on the mop head, Eliot said, 'Actually, I'm out tonight, Mike. So, I won't be having tea.'

Michael said nothing, just nodded.

'With psycho girl?' David teased, his eyes fixed on the mop head as Michael worked the floor.

'None of your business,' Eliot said, but smiled.

'Is she like your girlfriend now?'

He shrugged. 'Maybe, you'd have to ask her.'

'I bet she is,' David laughed. 'Hey, Mikey, Eliot's got a girlfriend.'

'Good for him,' Michael murmured, winking at Eliot. 'Eliot, put those socks back in the bowl, will you?'

Eliot nodded and grabbed the tangle of wet socks. 'They're still dirty,' he observed, dumping them back into the bowl.

'Yes,' Michael agreed. 'And getting them on the floor hasn't helped.'

David took the bowl from Eliot, who surrendered it up without protest and filled it with water from the tap.

'Here you are,' said Michael, taking out a box of powdered detergent from beneath the sink cupboard. 'You'll need this.'

'I know,' said David.

'Yes, I know you do,' Michael smiled.

'They'll need a good soak first,' Eliot observed. 'Before you scrub them.'

'Yes,' Michael agreed. 'I think you're right.'

34 Saturday, 10 April 1982

Two days to go.

'Really?' Claudine said, expressing genuine surprise. 'You've never given your mum an Easter egg?'

Eliot shook his head. They were walking along the beach, down by the water's edge, just out of range of the nibbling wash.

'Why ever not?'

The two of them had been meeting up quite regularly, mostly after school; the park on some nights, the seafront on other evenings.

'But Easter's for kids, isn't it?' he replied.

She laughed, 'So?'

'But,' he complained, 'giving your mum an Easter egg's just weird.'

Exasperated, Claudine shook her head. 'Eliot Thomas, you are a very strange boy.'

He picked up a pebble and turned it over in his hand. 'Look who's talking,' he said.

Claudine let that go. 'There's nothing to think about, Eliot. Just get her an Easter egg, do you hear?'

Nodding, he let the pebble drop from his hands.

'Good,' she declared. 'I'm glad we've got that sorted out.' She took him by the hand. 'Now then,' she sighed, clearly working her way through a well-thought-out prescription of things to be done.

'When are you going to stop being silly and let me meet your brothers? Properly meet them, I mean?'

Seeing the sudden alarm on his face, Claudine laughed out loud. 'I promise I won't bite them,' she grinned.

'Soon,' he mumbled miserably. When he looked over in her direction, she looked suspiciously pleased with herself.

Which did not make him feel any better.

Later that night, he spent a bit of time watching the street. In his diary, he wrote, *April 10 – Looks like Typewriter Man has finished his story. He doesn't look happy about it though, like he's written something he shouldn't have. Or gone somewhere in the story he shouldn't have gone.*

Old Man Vic seemed to agree. He was at his window, flapping his curtains and laughing his head off. Maybe he tried to write a story once and went mad in the attempt.

35 Easter Sunday, 11 April 1982

One day to go.

'What's this?' his mum croaked. It was about ten in the morning and she was sitting up in bed, numerous pillows keeping her propped up. She was so pale her skin had taken on an almost translucent quality. And she was horribly thin.

'It's yours,' Eliot replied, fidgeting, unable to keep his eyes on her for too long. 'It's an Easter egg.'

'I can see that, son,' she said quietly.

'Well, then,' he coughed, 'Happy Easter, Mum.' He watched apprehensively as she turned the Easter egg over and over in her hands, her expression unreadable.

After a moment, she motioned with her hand for him to come nearer.

But he remained where he was.

She sighed, 'Come here, son.'

He took a step towards the bed and leant forward, hoping that she would not touch him, but when he got close, his mum reached out her hand and gave his cheek a weak pat. Her palm felt leathery, warm against his cheek, but he tried not to flinch.

'It's wonderful, Eliot,' she said. 'Thank you.' And then she started coughing and her hand fell away.

He shuffled back from the bed, feeling awkward and ashamed.

'Michael has your Easter eggs,' his mum whispered when she finally finished coughing.

He nodded, wondering if he could leave now.

'Michael tells me you have a girlfriend?'

Caught off guard, he said, 'Why would he say that?'

His mum chuckled. 'Is it true?'

'Dunno,' he shrugged. 'I think so.'

He wanted to ask her the question then; one that had occupied his thoughts most nights for the past week. But he sensed it was a question you should never ask someone when they were poorly; not without frightening them—and frightening the asker.

This time her coughing fit lasted much longer, and he felt obliged to wait until it passed, wincing every time her clattering rattle tapered to an asphyxiated wheeze.

'She's a lucky girl, then,' she gasped, and then closed her eyes with a sigh. After that she stayed quiet, her chest neither rising, nor falling...

Perfectly still.

Perfectly still.

Nothing moving, twitching, rising, falling...

He whole body perfectly still. Dead still.

Eliot froze, not sure what to do.

Just then, Michael popped his head around the corner.

Seeing the look on Eliot's face, he quickly turned his alarmed attention to their mum.

But after a moment, Michael's terrified expression turned to relief and he smiled. 'She's asleep,' he said to Eliot. 'Just asleep. See?'

And he could: the blanket ever-so-slightly rising and falling again.

Eliot nodded. 'Yes. Asleep. That's all.'

Lying on his bed later that night, he closed his eyes, the unspoken question rising to the surface of his mind.

'Mum,' he asked. *'Do you believe in God?'* Or was it, *'Mum, are you afraid?'*

36 Monday, 12 April 1982

'Do you think we'll remember this?' the girl standing next to him asked, turning her bright eyes on him. She was wearing a close-fitting, light-blue, roll-neck jumper, a multi-coloured scarf and a brown Ra-Ra skirt—and of course, her big, black boots.

'Dunno,' he shrugged, as the mayor's voice droned on over the public address system.

Looking around at the bunting hanging from the hotel fronts, the Union Jacks snapping on the warm breeze, and the various coloured balloons bobbing high above the laughing heads of children hoisted onto their parents' shoulders, he was suddenly reminded of the scenes he had watched recently on the news, and all those ships sailing off to take back the Falkland Islands.

The tide was up and the doomed structure stood knee-deep in the water. All it needed now, he thought, was a knotted white hanky on its head.

'I really don't,' he said in a quieter voice. He supposed it would be difficult to forget an occasion like this, but then, he had always thought that memories were funny things. Recalling things often seemed provisional somehow, the *when* of an event, the *why* and *what* happened next, often leaving him with a vague suspicion that it might have happened to someone else, if indeed at all—and this was particularly true the further back in time his memory went.

'I hope so,' he said, gazing up at the pier.

This was it. The end. And yet these people were treating it like a celebration. The crowd of white faces gathered along the edge of the cordoned-off area were pressing forward and the delicate yellow tape, which swung from pole to pole, from the base of the esplanade down to the water's edge, was already bulging in places. Indeed, some of the cordon poles were beginning to lift out of the sand. What was wrong with these people?

'It can't be stopped now, I suppose,' Claudine said, sounding as wretched as he felt.

'I know,' he muttered, not feeling like talking. 'But it doesn't mean it's right, does it?'

'No,' Claudine sighed. 'No, it doesn't.'

He glared at the pressing crowds. No matter how hard he willed them back, the people kept pushing forward. He wanted to shout out, 'All of you, get back! Do you hear me? Get back! Go home; this isn't for you!'

Eventually, it became too much for him and he started looking around for a policeman or a soldier, someone who could make it all stop.

Just then, perhaps sensing that the mayor's incomprehensible speech was coming to an end, an excited buzz ran through the crowd. Eliot's gaze came to rest on the two small figures who were standing atop a crudely constructed scaffold platform up on the esplanade. The platform was gaudily adorned with bunting and flags and brightly coloured drapery. They should blow *that* up, Eliot thought moodily.

The two girls were stood behind a trellis table, upon which sat the detonator. Two men in yellow hard hats were talking to the grinning girls, explaining how things should be done.

You don't even live here.

'Go on then,' he muttered to himself. 'See if I care.'

'What was that?' Claudine murmured, her eyes on the platform.

There were more speeches from the platform, other dignitaries, and then the mayor, *again*—to groans.

And then a hush descended on the crowd.

As the two girls joined hands and pressed down on the detonator, every head turned expectantly towards the pier.

And then...

And then...nothing.

There was dead quiet for a few seconds, and then a puzzled murmur broke out, quickly moving through the crowd like a fat, blunt ripple. Some of the spectators exchanged baffled looks. Others frowned and turned their angry faces towards the raised platform.

Eliot noticed, however, that one or two children nearby were smiling.

Next to him, Claudine laughed in shock. 'Oh my,' she exclaimed. 'I don't think that was meant to happen.'

'What did happen?' he asked.

'Well, that's the question, isn't it?' Claudine chuckled.

The mayor's mumbling voice came over the public address system.

'What did he say?' Claudine whispered.

With a shrug, Eliot shook his head.

Confusion and ignorance unsettled the crowd. The two men in hard hats hurried forward and inspected the detonator. After a brief discussion, they bustled over to the mayor. Meanwhile, a group of adults stepped forward to reclaim the two girls, gently urging them away from the detonator.

Again, the mayor said something over the public address system, and again the crowd expressed their collective impatience; someone shouted out a generalised, good-humoured complaint. Another person hurled a more pointed insult directly at the mayor.

And the pier still stood, appearing almost apologetic against the blue April sky.

'Call it off!' someone shouted, before Eliot realised he had actually shouted it.

Next to him, he heard Claudine giggle. He laughed a bit, too. It helped ease the tension in his head.

A woman in front turned and glowered, disapprovingly.

Claudine giggled some more.

The two men in hard hats worked on the wires at the base of the detonator. Finished, they nodded to the mayor. The mayor straitened his jacket and stepped forward.

'He's just showboating,' someone close by muttered. 'What a prick.'

Eliot had to agree.

Once again, the crowd went quiet as the mayor finished his shortened speech. The two girls were invited to step forward once more. The mayor waved to the crowd.

Holding hands, the two girls pressed down on the detonator.

Once more, all heads swung around in the direction of the pier.

And then…

And then…and then…once more, nothing.

The murmuring in the crowd was louder this time, angry. Eliot did not share this sentiment. Not one bit.

Neither did Claudine. 'Something's not right, that's for sure,' she said, choking back laughter.

'You think?' he grinned.

Claudine gave him a jab of her elbow, her eyes wet.

The men with yellow hard hats were obliged to move in once again. After five more minutes and another attempt to rouse the crowd by the mayor, everything went quiet once more.

Eliot was still smirking. He was so proud of the pier suddenly. 'Go on, Grandad!' he yelled, suddenly feeling wild and reckless.

Angry and red-faced, the mayor looked over in his direction, like he had heard him. Claudine howled with laughter. *'Grandad?'*

The two men in hard hats—looking decidedly embarrassed, it should be noted—nodded something to the mayor and stepped back. The two girls were then invited forward once more, though they looked far from happy about it.

Hah!

As one, the people of the crowd turned their heads.

Holding hands, the two girls pressed down on the detonator.

There was a deep boom, then another. The sound seemed to move under the sand towards Eliot, and then up through the soles of his trainers and into his stomach. For a second the pier remained intact. A plume of smoke rose from beneath the structure but quickly dispersed.

It was quiet for a moment, and then the sound of cracking and snapping could be heard, like knees blowing out. Flakes of wood flickered and spun away from the central wood piles.

Nothing after that.

Seconds passed. An embarrassed cough from someone in the crowd.

And then, quite suddenly, two-thirds of the pier slumped into the water—not with a bang, but with a dull *whoosh*.

There followed a protracted period of silence. Balloons released at the moment of the explosion now drifted aimlessly on the wind, climbing higher and higher, and the odd flag swished lazily in the dying breeze.

The mood of the crowd was mostly subdued, but Eliot sensed a gathering swell of embarrassed dissatisfaction.

All around him, people shifted and stirred.

And then a child, high up on the shoulders of his father, cried the unspoken complaint of the crowd. 'Is that fucking it?'

'Tommy!' a woman nearby chastised, but her voice was so strangled with laughter it came out as a high-pitched squeak.

A stilted cheer went up from the crowd.

It was far louder than the explosion itself.

'What a bloody anti-climax!' a woman close by shouted.

Someone laughed.

'Oh, Mayor,' another woman declared loudly. 'Such a disappointment to a girl.'

The whole crowd was suddenly laughing and jeering and catcalling.

The mayor gave a quick wave to the crowd before hurrying away. The men with yellow hard hats hurried into view and started unplugging the detonator. Eliot grinned with vicious satisfaction as the two girls were hastily removed from the platform, probably by their parents, like it was their fault.

He stared at the dumped structure lying partially sunk in the water. It looked like the skeleton of some great beast; a dinosaur, or a vanquished dragon, like Smaug.

He picked up a pebble and threw it as far as he could into the water. He watched it arc and disappear with a faint *plop*.

'Plop?' he confirmed with a resigned nod.

Claudine slipped her hand into his. Smiling, she said, 'Come on, mister.'

'Where are we going?' he asked, properly not caring.

'You'll see,' she answered, a bit too smugly for his liking.

'Is that a fact?' he said, trying to act aloof and nonchalant.

But she just gave him one of her looks, and his pumped-up chest deflated.

Claudine laughed.

Girls.

When he finally worked out where she was leading him, Eliot tried to protest. But Claudine would not be dissuaded. And he followed, albeit reluctantly.

Once they had entered the woods—and when the hostile mob of marshals failed to materialise—he started to relax quite a bit. It seemed he was not going to be arrested after all.

After about half an hour of just wandering along the woodland paths, Claudine surprised him by leading him to the same glade where they had once sat and eaten sandwiches.

It felt like ages ago.

'I wonder what it must be like to be a tree,' she said in a quiet voice. Side by side, elbows touching, the two of them were now lying flat on their backs, staring up at the sky. The sun was right above them. He could feel it on his cheeks, his nose, his lips, and as it slowly warmed him, so he felt the restrictions of his body soften, dissolve, until he felt no real sense of physical being; like he was just a mind floating in the glade—belonging to, and of, the glade.

'Never really thought about it,' he murmured, glancing up at the nearby cherry blossom tree.

'I mean, I like trees,' Claudine said. 'But just imagine being rooted to the same spot for all time, going nowhere but upwards!' She wrinkled her nose. 'How *boring*.'

'Why would that be so bad? Least you wouldn't have to talk to anyone.'

Claudine sighed. 'People aren't that bad, you know.'

He turned his head towards her.

A soft laugh escaped her lips. 'Well, all right, they *are*. Well, most of them anyway.' She laughed. 'And boys in particular…smelly things.'

They both laughed.

When she next spoke, her voice seemed to have grown a good deal fainter, like she was asking him the question from the edge of the clearing. 'Eliot?'

'Hmm?'

Up above, a single cloud moved across the sky. It was joined by a second. They moved against each other, slowly circling, spools of soft white in a soft dance. He closed his eyes.

'Why do they call you gay boy?'

Her shadow fell across his closed eyelids, and he knew that she was sitting up, leaning over him, like she was trying to read him.

She did not speak for a little while after that, but he knew she would ask again, so he resisted the urge to open his eyes, and instead eased himself down into the silence where it was warm and smelled of new grass, and waited.

'Eliot?'

There it was.

'Why do they call you gay boy?'

The sun had grown suddenly so intense, he felt pinned down by it.

He breathed in. Breathed in again. Breathed in again.

Later, when he tried to recall this moment, he could never quite be sure if he had given her an answer. In fact, he was almost certain he had not. But the strange thing was, even when he decided that maybe he had said something, it never sounded like his voice (not when he replayed it in his head anyway), but rather some other boy, much older, far quieter.

It was a leafy estate, and hedges and trees concealed the surrounding houses.

The driveway ran up to an ugly red garage door. Gravel had replaced the front lawn. The floral curtains were drawn back, revealing a screen of white-laced netting.

The house itself was kept very warm, reminding him of his grandparents' bungalow.

Each week he returned to the same scene. Sitting in the recliner with his feet up, his eyes partially closed, was Mr Wilson's father, the Saturday newspaper across his lap, open at the sports section.

Sitting upright in an armchair opposite the television, whose volume was always very loud, was Mr Wilson's mother, a woollen tide forever flowing out from between the clash of her needles and tumbling over the sharp knobs of her knees.

The old woman slowly became aware of his presence in the room and she smiled. 'Gracious me,' she said, carefully setting down her knitting paraphernalia on the arm of the chair. 'Is it that time of the week already? Where does it go?'

As she slowly heaved herself out of the chair, one of her knees blew out and he flinched when he heard the crack.

'Would you like some tea?' she asked. When he shook his head, she suggested, 'Juice, perhaps? Maybe you'd like a slice of Madeira cake?'

He shook his head again, then remembering his manners he said, 'No, no thank you.'

He felt a hand on his shoulder, 'This way then, Eliot,' his teacher said, and Eliot nodded. As he climbed the stairs, he heard Mr Wilson's mother say, 'Nice boy, don't you think, George?'

'Hmmmm?'

'They all seem so pleasant.'

'What's that?' George said in a voice close to a shout.

'The boys! The computer boys. They all seem so nice!'

'Aye!'

'Cup of tea?'

'What's that?'

'Tea! A cup of tea, George? For goodness sake! Don't you ever listen?'

'Aye love, ta!' George said.

'Do you think I should fetch him some juice?'

'What's that? Juice! Not for me. Tea's fine, love.'

'No...I mean for the boy, George? Oh, never mind.'

'Aye. Just leave 'em to it.'

Eliot heard the slow, rumbling fart even from the top of the stairs.

'Oh, George!' the old woman muttered with a fond chuckle.

It was a small room. The curtains were drawn and it smelt of coffee and cigarette smoke. Mr Wilson guided him over to the desk that was set against the wall behind the door. The clutter of books and folders and files and pens and an assortment of floppy disks all seemed to swirl around the keyboard terminal and the computer monitor surmounting it. Two chairs faced the desk, one set behind the other, like on a bus or a train.

Eliot sat and placed his hands on his lap and waited silently.

On the dark screen in front of him he saw Mr Wilson's reflection remove its brown suede coat and drape it over the back of the second chair. Then he was leaning over him, his arms appearing either side of him. Hurriedly, his teacher tapped out a set of commands on the keyboard with long, nicotine-stained fingers.

'Here we are then,' Mr Wilson said, sounding like he was out of breath, as though he had run a great distance just to get to this point.

Mr Wilson sat down in the chair behind him.

The computer beeped and in the top right-hand corner of the screen, the green cursor slowly blinked and blinked and blinked.

Loading...

His computer lesson always started with a game. The same game, every time.

First to appear was the brick wall, which filled two thirds of the screen. Then the tiny figure of a man, the Defender, appeared on top of the wall, a pyramid of boulders materialising behind him.

Reluctantly, Eliot extended his arms over the keyboard, his right hand poised over the arrow keys, the left hand poised above the space bar.

He let his breath out quietly and waited.

Then the first small green man appeared at the bottom of the wall.

The creature began to climb.

And the computer beat out a dull, indifferent tone.

Beat...Beat...Beat...

He tapped the space bar and the little Defender hurled down a boulder. Eliot traced the blinking progress of the falling missile. A direct hit; the attacker fell from the wall and disappeared off the bottom of the screen.

Two more attackers appeared...and began to climb.

Beat…Beat…

Then a third. Beat…Beat…Beat…

Using the arrow keys to move left and right, he tapped away until the Defender was positioned directly above the lead creature.

A tap of the space bar sent down a boulder.

The boulder crashed into the slow, climbing creature and it fell back, taking with it the attacker directly below it.

Both fell and disappeared from the screen.

Seconds later…two, three…four new creatures were replacing the fallen on the wall…their climbing speed noticeably quicker.

It was a horribly simple game, and ultimately, unwinnable. Each time an invader fell, two more replaced it; and the urgency (the need) of the ascent, intensified.

Eliot toppled another invader.

Two more attackers appeared.

The hand he suddenly felt on his right thigh lingered there for a moment, then slid upwards.

The Defender took out two more invaders.

Eliot…well, he pressed his lips together, kept quiet—as he knew he must. As he knew also that this act of silence made things worse.

Eliot Thomas, Yes Boy.

Outside in the cul-de-sac he heard a boy shout out, and then the heavy bounce of a ball, and then some laughter, which soon faded as the frequency of the bounces quickened and the ball neared the window.

The hand slid higher.

And the whole world zeroed down to the wall and the lone Defender atop the battlement.

Beat…Beat…Beat…

Eliot's hands pressed and stabbed at the keyboard and the invaders fell; but always there were more. And they were quick, too quick. His eyes began to water, making it difficult to distinguish individual attackers through the wet swarm and his nose began to run.

Just in time, he spotted two attackers close to breaching the battlements and he sent them tumbling from the wall.

Up came the creatures, down went the missiles.

Beat…Beat…Beat…Beat…Beat…

Suddenly, there were just too many of them. First one and then a second creature breached the wall…then a third.

The first creature to reach the battlements raced across the top of the wall to get at the Defender.

Trapped, the Defender waited.

YOU LOSE!
YOU LOSE!
The screen flashed…
And then…silence.

The ticking of the wall clock was loud in his ears. After a moment he sensed the pressure of Mr Wilson's chair ease, heard his teacher cough. Eliot's hand reached for the Return key.

Just one more game. Just one more game.

Reflected in the dark screen, he saw his teacher stand. He felt a hand on his shoulder, 'Why don't you come and sit over here for a while, Ellie?'

He stood, and had no answer to the subtle shifts in pressure on his shoulder that guided him over to the bed.

As he sat, he asked his mum to make it stop, then God…then God…then God again—as he always did…as he always did—but it never worked.

Silence filled the glade. He could feel the beat of his heart in his ears.

'Stand up,' Claudine ordered suddenly.

He did as he was told. It was an effort. He felt remarkably sluggish.

After a pause, she gave him a very direct look. 'How far have you been with a girl?'

'Rhyl.'

'*Rhyl?*'

He nodded, 'With my cousin.'

Claudine rolled her eyes. 'I mean, how far have you *been?* Kissing and…you know?'

'Oh,' he said. 'Well…if you mean…' He dropped his head. 'Well, I haven't, not really.'

'What, never?' she said, but she was smiling, an intense, proprietary sort of smile.

'Well, I've kissed a few girls…at primary school.' He gave her an embarrassed laugh. 'But no, I haven't *done* anything, if that's what you mean.'

'It is what I mean,' Claudine nodded, sounding somewhat out of breath.

'I haven't even had a real girlfriend, to be honest. You?'

'A boyfriend?' She shook her head. 'No.'

He said, 'Funny, isn't it?'

She took his hand. 'You could be my boyfriend. Officially, I mean.'

'What, like go out together?'

She nodded.

'OK then,' he said.

There was a silence between them. He felt his heart banging in his chest.

'Well…' he finally said.

'Well,' she repeated.

'I suppose, girlfriend and boyfriend should kiss?'

Quietly, Claudine said, 'I think so.'

Quickly leaning forward, she put her lips on his mouth. They were soft, warm. It felt nice. Breaking free, they both laughed. After a brief pause it was his turn to lean forward and kiss her. Her arms reached out and clasped him around the waist, pulling him in. He kissed her some more, practising with his lips and tongue.

They broke for a second time. Claudine gasped, her eyes bright.

He felt it, too.

Giving him a very direct look, she said, 'I think we should.'

Eliot made no effort to conceal his nervousness, but he nodded, his heart softly thumping.

Quickly, the two of them undressed.

Naked at last, they stood for a second staring at each other, then rushed in for a kiss to hide their embarrassment.

The sun over the glade intensified.

After what seemed an age, they broke from their kiss and smiled at each other shyly.

When he placed his right hand over her left breast, which was small and pointed, a soft shudder ran through her body. And when she took hold of his small erection, a warmth unfurled in his stomach.

They stood like that for a long while, marvelling at the brightness of the day, triumph radiating from their small bodies.

All around them, petals from the cherry blossoms fell.

The End

Printed in Great Britain
by Amazon